T0354317

THE BANDITTI AND THE REGULATORS:

PASSION AND TERRORISM IN LINCOLN'S WILD MIDWEST

BY DONNA PATTEN GOLDSMITH-DAY

Order this book online at www.trafford.com
or email orders@trafford.com

Most Trafford titles are also available at major online book retailers.

Print information available on the last page.

ISBN: 978-1-4269-1611-3 (sc)
ISBN: 978-1-4269-1610-6 (hc)

Library of Congress Control Number: 2009937629

Trafford rev. 10/05/2021

 www.trafford.com
North America & international
toll-free: 844-688-6899 (USA & Canada)
fax: 812 355 4082

Acknowledgments

It took the knowledge of several people to compose this book with credibility. The wife of my mother's cousin was the one who inspired this research into my family history and gave me so much of her own research. She is referred to here as my "Aunt Dorothy." She passed away a year after our third interview, and I wish she were still here to see this result of her extensive research to clear her beloved husband's family name.

A visit to the Ogle County Historical Society after three visits to Dorothy Driskell started the paper trail that led to evidence of my ancestors' abolitionist activities. Ironically, historian Betty Obendorf in Ogle County was able to show me documents that pointed to the innocence of these ancestors. She was able to indicate this possible verification with many more facts than I had found in DeKalb County, the home county of these ancestors. She showed me pamphlets and books by Leonard J. Jacobs who later sent me further papers and court records leading to the corroboration of my Aunt Dorothy's belief in their innocence. I appreciate everything that they have done along with the patience and work of my cousin, Alice Ratfield and her husband Al. They took me to historical societies, museums and airports over several years with great devotion.

I appreciate the help of Leonard J. Jacobs who sent me pamphlets with the court records pertinent to the time of my ancestor's demise. He has meticulously assembled facts that point to their innocence of crimes ascribed to them.

My cousins, Julie and John Olson provided me with the genealogical materials regarding the Driskel link to the Pearces and Delamaters from the English royal line. Previously, I had no idea that we are descended from the line of Edward III. The Pearce genealogy points to why one of the brothers of William had the name Pearce, and the lost deed lends some suspense to the story.

Many thanks go to my daughter, Michelle Smith, chief of the states attorney's office in Annapolis, Maryland, who looked over the book and discussed it with me often.

I appreciate my fellow writer and friend of forty years, Judith Schwerein who perused my rough draft of the book along with another doctor of history and made apt suggestions, such as bringing the present into it with author's notes. This and their other astute ideas served to bring the events to life and educate the reader concerning the tenor of the times.

I am also grateful to historians in Maryland at the Talbot Historical Society who helped me with facts about famous Black abolitionists, such as Douglass and Tubman and also the history of Regulators as members of the Ku Klux Klan.

Many thanks go to Leonette Rawls, who with her Native American heritage, helped me through exhibitions and stories to gather facts for this book.

I am especially grateful to my counselor, Fred Mattis, who read this book several times and encouraged me to keep writing it.

Prologue

"Truth is generally the best vindication against slander."

"To stand in silence when you should be protesting makes cowards out of men."

"....by the operation of the mobocratic spirit, which all must admit is abroad in the land, the strongest bulwark of any Government, and particularly of those constituted like ours, may effectually be broken down and destroyed-I mean the attachment of the People... when ever the vicious portion of population shall be permitted to gather in bands of hundreds and thousands, and burn churches, ravage and rob provision stores, throw printing presses into rivers, shoot editors and hang and burn obnoxious persons at pleasure and with impunity; depend on it, this Government cannot last." The Perpetuation of Our Political Institutions: Address before the Young Men's Lyceum of Springfield, Illinois, January 27, 1838 Abraham Lincoln

One hundred and eleven vigilantes, called Regulators, murdered my great-great grandfather and his father in June of 1841 in Ogle County, Northern Illinois. My ancestors were "tried" in a "kangaroo court" by the Regulators, a term now known to pertain to the Ku Klux Klan, according to historians and television documentaries.

This terrible killing was considered a "skeleton in our family closet" and not discussed often. Recently, however, the truth surrounding this incident has begun to surface. The two men were accused of stealing horses and killing the head of the Regulators. The facts, however, indicate that they were actually stealing slaves.

The nearest town, now called Oregon, where a courthouse and jail were being built then, was later avoided by members of the Underground Railroad. Helping runaway slaves was an illegal activity then, and there were "a number of southern sympathizers in the Oregon-Mt. Morris area, including members of the Ku Klux Klan." (Henry Elsey, "The Tri-County Press," February 28, 1907.)

When we were growing up in a small town west of Chicago, my mother and her sisters mentioned that each of my eighteen cousins and I had one-sixteenth Native American heritage, Sioux blood to be specific.

"No wonder you act like little Indians," they would say with wry humor--Scotch and Rye, I should say. When they referred to our Indian blood, they were usually drinking from their individual fifths of Scotch, which they never shared but from which they frequently imbibed while together, until the wee small hours. They definitely had more Scotch than Irish in their blood by that time. I wonder if they would have been drinking so much if they had known that their ancestors were very reputable, brave and honorable abolitionists. Many people fall into depression because their families have been falsely accused of crimes. Knowledge of the truth in history often leads to greater self-esteem, especially if conveyed early to children.

I never guessed how that reference to our Indian blood tied into the disreputable claim that some of our ancestors were horse thieves. I had heard this from my cousins, and later, down near the Rock River near the small town of Oregon, I had observed the engraved stone plaque about our ancestors, called the Banditti. They had met their demise at the gun hands of the Regulators, our great-great grandfather having been shot fifty- three times and his son having sustained almost as many bullet wounds, only to die the next day. His pregnant wife and seven children were living in a corncrib for a week afterward, because their neighbors were too fearful of the mob of vigilantes to help them. Their home was burned as well as the home of their father whose wife, age 60, and of British royal lineage, was left to survive on the prairie for weeks.

I learned from research that because of public outcry, an actual trial was held several days later. I was yet to discover the outcome of that trial that would have meant so much to the men and women who remained alive in the family if our ancestors had been exonerated.

They say it was Abe Lincoln, himself, who may have been there at the second trial. Yet, the plaque with the story of the alleged outlaws is still there for all to see not far from the giant statue of the great Indian warrior, Black Hawk, overlooking the Rock River. In 1900, Mr. Virgil Red, a Civil War Veteran, placed a large granite boulder along the bank of Grove Creek. On the boulder he had inscribed a succinct message: "John and William Driskell, executed here. June 29, 1841." This may have been a tribute to their abolitionists activities.

Then, in 1969 for the bicentennial, in Chana, a part of Ogle County named after the first head of the vigilantes, a celebration was held, and the Illinois State Historical Society erected the road marker. It declared that our ancestors were criminals, although judged so by mob rule in a travesty of justice around a whiskey keg. They were allegedly accused of killing the head of the gang, John MacCade, whose descendants from Rockford had the plaque erected. The actual accusation was that of horse thievery.

3

Since the Underground Railroad was illegal and dangerous, few families kept records of all the people working on it as "Conductors" or protectors. Also, in the early 1830s, not everyone could read or write. Because of these facts, not all the families have been acknowledged for their abolitionist ideals and activities.

Rather than being ashamed about the charge of horse thievery, my cousins have often laughed about these "skeletons in our closet." Still, recently I have begun to wonder why these ancestors had stooped so low as to rob their own countrymen of such a vital necessity as horses, if that were indeed the truth. I learned that advertisements were posted for horse thieves when the men wanted were actually slave thieves. Since men often loved their horses more than anything, an alleged horse thief would be rapidly brought to justice.

Then, after doing a bit of research, I also learned that the Lakota Sioux were specialists in horse thievery. According to my Native American friend, they believed that the land and the wild horses they had obtained from the Spaniards were their own and that they were justified in reclaiming them. Our ancestors might have been implicated by association if they had been related to the Sioux. I suspected that there was much more to this story than met the eye of historical record, but there was no record that I could immediately find to substantiate that we were descended from Native Americans

Later, I did research at courthouses and libraries and spoke three times with my great aunt, Dorothy Driskel. A teacher for years, she had compiled briefcases of research on her husband's family from all over the nation, including the Ohio penitentiary where Old John was said to have spent five years. No record of this incarceration appeared.

She was quite ill at the time and passed away just months after our third meeting, but she was convinced that our ancestors should not only have been exonerated but that they were involved in a just and noble cause which led up the Civil War. This movement was the struggle to abolish slavery. That struggle in America has been used as a blueprint for freedom movements across the globe. Out of all the people in the Mid Atlantic area, 20 per cent were slaves in 1840. Unfortunately, today an estimated 27 million people are in some form of bondage, many in Southeast Asia. Most are in debt bondage as workers with limited or no prospect of buying their freedom. In looking back into how the freedom of Black slaves was won by a vast spectrum of diverse peoples working together, we may find a key to the liberation of others who are still enslaved around the globe because of human sex and drug trafficking.

Shortly after I spoke with my Great Aunt Dorothy for the last time, I learned through historians, knowledgeable regarding Black History, that the Regulator Clubs were actually the beginnings of the Ku Klux Klan. The British, concerned about tax issues, had come to Georgia and the Carolinas and between 1768 and 1771 had executed several Regulator vigilantes and had broken up the organization in the South, but it eventually covered nine states, as members of the group were in high positions of power. Anyone who refused to recognize the association and obey its laws was deemed a heathen, a publican and an outlaw to be treated as an outcast.

Aunt Dorothy had mentioned that Banditti is a Latin word, meaning a group banding together to protect the rights of each other. In Dekalb County, a group of settlers became a law unto themselves. They met September 5, 1835 in a cabin beside the Kishwaukee River near the present town of Kingston. Officers were chosen to insure an orderly gathering. There were many speeches to draft and present to the assembled settlers. The group drew up a preamble, constitution and bylaws that borrowed language from the DECLARATION OF INDEPENDENCE. The alleged bandits they chased definitely needed to band together to protect themselves.

Then, a few months later after reading the above, I found the diary of Margaret Lozier Driskel in my Aunt Margaret Larson's basement before she went into a nursing home. Here were her namesake's words, the account by our great-great grandmother, Margaret, concerning the relationship of her husband with our possible great-great grandmother, Tecumsehantas. More importantly, this was the history of her husband's abolitionist years. Were we part Native American? Were our ancestors horse thieves? Were they ever exonerated? Were they really abolitionists?

The following is a record of that diary, which makes for an astounding story and answers these questions. Margaret often starts entries with quotes from famous persons of the times in this way:

March 14, 1827

"Those who labor in the earth are the chosen people of God."

George Washington
First President of the United States
(Quotes from AN AMERICAN BIBLE, edited by Alice Hubbard, The
Roycrofters, East Aurora, N.Y., 1911.)

"I never mean, unless some particular circumstance should compel me
to do it, to possess another slave by purchase, it being among my first
wishes to see some plan adopted by which slavery in this country may
be abolished by law."
George Washington (1732-1799)
First President of the United States.

"I would define liberty to be a power to do as we would be done by. The
definition of liberty to be the power of doing whatever the law permits,
meaning the civil laws, does not seem satisfactory."
John Adams
Second President of the United States,
"A Defense of the Constitution."

My husband, William, has always wanted to help the "under-dog," as he
phrases it. He and his father, John, do have compassionate hearts, but
this tendency often gets them into trouble. As pioneers, they seem to
have a bond with the animals, the Negroes and the Indians, which keeps
them united with the earth itself. While they are productive farmers,
they are also always there to help when some creature is suffering or
some cause needs adherents. We have no Catholic churches here on the
plains, but they are true to this charitable part of their ancient religion
and have faced persecution because of this idealism and their daredevil
ways.

I fear for William and his new relationship with the Indian shaman
Tecumshantas, who is a member of a tribe near us here in southern
Illinois. William seems to be attracted to her in some strange way. His
background gives him more reason for this attraction than most men
would claim on the prairie.

His grandfather, Daniel, was born in 1760 in Pennsylvania and fought
in the Revolution. He knew of the runaway slave, Crispus Attucks,
who was among the first to die in the Revolution. Crispus died March

5, 1770, during the Boston Massacre when British troops panicked and fired into an unruly crowd of rebels.

Daniel's son, John, who is William's father, was born also in Pennsylvania in 1789. He felt that most of the founding fathers were hypocrites since they did not free their own slaves. He knew the Friends Society and felt a part of it. The family maid, a Negro woman, had raised him, since his mother had died in childbirth. He loved this compassionate surrogate mother and through her, knew David Walker who wrote "An Appeal to the colored Citizens of the World" in 1829. He also knew David's disciple, Moriah Stewart, and other Negro leaders. Moriah has recently been a guiding light to slaves. She says that Black Americans must uplift the race, and that they are "a nation within a nation."

Author's note:

In 1786 runaways from George Washington's plantation found shelter in a freed black community in Philadelphia. Perhaps Daniel and/or John Driskell participated in this shelter. They also may have had contacts with the Mother Bethel African Methodist Episcopal Church. In 1794 the Reverend Richard Allen started it and in 1830 organized the African American Convention in that city. A second church built there in 1805 was an underground station for 55 years and hundreds of slaves were hidden there. Between 1776 and 1781, The British Government freed over 25,000 slaves in southern counties, occupied by the British Army in the Revolutionary War, and many fled north to Philadelphia.

The Johnson House at 6300 Germantown Avenue, built in 1765 was used by Quakers to hide slaves sent to them by the Philadelphia Vigilance Committee. The slaves were later sent by wagons to Quaker villages in Norristown or Plymouth.

Louisa May Alcott's father, Bronson Alcott, was fired from his position as principal of a nearby school for admitting African-American students. It was rumored that he was working with the Johnsons in the Philadelphia Underground. Railroad.

Hosanna A.U.M.P. Church at Lincoln University, Chester, Pennsylvania is a tiny brick church founded in 1829 by freed Blacks. Abolitionist leaders such as Harriet Tubman and Frederick Douglass lectured there.

Longwood Meeting House, Route 1, Kennet Square, Pennsylvania was formed by radical Quakers who split off from the main church in 1854. Sojourner Truth, Susan B. Anthony and William Lloyd Garrison lectured there and runaways were often hidden there.

Most sites are open to the public.

Setting the abolition movement apart from the white-controlled Methodist Church, which encouraged abolition, was the emergence of free black women preachers such as Jarena Lee, Moriah Stewart, Sojourner Truth and Zilpha Elaw. They thought of themselves as instruments of God. Preaching at a series of camp meetings throughout the Eastern Shore of Maryland, Elaw and Lee operated with impunity under the watchful eyes of suspicious whites. Many Black women such as Charlotte Forten of Philadelphia were instrumental in the formation of female anti-slavery societies in the 1830s. These women were able to preach messages of salvation and liberation, unlike their male brethren who were often silenced by harassment or actual violence. The women often used the Old Testament examples of Jewish liberation and salvation. Their strength was that they were ignored. They must have influenced Harriet Tubman, as well.

Born March 15, 1822 near Cambridge, Maryland, Harriet Tubman helped scores of her Black fellow slaves to freedom and served in the Civil War with valor as a nurse and spy. Although a head injury, meant for another slave, caused her to have seizures all her life, these incidents and myriad other obstacles never deterred her from her mission. (Six Women Slave Narratives, Schomburg Library of 19th Century Black Women Writers, Oxford University Press, 1988.)

Black activists believed that the coming generation would see them as mentors. They felt that slavery would not die just because people were more enlightened. They said that only war would bring about the emancipation of slaves, that slaves are the most valuable "commodity" in the nation as they labor to make millions of dollars for their masters.

Old John felt that this situation must not stand. He married Mercy Aiken in Colombiana County, Ohio on January 29, 1803. It was a hotbed of abolitionist activity. She was as idealistic about the end of slavery as he was, although she was descended from the Plantagenets, the original kings and queens of England from the Scottish royalty. One of her ancestors was the famous Henry Percy, the closest contender for the English throne during the time of Henry VIII.

Mercy's family had held a deed to part of Manhattan Island, lost possibly to the Duke of York when the English took over New Amsterdam. Baron Resolve Waldron, Sr. had come to America with Peter Stuyvessant, the Governor of New Amsterdam, in the year 1646 and had settled on Manhattan Island with Tannekee Nagle, born in 1610. (This marriage may be one key to our Indian heritage.) Baron Resolve was born in 1608 in Hall, Holland and died in New Amsterdam in 1690. The deed to part of Manhattan Island, (land warrant 7610) may have been given to him by William of Orange, as my Aunt Dorothy mentioned. She also said that Resolve's daughter, Ruth Waldron, born in 1653, married an owner of the patent. Ruth did marry Jan Delamater in 1678. Jan, or John, owned the land north of the Hudson River, where the Palisades rise.

Our first American Pearce ancestor, John Pearce, was born July 18, 1647 in Boston, Massachusetts. He second married Eliza Carter and they had John Pearce in Flatbush, New York, who married Maria Delamater, daughter of John Delamater. John's son, James, married Sarah Van Horn, Mercy's grandmother. (Google Search, Cyndis list (now ancestry. com) and Bryans family Tree.)

April 7, 1827

"In every age, [liberty's] progress has been beset by its natural enemies, by ignorance and superstition, by lust of conquest and by love of ease, by the strong man's craving for power and the poor man's craving for food."

"By liberty I mean the assurance that every man shall be protected in doing what he believes his duty against the influence of authority and majorities, custom and opinion." "Historic responsibility has to make

up for the want of legal responsibility, Power tends to corrupt, and absolute power corrupt absolutely.."
John E. Dalberg, (Lord Acton)
English historian and statesman

My dear mother-in-law, Mercy, is very circumspect about any mention of her aristocracy or that she and John acted on their abolitionist beliefs in Pennsylvania and Ohio to form a network of safe-houses through family ties. This network was set up to bring slaves to Illinois and up through Wisconsin and Michigan to freedom in Canada. This abolitionist movement is illegal, and I have fears about our involvement in it.

Mercy and Old John and some of their sons live in Michigan, and we see them now and then. Others in the family live in Ohio and Pennsylvania. Pennsylvania was a part of Ohio Territory in the 1700's, and the Driskels had connections there with William Penn. Catherine Rambo, Old John's sister, born in August of 1785 in Pennsylvania, was a close friend of William Penn, who had been born in County Cork, Ireland, the birthplace of John's father, Daniel. William's brothers, David and Pearce, live near us here in southern Illinois.
Mercy is very loving and doesn't put on airs about her background. She is adamant that slaves should be free, and her son, William, my husband, is definitely of an independent, democratic bent in his love of people who are different, especially if they are persecuted. I feel very close to Mercy, perhaps because we come from the same area.

My ancestor Antjie Lozier was christened January 1st in 1662 in Hackensack, (Bergen), N.J. She may have been partly Dutch but was definitely French. One of my ancestors, Alexandre Lozier, married in 1685 in Pont D'Ain, France had a son Alexandre, married in 1728 there, who had a son, Albert, christened in Bergen, New Jersey in 1734, who married Anne, christened in 1746 in Bergen. Margaret Lozier, my great aunt, married Jacob Nagel in 1752. Could he have been descended from Tanekee Nagle who married Baron Resolve Waldron?

Nicholas Lozier married Mary Cruisea in Bergen in September of 1768. In 1796, Altie Van Horn, born in 1772 married John Lozier, born in 1776, and I was born in 1806. I am definitely related to the Pearce family through the Van Horns. (Google family search. Ancestry.com (films 0927765 Mercy Pearce Achens and films 0317527 Margaret Lozier.)

Author's note:

I can sympathize with Margaret, because I, too, have a friend who, like William, becomes involved with people who have been abused or who are disturbed. Now that I have found this diary, I can hardly put it down!

I think of how much killing there is in our own present era through the use of guns. Thirteen killed at an immigration center in New York... Eight murdered at a nursing home in North Carolina... Five killed in a house in California. These were among 57 killed in shootings in a 30day period this spring of 2009 in the U.S. And remember that we have had a Presidential assassination nearly every twenty years in this nation.

Our attacks on the native residents of this country were a beginning example of this history of violent tragedy. In general, most of the tribes welcomed us peacefully. The archeologists have now found that the settlement, two years before Jamestown, at Raleigh, North Carolina was not "lost" because of an Indian raid. Even though the natives were developing illnesses from the Europeans, they did not strike them. The English had pulled up stakes, literally, and moved north where there was fresh water "greener pastures" and probably fewer hurricanes.

Perhaps by the guiding hand of fate, I recently visited my son in New York who was living with a couple who are Sioux Native Americans. The man is a chef and the woman, an artist. They each have Mohawk hairstyles.

We stayed with them and enjoyed her lovely mosaic designs that decorated the apartment. We partook of his excellent fare in a nearby café and the Sioux philosophy, which I found in a book that was readily available on their coffee table. I feel that this is no coincidence and that I am being led mystically to write about Margaret, William and their thrilling but tragic adventures in defense of the Native and Black Americans. They had a background of persecution in the family, and County Cork stood for the rebellion of Richard, the Plantagenet son of Edward III against Henry VII. This may have been the reason that they were friendly to the Pearce line.

My great aunt, Dorothy, had saved this genealogy down through her years. Now, I am transcribing it here as follows:

"The ancient Gaelic surmane of the O'Driskell clan was O'h-Eidirsceoil which means 'the descendant of the Interpreter.' Annalists trace this name back to Eidirsceoil, 16th chieftain in descent from Lughaidh MacCon, High King of Ireland (195 to 225 A.D.) radition extends the genealogical tree of the tribe back to Ith, the uncle of Milesius, the warrior king who conquered the Tuatha de Danaans and established the Milesian race in Ireland.

In pre-Norman days the O'Driskells were dominant in the area bounded by Bantry Bay, the River Lee to Kinsale, south to the sea. They received Christianity from St. Ciaran of Cape Clear even before St. Patrick came to Ireland. The picturesque ruins of at least five ancient O 'Driskell castles, Baltimore, Lough Hyne, Ringcolisky, Castlehaven and Du-h-an-n-gall recall their historic power and sway in this part of County Cork. Baltimore is a picturesque fishing town there.

As a result of petty wars, family alliances, the Norman invasion and other factors down through the ages, the tribal lands were later restricted to the territory comprised roughly by the diocese of Ross. Powerful on land and sea, they still stubbornly defended themselves against encroachment by the English.

Their power began to wane in the sixteenth century as a result of the devastating Geraldine and Elizabethan wars. After the battle of Kinsale, their lands were confiscated and passed into the hands of Lord Castlehaven. They came into prominence again in the struggle against Cromwell.

Loyalty to the Stuart (Catholic) cause throughout the Williamite wars, however, brought the deathblow to their material fortunes. In 1690, Colonel O'Driskell, commander of the Old Fort of Kinsale, died in its defense against the Williamites, those loyal to William of Orange. Colonel Cornelius O'Driskell was another noted leader fighting for King James II to gain the English throne. However, after the infamous treaty of Limerick, he and all the other prominent members of the clan lost what was left to them of their hereditary lands. (The grandson of William of Orange, (1533-1584), alias the Silent Prince of Orange, did gain the English throne as consort with Queen Mary.)

Thereafter, the O'Driskell fighting men took their places with the "Wild Geese" in the service of France where many gained military and political eminence. Still, disaster and persecution failed to wipe out this hardy stock, and today they remain numerically strong in County Cork and particularly in their ancestral lands in Corcalee."

This is the history of the O'Driskell's that has appeared in our records. Our name was changed in Pennsylvania to Driskell but we know about our relatives in County Cork and receive correspondence from them from time to time.

Aunt Dorothy had mentioned that the name Driskell means a field of wild roses. They were rather wild and they had their thorny side when disturbed, but their essence was sweet and noble.

April 12, 1827

"First, you are to think always of the Great Spirit.
Second, you are to use your powers to help your people, especially the poor.
The Great Spirit is not always perfect; it has a good side and a bad side.
Sometimes the bad side gives us more knowledge than the good side......
We should be as water, which is lower than all things yet stronger than the rocks.
When we understand with our hearts, we will fear and love the Great Spirit.
He who serves his fellows is the greatest."
"Love yourself, get outside yourself; take action. Find the solution; be at peace."
(Adages of the Lakota Sioux Natives.)

I fear that the Indian shaman, Tecumsehantas, the granddaughter of the famous statesman, orator and warrior, Tecumseh, has been a dark influence on my husband since our move to the Illinois plains. If it hadn't been for my husband's Scotch-Irish charm, that shock of chestnut hair falling over his temples and the sapphire blue eyes I should have gone back to Pennsylvania long ago. I cherish the hope that he'll come to his senses and reform his ways by giving up this girl.

They met when he had fallen off his horse and sprained his leg. A hole in the trail had caused the fall, and his horse was down. He crawled near the horses' mid-section for warmth. When the Indian maiden came along the trail soon afterward, he was nearly frostbitten. She came to his aid, being a trained shaman, near the last stage of study. She made a splint for his leg and helped him back onto the horse, which had struggled to stand erect. Fortunately, the horse was not lame, so she leapt up behind to steady him and take the reins.

When they came back to our cabin, I was at the window, worried for him. I saw them in the distance and then watched as she dragged him down from the horse. I got my cape and helped her carry him into the cabin and into his chair by the fire. She glanced at me suspiciously as I went to make some hot tea. She was slender with the high cheekbones of the Sioux and the shining forelock over her brow. Her piercing eyes were large and full of fire, her nose straight and her lips full and ruddy in her glowing strangely fair visage.

She could speak a bit of English and took a pillow-like herb pack from around her waist to make a potion from the tea water that he drank to relieve the pain along with the stronger whiskey he had in reserve.

He offered her some from the bottle, but she wouldn't drink it. She said it weakened her healing ability, as did coupling with men. She would be a virgin for life, she said, and showed us the scars on her shoulder blades. Her mentor, the Prophet, Tensatawa, who is Tecumseh's brother, had slashed her there as an initiatory rite into the last stage of becoming a shaman. He had passed a rope through the gashes across her chest and then had hung her from a tree, until she had swung herself loose by tearing her chest open. The Mandan's annual O-kee-pa ritual was similar but was done to the most promising men in that tribe, she mentioned.

She said that much of this ritual was from the Lakota Sioux heritage. The Lakota, which actually means "allies" are often called "Sioux" an Ojibwe word for "enemy." This is a misnomer, perpetuated by 18th century French fur traders who asked who was to the west, and the Ojibwe said the "Sioux," or "enemy." The Lakota nation is comprised of seven culturally and linquistically related bands of people. The Prophet, Techumsah's brother has initiatory rites with the Sioux, and Tchumsahantas was of that Winnebago heritage on her mother's side. The Winnebagos are part of the Sioux Nation.

William told her he would accompany her to her camp, which he did after his leg healed. He said that, in gratitude for saving his life, he would bring food to her camp where the natives were starving because of the long winter snows, and so she told him where the tribe was wintering. That's how it started. I hope that my jealousy and fears have no justification.

I had our first baby, Morgan, whose name means morning or new beginning, just two years ago and he is a darling babe who favors his father's good looks. I was in labor three days, and the midwife thought that I was going to die, because the baby was breech, but she was able to turn him to go down into the birth canal by massaging my abdomen. I am just beginning to regain my strength now.

Morgan has bright strawberry blonde hair and an angelic smile as well as his father's sapphire blue eyes. We love him dearly. He is just beginning to toddle and is into everything! I was just churning butter, and he tried to get into it but is too little to reach the top of the churn. He is very strong, though, and he tried to push it over to get the creamy butter he loves.

Author's note:

I am amazed that Margaret could bear up under the threat of losing her husband to this native princess. I understand her trials of giving birth, because when I had my first child, the doctors thought they were going to lose me because they had to puncture the bag of waters. One doctor described this procedure as trying to puncture a bag, containing apples, while blind without puncturing any apples (the baby). Now I am eager to read on because my empathy is with her.

May 13, 1827

"Walk the good road, my daughter, and the buffalo herds wide and dark as cloud shadows moving over the prairie will follow you...
Be dutiful, respectful, gentle and modest, my daughter, and proud walking."
"If the pride and virtue of women are lost, the spring will come, but the buffalo trails will turn to grass.
Be strong with the warm, strong heart of the earth.
No people goes down until their women are weak and dishonored."
"There can never be peace among nations until it is known that true peace is within the souls of men."
(Lakota Sioux Legends)

I am still worried about Tecumsehantas' influence over my husband. The Indian princess was named after the famous Tecumseh, a Shawnee, who tried to keep the peace with the white race. He was born into a town on the Mad River in Ohio in 1768.

William's brother, Pearce, also likes Tecumsehantas and wanted to know how she was related to the famous Tecumseh.

This is what William told him:
"When he was around seven, Tecumseh's father, Puckeshinwas, was murdered by some settlers. Soon after his father's death, Tecumseh's mother left with his sister for Missouri. He was adopted by Blackfish, a sub-chief, but was raised mostly by an older sister, Tecumapease, and an older brother, Cheeseekau. His sister taught him the Shawnee golden rule: "Do not kill or injure your neighbor, for it is not he that you injure. You injure yourself. But do good to him and therefore add to his days of happiness as you add to your own."

According to my husband, Tecumseh was one of the greatest Indians, chivalrous, generous and honorable, a fine diplomat.

William went on to say:

"The Indians had always believed that a tribe was not bound by land cessions given by bribed Indians, but Tecumseh developed the idea that all the land belonged to all the Indians and that no tribe could sell a part of this common inheritance. He did not at first urge war on the whites, for he believed that if the Indians would unite in their common strength, they could uphold their heritage.

Tecumsahantas is the granddaughter of Tecumseh on her father's side and is of the Winnebago tribe of Sioux descent on her mother's side, but she may also have maternal roots in the Illinois Indians who had skin that was milky white. Hers is of the same lightness. Originally, the name Illinois meant "the most perfect man." This is fitting. The early Illinois were indeed men who were proud of being human beings. Many called them cowards because they did not fight. Their belief and trust in their fellow man was so great that they refused to fight many times.
The Illinois have nearly been killed off by the wars they hardly fought against the Iroquois Confederacy. This league was composed of the Mohawks, the Cayuga, the Seneca, the Onieda , the Onondaga and the Tuscarora. Comprised of six nations, it is the oldest living participatory democracy in the world, and the American system of government drew much inspiration from this confederacy.

Tecumsahantas was taught to be a shaman by The Prophet Tenskwatawa, Tecumseh's brother. This is how Tecumsehantas' greatest influence was from Tecumseh, a Sauk, but her mother had been Sioux, a Winnebago from Wisconsin. The Winnebagos were at times allied with the Sauks, although the main Sioux tribe, the Lakotas, were the Sauk's enemies. The Winebagos speak a Siouian language.

They became French allies and helped Pontiac, an Ottawa, in his efforts against our settler movement. The Winebago name sprang from the salty water of the shores of their first home far to the west. They call themselves "people of the sea." Perchance, they came from Asia.
Women in the Plains Indian tribes do not have farming duties but have a very important place in the tribe as healers, herbalists and holy people who give advice. When bands lose their male leaders, women become chieftains. Women carry knives and shoot small bows, because, among the Sioux, a woman is supposed to be able to defend herself against attack."

Considering what William was saying, I began to think about a woman's place as an Indian and as a pioneer wife, compared to her place in the society of the East. The puberty ceremony of the Sioux is such as to give pride to a young maiden. Sioux women are not treated exactly as equals of their men, but they are respected. We pioneer women are also respected more than women are back East. Perchance it is because we share the work of building a life in the wilderness with our men. We have more special respect because we are needed more here. There is much more danger here, and when the men pass from this life, the women often take up the men's work as well.

Author's note:

I was interested to see that Margaret, or Peggy, as they called her, was so staunch even though she sometimes didn't like her pioneering life. She may have longed for the "buttons and bows" of the East, but she wanted to show William and others that she could take whatever the reality of the plains states "dished out to her." I see why my aunts could take two wars and a depression in their stride. They had the Driskel Irish tenacity of spirit and the Byers' attitude of "Walk in like you own the place" "savoir faire."

June 1, 1827

"All, too, will bear in mind this sacred principle, that though the will of the majority is in all cases to prevail, that will, to be rightful, must be reasonable; that the minority possess their equal rights, which equal laws must protect, and to violate which would be oppression."
Thomas Jefferson. First Inaugural address 1801

"We hold these truths to be sacred and undeniable, that all men are created equal and independent, that from the equal creation they derive rights inherent and unalienable, among which are the preservation of life, and liberty, and the pursuit of happiness."
Original draft of the DECLARATION OF INDEPENDENCE
Thomas Jefferson

"This abomination, Negro slavery, must have an end." To Edward Rutledge.
Thomas Jefferson

I have heard that Thomas Jefferson, who died on July 4th last year, had a Negro mistress named Sally who stayed by him to the end of his life in bankruptcy, even though she had been set free by him just shortly after the French Revolution in 1789. She returned with Jefferson from France and stayed with him ever afterward, bearing several children who never inherited his name.

Near the time of his death, Jefferson had to sell some of the slaves and said that he regretted not having freed them long before. When he bade them farewell, he said that he was sorry to them and also apologized to Sally on his deathbed.

Author's note:

In 1776, following heated debate, language for the elimination of slavery was deleted from the DECLARATION OF INDEPENDENCE.

June 10, 1827

"The moment the idea is admitted into society that property is not as sacred as the laws of God, and there is not a force of law and public justice to protect it, anarchy and tyranny commence."
John Adams

Pearce, William's brother, who was visiting with us from Wisconsin, wanted to know about Tecumseh and how he had planned to make peace, so William told Tecumseh's story around the fire the other evening, and this is what he related to us:

"Tecumseh's sister Tecumapease and his brother, Tenskwatawa, the Prophet, started a kind of native religion through trances and stories of spiritual happenings. Their belief is a little like our Christian Golden Rule and like the Scotch Irish philosopher Hutchinson's. He wrote while living in Ulster, that each man, even in his native state without trappings of civilization and its formal laws, has a divine spark within him that knows right from wrong.

As Bobby Burns the Scottish writer and poet said, "A man's a man for all that."

20

"What though on homely fare we dine,
Wear haddin-grey and a' that; g'ie fools their silks and knaves their wine-
A man's a man for a' that, their tinsel show and a' that,
The honest man, though ne'er sae puir,
Is king O'men for a' that.
The man of independent mind,
He looks and laughs at a' that.
It's comin' yet, for a 'that.
When man to man, the world o'er
Shall brothers be for a 'that."

Very like the Indians, The Scots in the old country lived in tribes called clans. They actually originated from the people of Ireland who crossed the sea, into the land north of Ireland, to Scotland. They were similar to Old John's people but believed that man had the divine spark within him and could look inside of himself to find a faith that did not need the intervention of priests.

The Prophet, Tecumseh's reformed brother, had definite divisive ideas about all of the white men. Even while holding the ideal about a spark of divinity in most humans, the Prophet held that the white Americans "grew from the scum of the great water, when it was troubled by an evil spirit and the froth was driven into the woods by a strong east wind. They are unjust; they have taken away our lands, which were not made for them." But the Indians, he said, had also sinned by adopting white ways. Because of that sin, He, the divine spirit, had shut the game up in the ground to punish them. They should throw away all these corrupting influences: drunkenness, domestic animals, traders' products, even guns, and join in the songs and dances of this new kind of revival meeting, he maintained.

Still, Tecumseh wasn't as radical as this brother, the Prophet, who had lost an eye as a child and became an alcoholic and wife abuser. Then suddenly, his brother was burned as he fell into a camp fire, had an epiphany, and saw himself as a prophet for his tribe and all Native Americans. In a complete about face, he became almost an aesthetic. It was said that he could "make rain" and perform other so-called miracles. He knew that alcohol led to the downfall of the Native

21

Americans. They were told to pay for it in cash, as everyone else did, but some of them could not. They paid a down payment in wampum or furs and thus, incurred tremendous debt for which the whites exacted land from them.

Tecumseh also had two white foster brothers whom Blackfish had captured. One was Stephen Ruddell and the other was Richard Sparks who became a captain under General Anthony Wayne. Tecumseh was not aroused to hostile feelings until 1780 when George Rogers Clark destroyed the Shawnee towns and forced his people north. Later, Tecumseh was more disillusioned by the brutal slaying of Cornstalk by an American mob. Then, the massacre of ninety-six praying Christian Delawares at Gnaddenhutten, Ohio in 1782 was the crushing blow to make raw his bitterness.

William said that his father, John, remembered learning about this from his father, Daniel. It had occurred just one year after William's birth in Pennsylvania.

William declared:
"Old John was outraged by the injustice toward these Indians, since he had a friend in Ohio named Kilbuck who was a Native American, and John, an Irish Catholic, had already experienced much prejudice. He named the acres near his house "Kilbuck." Old John's brother, Phoenix, later married Kathryn Rambo whose family could call William Penn a personal friend as well as a leader of the Friends Society.
In that way, back then, our family had a close connection with the Society of Friends or Quakers as they are called in a disparaging way. Most of them were abolitionists and wanted to stamp out injustice in all forms. One of their songs stated that they were "gentle, angry people, fighting for justice.""

Many Societies of Friends existed in County Cork, Ireland before Daniel emigrated from Ireland to New Jersey. Later, the family moved to Ohio, where the story about the murder of the massacred Christian Delaware Indians was told to William.

Author's note:

John and Phoenix were in Pennsylvania in Washington County, which was considered part of Virginia, and land records show that they bought land in Alexandria. The records of this transaction are in the Alexandria, Virginia, U.S. Department of the Interior, Bureau of Land Management, Eastern States Office, 350 South Pickett Street.

June 15, 1827

William was in Harper's Ferry before Nat Turner's uprising there. He had heard him speak. Nat had encouraged his brothers to have pride. Saying that they were men not dogs, he used the analogy of Moses leading the Jews into the promised land as men who would stand up for themselves.

William looked bemused by the memory of that day, and then he gave us a start, saying, "I guess I should tell you now that we're on the subject. Old John is fixing to send us a hay wagon filled with fugitive slaves. We're going to hide them and then run them up to Pearce's house in Michigan.. He'll send them on to Canada, where they can be free. It's in the family tradition."

Amid a flurry of questions about where the slaves would be hidden and how long they would be with us, William's brother, David, asked how this tradition had gotten started.

"It was in Ohio that Old John met his wife-to-be, Mercy Ackin. I was their first- born son. Their son, Pearce, our brother, was born in Morgan County, Ohio where we owned a home. At that time they had one indentured servant named Henry but no slaves. Pennsylvania was part of the Ohio Territory back then. John's brother kept slaves, but John never did. Old John's father, Daniel, our grandfather, was in real estate in Holmes County, Ohio. He couldn't write. He and John always signed with an "x". He helped to build a school there.
We had a brother, Daniel, named after him, who died in Ohio in 1820.

We came from Jefferson County, which marked a line between the free and enslaved. parts of Ohio. If the slaves could get over the Ohio River, they usually were able to make it to freedom. The bloodhounds couldn't track them in the water. We started helping them get through the water, then on to freedom on horseback.

The upper end of Ohio County just below Brooke also fronted on Jefferson County and in that portion there are probably a dozen slaves to one hundred people.

The grandmother of my mother, Mercy, was Sarah Pearce whose husband, James, was descended from Countess Phillippa Plantagenet of Ulster whose daughter, Elizabeth Mortimer (1370-1417), granddaughter of King Edward III, married Sir Henry Percy. He was called Hotspur. Don't ask me why. I don't know. Shakespeare wrote about Hotspur in his play HENRY THE FOURTH. Hotspur tried to start a rebellion against King Henry, as he was in direct line for the throne, but it was put down. I guess we've got that rebel blood in our veins.

Your grandma, Mercy Pearce, was born in New Jersey in the thirteenth generation from Hotspur. They had plantations in Virginia and the deed to Manhattan Island. But that's another story for another day. I'm tired and need some sleep. No doubt, the baby will start crying in the middle of the night again." William muttered through a yawn.

Author's note:

As I read this diary, I was amazed to see that our family was descended from the original English royalty! I was also astounded to find that this descent was through an unassuming abolitionist grandmother named Mercy Achen Driskel.

Hot Spur's son was Henry Percy, Earl of Northumberland II, who married Eleanor Neville. They had ten children and we are descended from the second, Ralph (1425-1464). Since he was the second son, he could not inherit the title or lands.

He married Eleanor Acton, Daughter of Lawrence Acton, born about 1429 and a possible ancestor of Lord Acton, famous English historian and statesman. After his son, Peter, and a grandson and great grandson named Richard who all died in Pearce Hall, England, Richard Pearce was born in 1590 in Somerset, England. He died in Newport, Road Island, 7 October 1666. His son, William, born in England, had one child, John, born in Boston. His son John Pearce and Maria Delamater had the twins James and John In 1724 James married Sarah Van Horne, born in 1721 to John Van Horne and Rachel Webber.

Aunt Dorothy knew that John Delamater owned the land in the northern portion of Manhattan Island near the Palisades. Perhaps James owned some of that expensive real estate also. It was valuable even then, because it was thought to be the gateway to the West and even possibly to the Orient. There were thirteen patents to this land.

It may have been that Sarah Van Horne, herself, had this deed, given to her Dutch family from William of Orange, as Aunt Dorothy surmised. She first married James Pearce and had Sarah Pearce, Mercy's mother, born about 1761. Then Sarah Van Horne married Freegift Taylor. In her rush to leave James, she may have left or lost the deed. Or Freegift Taylor may have owned the deed and lost it on the way out west. The Taylors and Bogarts were also related to the Delameters through Sarah Bogart who married Abraham Delameter in 1711. A Taylor/Bogart farm still existed near South Grove in Margart's time and on into the mid -1900s.

Looking back in the genealogy, I could see that Old John's father, the settler, Daniel, Driskell had had a daughter Sarah (Sally) who married William Gibson in Ohio and had the son, Phoenix. My Aunt Dorothy proudly informed me that Phoenix had donated the land for Wheaton College, one of the foremost theological colleges in the country. Also Anne Funo, descended from Old John's youngest child, Little John, a foster child, donated 3 million dollars for an executive education center and for a scholarship in Madison for Wisconsin University. Her husband was governor of the Chicago Stock Exchange. Little John was the youngest of the twelve children that Mercy and Old John had raised.

At the time of William and Old John's impending murder, William had tried to tell his brother, Pearce, where the money was that he had saved for his children's education, but the mob attacked him too soon.

The children of Old John have definitely made up for that twist of fate in the prominence that they were able to claim and the good that they were able to effect in their area. Theodore Decatur had been with his mother, Margaret, in the corncrib after his father and grandfather were murdered. One of his sons was Jesse, my grandmother's brother. To Jesse and Edith Driskell, his remarkable wife, is dedicated a statue to the Sycamore Library. It rests today on a three foot pedestal at the street level entrance and is entitled "Girl With Book" by Helen Merritt.

Edith was a nationally published poet. Her poems stated witty remarks about the politics and social life of the mid twentieth century through which she lived vibrantly. She bore Jesse twelve children, two of whom were blind. Cheerful, loving Carol taught brail and the other blind sister had a PhD from a college for the deaf and was a professor there. Dr. Mabel Driskell Bailey was former president of the National Association of Blind Teachers and wrote three books. Her book, MAXWELL ANDERSON, THE PLAYWRIGHT AS PROPHET, gained wide recognition. She earned her doctorate at the University of Iowa. Her mother, Edith lived to be 101.

When Edith asked me why she had lived so long, I said that it probably was because she was an excellent example for us all. When Jesse had gone bankrupt in the Depression, she had started a clothing boutique in Sycamore without any prior business experience. On the farm as a wife, she always rose before six to bake bread in a business suit. She ran her family like a business but with love and compassion.

Her daughters wrote a very sophisticated cookbook, featuring her gourmet recipes, which they lovingly dedicated to her.

Author's Native American friend, Leonette, and African American friend, Olivia - the grand niece of Maya Angelo.

June 17, 1827

"Somehow and somewhere there germinated in his (man's) mind the idea that association, cooperation, would serve his ends better than unbridled egoism in the struggle for existence. Instead of "each man for himself" his motto became "each man for his family" or his tribe, or his nation or-ultimately- 'for mankind.' And at a very early stage, what made for association, cooperation, brotherhood, came to be designated a 'good' while that which sinned against these upward tendencies was stigmatized as 'evil'".
William Archer (1856-1924)
Scottish critic

Today the slaves arrived in the hay wagon drawn by a pair of huge Belgian draft horses. We took them into the basement with hay from the wagon for their bedding. Then we gave them soup down there. And didn't they have stories to tell of savagery and desolation!

One man, who could hardly speak intelligibly, said that the daughter of his master in Tennessee had chosen him to father his master's first grandchild. He was tempted by the white woman and knew that if he didn't cooperate, she would malign him to her father. When the child was born, the eyes became brown and the skin dark soon enough.

The white grandfather, half mad with rage, wanted to get his revenge on the black man but his daughter had given him free papers and had sent him away from Tennessee. He was denied the free status in Tennessee, but found people who would shelter him and send him in the hay wagon to our safe house. Even though he was legally free, he feared being apprehended for mating with a white woman, and he wished to be free of the country and sent to Canada. He said that the child of this white woman and himself would probably be smothered or sent where its lineage would not be known. William said the hay wagon was called a "coach or train," the slaves should be called "cargo" or "passengers" or "packages" whenever we referred to them from now on. Our log cabin was a "station" or "stop" along the "line" or route the runaways take. We use the positioning of lanterns in windows to tell them that we are a safe house and if the law might be nearby. Quilt patterns that we made at quilting bees depict the different routes that could be used to gain freedom.

If two white men driving wagons happen to approach each other, one might say "Hello, friend of a friend," which meant he was driving a load of runaways and was checking to see what was up ahead. The other if he was sympathetic might reply by raising his right hand to his ear, or he might grasp his hat between his thumb and finger. Either response meant that all was well. If the response was a palm extended outward, however, it would mean to beware.

Author's note:
We can see that the two minorities, Native and African Americans, definitely have history that ties them together in many ways. Even as early as 1816, hundreds of runaway slaves found refuge within the borders of the Seminole Nation, in Florida, following the Seminole War. This tribe of Native Americans was not removed, because they could hide in the swamps, and they also hid the Blacks.

In 1822, Denmark Vesey led an abortive slave revolt in Charleston, South Carolina after which 36 slaves were hanged. Rebellions did not liberate anyone, but they symbolized a new determination of slaves to be free, ending the idea that all slaves were docile and satisfied with their condition. This also spurred the development of anti-slavery organizations in each northern state.

June 18, 1827

"In democracy, liberty is to be supposed; for it is commonly held that no man is free in any other government."
Aristotle 938-322 B.C.
Greek Philosopher

"Talk about Slavery! It is not the peculiar institution of the South. It exists wherever men are bought and sold, wherever a man allows himself to be made a mere thing or tool and thus, surrenders his inalienable rights of reason and conscience."
Henry David Thoreau 1817-1862 Journal

"All men recognize the right of revolution, that is, the right to refuse allegiance to, and to resist the government when its tyranny or its inefficiency are great and unendurable. But almost all say that such is not the case now. But such was the case in the Revolution of '75."
"On the Duty of Civil Disobedience."
Henry David Thoreau

I went down in the cellar to take some porridge to the slaves. One striking mulatto girl caught my eye, and I noticed that she was writing in a rustic diary. I asked her for her name and how she had learned to read and write. She said her name is Emily and that the great aunt of her lawyer master had taken a liking to her grandmother and had taught her to read and write, but after she reached the age of fifteen, her master began to whisper "nasty" words.

She tried to ignore him or treat him with contempt, but he persevered. Sometimes he angered, and it made her tremble. Sometimes he used gentleness to try to get his way and make her forget the character training of her grandmother. He told her that she was his property and subject. She had to live under the roof of this man who was a fiend and only had the shape of a man. The mistress, his wife, who should have protected her, bore her only jealousy and rage.

She said that the little child who waits on her mistress learns why the mistress hates certain slaves, and the child learns bad things before her time. Her innocence is stolen from her and she is not a pure child any longer. If she has beauty, it is a curse. What is praised in a white woman is the cause for the downfall of a black slave girl. She said that her master crept up on her. If she tried to sleep, she lay in fear. When she tried to go outside for fresh air, he dogged her. Even when she knelt at her mother's grave, he rose up behind her. She was afraid to tell her grandma, as it shamed her, but she knew that she had chased one white man away from one of her daughters with a gun. Lisa said that many women of the north kept quiet about such things, but that I am different and a gift from God..

Runaways traveling alone have to be extremely careful when approaching a home. Many knock on what they think is a friendly door only to find themselves roughly bound and gagged and turned over to authorities for the reward money which is sometimes as much as $75. Free blacks are not immune from slave-hunters either. By law, a slave-hunter does not have to verify whether he has a slave or a free man taken by accident.

I decided to take Emily as a maid, since she became devoted to me in a short time and was a bit afraid to go on into Canada. I needed help with the new baby, Morgan. William said that he would take the chance of keeping her although she might be pursued over state lines. When she learned more of world events she said that she would rather be half starved as a pauper in Ireland, the way Old John's father had been, than to be the most pampered among slaves in America. She would have rather drudged out her life in the fields of the plantation than to live with that unprincipled master and his jealous wife. A felon in a jail might repent from his ways and gain peace, but a favorite slave is not allowed to claim a virtuous life.

Her mistress could have used the knowledge of her husband's ways to screen and counsel the young and innocent among her slaves, but for them she had no sympathy. She watched her husband carefully, but his schemes evaded her vigilance. When he discovered that Emily could write, he began passing notes to her. She said that she couldn't read them, but then he said that he would read them to her. On and on he used insidious methods to lure her away to a secret place. When she finally said that she must apply to her grandmother for protection, he threatened her with death and even torture that would be worse than death.

The secrets of slavery are like those of the Inquisition. Emily's master was, to her knowledge, the father of eleven slave children. But the mothers did not dare to tell who was the father of their babies. The other slaves did not tell either, except in whispers to each other. They knew too well the consequences of this kind of talk.

Southern women often marry a man knowing that he is the father of many little slaves. They look the other way and regard such children as property, as marketable as the pigs on the plantation. They often make the children aware of this by passing them on to the slave trader as soon as possible to get them out of their sight. I'm glad she said that there are some exceptions. She knew of two Southern wives who asked their husbands to free those slaves who were their children, and their requests were granted. Though slavery as an institution deadens the moral sense, even in white women, to a deplorable extent, I have heard Southern women decry the fact that Southern men not only father these black children but are not ashamed to call themselves their masters and that this situation should not be tolerated in any decent society.

July 1, 1827

"The law will never make men free; it is men who have got to make the law free. They are the lovers of law and order who observe the law when the government breaks it. I hear many condemn these men because they were so few. When were the good and the brave ever in a majority?"
"Slavery in Massachusetts,"
Henry David Thoreau

"Is it not possible that an individual may be right and a government wrong? Are laws to be enforced simply because they are made? Or declared by any number of men to be good if they are not good?"
"A Plea for Captain John Brown,"
Henry David Thoreau

Because of his ideals about emancipation for slaves, I trusted William not to violate Emily's trust. Her story was so heart rending and outrageous, that I felt sure that William would have a pure relationship with her. It also had a cathartic effect on his involvement with Tecumshantas in my mind. Hearing Emily speak of how she had been violated, made me feel that William would regard Tecumshantas with respect.

We were sitting around the dining room table and David, William's brother, was visiting. from down the road where he lives.

"You still haven't told us how Tecumshantas was born," David said to his brother after William stoked up our corncob pipes and poured us whiskey.

"Well, I can tell you this," William began.
"Tecumseh had married Manete who came from mixed tribes. Around 1796, she bore him his only son Pugeshashenwa, who was Tecumsehantas's father. Manete was the sister of Chief Naw Kaw of the Winebagos, who had moved his tribe close to Fort Dearborn. Naw Kaw had become one of Tecumseh's personal attendants during Tecumseh's height of power. He was with Tecumseh for about twenty years before Tecumseh was killed at the Battle of the Thames.

In 1808, the brothers had built a Prophet's Town on Tippecanoe Creek in Indiana, where their converts lived in the so-called purity of the old ways. The next year, Tecumseh visited the Southern tribes to convert them and while he was away, Governor Harrison called a few chiefs to Fort Wayne, "mellowed them," he said, with alcohol, and got their signatures to a treaty, ceding three million acres of land in Indiana, some of it belonging to tribes not even present at the council. When Tecumseh returned, he condemned the fraud.

By the spring of 1810, he had one thousand warriors at the Prophet's Town, including six Sioux warriors, training them to repel any attempt to settle the land, but his plan for peace and unity had not been strong enough to be maintained.

In August, with 300 followers in war paint, he went to see the governor at Vincennes. The meeting was held under the trees with Harrison's soldiers and Tecumseh's warriors standing by. Winnemac, a Potawatomi chief and friend of Tecumseh who was lying on the ground, held a loaded pistol beaded at the governor.

The Governor invited Techumseh to take a chair.
'Your father requests you to take a seat by his side,' he instructed.
'The Great Spirit is my father,' the chief answered. 'The earth is my mother, and on her bosom I will recline.'

Then he sat down on the ground. Later he spoke, presenting the Indian cause so eloquently that an interpreter was hard pressed to follow him:
'Sell a country!" he hollered. "Why not sell the air, the clouds and the great sea, as well as the earth? Did not the Great Spirit make them all for the use of his children?
The States have set the example of forming a union among all the fires- why should they censure the Indians for following it?'

Harrison then spoke, saying the United States had always been fair to the Indians. Tecumseh, springing to his feet, shouted, 'It is false! He lies!'

Captain Floyd drew his dagger and Winnemac immediately responded by cocking his gun.

The warriors drew their tomahawks; the governor unsheathed his sword.
Then, just as suddenly, when a fight seemed near at hand, he abruptly dismissed the council.
That was the white way of gaining peace.
Now, I am weary and wish you a good night," William said, blowing out the candle.

July 2, 1827

"Anybody can become angry-that is easy, but to be angry with the right person and to the right degree and at the right time and for the right purpose, and in the right way-that is not within everybody's power and is not easy."
Aristotle (384-322 B.C.)
Greek Philosopher

This evening, I continued the story from the history book that William had been following. William and I and David were drinking whiskey and smoking our corncob pipes while I read the following story:

"The next day, Tecumseh visited the Governor, apologizing for his outburst. He sat on a bench with the governor and kept crowding Harrison, who kept moving over. Tecumseh laughed and said that was what the white men were doing to the Indians. He said he was going on a unity mission to other tribes and asked for a truce. Harrison agreed.

As soon as Tecumseh was safely away, Harrison marched against the Prophet's town with a force of 1,000 men. The Indians held an excited council. Tecumseh had told them to keep the peace but some Winnebagos wanted to fight, and the Prophet yielded. Some 450 Indians made the attack before dawn, then they withdrew. Harrison went on and burned the town.

Here, Tecumseh discovered that he was at war before he had concluded his Pan-Indian union. The tribes whose warriors had been killed fell on the settlements. Many settlers were killed, farms were abandoned throughout Indiana and one family was killed within about two hundred miles from us, near Ft. Dearborn."

I decided to read the boys from a history book I had about the War of 1812 in which my ancestor, Stephen Decatur was an admiral:

"Meanwhile, on June 18, the United States declared war against Great Britain. Both sides then sent agents throughout the Northwest to enlist Indian allies. Gathering a huge war party, Tecumseh marched to Fort Malden and joined the British. Thus, it was an Indian, Tecumseh, who began the fighting in the War of 1812. Soon Major General Isaac Brock arrived with British reinforcements, and Tecumseh helped materially in his capture of Detroit and Hull's entire army in August. At the same time, the Potawatomis captured Fort Dearborn and massacred the garrison, just two hundred or so miles from us!" I added, looking up at the boy's amazed faces.

"In April of 1813, " I continued, "Tecumseh returned to the North with 600 recruits from the Illinois tribes, the Fox, Sauk and Illinois. He now had about 3,000 men under his command. But in January a force of

850 Kentuckians advancing against Detroit had been annihilated by the Indians under Procter, those not killed being butchered after their surrender. When Tecumseh learned of it he was equally angry with his Indians. Harrison marched north to avenge this outrage and Procter and Tecumseh besieged him there and the warriors cut off some 800 Kentuckians on their way to reinforce him. Most were killed, but about 150 surrendered. The Indians scalped them.

Tecumseh galloped to the camp and hurled himself on the killers. The massacre stopped instantly. Then he went to Procter. 'You are not fit to command,' he raged. 'Go put on petticoats!'"

(THE INDIANS OF ILLINOIS, Helen Cox Tregillis, Heritage Books, Inc., 1983.)

Here, the boys laughed uproariously.

"Tecumseh realized then that his men were not yet adept in civilized warfare." I went on from the book.

"On August 30 the hostiles brought the U.S. into the war by falling on Fort Mims, a few miles above Mobile. The Indians rushed in through an unguarded gate and killed 107 soldiers, 160 civilians and 100 Negro slaves. But on September 10 came Perry's famous naval victory on Lake Erie, cutting off the British supply route from the east. Procter then abandoned the Detroit area and started to retreat along the north shore of the lake with Tecumseh protesting every step. Harrison caught up with them. And Tecumseh was killed fighting in the Battle of the Thames on October 5, 1813. A monument with a Canadian flag flying above it now marks the place where his great design collapsed far from the homeland he had devoted his life to keep.

Naw Kaw told the historian, Atwater, that Tecumseh "fell at the front line of Kentucky Dragoons pierced by more than 30 bullets.

He was carried four or five miles into the thick woods and buried by warriors."

"On that solemn note, we need to get you to bed," I told the boys.

Later, watching William stare into the glowing embers of the dying fire, I wondered what his thoughts might be.

This was the end of the story of the great chief. The rival for my husband's affections is his namesake. She may be of comparable fighting valor. Yet, she may not have the noble peace keeping intentions of the honorable chief. Is she intent on breaking up my home and family?

Indiana became a state in 1816 and Illinois in 1818, seven years before we were married. Then Missouri became a state in 1821, and its Indians were removed to Kansas. Georgia and Mississippi passed laws extending their jurisdiction over the Indians within their borders. After the War of 1812, Shaubenee, who fought with Tecumseh's forces against us, had reluctantly pledged his allegiance to the United States. For this pledge, he was granted land.

But now in 1827, Shaubenee, who was with Tecumseh when he was killed in the Battle of the Thames, still has the land granted to him north of us in a place called Shabbona's Grove west of Ft. Dearborne. That's where my rival, Techumsahantas was born, since her mother was a Winnebago Sioux princess.

Later, William pulled on my skirt as I brushed by him where he lay on our bed. He pulled me down to him and kissed me hard, but I was reluctant. Then, he held my face in his rough hands, still kissing me deeply. Finally I relented as he untied my corset and set me free of its daytime binding, He ran his fingers over my breasts and set my soul on fire. I am a prisoner of circumstance here.

July 7, 1827.

"From the use of the word free-will, no liberty can be inferred of the will, desire or inclination, but the liberty of the man; which consisteth in this, that he finds no stop in doing what he has the will, desire or inclination to do. "
Thomas Hobbs (1588-1679) English Philosopher

"Speak the truth in humility to all people. Only then can you be a true man. Do not only point out the way but lead the way."
"Lying is a great shame. There is a hole at the end of a thief's path."
"Is it not better for a hundred to pray for one than for one to pray alone for himself?"
(Legends of the Lakota Sioux)

Our story hours seemed pertinent now to current history. We just heard a news flash via the community "grape vine."

William came home for supper and repeated the news to us this way:

"During the War of 1812, Billy Caldwell, born around 1780 in Canada to an Irish officer and a Potawatomi woman, was Tecumseh's aide and also his secretary, since the chief spoke little English. Caldwell saved many prisoners at Ft. Dearborn from the massacre. In 1816, he wrote a commendation for Chamblee (or Shaubenee), for his service during the war, and next week he and Shabona are supposed to meet with Big Foot to prevent a Winnebago uprising north of here."

The Indians have for a long time had quite a large camp on ninety to a hundred lodges on the west side of West Four Mile Branch. The Indians camped there are part of three tribes, the Kickapoos, Pottawatomies and Delawares. These Indians are very friendly and considered honest. The camp is a lively place on Sunday, made more so by the presence of a great many white people, who come from settlements for miles around to spend the day. They all enjoy horse racing, shooting, foot-racing, jumping and "Indian wrestling." But suddenly the Indians left their hunting grounds and have not been seen again.

Last week some boatmen north of Galena kidnapped some Winnebago women. The Illinois Governor, Reynolds, said they were kidnapped for "corrupt and brutal purposes". Now, there is talk that the Winnebago husbands will retaliate. I am remembering that Techumseh's wife was partly Winnebago as was Techumsehantas's mother, a Winnebago Lakota Sioux.

July 12, 1827

"Let us not be unmindful that liberty is power, that the nation blessed with the largest portion of liberty must in proportion to its numbers be the most powerful nation upon earth. America in the assembly of nations has uniformly spoken among them the language of equal liberty, equal justice and equal rights."
John Quincy Adams 1821
6th President of the United States (1767-1848)

Last night it happened! The Winnebagos attacked our community in defense of their women. Hearing sudden war whoops, my husband reared up out of our bed and rushed to the window in his nightshirt. I followed and saw them carrying firebrands to burn our homes. Some had already been torched, and people were dousing flames with buckets. Then, an astounding thing occurred. Out from the shed on the hill came Tecumseh's granddaughter striding purposefully, her milk white face glowing in the firelight. She held up her hand when the chief came riding toward her to swoop her onto his horse and hold her hostage, thinking she was a white woman. Then, I saw him look into her jet black eyes, burning with defiance. He recognized her then and appeared to be asking what she was doing there. We learned later that she asked him to spare the village. She said her friends here were not responsible for treating the natives with disrespect. She also said that she knew the men who were responsible and would point them out.

Even I was grateful for this act, which was a return of my husband's kindness to her. I have to admit that we were witnessing another valiant act similar to that of Pocahontas, but this was not the mild mannered John Rolfe the Indian maiden was defending. This was my degenerate husband. And she would not have the chief, her father, consent to a marriage with this married man. She would be an exile in disgrace among her own tribesmen, since she had been a priestess, and now they would consider that she had lost her healing powers.

We wondered if Tecumsehantas knew of Pocahontas' fate and how, after converting to Christianity and taking the name Rebecca, the Indian princess was placed on display in England and subjected to the myriad diseases the whites are heir to, dying early. She was the only Native American to be abducted, but more abductions had been planned in Jamestown where the citizens were planning to set up a school near Henricus. They planned to convert the Indians there, but the school was destroyed before it could be completely erected.

I didn't ask my husband that night about what Tecumsehantas knew regarding Pocahontas. I just uttered a prayer of thanksgiving that we had been saved from the fate of that school.

Alexander Robinson has lived around Fort Dearborn for some time. He is the son of a Scottish trader and an Ottawa and has become prominent as an interpreter and mediator. He and others are responsible for keeping the Potawatomi from joining the Winnebagos against us.

Author's note:

I was interested in Pocahantas because while I was writing this book about my ancestors I had met a woman descended from Pocahantas' tribe, named Leonette. She had come to my doorway with her son for a world peace meeting. Her son had learned about these meetings years before. We were chanting for peace in our own lives and for the peace of the entire world. Leonette had a manic-depressive husband who was abusing her. He had broken into her townhouse and had beaten up one of her sons. She was looking for a practice that would keep her safe.

Later we went to powwows, where she and her brilliant daughter did fancy dancing. Finally that daughter graduated magna cum laude from a university in Maryland As I wrote about my ancestors, she informed me more about Native Americans, past and present.

September 1827

"They (Americans) must win gold, predominance, power, crush rivals, and subdue nature. They have their hearts set on the means and never think of the end. They are eager and restless and positive, because they are superficial. To what end all this stir, noise, greed, and struggle?"

"Philosophy means the complete liberty of the mind, and therefore independence of all social, political or religious prejudice. It loves one thing only-truth. If it disturbs the ready-made opinions of the Church or the State of the historical medium in which the philosopher happens to have been born, so much the worse, but there is no help for it." "The art of achieving the true is very little practiced, because there is no personal humility or even love of the true. We desire, as a matter of course, the kind of knowledge that strengthens our hand or tongue and serves our vanity or our desire for power, but criticism of ourselves, of our prejudices and inclinations is antipathetic to us."
Henri Frederic Amiel (1821-1881)
Swiss poet, philosopher

It has taken a long time to clean up our village and restore the burned homes. In the meantime Tecumsahantas has testified that it was boatmen who insulted the Indian maidens. They were not the men of our village. She has pointed out the guilty men in Galena to Judge Peoria, who also has Indian blood. William and the others have been thus exonerated of the crimes of which they were accused.

Some people are saying that I have Indian blood, because my father is French and I sometimes smoke a corncob pipe, but I don't believe there is a drop of savage blood in my veins. My great grandfather helped La Fayette aid the Americans in Revolutionary times, and I come from honorable stock from Pont d'Ain, France. I still wonder about Tanekee Nagle though. Was she an Indian who married Resolve Waldron, and am I related to her through my Nagle bloodline?

Regardless of this nation's debt to Lafayette and others of French blood, there is talk of exiling French people west of the Mississippi with the Indians, because so many French traders married Indians, and some think we might all be half-breeds. I wonder often how they can be so blind to our history? After all, it was Jacques Marquette, the Jesuit missionary, and Louis Joliet, the explorer of the Mississippi area, who first discovered Fort Dearborn area.

November 5, 1827

"Force no matter how it is concealed begets resistance."
"Power does everything in a circle."
(Lakota proverbs)

I have morning sickness now because I am expecting a baby again. I am now twenty one and have some silver in my auburn hair, which I wear curled in a chignon at the crown of my head during the day, but when I let it down at night, it reaches my waist. William used to like to brush it until the "firelight gleamed in it," as he used to say. Then, he would wrap his arms around me from behind and pull my white nightdress up, all the while whispering endearments and kissing my ears, while caressing my breasts until his manhood grew strong within me. His Irish magic was irresistible. And it still is.

As I mentioned earlier in this journal, I nearly died giving birth to our son, Morgan, two years ago. He is named after William's youngest brother who was born in Morgan County, Ohio.

In our cemeteries are so many graves of women who died that way. Morgan was breech, and the midwife came all the way from Springfield. I was already in hard labor three days, and nearly dead then. Still, she massaged my abdomen and encouraged me to push one last time. Then, she reached in and found a foot, then reached up through my searing pain to find the other. With a powerful pull she brought out the feet. She shouted to me that she had a foot, and then she twisted the body to set the shoulders vertical.

William said that he would never forget my last unearthly scream as the head emerged. He thought I had vanished from this existence, but then in a few minutes he was called and found the blonde baby in my arms, nursing as I slept at last.

The doctor had sewn me where I was torn, but I had internal tearing and have not been the same in our marital bed since then. It is so painful, but I do try. My blood and spirit are willing even though my body is not. And then, there is the trouble about Techumsahantas....

I have time to think of these things since William has gone to drive the cattle up north to Fort Dearborn. The papers say that this year the turnpike gate at Cumberland Gap saw livestock worth a million dollars go through it. Horses, mules, cattle and hogs are connected with markets across the country by foot. Sometimes four and five thousand hogs are driven at once on horseback.

January 1828

"The ardor of the men could not be repressed; they abandoned their mired horses and pursued the savages on foot, through mud and water up to their waists every step, and many penetrated through the bank of the river, a distance of three miles, where they found and burnt a Potowatomy village, together with a great heap of corn & property. 20 or 30 Indians were killed and a number wounded, four prisoners taken; six American scalps and some horses that had been lately stolen from St.

Clair County were retaken." (Governor Edwards from THE INDIANS OF ILLINOIS, Helen Cox Tregillis.)

"Poverty is a noose that strangles humility and breeds disrespect for God and man."
(Santee Sioux Proverbs)

William had just returned from Ft. Dearborn, up north, where he drove the cattle to be slaughtered. He was covered with soot and was hardly able to relate what happened there. His black beard is singed and his dark blue eyes are clouded by anger.

"The fort is almost completely burnt up from being stuck by lightening! Big Foot, called Maungeezik as the Potawatomi chief, and his men were outside the stockade," William said breathlessly

"They were there for a peace treaty. They stood by while the city burnt. Then they left and several men outside the fort gathered and hurriedly decided to send Shaubenee and Billy Caldwell to talk to Big Foot who sympathized with the Winnebagos' plan to attack the fort while it was weakened."

My husband stayed over night at a tavern near the fort called the Saganash Inn where he saw couples fornicating in the back yard, which was like a mud hole. He heard from the scuttlebutt that Shaubenee was seen riding into Big Foot's village alone. Big Foot and Shaubenee argued. Shauabenee refused to help the Winnebagos take the Fort. Big Foot, became enraged with Shaubenee and all but killed him. Shaubenee was thrown into a wigwam as a prisoner under guard. When his friend had not returned in a full day, Caldwell finally rushed into the village to help Shaubenee get released. He presented a plea to Big Foot, reminding him of Gomo and Black Partridge's treaty of 1815.
Finally, Shaubenee was released.

Black Partridge was a Potawatomi chief on the edge of Peoria Lake who often made visits to Ft. Dearborn where he knew Captain Heald, who commanded the Fort. He did not join Tecumseh in the confederacy to slow the movement of the settlers going west. In 1812, when Captain Heald was ordered to abandon Ft. Dearborn and emptied the liquor supply into Lake Michigan, the Potawatomies became furious since they had expected to receive most of the goods as gifts. Black Partridge warned the captain about the young braves and that he could no longer control their actions.

On a famous occasion in August 1812, Black Partridge had handed Heald his medal that he wore around his neck. Then the captain was escorted from the fort. They began their way to Detroit but were attacked by some angry Potawatomi. Mrs. Linai Helm, one of the soldier's wives, was seized by a young warrior. Fortunately, the brave was Black Partridge.

She was taken to a place of safety until the firing ceased. Her husband, Lieutenant Linai Helm, was taken to a village on the Kankakee River and was held prisoner there for two months before Black Partridge discovered where he was. Black Partridge collected some money from a white trade stationed at Peoria and bought the Lieutenant from the village. The money was not enough, so Black Partridge offered his own horse, his rifle and his gold nose-ring to satisfy the kidnappers. Her husband was released then and returned to her.

Unfortunately this good deed was returned by white cruelty. Just a few months later, Governor Edward's men destroyed Black Partridge's village.

When my husband told this story about Black Partridge, his brothers all sided with the Indian chief who had saved the lieutenant and his wife. They mused over the injustice perpetrated on other tribes, which involved Governor Edwards.

March 1828

"The General immediately made the necessary arrangements, and leaving the sick and a few who had lost their horses, we marched the next morning for Gomo's town. Here we found the enemy had taken water and ascended the Illinois. We burnt their village and two others in the neighborhood and encamped on the ground two nights. The general, finding they had declined giving us a fight, marched back to Peoria.

(Ibid.)

Gomo, another chief of the Potawatomi during the War of 1812, also did not agree with the Prophet's attempt to stir up the tribes against the white man and met for a treaty in Peoria, near here, but that winter the game was scarce and tribes resorted to stealing horses, since the traders would not supply goods. British interference was a scapegoat, but the truth was that Gomo did not answer requests for return of stolen horses. By 1812, Governor Edwards was desperate to make peace with the tribes. These efforts were thwarted when settlers killed an Ottawa and captured two others on the mouth of the Illinois River and Governor Edwards burnt Gomo's village.

Then, during the summer of 1814, Gomo and others returned to the Illinois River area. Gomo, Black Partridge and Pepper assured the Americans they wanted peace. In 1815 a treaty was signed, but this year, Gomo died.

My husband sided with the Indians, since he believed that the horses were originally theirs, having been given to them by the Spaniards. He has a way with horses and is able to whisper in their ears to train them rather than "break" them. When the wild one is in a corral, he walks away from him until the horse is not afraid of him. When he gets close enough, William shows him a carrot or piece of sugar, and he comes closer. Days later he is able to lasso the bronco and finally, after much longer, to place a blanket on him. He never uses a saddle or bridle, but, like the Indians, rides bareback. His horses never feel the hard, cold bit in their mouths. But he is one with the horse when he rides, and he guides it with the mane, again like the Indians. In the summer, he takes them up in the hills to a cooler place, as the Indians do also.

Author's note:

The horse made the nomadic Indians better fed and housed and allowed the sick and old to travel in greater comfort. It became the center of Plains nomadic life. The Indians traded and raided for horses. The Comanche, the Sioux, the Arapahos and others all are better understood as nomads, traveling with their horse herds, than as mere buffalo hunters.

So much did the horse become a part of their lives that some plains Indians denied that there had ever been a time without horses. But the southernmost group of the Blackfoot confederation kept alive the legend of the arrival of the first horses or "sky dogs" as many western plains Indians call them. A kutenai, or enemy, brought the first horses to a Blackfoot camp whose headman was named Dog. The Kutenai and his family were starving. For some reason they had been unable to kill buffalo. The Kutenai brought the horses in a desperate attempt to appease his enemies and get food. On seeing the horses, the Blackfoot Tribe thought they must have come from the heavens or from beneath the earth. Over time, both the horses and Dog prospered. Dog finally became a leading chief named Many Horses, and mounted on the horses, drove them west of the Rockies.

There were pros and cons to the arrival of the horse. Like Europeans themselves, horses and cattle harbored diseases previously unknown in North America, diseases that could kill native species. Strange grasses were mixed in their excrement. Consider the snake grass eaten by cows which when consumed in their milk led to "the milk sick", which may have killed Lincoln's mother, first love, Anne Rutledge, and many other pioneers. Now it is thought that Anne Rutledge probably had typhoid fever.

Even as the Indians created a new world based on the mixture of horses, buffalo and grass, that world, unbeknownst to them, began to unravel ecologically. Before the white hunters ever arrived, it appears that disease and habitat destruction began to seriously cut into bison numbers. The whites would only administer the crowning blow.

August 25 1828.

"Every wanton and causeless restraint of the will of the subject, whether practiced by a monarch, a nobility or a popular assembly, is a degree of tyranny."
"No laws are binding on the human subject which assault the body or violate the conscience."
Sir William Blackstone
(1723-1780)
English writer on law

"It is difficult to discover what is meant by the landed interest, if it does not mean a combination of aristocratic landholders, opposing their own pecuniary interest to that of the farmer, and every branch of trade, commerce and manufacture. In all respects, it is the only interest that needs no special protection. It enjoys the general protection of the world."
(Thomas Paine)
American Revolutionary and Statesman

"Every individual, high or low, is interested in the fruits of the earth; men, women and children, of all ages and degrees, will turn out to assist the farmer, rather than that a harvest should not be got in; and they will not act thus by any other property. It is the only one for which the common prayer of mankind is put up, and the only one that can never fail from the want of means."
(Ibid.)

Since I am the granddaughter of an officer, who fought in the War of 1812 as well as the Indian War, I could not side with the "savages" as I referred to them in my thoughts. I remember always that my uncle was a naval hero of that war. This bias I have against the Indians has caused a rift between William and myself for some time. Now, although William does not know that I am aware of his meetings with Tecumsehantas, in the sweat lodge a few miles from our house, I can scarcely contain my grief and outrage. He says he is learning healing from her, but I don't believe him at all. At the same time, I'm afraid I'll turn him away even more with my jealousy.

It is strange how many people are attracted to the Indians. They have a closely integrated and wild culture. Those who are captured very rarely want to come back to our society with all of its prohibitions and strictures. The Strong family lost a daughter in that way. She was stolen in an Indian raid, married a brave and when they went to rescue her, she would not return.

Also, our Irish men have ties to the land, similar to the Indians. They staked their claims in the midst of much danger, dug their furrows and cleared the land. Now, other settlers think that they have a claim to that land. People like the Phipps are always trying to get land at a cheap price, which diminishes its value. They did the same when they were in Canada. When a new settler wants to buy our land, we have to fight to sell it for $1.25 per acre. Then, people like the Phipps turn around and sell it for $3.50.

"Pleasant it looked,
This newly created world.
Along the entire length and breadth
Of the earth, our grandmother,
Extended the green reflection
Of her covering
And the escaping odors
Were pleasant to inhale."
(Winnebago Poem from THE WORLD OF THE AMERICAN INDIAN)

"One must learn from the bite of the fire to leave it alone."

"A child believes that only the action of someone unfriendly can cause pain."
(Sante Sioux Proverbs)

"Creation is on-going"
(Lakota Sioux Proverb)

Sept. 10 1828

The Treaty of Green Bay, the Winnebago Conveyance, has given the United States over 750,000 acres of land in Illinois. The payment by us was $20,000.in trade goods.
I hope that we can move away from here up north near Fort Dearborn now that the U.S. owns that land.

I am torn by a dichotomy in my emotions. I am jealous because I do not want to share my husband. I am especially appalled about his possible adultery with a native. The strange conflict in my thinking comes about because I sympathize with Tecumsehantas in part.

Author's note

During the early years of this century in a rapid succession of treaties, the Southern tribes had ceded tract after tract of land as the settlers overran them, each time assured that the new boundary would be permanent. At first President Jefferson had the policy of showing the Indians how to live on smaller areas. He suggested this to the Choctaws and Chickasaws without result. Then, he had some success with the Cherokees. In 1809, they sent out an exploring party, and the migration began that year. Soon 1,130 Cherokees were living in northwestern Arkansas. They developed farms, towns and a written language as Jefferson had suggested.

Then when Jefferson acquired Louisiana, he wanted to move the Indians beyond the Mississippi. This expulsion of the Cherokees was an abomination.

The Cherokees were always sympathetic to the Black slaves. They intermarried with the ones who had escaped into their midst. On the " Trail of Tears" when the Cherokees were removed farther West, they told the white militia that the Black family members were their Slaves so that the Blacks would avoid being recaptured.

On their farms, when they had tried to blend into white society, they often had had slaves. At first the tribe held the land in common, but a man could have as much as he could work or find people to work it for him.

The Cherokee nation also formed a government, and Chief Justice Marshall sent down a judgment from the Supreme Court that the Cherokee land was impregnable and completely theirs. But President Jackson refused to enforce the decision. Indian removal was his top priority. John Ross had created a constitution for the tribe, but the government gave them 5 million dollars to leave. John Ridge, the original founder of the tribe, wanted them to leave in order to protect them, but John Ross, a Scotsman married to a Cherokee, wanted them to remain where they had established a government.

Only a few left of the 14,000. They believed, along with Ridge, that it was more important to remain a sovereign nation than to own land. Sixteen thousand people wanted to stay

And they were the ones who were forced onto the Trail of Tears where 4000 people died. Twelve thousand people were herded into stockades. One half of the infants and all the old people died in ice storms during this death march.

In comparison, the tribes of the northwest were too disorganized. All the area west of the new state of Ohio had been organized as the Territory of Indiana, and William Henry Harrison had been appointed as governor. This is when he had come into conflict with Techumseh.

September 20,1828

"Driven from every corner of the earth, Freedom of Thought and the Right of Private Judgment in matters of conscience direct their course to this happy country as their last asylum."
Samuel Adams

"Our contest is not only whether we ourselves shall be free, but whether there shall be left to mankind an asylum on earth for civil and religious liberty."
Samuel Adams (1722-1803) American Revolutionary leader Speech, Philadelphia, August 1 1776

My uncle was a trapper. He told me of a famous mountain man, Jim Bridger, who lost his Ute wife in childbirth. He brought up his infant daughter by shooting buffalo cows for milk. When she was five years old, he sent her to St. Louis, Missouri where he placed her in a convent. Later he met a Shoshone woman. He finally returned to Missouri to live, taking her along and marrying her according to the white man's law.

It was in St. Louis, where the weary party of Lewis and Clark concluded its journey in September of 1806. During much of the trip, Sacagawea, the beautiful Indian woman, led them. What kind of a relationship did Clark have with her? He adopted her son and sent him to Europe recently to broaden his education, but now the son is still an Indian guide, as his mother was. She had come from the Shoshone nation.

Just a few years ago in 1825, the St. Louis fur companies began to replace the permanent fortified trading post with the "rendezvous."

Caravans of trade goods were sent overland to selected places near the Continental Divide. In a festival atmosphere of drinking and carousing, horse racing and gambling and storytelling, the traders and trappers and Indians came with their beaver to exchange for supplies and luxuries. At the first rendezvous, $25,000 worth of furs was hauled back to St. Louis, This year, the profit reached $500,000.

Years ago, if any of the traders, trappers or explorers ventured too far south, they are captured by the Spaniards and imprisoned or finally expelled, but in 1821, Mexico became independent, and traders were welcomed. The famous Santa Fe Trail connecting Independence, Missouri and Santa Fe has become an important highway of frontier traffic, but the South Plains tribes sometimes raid the caravans.

November 20 1828

"Liberty and good government do not exclude each other; and there are excellent reasons why they should go together. Liberty is not a means to a higher political end. It is itself the highest political end."
Lord Acton

The most certain test by which we judge whether a country is really free is the amount of security enjoyed by minorities."
Lord Acton (John E.E. Dalberg) 1834-1902
English historian and statesman

Two days ago, I birthed our second child, a sweet little girl we named Elizabeth after William's aunt, Elizabeth Cedelia. Through the pregnancy, I had false labor, lying on the bed moaning from time to time. This birth was not as bad as the breech one, although I am torn a little more.

William came to see me today and kissed me as well as the baby. I was very grateful for this tenderness. I should be up on my feet in about a week. Perhaps the birth of this little girl will round out our family and bring us closer in communion.

William is incensed about the policies of our President Andrew Jackson.

Even though Andrew Jackson is as Scotch-Irish as William is Irish, William will give no portion to his policies. He was talking about it to us around the fire the other night.

He declared this about the President:

"Often compared to Daniel Boone, he was an Indian fighter way back when. Jackson believes in the right of Eminent Domain declared by the government, and I believe that once I staked my claim to my land, plowed furrows around it and cleared it, no one could contest my right to it."

The Indians owned the land and had ceded it to the white men who arrived first and staked their claims. This was a promise from the U.S. government. But then some families, such as the MacCades and Phipps who had some years ago tried to grasp power and land in Canada and had been defeated, attempted to do the same land- grabbing on the plains of this country. That attempt frustrates not only us as early settlers but especially the remaining Indians. These Scottish rebels had tried to take over the government in Canada and when they failed, they came down here to try to take over our land and change our forms of law and order. Some of the Scots live in a town named Polo here, but most of its inhabitants are imbued with the ethics and morals of its founder Zenus Aplington, a good friend of Lincoln. A few of them are out for whatever they can get legally or illegally."

I started to think more about the land grabbers around us because of my husband's words.

One land-grabber is a man named John Phipps. He had fought during the War of 1812 under Andrew Jackson in the Battle of New Orleans, and you can imagine how every one was impressed with that! He was known as a true patriot! Of course, my husband, didn't give any credence to that. He was disillusioned with Jackson anyway.

Phipps had been born in Virginia and then moved to Tennessee. He was an original Tennessee Volunteer. When he got back from New Orleans, he married Sarah Carlin.

Later on, Sarah's cousin, a Carlin, became a governor of Illinois.

There was no question that John "knew" a lot of people. Maybe it was something that occurred to him when he was in service, that if he had something the people needed, and he could make it available for sale to them. "Some big money could be made by getting there first with the most," he thought. The idea he had in his mind was "think big; be a wheeler-dealer!"

Phipps is a self-promoting anti-abolitionist.

William doesn't like these traits and wonders what the Phipps family will do next.

(Leonard J. Jacobs, Arson on Second Thought.)

Jan 1829

"They are children. They need the strong guiding hand of a father, who knows what's best for them."

Andrew Jackson on the Native Americans.

(THE INDIANS OF ILLINOIS)

It helps little that we have a ruffian, Indian hater in the White House who believes in Manifest Destiny and the right of men to take the law into their own hands and to acquire land by warfare and pillaging.

Andrew Jackson was one of the main detesters of the Indians since he had fought them in the War of 1812 and several times after that. One experience with the Creeks was bad.

In the South the winter of 1813-14 saw two invasions of Georgia militia and pro-Hawkins Creeks from the east; a federal army with a Choctaw contingent under Pushmataha up the Alabama River from the south; two Tennessee armies from the north, one of these under Andrew Jackson with six hundred Cherokee auxiliaries.

This was a new experience for the Creeks. Their unpalisaded towns had seen no foreign invader since DeSoto had made his trail of death and rapine across their country three centuries before. They fought desperately, relying for the most part on native weapons.

And they did drive back the invaders. Even Jackson had to retreat twice and reorganize his forces. Then he advanced the third time, and the final catastrophe came on March 27.

The religious renewal among the Creeks coupled with Tecumseh's calls for pan-Indian resistance to the Americans, led to what amounted to a sacred revolt. When, at the town of Tohopeka on March 27,1814, one thousand Creek warriors, known to the Americans as "Redsticks," barricaded themselves in a horseshoe bend of the Tallapoosa River to face fifteen hundred Anglo-Americans and five hundred Cherokees, plus one hundred of their countrymen who were with the attackers. Only about a third of the Redsticks had firearms, but they possessed, they thought, a greater power. They believed that enemy gunfire could not harm them. They thought their prophets would make the very earth oppose the invaders.

Rifles and cannons did, however, prove more powerful. Eighty percent of them died on the fields or in the river trying to escape. It was one of the greatest defeats Indian peoples were to suffer in their resistance to the United States. It broke the rebellion.

Jackson went on from the removal of the Pushmataha and Choctaws to the capture of Pensacola and to winning glory for the defense of New Orleans against the British. Then, with the war over, he had commissions to make treaties with his other allies. In doing this, he had no compunction or feeling of war guilt for them. By intimidation, bribery and pressure and using their admiration for him, he is despoiling the Choctaws and Cherokees almost as effectively as he had despoiled the Creeks.

For all of his disdain for the natives in general he is kind to individuals but patronizing.
When the war that Andrew had longed for came and when they had destroyed the village of Talluhatchee and killed two hundred braves, they brought Andrew a little Creek boy, whose parents were dead. The women would not look after him. Andrew took the boy to his heart, called him Lincoyen, sent him to Rachel, his wife, and made him part of the family.

Perhaps this was just a "show" to try to make up for all of the lives he had taken.
He and Rachel had never had children together. They had adopted several before this. She had been married before to a man who had abused her, and there was disparaging talk about her, which Andrew has avenged in staged duels to the death.

Now, he is bored with Nashville, though he loves the town. He hates peace and true to his frontier heritage, is always looking to prove himself in a new war or other challenge.

In Philadelphia, then the capital, he criticized George Washington, was the bane of the financial committees and became close friends with Aaron Burr. His grateful state appointed him to the Superior Court where he was a tough judge, dedicated to rights of the individual against the state.

Then his old friend, Aaron Burr, proposed a wild scheme to persuade the British to aid him in a rebellion. He suggested a plan to free the Mississippi Valley, or Florida or anywhere from the governance of or alliance with the United States and make himself ruler of that new country.

Andrew was willing to listen, but ducked out at the last minute. He encouraged Burr but kept his options open. Perhaps he believed in Burr's vision, but detested Burr's readiness to parlay with Britain, the country he blamed for his mother's death of the plague, which he attributed to the intolerable circumstances caused by the Revolutionary War. He should have hated war but his restlessness demanded wars.

In any case, Burr failed, was tried for treason and was eventually acquitted, in spite of the influence of Thomas Jefferson, but was forced into exile. Although Andrew was never directly implicated in Burr's plot, the taint of the scandal is still with him.

February 1829

"These are people who have been invaded, their morals corrupted by strong drink, their lands wrested from them, their customs changed, and therefore, they are lost to the world."
(George Catlin, I HAVE SPOKEN)
Memoir

We have met an artist named George Catlin who is here to paint portraits of the Indians.
Some say he is exploiting them for his own profit, but I read in his eyes that he has a mission to explain their sad lot to all of us. He has made a powerful impression on me. Along with the explorer Clark, he seems

to be really sympathetic to the cause of these first Americans, and I am trying to understand their history. He had created a portrait of the Prophet, Temskwatawa, while this brother of Tecumseh was living with the Shawnee band in Kansas. He has beads in his hand and a spear in the other hand. A ring is in his nose, but on his shoulder are feathers rather than in his headdress, which is a simple band.

He certainly looks savage with gold armbands and necklace.
Yet, he has depicted Tecumseh in a white man's suit with his hair cut as a white man. Did he appear this way, because he was a diplomat who spoke with the white man to defend the heritage of the natives?

Catlin, himself, looks rugged enough with a long beard, huge fur hat, deer skin coat, paint spattered trousers and moccasins.

He had little training as an artist, but he grew up hearing tales of Indians from his own mother, who at age seven had been abducted along with her mother by Iroquois during a raid along the Susquehanna in 1778. They were soon released unharmed, and Polly Catlin often told her son about the experience. On top of this, in 1805, the nine-year-old boy was exploring the woods along the Susquehanna River in south central New York and came face-to-face with an Oneida Indian. The boy froze, terrified. Towering over him, the Indian lifted a hand in friendship. The boy never forgot the man's kindness, which may have been the foundation of his life's mission.

He earned commissions to paint famous figures, including Sam Houston and Dolly Madison, but found that being a portrait artist to the famous did not fulfill his mission.

He found his reason for being in 1828 when a delegation of Indians stopped in Philadelphia en route to Washington.

He had recently married Clara Gregory, daughter of a prominent Albany, New York family, but he packed up his paints, left his new wife and headed west. He said that he adored her and wrote to her each week. He was torn between devotion to her and his artistic cause. This reminds me of my husband, who does not want to leave me, but wants to keep Techumsahantas.

July 1829
"I was captivated by their classic beauty. Nothing short of loss of life will prevent me from visiting their country and becoming their historian." (Ibid.)

William has asked Catlin to speak with Tecumsehantas. Catlin said to William that General Jackson had called the leading chiefs together after the War of 1812 for peace. All but possibly one belonged to the majority party that had fought for the United States through the war. Still, they were all made to sign a confession of war guilt and to cede two-thirds of their territory-an immense tract to the west of their heartland comprising about half of Alabama and a wide strip along the south to cut them off from the Seminoles. He tried to persuade the Cherokees to exchange all their land for a western tract. About one-third of the tribe did remove to Arkansas, but the rest remained on their reduced holdings.

Techumsahantas told Catlin that they had begun to ask for schools. The Moravian Brethren had come in 1801, and the Scottish Presbyterians opened a school a little later. The Scottish believe in educating everyone so that they could learn to read the Bible. Some progress began when the American Board of Commissioners for Foreign Missions began its work there in 1817. Then the educational work of the missionaries was simplified when just at this time the Cherokee genius Sequoia had reduced the language to the written word.

He knew that the white man had a system of conveying messages by making marks on paper. He said, "I thought that would be like catching a wild animal and taming it." Working for years, he finished in Arkansas in 1821. He had isolated eighty-six Cherokee syllables and assigned a character to each one. Thus, the Indians simply memorized the characters; then they could read or write anything in the language. Almost immediately, the whole tribe became literate, and the Western and Eastern divisions began to communicate with each other in writing.

The great American Board missionary, Samuel Austin Worcester, went to Boston and had special type made for a printing press. Last year, the tribe began to publish a newspaper with columns in English and

Cherokee, and the natives in the remote settlements became informed on current happenings.

At the same time, Worchester-with his board paid the tribe for the use of the press-published books of the Bible, religious tracts, and hymn books in the Cherokee language. Now, mission schools have become common, and adult Indians are joining Presbyterian, Methodist or Baptist churches. Presbyterians have to learn English in order go on with their faith, which is why the Scots all know how to read when they come here. The Presbyterians even started colleges in the East, such as Princeton, when only Anglicans could attend Harvard University.

August 1829

"No iron chain, or outward force of any kind, could ever compel the soul of man to believe or to disbelieve."
Heroes and Hero-Worship.
Thomas Carlyle

"The first duty of man is that of subduing fear.
"We must get rid of fear; we cannot act at all till then. A man's acts are slavish, not true but specious; his very thoughts are false, he thinks too as a slave and coward, till he have got fear under his feet."
Thomas Carlyle (1795-1881)
Scottish historian, critic, sociological writer

Techumsahantas told William and George that the Cherokees had begun to formulate a legal code in 1808 written in English. Then, step-by-step, they developed a responsible government, taking the place of the unformulated rise of chiefs, just as the Scottish Highlanders have tried to form links with government. Last year, they elected delegates to a constitutional convention, which created a government with a principal chief, a bicameral council and a system of courts with orderly procedures and jury trial. Their government is functioning smoothly and effectively, financed by council appropriations of the $6,000 annuity paid by the U.S. under various treaties.

They laid out a capital named New Echota, erected public buildings and began to publish their newspaper there. They were a united people and hoping to be safe from further land cessions by bribed or intimidated chiefs.

As soon as the American Board began its mission among the Cherokees, the Choctaws petitioned for one in their own country. The first station, named for the pathetic John Eliot, was established in 1818. Then, the next year a demonstration farm and school was started there, and the warriors appropriated their annuities and donated $1,800 and eighty cows and calves for its support. The missionaries reduced the language to writing, and the children received the schooling in English while the adults were reading religious works in their own tongue. Soon after, the missionaries work with the Chickasawas.

Now the Cherokee, Choctaw, Creek and Chickasaw Indian tribes are charged with "an attempt to establish an independent government" and are being driven off their rich, wide tracts of land to make room for the cotton crops. The Catawaba branch of the Sioux were Once in the Carolina Piedmont area but were driven further and further west. That way/

The Creeks were a dispirited and divided people still, but slowly, under the Cherokee influence, they began to summon their ancient unity and even adopted some of the hated white man's ways. In 1822, they gave reluctant consent to the establishment of two mission schools, Methodist and Baptist, but they strictly forbade the conversion of adults.

(A HISTORY OF THE INDIANS IN THE UNITED STATES)

October 1829

"I have seen him shrinking from civilized approach which came with all its vices, like the dead of the night, upon him... seen him gaze and then retreat like the frightened deer. I have seen him shrinking from the soil and haunts of his boyhood, bursting the strongest ties, which bound him to the earth and its pleasures. I have seen him set fire to his wigwam and smooth over the graves of his fathers...clap his hand in silence over his mouth, and take the last look over his fair hunting ground, and turn his face in sadness to the setting sun."

George Catlin, I HAVE SPOKEN

"To touch the earth is to have harmony with nature."

"Great men are usually destroyed by those who are jealous of them."

Sioux philosophy

Catlin said that in a council at rebuilt Tuckabatchee they adopted a solemn declaration of policy, which began with a reference to the Indians' past greatness and admitted the terrible results of their division and war. "Our fathers never spent a thought on what was to be their end, or what was to become of their offspring." But now they said they could support themselves only by agriculture and they resolved to acquire these skills and remain in their ancestral homes:

"This is the land of our fathers; we love it…and on no account whatever will we consent to sell one foot of it, neither by exchange or otherwise."

In spite of some migrations to the West, however, the four great Southern tribes as a whole have remained intact in their homeland thus far. They have shown that they could make the adaptations necessary for survival in the surrounding white society. It remains to be discovered how the tribes will do here in the heartland.

December 1829

"Our reliance is on the love of liberty, which God has planted in us. Our defense is in the spirit, which primed liberty as the heritage of all men, in all lands everywhere. Destroy this spirit and you have planted the seeds of despotism at your door. Familiarize yourselves with the chains of bondage and you prepare your own limbs to wear them. Accustomed to trampling on the rights of others, you have lost the genius of your own independence and become the fit subjects of the first cunning tyrant who rises among you."
Abraham Lincoln, Speech, Edwardsville, September 13, 1858

We have a Christmas baby, born in the night this 24th day of December. She was turned the right way, thank God. So there was no need for the doctor to come through the snow on his sleigh. My neighbor and a midwife helped to deliver her. She is only five pounds but had a good hollering voice, as she greeted us, fresh out of the womb.

We decided to call her Mercy, another name for Mary, because of Christmas and in honor of her grandmother, the heir to the Manhattan fortune, if only someone could find the lost deed.

The children got oranges in their stockings, brought from Ft. Dearborn at great expense by their father. He also bought some apples, which are less expensive and in season here, thanks to Johnny Appleseed.

For more than twenty years, Johnny Applesee has been making his name between the Ohio River and the northern lakes. In 1806 he had loaded two canoes with apple seeds in Western Pennsylvania, floated down the Ohio River and made a visit to the borders of Licking Creek, where many farmers are grateful to him for their orchards. When he ran out of seeds, he rode or walked back to western Pennsylvania to fill two bags with apple seed. He went barefoot till winter came, and was often seen walking in mud and snow. Neither snakes, Indians nor foreign enemies have harmed him. Asked if he wasn't afraid of snakes as he walked barefoot, he pulled a New Testament from his pocket and said that the holy book is his protection

A hornet stung him and he let it go free. What little money he needs comes from farmers willing to pay for young apple trees. As settlements and villages came thicker, he has moved west with the frontier, planting seeds, leaving orchards in his path over a territory of a hundred thousand square miles in Ohio and Indiana. We just heard that he had built a campfire, which drew many mosquitoes that were burning in it; he quenched the fire.

Sometimes, I put apples in the boys' stockings at Christmas and think of him. Also, when we make apple pies for lunch or dinner, he is on my mind.

January 1830

"I love a people who have always made me welcome to the best they had… who are honest without laws, who have no jails and no poor houses…who never take God's name in vain…who worship God without a Bible, and I believe God loves them also,…who are free from religious animosities…who have never raised a hand against me or stolen my property, where there is no law to punish either…who never

fought a battle with white men except on their own ground...and oh, how I love a people who don't live for the love of money! "
(George Catlin, I HAVE SPOKEN)

Now Catlin, the wondering artist, has wrangled a meeting with the city of St. Louis' most illustrious citizen, General William Clark. He and Meriwether Lewis have already explored the Louisiana Purchase, and Clark is the government's Superintendent of Indian Affairs for Western tribes. Catlin presented his early portraits to the general and asked his assistance in making contact with Indians in the West. Clark was skeptical at first, but Catlin convinced him of his sincerity.

This summer, Clark took Catlin some 400 miles up the Mississippi River to Fort Crawford, where several tribes-the Sauk, Fox and Sioux among them-are having a council. Surrounded by gruff soldiers and somber Indians, Catlin took out his brushes and began work. The other day, he wrote about how the Sioux medicine men predict dire consequences for those whose souls are captured on canvas, yet Blackfoot shamans readily allow themselves to be painted. Once among the Hunkpapa Sioux on the Missouri River, he painted Chief Little Bear in profile. When the portrait was nearly finished, a rival saw it and taunted the chief saying, "The artist knows you are but half a man, for he has painted but half of your face!"

The chief ignored the affront, and when the portrait was done, he presented Catlin with a buckskin shirt decorated with porcupine quills, which he cherished. Yet, the insult led to an intertribal war that claimed many lives. Some Sioux blamed Catlin and condemned him to death, but by then, he had moved quickly up river.

March 1830

"Neither let us be slandered from our duty by false accusations against us, nor frightened from it by menaces of destruction to the government, nor of dungeons to ourselves. Let us have faith that right makes right, and in that faith let us to the end dare to do our duty as we understand it."
Abraham Lincoln,
Address, Cooper Institute, N.Y., February 27, 1861

Catlin has told us about his friend Jean Audubon. He is a rugged sort with long hair like an American trapper. He also carries a dagger, to fend off Indians in their own way, I guess. He was born in Santo Domingo in 1785, the son of a French naval officer, Jean, and a Creole mother on his father's sugar plantation on Saint Dominque, soon after named Haiti. His mother, a 27 year old chamber maid, died of an infection within months of his birth. The stirrings of slave rebellion in 1791 prompted Jean Audubon to sell what he could of his holdings. Later, the father took the boy home to be raised by his wife.

When the Reign of Terror that followed the French Revolution approached Nantes in 1793, the Audubons formally adopted Jean Rabin to protect him and christened him Jean Jacques or Fougere Audubon. Fougere, meaning Fern, was an offering to placate the revolutionary authorities, who scorned the names of saints. The revolutionary envoy ordered the slaughter of thousands in Nantes, and Jean and his family were thrown into a dungeon. After the terror, Jean decided to escape entirely to the new land of America.

The name Audubon came to epitomize the ideal of American individualism. He married Lucy Bakewell from a distinguished English family with whom Erasmus Darwin, a respected poet, physician and naturalist was on familiar terms. They married and moved to Kentucky in 1808.

In the Panic of 1819, Audubon's mill and general store defaulted, and the family lost everything except John Jacque's portfolio and his drawing and painting supplies. Before he declared bankruptcy, he was even thrown in jail for debt. Lucy's fidelity never failed. By spring of 1820, Drake's museum owed Audubon $1,200, most of which it never paid. The artist scraped together funds to support Lucy and their three children by drawing and teaching art. Finally the family moved in with relatives again, and Audubon recruited his best student to draw backgrounds, and in October floated off down the Ohio and the Mississippi.

For the next five years, he labored to compose a definitive collection of drawings of American birds. His decision to produce this great ornithology was condemned by Lucy's relatives as derelict. THE BIRDS

OF AMERICA would comprise 400 two by three foot engraved, hand-colored plates of American birds of life-size dimensions to be sold in sets of five and collected into four huge, leather-bound volumes of 100 plates each with five leather-bound accompanying volumes of bird biographies. He raised almost every cent of the $115,640 it cost by painting, exhibiting and selling subscriptions and skins. Lucy supported herself and their children by teaching in her school in Louisiana while he established himself in England. After that, he supported them all and the work as well.

Like Abraham Lincoln, he once kept a store in Kentucky and traveled the Ohio and Mississippi River regions hunting birds to paint them in oil on canvas trying to capture in his mind their best characteristics. He was among pioneers who moved from Kentucky and settled at Princeton, Indiana, who walked on thousand-mile trips, leaving his wife to stay with friends while he lived with wild birds, shot and sketched them.

Audubon went east to Philadelphia in 1834, gave an exhibition of his paintings, sold less than enough to pay for the show and was told not to publish his work.

In 1827, he began his issues of a work THE BIRDS OF AMERICA which, when finished, was in eighty-seven parts. That same year he reached London. While in London, he became an international authority, and sat up till half-past three one morning writing a paper to read the next day before the Natural History Society of London on the habits of the wild pigeon and how it loves its young as human women love their own babies.

He and Lincoln had footed the same red clay highways of Hardin County, floated on the same rivers and fought in the night against predators that came to kill. Both had spirits that were of gold.

Author's note:

Some Underground Railroad workers were famous men who could travel through the South on business without suspicion. One of these men was Dr. Alexander Ross. He was one of the world's leading ornithologists as well as being a Canadian physician. His research on birds was often described in American and European journals and books. The doctor often stayed as a guest at some of the largest slave plantations in the South. He quietly talked to thousands of slaves, and was never detected as an abolitionist as he traversed cotton and tobacco fields, ostensibly looking for birds. He offered slaves advise on how to escape, told them the location of safe houses and gave them small sums of money for their trip. Planters often mentioned to friends that slave escapes from their counties often came a few weeks after the ornithologist's visits but never connected the two events.

May 1830

"I am for the people of the whole nation doing just as they please in all matters which concern the whole nation; for that of each part doing just as they choose in all matters which concern no other part; and for each individual doing just as he chooses in all matters which concern nobody else."
Abraham Lincoln. Speech, October 8, 1858

"As I would not be a slave, so I would not be a master. It is the same principle. This is my idea of democracy."
Abraham Lincoln.

We hear from some of Pearce's buddies that Lincoln has moved to Macon County Illinois. They crossed the Wabash River in October of last year and then the state line of Illinois on a two-week trip.
Lincoln was selling needles and notions and wrote back to Indiana that he doubled his money; he earned a pair of jean trousers by splitting four hundred rails for each yard of the cloth.

Finally after a rough winter, the family settled in the southern part of Coles County a hundred miles from Decatur, a county-seat settlement, named after my ancestor.

The weaver has come to my house on his rounds. I've been saving up old bits of fabrics to have him make into rag rugs. I only use my spinning wheel once in a while now, since he can make several articles of clothing when he gets around to our house. We put him up for a couple of days, and I make extra food, especially pies, which he favors.

He mentioned that in the South the fabric of an empire, a pastoral and agricultural nation is being woven. Its foundations rested on three chief conditions:

1. The special fertility of a certain strip of land for cotton crops;
2. The raising of the cotton crop by Negro slave labor; and
3. The sale of that crop to northern American and to English cotton-mills, which sell the finished product to an ever-widening world market.

The planters who have control of its destiny are men of pride, valor, and cunning; they live on horseback, accustomed to command.

July 1830

"Slavery is founded in the selfishness of man's nature-opposition to it is his love of justice."
Speech, Peoria Illinois,
October 16, 1854
Lincoln

In the state of Maryland, the old-time tobacco planters speak in muffled farewells to the power they once held. In some counties in Virginia, half the population had been swept out and away downward into the Cotton Belt; the stately white home of Thomas Jefferson was bidden in for $2,500. The speech, the tone of voice and the human slant of the Declaration of Independence is fading out from approved conversation. My father's home is being sold for about $1,500 and old John's beautiful mansion in Maryland was sold for $1,700.

Now, he has moved to Michigan in order to intercept slaves in a safe house near Canada.
He established residency in Ohio, purchasing 50 acres for $1.25 per acre.
William and I were married there in 1825 in Chester Township, Wayne County, Ohio.

Ohio is a great abolitionist stronghold. Its center, the Ohio River Valley, where scores of river crossings serve as gateways from slave states to free; they allow slaves to cross at less peril. Once across the Ohio, the fugitives can hope to be passed from farm to farm all the way to the Great Lakes in a matter of days. Old John was very active in this Underground Railroad whose only rule or law was the 'Golden Rule' and every man does what seems to be right in his own eyes. The term is derived from the story of a frustrated slave hunter who, having failed to apprehend a runaway, exclaimed,

"He must have gone off on an underground road."

Author's note:

In Wilbert Seibert's 1898 book, THE UNDERGROUND RAILROAD, based on first- hand accounts, the movement in Illinois actually started in Ohio.

"In 1819, a small group of devout abolitionists moved from Brown County, Ohio to Bond County in southern Illinois. They later relocated to Putnam county and then Bureau County. Each time, the group set up new stations for the "underground railroad" to operate."

Perhaps Old John and his sons had moved in this group and had association with some of the following abolitionist leaders:

One of the most active underground centers was in Ripley, Ohio, about 50 miles east of Cincinnati. It is one of the busiest ports between Pittsburgh and Cincinnati, its economy fueled by river traffic, shipbuilding and pork butchering. To slave owners it is known as "a black, dirty Abolition hold"-and for a good reason: Since the 1820's, a network of radical white Presbyterians, led by the Rev. John Rankin, a flinty man from Tennessee who moved north to escape the atmosphere of slavery and collaborated with Negroes on both sides of the river. The Rankins' austere brick farmhouse was visible for miles along the river and well into Kentucky; thus many of the slaves taken in there were sent almost immediately to the next "station," but Rankin had a lighthouse in his yard about thirty feet high.

John Brown's Home is at 514 Diagonal Road in Akron, Ohio. The passionate abolitionist lived there during the 1840s, and many artifacts pertinent to his life are on display.

Professor James Monroe was a very vocal abolitionist leader and state legislator. During the war he was a leader in efforts to win the vote for freed slaves. His home is at 73 South Professor Street in Oberlin, Ohio.

Benjamin Lundy was an abolitionist leader who traveled far and wide speaking out against slavery. The editor of one of the nations first abolitionist newspapers, he also published several anti-slavery books. William Lloyd Garrison was his disciple.
His home is at the corner of Union and Third Streets in Mount Pleasant, Ohio.

John Monteith, the first President of the University of Michigan moved to Elyria, Ohio and started a girls' high school there. By night he was an underground leader. His home is at 218 East Avenue. Beginning in the 1840s slaves hid there in the basement or in 3 feet deep closets and fled via a secret tunnel to the riverbank. ·

Thomas Garrett was born in Philadelphia and moved to Wilmington, Delaware in 1822. During the next forty years he helped slaves fleeing from Maryland, hiding them in friends' homes as he arranged their passage north to Philadelphia or New Jersey. He said if he had more money he would build another floor in his home to hide more fugitives. He never denied that he worked for the railroad although several southerners threatened to kill him.

One of the most successful Underground Railroad workers was businessman Levi Coffin, who owned small factories and stores. He assisted runaways from the time he was fourteen, living in North Carolina. He decided to make it his life's occupation when he moved to Newport, Indiana in 1826 and opened a general store. He made several southern friends because of his upbringing in the South. He built a large home outside of Newport and sheltered runaways in the late 1820s. Later, he moved his business to Cincinnati, Ohio, where he lived in another large house and harbored more slaves. He estimated that he assisted over two thousand runaway slaves during his thirty-four years as the Midwest leader of the railroad.

July 10, 1830

"The world has never had a good definition of the word "liberty," and the American people, just now, are much in want of one. We all declare

for liberty; but in using the same word, we do not all mean the same thing. With some, the word "liberty" may mean for each man to do as he pleases with himself and the product of his labor; while with others, the same word may mean for some men to do as they please with other men and the product of other men's labor. Here are two, not only different, but incompatible things, called by the same name, liberty. And it follows that each of the things is, by the respective parties, called by two different and incompatible names, liberty and tyranny."
Speech, Sanitary Fair
Abraham Lincoln

I remember Arnold Gragston, telling us that as a slave in Kentucky he ferried scores of fugitives across the 500 -1,500 foot-width of the Ohio River. I know that there were antislavery men in Kentucky and also proslavery men in Ohio, where a lot of people had Southern origins. Frequently, trusted slaves were sent on their own from Kentucky to the market at Ripley. For families like the Rankins, the clandestine work became a full-time vocation. I remember Jean Rankin, John's wife, said that she was responsible for seeing that a fire was burning in the hearth to warm the runaways and that the couple's nine sons remained on call, prepared to saddle up and hasten the charges to that next station.
One of the sons said, "It was the custom among us not to talk about the fugitives lest, inadvertently, a clue should be obtained of our 'modus operandi.' 'Another runaway went through the night' was all that would be said."

One Rankin collaborator, Methodist minister John B. Mahan, was arrested at his home and taken back to Kentucky, where after 16 months in jail he was made to pay a fine that impoverished his family and may have contributed to his early death.

Not even the Rankins would cross the river into Kentucky, where the penalty for "slave stealing" was up to 21 years in prison. One Ripley man who did so repeatedly was John P. Parker, a former slave who had bought his freedom in Mobile, Alabama. By day he operated an iron foundry. By night, he ferried slaves from Kentucky plantations across to Ohio.

The slaves used the colors blue and white in quilts to spell out spiritual safety and a safe place for a runaway to stop. A drinking gourd or the Big Dipper was a reminder to follow the North Star. Flying geese were a reminder to leave in spring, since in the North deep snows made travel impossible in the winter months. A quilt with a "drunkard's pattern" was a warning to be careful that danger lurked ahead, so zigzag. Don't go in a straight line. Other signs were a brightly lit candle in a certain window or a shimmering lantern strategically placed in the yard.

The Reverend Theodore Weld was a fierce anti-slavery lecturer. He was often pelted with eggs, tomatoes, and rocks. There were many threats on his life and on many occasions he was hurried into a buggy to be driven swiftly out of town.

Another minister was Reverend Theodore Parker, of Boston, who told parishioners, pro-or anti slavery, that when he wrote his sermons he kept a Bible on the left side of his desk and his rifle on the right.

Other abolitionists of New England were Dr. Samuel Howe and his wife, Julia Ward Howe, Wendell Phillips, and Henry Ward Beecher, brother of Harriet Beecher Stowe.
Writers and artists included John Greenleaf Whittier, Henry David Thoreau, Walt Whitman and Ralph Waldo Emerson.

One time, John P. Parker from Ripley learned that a party of fugitives, stranded after the capture of their leader, was hiding about 20 miles south of the river.
"Being new and zealous in this work, I volunteered to go to the rescue," Parker recalled.
Armed with a pair of pistols and a knife and guided by another slave, Parker reached the runaways at about dawn. He found them hidden in deep woods, paralyzed with fear and "so badly demoralized that some of them want to give themselves up rather than face the unknown." Parker wrote to us that he led the ten men and women for miles through dense thickets.

With slave hunters closing in, one of the fugitives insisted on setting off in search of water. He had gone but a short way before he came hurtling through the brush, pursued by two white men. Parker turned to the slaves still in hiding.

"Drawing my pistol," he recalled, "I quietly told them that I would shoot the first one that dared make a noise, which had a quieting effect."

Through thickets, Parker saw the captured slave being led away, his arms tied behind his back. The group proceeded to the river, where a patroller spotted them. Bloodhounds baying in their ears, the runaways located a rowboat quickly enough, but it had room for only eight people. Two would have to be left behind.

"When the wife of one of the men picked to stay behind began to wail," Parker recalled, "I witnessed an example of heroism that made me proud of my race." One of the men in the boat gave up his seat to the woman's husband. As Parker rowed toward Ohio and freedom, he saw slave hunters converge on the spot where the two men had been left behind. "I knew," he wrote, "the poor fellow had been captured in sight of the promised land."

Author's note:

President Obama's Inaugural Speech has inspired me. In its depth, it shows the spirit of our first president of mixed white and black blood, preparing to embark on the bleakest economic era since the Great Depression. These are my incomplete notes from this time when he took the oath on the Lincoln Bible, held by his wife, in the presence of Chief Justice John G. Roberts, Jr. It was addressed to more than four thousand people, standing in Washington, D.C.

The speech went something like this:
He said that he was humbled by the task, grateful for the trust, mindful of the sacrifice of our ancestors. He also remarked that we are the people with the ideals of our forefathers. Our economy is badly weakened, our health care has failed too many. Each day strengthens our adversaries.

Yet, he said that we are children of hope over fear, unity over discord. We remain a young nation. The time has come to choose…All are equal, all are free to pursue their full measure of happiness.

He reminded us that we have never been ones of faint-heartedness. We are risk takers.

For us, our ancestors traveled across oceans, toiled in the fields, fought at Gettysburg that we might lead a better life. The time has surely come, he remarked, to 'pick ourselves up, dust ourselves off' and remake America. We will create new jobs for growth, harvest the wind and soil for conservation, transform our schools and colleges.

He deplored that so many doubt; they have forgotten what free men and women can achieve with unity of purpose.

He declared that the nation cannot prosper long that favors only the prosperous.

Instead, he remarked that we must cherish the root for the common good, the rule of law and the rights of men; we must let the world know that America is the friend of all nations and that we are ready to lead once more.

He indicated that we can roll back the specter of a warming planet. We know our heritage of strength; our common humanity will reveal itself.

He said that people will judge you on what you can build, and we will extend a hand not a clenched fist.

He asked us to remember those brave Americans who have fought for us and have a willingness to find meaning in this moment that will define a generation.

He urged us to return to these truths of honesty hard work, fair play, tolerance and curiosity...and create a new era of responsibility, to face uncertain destiny, defining our character.

He challenged us to take a most sacred oath, keeping in mind memories of who we are and how far we have come. From a moment when nothing but hope and virtue could survive, he said that we must determine to endure what storms may come, eyes fixed on the horizon and god's great gift of freedom.

August 10, 1830

"It behooves every man who values liberty of conscience for himself to resist invasion of it in the case of others." 1803
"Those who labor in the earth are the chosen people of God, if ever He had a chosen people."
Thomas Jefferson

The weaver has left me with some interesting and dismal facts:
Cotton is now king. As a region, the South covers 880,000 square miles; less than one-fourth holds in its grip the controlling economy. In the strip of land, where cotton crops laugh with snow-white harvests, there live about a million and a half people. One in three is a Negro. Massachusetts, Connecticut, New York, Great Britain and France send more and more ships each year for this cotton crop; its bales in this year are worth $290,000.

On a crisscross neck of land running from lower North Carolina to the Red River counties of Louisiana and Arkansas is rising the cotton civilization. The talk of the world is the South. Potluck hunters come from states north, from Britain, and Ireland and the continent hoping a small gamble will bring quick rich rewards. Land is wearing out and the soil is mined and exploited without care or fertilizer. So the worked-out land is left empty or rented to poorer whites, while the big planters turn west and further west.

They seek fresh virgin soils. This is why the covenants of the Federal Government with the Red Indian tribes were torn to scraps of paper while the Cherokee, Choctaw, Creek and were driven off their rich and wide tracts of land to make room for cotton crops and the cotton civilization.

My husband, William, his father and brothers are dead set against this civilization and empathized with the Indians because their land in Maryland had been cheapened and the value of work as farmers lessened due to the "free" labor of slaves. It wasn't only an idealistic cause that made them abolitionists; it was economic. They wanted to send the slaves to Canada as well as having the idealistic compassion to free them.

If my father had not been a military officer by profession, if he had been a farmer, he might have had just as strong sentiments.

I know that in Maryland, for "rambling, riding or going abroad in the night or riding horses in the daytime, without leave," a slave could be whipped, have his ears cropped, be branded on the cheek with the letter R or punished by any method which would not render him "unfit for labor." The fourth time a slave escaped and was captured, he would be castrated

Author's note:

The following are some sites in Maryland and Washington, D.C., which commemorate the Underground Railroad;

The Orchard Street Church at 512 Orchard Street, Baltimore, Maryland was built in 1882 and stands on the site of two former structures believed to have been built in 1840 by the freed black congregation. After the Civil War, freed blacks said that the church had harbored fugitives from plantations nearby. Construction crews working on the church in the 1970's uncovered an underground tunnel. It was thought to have been used in the pre-war era since nearby was the home of freed black leader William Watkins, an influential abolitionist who hid runaways.

President Street Station at President and Fleet Streets, Washington, D.C. gained fame when Abraham Lincoln arrived there secretly on his way to Washington in order to avoid assassination, rumored to take place at a Baltimore train station. Many slaves posing as freedmen forged papers and used the President Street Station because they would not be so evident in the crowds there. Frederick Douglass used this station as well.

The Banneker Douglass Museum at 84 Franklin St. in Annapolis is dedicated to preserving Maryland's African American heritage and serves as the state official repository of African American material culture. The original museum was housed in Mount Moriah African Methodist Episcopal Church, built in 1874 in the heart of historic Annapolis.

"Deep Roots, Rising Waters" is a permanent exhibit overview from 1633 through the Civil Rights Era. It begins with the arrival of Mathias de Sousa, the first Maryland African American colonist, who was an indentured servant and later a sailor.

The famous Marylanders, Banneker, Tubman and Douglass are, of course, emphasized.

Then, it highlights the life of James Pennington, who published his autobiography, THE FUGITIVE BLACKSMITH, still in print today. This book tells how he was able to use his trade to support his underground activities. The exhibit also depicts the struggles of Leo Green who shipped herself in a box from Baltimore to Philadelphia, and after many trials finally arrived in New York.

Displays of African American art and culture change seasonally. The museum is open Wed.-Sun. Summer and Tues.- Saturday after Labor Day. Call (41O) 216-6180 for tours.

Kennedy Farm, headquarters of John Brown at 2804 Chestnut Grove Road, Sharpsburg, Maryland, was the place where fiery abolitionist leader John Brown and his men hid just a few miles across the Potomac River from Harper's Ferry. It was before their attack on the federal arsenal on October 16, 1859 that Brown rode a few miles to meet Frederick Douglass to let him know his plans. He hoped that Douglass would lead a huge slave revolt, which did not occur. Dozens of men, his son and a runaway slave were with him in this attack that ignited the Civil War in 1861.

Cedar Hill, Frederick Douglass' Home, at 1411 W. St., S.E. Washington, D.C. was not a safe house. Douglass moved there in 1877 after his controversial marriage to Helen Pitts, a white woman, who had the home preserved as a memorial. Call (202) 426-5961
for information on tours.

Harriet Tubman Museum and Learning Center at 424 Race Street, Cambridge, Maryland gives tours of the town of Cambridge and out to Bucktown Road where Harriet lived and where a marker tells about her. Call 410 228-0401

All of these homes and museums are open to the public.

August 20, 1830

"...a wise and frugal government which shall restrain men from injuring one another, which shall leave them otherwise free to regulate their own pursuits of industry and their own improvements and shall not take from the mouth of labor the bread it has earned."
Thomas Jefferson

William has told us that his grandfather mentioned to Old John the fact that in the 1750s nearly five thousand slaves were brought into the country by ship each year.
Sometimes masters injured slaves beyond recall or killed them, knowing that more would be arriving. They also put all kinds of contraptions around their necks so that they would not be likely to escape.

A church association in Georgia had formally decided that when slave husbands and wives were separated by sale, either could marry again as though the other had died.
They issued a proclamation stating:
"Such separation, among persons situated as our slaves are, is civilly a separation by death, and in the sight of God, it would be so viewed."

In South Carolina and Georgia, any person finding more than seven slaves together in the highway without a white person could give each one twenty lashes.
For 200 years, ships have sailed to the West African coast, shackled their loads of live- stock and hauled them to American harbors. John Rolfe who married the Indian princess Pocahantas, recorded in his diary in 1619 the arrival of a ship in Jamestown, "a Dutch man of war that sold us twenty Niggars."

An African prince from Timbucktoo was shipped over to Carolina and then sold down to Mississippi to a Calvinist Scotsman named Foster. The slave was wise in the ways of planting and became an indispensable over-seer for Foster, married Isabella and started a family. As he grew old, Foster's son, to whom his children were willed, had an affair with one of his daughters and some of his grandchildren were born from that union.

He is now seeking asylum for himself and his nine children in his birthplace, Africa.

He wrote to Henry Clay and visited Washington, pressing his case to the Capital, but neither John Quincy Adams nor Jackson would allow the manumission of his children born in this country. Only he and his wife were allowed to sail away to Africa.

Mournfully leaving their family, they passed away far from them in that distant land.

(We hear that Lincoln might favor sending black slaves to freedom in Liberia, but it doesn't seem as though that would be a good idea to us.)

Another one-time slave from South Carolina was Francis "Free Frank" McWorter, born in 1777. He eventually migrated to Kentucky where, for years, he labored in a saltpeter mine. Finally at age 40, he had "salted away" enough money to buy his wife's freedom for $800. The couple traveled 400 miles, between Pulaski County in Kentucky to Pike County in our area of west-central Illinois.

Masters sometimes asked one slave to kill another runaway. One slave is recorded as saying, "I'ze suppose to kill you, but I ain't no Massa...My hands ain't stained with no blood. I'ze make up my mind I'ze gonna run away first chance I git. I'ze travels all that day and night. Bloodhounds done tree'd me. I kept wishen' I meets up with that Tubman woman. I saw a big lighthouse in Ripley, Ohio. A tall man took my arm. 'Hungry, boy?' he asked. I went back across. I made three or four trips a month in the black nights of the moon takin' runaways across the river. Walk along free one night and a hand over your mouth and you're back in slavery. My grandkids never git tired of hearin that their grandpa rowed hundreds of slaves to freedom and never knew who they were."

A revolt had taken place in South Carolina in 1772, inspired by the rebellion that was a success in Haiti earlier. Many fugitive slaves were almost successful in South Carolina. If they had been able to run only about 24 more miles, they would have made it to freedom.

Now the census takers reckon two million and more Negro slaves in the South. The approved unit is a hundred slaves to a thousand acres. On a single plantation might be found coal-black Africans with slant skulls and low foreheads, direct from the jungles, men and women of brown or bronze shades with regular features; some who came evidently from Arabia or northern Africa, with flashes of intelligence and genius from old civilizations and persons of thirty percent white blood with manners, skill and accomplishments. All are held as slaves.

Most of the Negroes are on large plantations, but a slave-owner might be a small farmer raising crops with the help of one or two slaves who work side by side with him. My husband has disdain for these farmers, and it's bound to cause us trouble.

From thousands of farms in the North, people are moving into the industrial cities to go to work in the mills. The Southern plantation system is based on the sale of that crop to northern American and English cotton-mills. Some farmers, like us, are selling out and moving over into the Mohawk Valley and western New York or out to Michigan, where Old John has his safe house.

Some tell of the New England farmer who called a minister to pray for better crops from the soil; the minister, after looking over the stony and stingy soil said, "This farm doesn't need prayer; what this farm needs is manure!"

People want to stay on their farms because the life in the cities is so harsh. Farmers' daughters fill the cotton mills in Lowell, Massachusetts; they start work at five o'clock in the morning and work till seven o'clock in the evening with a half-hour off for breakfast and forty-five minutes off at noon for dinner. They spend fourteen hours a day at the factory and have ten hours a day left in which to sleep and to refresh themselves or to improve their minds and bodies.

Authors note:

A rebellion at Fort George, New York took place in 1774 when the pre-revolution foment was in the air. When the slaves were apprehended, fourteen were burned at the stake and seventeen were hanged.

The following are some important anti-slavery sites in New York:

The Isaac Hopper Home at 110 Second Avenue, (Manhattan), New York was owned by Isaac Hopper, a Quaker. He began aiding runaways in Philadelphia as a teenager in the 1790s and moved to New York City in 1829. Fugitives met him in his store on Pearl Street and then were sent to the homes of friends or his own home.

Bridge Street African Methodist Episcopal Wesleyan Church at 273 Stuyvesant Avenue, Brooklyn, New York was a major stop on the Underground as early as 1828. Its middle class black members gave support in shelter, food and money for fugitives.

Siloam Presbyterian Church at 260 Jefferson Ave., Brooklyn, New York was a refuge for slaves. Members also donated money to the New York Vigilance Committee.

Mother Zion African Methodist Episcopal Church, now at 140 137th Street, New York was the first African-American church in New York State. Its pastor, the Reverend James Varick, lectured against slavery for years and harbored fugitives in the church's basement and rooms. On Leonard Street in 1800, it was later moved to Harlem.

Plymouth of the Pilgrims Church, 75 Hicks St., Brooklyn, New York attracted members throughout New York to the passionate speeches of Henry Ward Beecher, brother of Harriet Beecher Stowe, against slavery. They were often complemented by theatrical displays. Several tunnels beneath the church probably served as underground refuges.

The William Seward Home at 33 South Street, Auburn, New York is open as a museum.
William Henry Seward was the leading radical, anti-slavery politician in the country in the 1850s and supported publishers of abolitionist books. He was the runner-up to Abraham Lincoln at the 1860 Republican Convention and became Lincoln's Secretary of State. The museum's telephone number is (315) 252 1283.

The Harriet Tubman Home at 180 South Street, Auburn, New York, was purchased from Seward by Harriet for a minimal amount due to her amazing services for the cause. She bought it for her parents and lived in it most of her post-slavery life. She was buried with full military honors in Auburn's Fort Hill Cemetery.

The Abolitionist Hall of Fame on Main Street, Peterboro, New York commemorates Gerrit Smith, one of the East Coast's most active supporters of the anti-
slavery cause. He arranged for many freed slaves to serve as tenant farmers on his estate hid dozens and donated large sums of bail money. He paid for the guns of John Brown used on the attack on Harper's Ferry and had himself committed to an insane asylum after Brown was arrested in order to appear mentally unsound to obtain leniency.

The museums with phone numbers are open to the public.

September 1830

"I go for all sharing the privileges of the government who assist in bearing its burdens. Consequently, I go for admitting all whites to the right of suffrage who pay taxes or bear arms (by no means excluding females.)
Abraham Lincoln Letter to Sangamon Journal, dated in New Salem, June 13, 1836.

A pastoral letter from the General Association of Ministers of Massachusetts commands ministers to forbid women to speak from pulpits" "When she assumes the place and tone of man… we put ourselves in self-defense against her."

Sarah Grimke wrote, in response, a series of articles: "Letters on the condition of Women and the Equality of the Sexes."

She said: "I ask no favors for my sex. I surrender not our claim of equality. All I ask of our brethren is that they will take their feet from off our necks and permit us to stand upright on the ground, which God has designed for us to occupy…. To me, it is perfectly clear that whatsoever it is morally right for a man to do, it is morally right for a woman to do."

Sarah could write with power; her sister Angelina was the firebrand speaker. Once she spoke six nights in a row at the Boston Opera House. To the argument of some well-meaning abolitionists that they should not advocate sexual equality because it was so outrageous to the common mind that it would hurt the campaign for the abolition of slavery, she responded:

"We cannot push abolitionism forward with all our might until we take the stumbling block out of the road. If we surrender the right to speak in public this year, we must surrender the right to petition next year and the right to write the year after, and so on. What then can woman do for the slave, when she herself is under the feet of man and shamed into silence?"

The African Meeting House at 8 Smith Court, Boston, Mass. was the center of black cultural life in Boston. Built in 1806, it was here in 1833 that William Lloyd Garrison and others founded the New England Anti-Slavery Society. Members of the congregation housed fugitives.

TheTwelfth Street Baptist Church at 150 Warren Street, Boston, Mass. served as an underground station. Freed black members included Anthony Burns, Shadrach (Fred Wilkins), whose rescue efforts drew much national attention, and pastor Leonard Grimes.

Faneuil Hall at Faneuil Hall Square in Boston was ironically a gift to the city by a man who had been a wealthy slave trader. It was a meeting hall for the Sons of Liberty and other revolutionaries in the 1770's and then gained fame in the 1850's when anti-slavery meetings were held there. In 1851, it was here that the crowd that freed Shadrack first met. It is next to Quincy Market, a collection of shops, restaurants and food emporiums.

The William Lloyd Garrison Home at 125 Highland Street, Roxbury, Mass., was the home of the founder and editor of the first nationally distributed anti-slavery newspaper, the" Liberator". He was not an organizer in the underground but a great proponent.

In the Jackson Homestead at 527 Washington Street, Newton, Mass., the Jackson family built a dried up well in their basement between two chimneystacks to hide slaves. Ellen Jackson wrote a memoir to tell historians that the homestead was a station on the underground. The women in the family and others held a sewing circle to make clothes for fugitives. Call (617) 796-1450 for tours.

The African Baptist Church and African Meeting House, Pleasant and York Streets, Nantucket Island, Mass. was the church attended by Frederick Douglass in 1841where he made his unannounced fervent speech. It made him a regular speaker at rallies. Fugitives were sheltered here pending being sneaked away aboard ships to Boston.

In the Johnathan Ball Home, 37 Lexington Road, Concord, Mass. Ball, a local goldsmith built a small hidden room inside a large beam and paneled chimney in his living room to hide fugitives. Henry David Thoreau and a local doctor drove these slaves to West Fitchburg from this house.

Those museums with phone numbers are open to the public. Others may be open also.

October, 1830

"The real democratic idea is, not that every man shall be on a level with every other, but that every one shall have liberty, without hindrance, to be what God made him."
The Dishonest Politician

"Life represents the efforts of men to organize society; government, the efforts of selfishness to overthrow liberty."
Proverbs from Plymouth Pulpit
Henry Ward Beecher
(1813-1887)
American clergyman, writer

The weaver has come to our home to weave some of the clothes for the fall.
He has many more stories to tell.

One girl, operating a single spinning-machine, carrying 3,000 spindles, spins as much cotton cloth as 3,000 girls working by hand a single thread at a time on the old-fashioned spinning wheel. In fifteen years the price of ordinary cloths for sheeting has dropped from forty cents a yard to eight and one-half cents a yard. Overseers in some textile mills crack a cowhide whip over women and children.

The itinerate weaver says that a new form of world civilization is developing, based on power-driven machinery and the selling of merchandise in markets as far off as cargoes can be carried by sailing vessels and by the new in-coming steamboats. This was a large fact of history, before which, it seems, all other facts bend and crumple. Old sleeping, mysterious dynasties of Asia have even given way before it. Let their arabesque portals open to the world.

Yet it is happening that the millions of new customers for the factory-made goods of Europe are not able to buy all that the new power-driven looms and spindles turn out. Factories in the East have shut their doors and turned workmen out. One day in Lancashire, the weaver said, an army of men, out of work, broke into the factories and smashed a thousand looms. In Paris, he says, a tailor invented a chain-stitch sewing -machine worked with a treadle, and workmen who hate laborsaving machines wrecked a new factory with eighty of these sewing machines in it. At Lyons, France, workmen out of jobs rioted with banners inscribed, "Live working or die fighting." Leaders and members of this Free Labor movement began to see slavery as a wrong because factory bosses, they believed, could treat free white workers as "wage slaves" as long as slavery existed.

This is how in the ferment and stew of human conditions, sections of the people of Europe are so restless that they look to see where else on earth they can go. There is an appeal to them in "land uncultivated to an extent almost incalculable" land at $1.25 per acre. That appeal sends millions on the long suffocating voyage across the ocean to make their gamble in the new country.

The people live in three sections, each with a character of its own. There is the North with a long belt of factories, shops and mills, running from southern Maine to the Chesapeake Bay. There is the South with its cotton, tobacco, rice and slaves. There is the West, our area, with its corn, wheat, pork, and furs. In some respects, these sections are like three separate countries with different ways of looking at life.

October 1830

"Let me not be understood as saying that there are no bad laws, or that grievances may not arise for the redress of which no legal provisions have been made. I mean to say no such thing. But I do mean to say that although bad laws, if they exist, should be repealed as soon as possible, still, while they continue in force, for the sake of example, they should be religiously observed."
Abraham Lincoln
Address, "The Perpetuation of Our Political Institutions," Young Men's Lyceum, Springfield, Illinois, January 27, 1837

Pioneers are like vagabonds. They look out on horizons for happiness in ripe cornfields or with sickness, mortgages or rheumatism, rust and bugs eating crops.
Pioneers are luck-seekers. Luck is yonder, over the horizon; it's there summoning, especially to the Irish like my husband, William.

The farmer, who puts in crops and bets on the weather and gambles in seed and hazards his work against so many fateful conditions, has a pull on him to believe he can read luck signs, and tell good or bad luck in dreams in changes of the moon, in manners of animals we often notice certain coincidences operating to produce certain results. And when again those coincidences arise we say that what happened before is liable to happen again.

Pearce told us that Abe Lincoln's father had had a dream about a woman who was the woman to be his wife after Nancy Lincoln had died of the "milk sick." This was the dream that haunted him till he went down a path to a cabin and there saw the woman, Sarah Bush Her face was the one he had seen so often in his dream. The boy, Abe, often questioned his dreams for relevancy. He loved his new stepmother, and she said that their thoughts are often the same; their minds are in communion.

Pearce is seeing a flaxen haired girl named Mary Brody. He is shy with her, and they say that Lincoln is also shy. Her mother is Hannah Kinney, whom I knew from Kilbuck, Ohio, now called Columbia, near William's brother David's home. David is thinking of moving here.

I miss my own mother since she died in childbirth when I was only 12 years young. She wasn't superstitious, but many are out here on the frontier. Luck is what they count on most of the time.

It might have been that the white men took a cue from the Indians, who always watch the actions of creatures for prophesy.

But setting himself apart from superstition, Abe Lincoln wants to know the facts of things from books.

They say that Abe's mother, Nancy Hanks, read to him and sang Scottish ballads. She was an intellectual woman, reflective and sometimes sad. I can relate to that. There are not many intellectual people here on the prairie. She was tall, dark haired. She thought carefully, spoke well and told stories. Perhaps from her he learned to be a raconteur, entertaining all around him with jokes and tall tales.

Thomas Lincoln was a plainspoken man and discouraged Abe from educational pursuits. Several families lived on Nob Creek. They were poor and everyone felt equal to his neighbor. Lincoln saw slaves, driven to the south to be sold. His mother and father first belonged to a Methodist Church and then belonged to a fundamentalist, Baptist group and were against slavery.

When Lincoln was nine, the family moved to Indiana. Thomas was tired of the disputes over slavery. While Thomas built the cabin, they lived in a cave-like place. They huddled around a fire, and Abe recalled wolves howling and mountain lions roaring.

Nancy Hanks was only 34 when she died, and Lincoln was nine. He suffered deeply. Her death led him to a kind of fatalistic philosophy that everything ended in death with no recourse.

He said that his mother was like an angel, and everything he was, he owed to her.

November 1830.

"Abraham Lincoln is my name
And with my pen I wrote the same.

I wrote in both haste and speed
And left it here for fools to read."

"Abraham Lincoln
his hand and pen
he will be good but
god knows when"
Abe Lincoln
Verses in his boyhood sum book c. 1824-1826

Some say that Sarah Bush Lincoln saved Abe. None of his questioning bothered her. His experiences with these wonderful mothers colored his attitude toward women in lovely tones for the rest of his life, but he was shy and awkward with women later in his youth.

November 1830

"The philosopher and lover of man have much harm to say of trade, but the historian will see that trade was the principle of liberty; that trade planted America and destroyed feudalism; that it makes peace and keeps peace, and it will abolish slavery."
Ralph Waldo Emerson,
"The Young American," 1844.

A transportation revolution is happening! An American-made horizontal-boiler engine is running on the first stub line called the Baltimore & Ohio Railway. Processing for smelting iron with anthracite coal by use of a hot-air blast is almost ready. That means no hunting for iron ore and the arduous task of mixing it with other imported elements and shoving all into a furnace in the woods. Iron production has jumped from 54,00 tons in 1810 to 165,000 tons this year. In the little narrow Atlantic States the dinky B & O engines puff along at fifteen miles an hour and slip on the uphill drag, but out here in the Great Plains where it's flat, the miles are measured in thousands. Also, McCormick, Hussey and other men are fixing their wits on making harvesting machines so that one farmer alone on a mower can cut as much grain as a gang of field hands with scythe and cradle.

Ads and flyers I see tell me all of this along with an occasional newspaper from the East.

December 1830

"This gradual and continuous progress of the European race toward the Rocky Mountains has the solemnity of a providential event, it is like a deluge of men rising unabatedly and daily driven onward by the hand of God!"
Alexis de Tocqueville 1805-1859
French statesman and political writer

Thanks to the weaver and his industry, everyone has a new outfit for Christmas in our family this year. Over New England and the Middle States has sprung up, without forewarning, the beginnings of a civilization of power-driven looms, wage-earning labor, of iron, coal and fast transport. So soon we won't need the weaver; we'll buy ready-made clothes at the general store. The big word in the South is Chivalry. In the North it's improvements. But still in the West the word is Freedom or independence or a slogan, "Hands Off." Pioneers in waves are always crossing this stretch of country.

May 12,1831

"This man (Black Hawk), whose name has carried a sort of terror through the country where it has been sounded, has been distinguished as a speaker or counselor rather than as a warrior; and I believe it has been pretty generally admitted, that 'Nah-pope' and the 'Prophet' were in fact, the instigators of the war (Black Hawk War of 1832) and either of them with much higher claims for the name of warrior than Black Hawk ever had.

When I painted this chief, he was dressed in a plain suit of buckskin, with strings of wampum in his ears and on his neck, and he held in his hand, his medicine-bag, which was the skin of a black hawk, from which he had taken his name, and the tail of which made him a fan, which he was almost constantly using."
(I Have SPOKEN, George Catlin, a memoir)

George Catlin came to supper and spoke to us about the Black Hawk dilemma. He said:

The United States has been reimbursing Indian tribes for horses stolen from them. After moving from Michigan territory, Aptakisic a great orator of the Potawatomies, once lived near cornfields on the Des Plaines River near Indian Creek. As chief he was one of many who signed for the Potawatomies and gave up 565,000 acres to the government. In payment, they were given $32,000 in goods and were promised $10,000 in goods this spring. He was not one of the chiefs reimbursed for a stolen horse. He was however still permitted to hunt, fish and plant on any land, which still belonged to the U.S. as long as the tribe did not molest the settlers.

Techumsahantas says that the Sauk chief, Black Hawk, is instigating the war, but the Prophet may actually be the one behind it.

In 1804, as Lewis and Clark began their journey, Black Hawk opposed the Treaty of St. Louis in which the Sauk and Fox ceded all their lands east of the Mississippi to the United States. In later years Black Hawk viewed that act as the beginning of the end of his race. He tried to enlist the aid of White Cloud, a medicine man, to create a confederation of tribes, which would counteract the flow of Americans west. His efforts are failing.

White Cloud was the son of a Winnebago father and a Sauk mother, like Techumsahatas' blood, but the reverse. Tall and fat with long gray hair and, rare among Indians, a scraggly black mustache, he is a great shaman, tending to the spiritual and medical needs of the Winnebago, the Sauks and the Mesquakies. All three tribes knew him as the Prophet, but White Cloud had no comforting prophecy to offer Keokuk, chief of the Sauks, who already knew the Americans were too many for him.

Seven hundred horse soldiers came and camped below Sauk-e-nuk, their capital. At the same time, a steamship belching smoke chugged up the Rock River. The ship grounded on some of the rocks that gave the river its name, but the Mookamonik freed it and soon it was anchored, its single cannon pointed directly at the village.

The war chief of the whites, General Edmund P. Gaines, called a parley with the Sauks. Seated behind a table were the general, the Indian agent, St. Vrain, and the trader, Davenport, who interpreted.

General Gaines said that the treaty of 1804 that had set up the fort on Rock Island also had given the Great Father in Washington all the Sauk lands east of the Mississippi-fifty million acres. He told the stunned and puzzled Indians that they had received annuities, and now the Great Father in Washington wanted his children to leave Sauk-e-nuk and go to live on the side of the large river they called Maseibowi. Their father in Washington would give them a gift of corn to see them through the winter.

'When Davenport gave Keokuk these words, it seemed that his face fell as though a great grip was placed on his heart,' Techumsahantas said. "The others looked at him to answer, but he remained silent. Instead, a man rose to his feet. He had learned enough language while fighting the British, and spoke for himself saying:

'We never sold our country. We never received any annuities from our American Father. We will hold our village'"

General Gaines looked at this Indian, almost old, without a chief's headdress in stained buckskins. Hollow-cheeked, with a high, bony forehead and more gray than black in the roached scalp lock that split his shaven skull, he had an imposing beak of a nose leaping out between wide-set eyes and a sullen mouth over a dimpled lover's chin that didn't seem to belong in that ax of a face.

Gaines sighed and looked with a question in his eyes at Davenport.

"Name of Black Hawk." The interpreter said.

"What is he?" the general asked.

"I am a Sauk." Black Hawk said proudly. "My fathers were Sauk, great men. I wish to remain where their bones are and be buried with them. Why should I leave their fields?"
"I came here not to beg nor to hire you to leave your village," replied Gaines.
"My business is to remove you, and if you don't cross the Mississippi in two days, I will force you away."

They talked among themselves and with White Cloud. They had old rifles, few bullets and no reserve of food. White Cloud said the militia was a superior force and Gaines would not listen to reason. Davenport met with the chief and the shaman and urged them to do as they were ordered before the dispute became bloody. So on the second night of the two days the People had been granted, they left Sauk-e-nuk like animals that were driven away and went across the river into the land of their enemies, the Iowa.

According to Black Hawk, the treaty of 1804 gave the Indians a promise on paper, a sheet of writing saying that they could hunt and plant corn in Illinois, until the lands were surveyed and open to settlers.

That winter the corn delivered by the Indian agent to the new village was of poor quality and not nearly enough to stave off hunger. The People couldn't hunt enough meat, for many in their depression bartered their guns and traps for Whiskey. They mourned the loss of the crops left in their fields. The rich pumpkins, the huge sweet squashes and the mealy corn was their hearts' desire.

Wakieshiek or White Cloud is a medicine man and advisor to Black Hawk. His mother is a Winnebago, as Techumsahantas' mother is, and like hers, his father is a Sauk.
One of Black Hawk's chiefs, Nah-pope, deceived Black Hawk into believing that the Prophet had invited Black Hawk to come to the Prophet's village to plant corn and that Black Hawk's people would be protected.

One night five women crossed the river once again and went to their old fields to pick some frozen ears of the corn they had planted themselves the previous year. While picking it, they were discovered by white homesteaders and severely beaten.

A few nights later, Black Hawk led a few men on horse back to return to Rock Island. They filled their sacks with corn from the fields and broke into a storehouse, taking squashes and pumpkins. Through the terrible winter, a debate continued. Keokuk, the chief, argued that Black Hawk's action would bring the white armies. Black Hawk said white-skins would push the Sauks as far as possible and then destroy them. The only choice was to fight. The only hope for all the red men was to forget tribal enmities and join together from Canada to Mexico, with the help of the English Father, against the greater enemy, the American.

In 1826, an uneasy peace had been finally settled among the Winnebagos, Sauks, Foxes and Pottawatomies. They had wrestled for two centuries and the Winnebago finally have the northwest of Illinois.
Remember that it was the Winnbago faction of the Sioux in 1808, which had wanted to fight when Tecumseh had told them to keep the peace. The prophet yielded to the Winnebagos and some 450 Indians attacked Harrison's camp before dawn. In the battle Harrison lost 61 killed and 127 wounded. The Indians suffered fewer casualties, but they withdrew, and Harrison went on and burned the town.

William, Pearce and David were very interested in Catlin's insights. Now, we have the threat of the Black Hawk War. The Sauks argued at length. By spring most of the People had decided to stay with Keokuk west of the river. Only 368 men and their families are linked with Black Hawk.

May 20 1831
"My reason teaches me that land cannot be sold. The Great Spirit, Man-ee-do, gave it to his children to live upon. So long as they occupy and cultivate it, they have the right to the soil. Nothing can be sold but such thing as can be carried away."
(Black Hawk THE INDIANS OF ILLINOIS, Helen Cox Tregillis, Heritage Books, 1983)

"Guard your tongue in youth and in age you may mature a thought that will be of service to all people."
"When you choose a counselor, watch him with his neighbor's children."
Sioux Philosophy

From the beginning in this country, the Native Americans did not believe that they were yielding their land to the white men. In their eyes, it was more like renting it in exchange for alliances against other tribes, namely, the support, knowledge and guns of the white men.

They continued to live on the land and could not conceive that they had actually relinquished it.

Techumsahantas is keeping us up to date on Black Hawk's movements. Canoes were laden. Black Hawk, the Prophet and Neosho, a Sauk medicine man, set out in the lead canoe, then the others pushed off, paddling hard against the mighty current of the Mississippi, Techumsahantas had observed. She had heard that Black Hawk wanted no destruction or killing unless his force was attacked. As they moved downstream, approaching a white town, he ordered his people to beat their drums and sing. With women and children and the old, he had about thirteen hundred voices. Settlers fled the terrible sound. In a few settlements they could collect food, but they had many mouths to feed and no time to hunt.

William has enlisted the aid of Techumsahantas against old Black Hawk who has declared that added to his problems was the fact that at the mouth of the Rock River was the tribe's old burying ground, where the fathers and mothers of hundreds of years back were buried. This was sacred ground.

To all Indians, this point was a matter of utmost importance, but Techumsahantas still has prestige among those of her Winnebago Sioux tribe. Even though she had disappeared for some time, she was still a priestess, who had ripped open her chest in sincere devotion to the tribe. The Winnebagos had induced the War of 1812 against the whites, when her grandfather had been still interested in peace, but some how through her great love for my husband, she might turn their savage thoughts toward peace.

She must counsel the chief for peace with the whites, because of the white man's superior strength and the logic of having him on the side of the Sioux nation for the future. She must make the Sioux, her mother's tribe, scouts for our people against the ambush of the Sauk, her father's people. What a difficult dilemma she was asked to face! All of her tradition of culture was from her maternal line, her inherited prestige, but her very name and her sympathies of honor were with Techumseh, her great grandfather.

Black Hawk is now sixty-seven years old and can look back on forty years as chief of the Sauk tribe. On his blanket was a blood-red hand, the sign that he had killed and scalped an enemy when he was just fifteen year old. Now he felt the Great Spirit telling him to scare and scatter the squatters and settlers, and then ambush and kill off all the pale-faced soldiers. The Fox, Winnebago, Sioux, Kickapoo and other tribes who had recent grievances against the whites had sent word that they would join him in driving out the palefaces. Already, we had heard that the fast ponies had circled among settlers around the Rock River up north, leaving cabins in ashes and white men and women with their scalps torn out. Our friends wake in their cabins at night to hear yells, to see fire and knives and war-axes burn and butcher, to see their families killed horribly. Copper-faced men have tumbled off their horses with the rifle bullets of white men in their organs.
Across all northern Illinois any strange cry in the night sends shivers of terror to the white people in their lonely cabins.

Finally men on horses, picked for speed, rode to the governor down here in Springfield and asked for help.

Soon, the Washington government, a thousand miles away, was sending the pick of its young regulars to handle the revolt of the Indian chief who would sell land and afterward raise the point that land cannot be sold. Sons of Alexander Hamilton and Daniel Boone are helping young commanders named Albert Sidney Johnston, Zachary Taylor and Winfield Scott. And now our sons and my husband must go also. The white civilization of firearms, printed books, plows and power-looms has resolved on a no-compromise war with the redskin civilization of spears, eagle feathers, buffalo dances and the art of ambush.

I am six months pregnant again, in my second trimester, the calmest part of the ordeal. William has told me that I must go to Michigan to Mercy and Old John where it is safe. We must leave now in the spring, while traveling is better. We are going on a steamboat up Lake Michigan to their home. Mary, Pearce's wife, is there already. They have no children yet, so she will help me with little Mercy.

My husband has been pale and tense for a week, on tender-hooks about how Techumsahantas will persuade the Sioux to use reason and help us. Finally, tonight, he walked in the house without the strain on his face, and some of its color had returned. He said: "I believe that we will have victory with the Sioux scouts on our side. Maybe my brothers and I will come out winners."

I rushed to him without drying my hands from plucking chickens and embraced him. Then, he loaded us with our grips and a trunk on to the buckboard to head for the lake and the steamboat.

July 30, 1831

"I do not mean to say we are bound to follow implicitly in whatever our fathers did. To do so, would be to discard all the lights of current experience-to reject all progress, all improvement."
Abraham Lincoln. Address, Cooper Institute, N.Y. February 27, 1860.

We arrived safely and were greeted warmly by our extended family on the shore. Soon I received a letter from William. He wrote the following:

"Moving with his band up the Rock River, Black Hawk was overtaken by a messenger from General Atkinson ordering him to return across the Mississippi.
Black Hawk said he was not on the warpath, but going on a friendly visit to the village of White Cloud, the Winnebago Prophet, and continued on the journey. General Atkinson had sent imperative orders for him to return at once or be pursued by his entire army and driven back. In reply, Black Hawk said the general had no right to make the order so long as his band was peaceable and that he intended to go on to the Prophet's village"

Now, William and his brothers have volunteered as members of the militia under Captain Abraham Lincoln. He had been raised in Indiana and Kentucky, sometimes even in cave-like shacks, I've heard. The family moved to near Decatur, Illinois.

Abe's ancestors had a great deal to do with Indian fighting. In 1776, one Abraham Lincoln was a captain in the Virginia militia living in Rockingham County. He was a farmer with a 210 acre farm, deeded to him by his father, John Lincoln, one of many English, Scottish,

Irish, German and Dutch settlers in the Shenandoah Valley. In the summer of 1776, Captain Abraham Lincoln's company took a hand in marches against the Cherokee tribes to drive them out in order to farm in peace.

To the northeast was a regiment of British soldiers and Virginia was sending young men to the colonial soldiers under General George Washington. Amos Lincoln, a kinsman of Abraham, up in Massachusetts, was one of the white men who dressed as an Indian, went on board a British ship and dumped the cargo of tea overboard in defiance of British rule. Abe's first cousin, Hananiah Lincoln fought at Brandywine under Washington and became a captain in the Twelfth Pennsylvania regiment. Jacob, a brother of Abe was at Yorktown, a captain under Washington at the finish of the Revolutionary War. These Lincolns in Virginia came from Berks County in Pennsylvania. Although they were fighting men, they had a strain of Quaker blood running through them. They came from people who held war to be a curse from hell; they were a serene but obstinate people. Abraham Lincoln took a wife named Bathsheba Herring. She bore him three sons, and they were named Mordecai, Josiah and Thomas. She also bore two daughters named Mary and Nancy. Abraham Lincoln had wanderlust, because his friend, Daniel Boone kept coming back from Kentucky, telling about this lush land of black, rich land and blue grass with game and fish galore and tall timber with clear running waters. Boone said that this land was all his for forty cents an acre. Abraham waited until a land office was started in Kentucky to straighten out tangled land-titles. In 1781, he and his family started out on the Wilderness Trail that Daniel Boone and his friends had worn, following an old buffalo path down the Shenandoah Valley to Lexington and around to the Cumberland Gap in Tennessee, then northwest into Kentucky.

Abraham Lincoln located on the Green River, where he filed claims for more than 2,000 acres. He had been there three of four years when, one day as he was working in a field, the rifle shot of an Indian Killed him. His children scattered across the Midwest.

Tom Lincoln, Abe's father, lived in different places in Kentucky, sometimes with kin, sometimes hiring out to farmers and sometimes learning the carpenter's trade and cabinetmaking. He bought a farm on

Mill Creek in Hardin County. He was a slow, careless man with quiet manners who would rather have people come and ask him to work than to hunt for a job himself.

Lincoln never identified with his father's life as a farmer. He wanted to "make something of himself." His mother, Nancy Hanks, always encouraged him to do so.

Then, when Abe was about 21, he set out on his own for New Salem in a canoe. New Salem is a town of only about a hundred people but they are almost sophisticated compared to Abe who looked like a "hayseed."

He had been working for Denton Offut, in charge of a new store rented from the Rutledge and Cameron gristmill. It is said that he is in love with the beauty Ann Rutledge and that he could outrun, out lift, outwrestle and throw down any man around The Clary's Grove Boys had put their champion, Jack Armstrong up against him,. He said Abe had won fairly.

Lincoln also enjoys the barbering of a colored man. Billy Florville. He swaps stories with friends while having him cut his hair. William Florville is three years older than Lincoln, according to William. Born in Haiti, he came to Illinois this year. On his way to Springfield, and out of funds, he had met Lincoln in New Salem wearing a red flannel shirt and carrying an ax on his shoulder.. Lincoln has rounded up enough customers so that the barber can continue on his way.

Even the son of the famous explorer George Roger Clark is in the militia of which his father was once Brigadier General. Clark's romance is rumored to be ongoing with the lovely Indian guide, Sacagawea, who with her baby on her back, took him through the wild country of the West.

August 1831

"What country before, ever existed a century and a half without a rebellion? And what country can preserve its liberties, if its rulers are not warned from time to time that this people preserve the spirit of resistance? Let them take arms. The remedy is to set them right as to facts, pardon and pacify them. What signify a few lives lost in a century or two?

God forbid we should ever be twenty years without such a rebellion. The tree of liberty must be refreshed from time to time, with the blood of patriots and tyrants. It is their natural manure."
Thomas Jefferson to Colonel William S. Smith, 1787

William went to Harpers Ferry Virginia driving some steers to sell there. He came back with fervent eyes, saying that a black man named Nat Turner led seventy slaves in a two-day armed rebellion in Virginia. Fifty-seven whites were murdered. Turner, claiming visions from God, gathered some seventy slaves who went on a rampage from plantation to plantation, murdering men, women and children. They gathered supporters, but were captured as their ammunition ran out. Nat Turner was tried and hanged, along with twenty others. Before Turner died, he explained how he had gotten the idea to lead the uprising.

He said that books had stirred his imagination and one day while praying, he felt a spirit that had spoken to the prophets telling him to seek the kingdom of heaven. He believed he was ordained by God for some high purpose. He said that several years later he heard a loud noise and the spirit appeared, saying that an eclipse of the sun would make known to him the time when he should arise and slay his enemies with their own weapons.

October 1831

"Ours will be the follies of enthusiasm not of bigotry, not of Jesuitism. Bigotry is the disease of ignorance of morbid minds, enthusiasm of the free and buoyant. Education and free discussion are the antidotes of both. We are destined to be a barrier against the return of ignorance and barbarism."
Jefferson to Adams, August 1, 1816

Nat Turner's rebellion horrified white Southerners. They are amazed that blacks were willing to kill and die for freedom. Now, they have become convinced that reading and writing are dangerous tools, since it was Nat Turner's reading of the Bible that convinced him that God had chosen him to lead his people out of slavery. Fearing more rebellions,

Southern lawmakers have passed harsher slave codes, and it has become illegal to teach blacks to read or write.

Did such rebellions set back the cause of abolition? The South did not answer this rebellion with surrender. Why would they give up millions of dollars in the value of slaves and depreciation of their own lands.

They are almost ready for such a rebellion. In this year Virginia is an armed and garrisoned state. With a total population of 1,211, 405, the state of Virginia was able to field a militia force of 101,466 men, including cavalry, artillery, grenadiers, riflemen and light infantry. This in a time when the neither the State nor the nation faced any sort of exterior threat is truly astounding. Virginia, because of its slaveholders feels the need to maintain a security force roughly ten percent of the total number of its inhabitants.

The other day my father wrote that when William Lloyd Garrison called for abolition in his Boston newspaper, a proslavery mob dragged him through the streets and lynched this famous writer.

Also in Massachusetts, David Walker wrote "An Appeal to the Colored People of the World", based on a defense quoting the DECLARATION OF INDEPENDENCE. He gave it out in pamphlet form but he was killed in a suspicious turn of events. Moria Stewart, his disciple, took up the cry after his death and that of her own husband, who had been wealthy but was swindled by white associates. She made speeches and risked her life repeatedly for the sake of the abolitionist cause.

Slavery became legal in Massachusetts in 1641 and between 1650 and 1750 other colonies followed. The first twenty African settlers had arrived in Jamestown, Virginia as indentured servants in 1619, and slavery did not become legal there until 1661, eleven years after it was legal in Connecticut, three years before Maryland, New York and New Jersey. It was legal in South Carolina in 1682; Rhode Island and Pennsylvania in 1790, North Carolina in 1715 and Georgia in 1750.

By 1804 all of the Northern states, north of Delaware abolished slavery. In 1787, Congress adopted the Constitution. The "Three-fifths Compromise" allowed the Southern states to count three-fifths of their slave population to determine representation in the House of

Representatives. The Northwest Ordinance, passed in the same year, barred slavery in the Northwest Territories.

Just as I had home-schooled Pearce, who is now fighting with Lincoln's band. I attempted to home school the children of our black cook, Matty, and several other colored children on our farm, just one by one-not in a group school. Sometimes, I even try to teach them some French, but my husband seems to free them faster than I can teach them to read. This teaching is also against the law, and I could end up in jail for it.

Still, my ability to teach is one stronghold that I have in the family. Even though William doesn't trust my intellectual questionings, he is glad that I can read and write for the farm business and that I can educate his children.

Emily is helping the fugitive slaves who pass through here to read and write a bit before going on. One man told her that they had had another muster after the annual one on his plantation. The poor slaves rejoiced; they thought it was going to be a holiday. He said that people rushed in from miles away. The houses would be searched by country bullies and poor whites, who had no slaves of their own and exulted in the chance to show a little authority and subservience to the slave holders. They didn't reflect that it was the power of the rich that also kept themselves in poverty, ignorance and moral degradation. It happened that Joseph could read and his wife had kept some letters from abolitionists and other white people. When found, the searchers asked her whom the letters were from. "Are these from half-free coloreds?" She was asked.

"No, most of them are from white people who ask me to destroy them after reading," she replied, bringing on an exclamation of surprise from the company which brought a halt to the questioning.

This was a search beyond the belief of most people. Sometimes the searchers scattered powder and shot in the clothes of colored people and then sent other scouts to find them and bring them forward as plotters of further insurrection. Everywhere men and women were whipped until the blood stood in puddles at their feet. Their dwellings, unless protected by influential white persons, were robbed. All day these wretches went about tormenting the helpless Negroes.. Many women hid in the swamps and were bitten by snakes and insects if not found and raped. If any fathers or husbands told of these outrages, they were tied to the whipping post and scourged for telling "lies" about white men. Night with its infusion of liquor brought on more atrocities.

One old respectable colored minister was hauled to the courthouse green because they had found shot in his wife's kitchen which she used to balance her scales. They were going to shoot him for this "crime." What a spectacle this was in a so called civilized country: a rabble of intoxicated ignorant men assuming that they could administer justice.

The gentry of the city tried to save some of the persecuted people and placed them in jail to do so until the rabble stopped. But it had gone too far and the whites found that their own property was not safe from the drunken hoards. They finally drove them back into the country and set a guard on the town.

Then the hateful swarm was set upon the country coloreds and every day for a fortnight. she said that she would see some poor panting Negro tied to their saddles and compelled by the lash to be taken to the jail. Nothing was proved against any of the colored people and the scourge was slightly abated with the capture of Nat Turner.

The imprisoned were released and slaves were returned to their owners. The slaves begged the privilege of again returning to the little church they had built in the woods. They had no better joy than to meet there and sing hymns together and pour out their hearts in spontaneous prayer. Their wishes were denied and their church demolished. They were permitted to meet only in the galleries of the white churches, since sermons were geared to keeping them passive and in subservience. After everyone else had been given communion, the minister would say, "Come down now, colored friends."

Then they would obey the summons and partake of the bread and wine celebration of the meek and lowly Jesus who had declared that all men are brothers.

In 1820, the Missouri Compromise admitted Missouri to the Union as a slave state and admitted Maine as a free state. Slavery was prohibited north of 36 30 latitude. In other words, the western states west of

Missouri and north of its southern border were declared to be states where slavery was prohibited. Every state in the Louisiana Purchase was to be free north of the southern border of Missouri except for Missouri itself. After England past a law against slavery, a federal law here ended the legal importation of slaves in 1808. Still they are coming in illegally in huge numbers.

Meanwhile, "Free Frank" McWorter, who freed his wife after working in the saltpeter mine for years, has started a community in Pike County, about 20 miles from the Missouri-Illinois border. He picked up the name "Free Frank" in his move to our non-slave state. He bought 80 acres from the federal government for $100. He platted the parcel into 144 lots and sold them to African-Americans and Caucasians alike. I guess the community will be a part of the "railroad". He is probably part Irish, with a name like McWorter.

Nathaniel Benford of Charles City Co. Virginia has liberated 7 of his slaves and sent them to Ben Ladd at Smthfield.

I have asked William that we no longer be part of the underground railway since I am pregnant again and fear for our children.

December 1831

"May it [The DECLARATION OF INDEPENDENCE] be to the world what I believe it will be…The signal of arousing men to burst the chains under which monkish ignorance and superstition have persuaded them to bind themselves and assume the blessing and security of self-government. That form which we have substituted, restores the free right of the unbounded exercise of reason and freedom of opinion. All eyes are opened or opening to the rights of man. The general spread of the light of science has already laid open to every view the palpable truth that the mass of mankind has not been born with saddles on their backs, nor a favored few booted and spurred ready to ride them legitimately by the grace of God. These are grounds of hope for others."
Jefferson to Roger C. Weightman,
June 24, 1826, the 50th anniversary of the Declaration and ten days before Jefferson's death.

Well, I've had an awakening experience. With Old John gone up to town for some provisions, I decided to go out to the shed to find some more logs that he stores there for the cook stove. Since my belly was so big from my pregnancy, I picked up a log and lost my balance because my legs were nearly frozen stiff. I fell against the cliff side of the shed and it gave way to open a rugged door and disclose an opening about four feet high dug into the cliff. There I found a cup and a blanket rolled up. Back further in the hole, I found a girl who was shaking with fear

The golden skinned girl is only about six years old. She is singing to herself: "Didn't my lord deliver Daniel, deliver Daniel, deliver Daniel and why not every man." Her eyes are glowing with hope. She is clutching a quilt with a bear paw motif. This is to remind her to follow the tracks of animals if she is lost in the woods. She was following the tracks when she said the "master of the house came with a lantern, a signal, that he is a station master" and put her in the shed.

Here was a secret compartment, and I now know that my father-in-law has been hiding slaves here. How many nights has he been laboring in a compassionate endeavor to save these miserable people?

Now, I realize that he has placed himself in danger's way, and I see why he has such a passion to train wild horses and why the horses disappear as soon as they are trained. He is following in his father's footsteps and has endangered us all.

It's not bad enough that we're involved in this war with our men's lives at stake, but he may be creating another great disaster for us all. The revelation of the bedlam after Nat Turner's insurrection has alerted me to the danger of harboring these people

I took the colored girl in with me to the house and fed her some soup. She said that her parents had been on a slave ship and had watched friends from Africa being thrown overboard so that it would not be considered a slave ship when the English came aboard. There she was sitting beside the fire when he came home. There was the evidence.

I turned on Old John as he came into the house out of a snowstorm that had been gaining in intensity through the evening. The fury in my eyes and the girl by the fire told him that he had been found out.

He tried to hold my hand and explain but I turned in dismay and fled to one of the hired hand's rooms, abandoned now as the hand had fled on a horse from the shed. I slept very little that night. It was a long, bitter night.

January 1832

"This declared indifference, but, as I must think, real, covert zeal, for the spread of slavery, I cannot but hate. I hate it because of the monstrous injustice of slavery itself. I hate it because it deprives our republican example of its just influence in the world, enables the enemies of free institutions with plausibility to taunt us as hypocrites, causes the real friends of freedom to doubt our sincerity, and especially because it forces so many good men amongst ourselves into an open war with the very fundamental principles of civil liberty, criticizing the DECLARATION OF INDEPENDENCE, and insisting that there is no right principle of action but self-interest."
Abraham Lincoln.
Reply to Senator Douglas, Peoria, Illinois, October 16, 1854.

It is now a few weeks later, and I have delivered another baby girl, whom I named Sarah Jane. This time William was not there to greet her, since he is fighting in the war, and I am up here in Michigan in the icy cold winter. Pearce's wife, Mary, helped me as I screamed, pulled on a cord hooked to the bed and finally had a last burst of strength to push out this six-pound daughter of ours. Her flaxen hair is streaked with my blood. I am terribly torn and wonder if I can heal this time. I hope that this little girl is our last child. I have grown very close to Mary Brody Driskel, Pearce's wife, and would rather stay here for the rest of my days. But then I worry about William in the war and miss him. The Brodys have been connected with our family for generations. They are not the same Groadys, who were here in Groadys Grove and robbed salesmen before we came here.

January 1832

"A representative form of government rests no more on political contributions than on those laws which regulate the descent and transmission of property."

Address, Massachusetts Convention

"Labor is the great producer of wealth it moves all other causes."
House of Representatives April 2, 1824.
Daniel Webster (1782-1852)
American statesman, lawyer, orator

Well, I am back home with my baby, and I am glad to see William and the children The rift between William and myself because of Techumsahantas and our separation has not engulfed us. We have weathered through worse impasses in our stormy marriage, and I can see that my husband has a compassionate nature even though this good character trait, his compassion, may lead to terrible trials for us all. Still, I continue to write to him. It was a bleak holiday season without him and Pearce and David. I hope this preparation of troops ends soon.

William is amazed at the news that William Lambert, who died in Detroit, helped 30,000 slaves to freedom in 33 years-nearly 1,000 per year, Mercy told me. He is buried in Elmwood Cemetery.

William has finally told me that Old John's father, Daniel, had had an affair of many years with a black woman after his wife's death in Pennsylvania. After John was left motherless, this beautiful Negro woman had mothered him. She was such a warm, imaginative and gentle woman that John had never forgotten her tenderness toward him. Because of her, he had determined to free slaves wherever he went.

When he met Mercy Acken in Columiana Co. Ohio where he was setting up a free house, she joined him in this endeavor. Mercy's mother, Sarah Pearce, had been born in Bergen, New Jersey, a town near Pennsylvania, where my ancestors lived at one time. They were all members of the Friends, or as some say, they were "Quakers", a derogatory term, which meant that they were afraid to fight. Some were Mennonites. Most of these simple people were against slavery. Some of them formed under ground passages to the sea in order to free slaves.

At least William and I have this heritage in common. I should be more of an abolitionist, I suppose, but it is such hard work on the plains without help and with little money to hire people. My ancestors were French Huguenots. We do have this common strain of historical persecution.

Author's note:
It was truly a historic and sad year in 1793 when Congress passed the Fugitive Slave Act, permitting owners of runaway slaves to retrieve them in free states or territories. In the same year the cotton gin was invented, and Southern slave owners started to buy more slaves, but also gave them better treatment in many cases in order to have higher profits. In the same year under intense pressure from Quakers in Canada the government of Upper Canada (now Ontario) passed a law that eliminated slavery there. Quebec Province ended slavery in court ruling in 1800. Slavery was outlawed in the rest of Canada in 1833. So it was that in the next year of this diary, American runaways had a home beyond the northern states where they could be completely free.

There were some landowners, living in Canada, who resented this law and who with American comrades rebelled against the English government. They were called Chasseurs. In Montreal many were jailed and twelve were hanged. Whether or not this rebellion had to do with the slavery issue, I do not know, but several of the rebels returned to the States and were against abolition. They had tried to take over the government and grab land in Canada and continued to try to do so here.

March 1832

"Every man is said to have his peculiar ambition. Whether it be true or not, I can say for one that I have no other so great as that of being truly esteemed of my fellow men by rendering myself worthy of their esteem."
Abraham Lincoln
Letter to the people of Sangamon County, March 9, 1832

With the Christmas card from my parents, my father has written that this is a historic year and decade:

John Keats, the poet, died in Rome. He was buried with his own epitaph on his gravestone:
"Here lies one whose name was writ in water."

"Beauty is truth, truth beauty, that is all ye know on earth and all ye need to know."
"Ode to a Grecian Urn." John Keats (1795-1821)

The next year Shelley drowned in the Mediterranean and his ashes were placed next to the burial urn of Keats. The year before he had written of Keats, " I weep for Adonis-he is dead."

The poet Lord Byron fell, fighting in Greece far from home, and died of fever two years later. Shelley had written of him, "Space wondered less at the swift and fair creations of God when he grew weary of vacancy, than I at this spirit of an angel in the mortal paradise of a decaying body."
Percy Shelley (1792-1822)

"Hereditary bondsmen! Know ye not
Who would be free, themselves, must strike the blow?
By their right arms, the conquest must be wrought.
I wish men to be free, as much from mobs as kings-from you as me."
Lord Byron (1778-1824)

May 1832

"The love of property and consciousness of right or wrong have conflicting places in our organization, which often makes a man's course seem crooked, his conduct a riddle."
Abraham Lincoln.
Hartford, Connecticut. March 5, 1860.

Our brother, Pearce, has come home for a short stay.
He has returned alive, thank God! When he could catch his breath finally, he said this:

"Abraham Lincoln had reasons for going into the Black Hawk War. His job as a clerk would soon be over since the store was sold and he was running for the legislature. Also, a war record would count in politics."

Pearce said that the men in the Fourth Regiment of Mounted Volunteers, all of whom were on foot, had elected Lincoln captain by forming a line behind him that was double the length of his rival, Kilpatrick's.

"He was now Captain Lincoln, and made a speech thanking the men for the honor, saying the honor was unexpected and undeserved, but he would do his best to merit the confidence place in him. Later in life, he said, "Not since had any success in life afforded me so much satisfaction." Yet later, he also never failed to make light of his soldiering days, claiming that his most ferocious foes were the mosquitoes," Pearce said laughingly:

"The first military order he gave as captain got the reply, 'Go to the devil, Sir!' He knew our company could fight like hell but that we would never understand that we had to obey. Other volunteer companies said that we were a tough group of men. One time our men opened officers' supplies and found a lot of "moon-shine." The morning after, the officers had a hard time getting us men up and out. A court martial ordered Captain Lincoln to carry a wooden sword for two days.

An old Indian drifted into camp one day. We men started to attack him since we were out in an Indian war. Lincoln jumped to his defense saying that he should not be killed by us.

We marched in cold rain to the Mississippi, then to Dixon on the Rock River. One company refused to cross the line toward the north. Colonel Zachary Taylor, in command, made a speech, saying he had orders from Washington to follow Black Hawk with the Illinois troops. Behind us he drew up lines of regular soldiers. Ahead were the flatboats to cross the river and leave Illinois; they had a choice. They decided to get into the flatboats and fight Indians rather than fighting the regular soldiers.

Another time, Captain Lincoln went to the regular army officers of his brigade and told them that there would be trouble if his own volunteers didn't get the same rations and treatment as the regulars."

June 1832

"I think the authors of that notable instrument (DECLARATION OF INDEPENDENCE) intended to include all men, but they did not

intend to declare all men equal in all respects. They did not mean to say all men were equal in color, size, intellect, moral or social capacity. They defined with tolerable distinctness in what respects they did consider all men created equal-equal with 'certain unalienable rights among which are life, liberty and the pursuit of happiness.' This they said and this they meant. They did not mean to assert the obvious untruth that all were then enjoying that equality, or yet that they were about to confer it immediately upon them. In fact, they had no power to confer such a boon. They meant simply to declare the right, so that enforcement of it might follow as fast as circumstances should permit."
Abraham Lincoln.
Speech on The Dred Scott Decision

Our brother, David, wrote a letter about Lincoln:

"Near Kellogg's Grove, Lincoln helped bury five men.
He and us men rode up a little hill toward five corpses.
Each of the dead men had a round spot on the top of his head about as big as a silver dollar where the redskins had scalped him. It was frightful!"

On those green hills along the Rock River, the red man and the white man hunted each other.
As they hunted, they looked quite small and were hard to see. Only keen eyes could spy,- eyes that knew those lands perfectly, -the eyes of the Sioux scouts that had betrayed The Prophet and Techumseh. They could put together the movement that appeared, faded, came again, and flashed in the reaches of rolling prairie and slopes of timber.

The Sauks shaped and reshaped their army as a shadow, came and faded as a phantom, spread out false trails, mocked their enemy with vanished from places they had just filled. An ambush was their only hope. But the Sioux knew their every trick. By zigzag and crisscross paths, with the Sauks and Foxes the only tribes actually fighting, Black Hawk was driven north out of Illinois and into swamp and island battles on the Wisconsin and Bad Axe Rivers. His men tried to hold off the whites, who took the island and shot those swimming Indians trying to get to the western shore.
Fifty prisoners only were taken, mostly squaws and children

The Sioux had virtually eliminated the Sauks, their competitors for hunting grounds.

Late June 1832

"The frog does not drink up the pond in which he lives."
Sioux Proverb

My husband found Techumsahantas weeping, utterly distraught. She felt that she had betrayed her Sauk heritage.

She told him a sad story, one of a long cycle of stories of the coming of the Peacemaker:

"Many Hundreds of years ago before the Europeans came The five Nations of the Iroquois, Mohawk and Oneida, Onondaga, Cayuga and Seneca were always at war with one another.

Although they had a common culture and languages that were much the same, no longer did they remember they had been taught to live as sisters and brothers.

Once they had shared the beautiful land from Niagara to the eastern mountains, but now only revenge was in their hearts and blood feuds had made every trail a path leading to war.

So it was that the Great Creator sent once again a messenger, a man who became known to all the Five Nations by the name of the Peacemaker.

To help the people once again make their minds straight, he told them stories about peace and war. This is one of the tales:

'Once there was a boy named Rabbit Foot. He was always looking and listening.
He knew how to talk to the animals so the animals would talk to him.

One day as he walked out in the woods he heard the sound of a great struggle coming from a clearing just over the hill. So he climbed that hilltop to look down.

What he saw surprised him. There was a great snake coiled in a circle. It had caught a huge frog and although the frog struggled, the snake was slowly swallowing its legs.

Rabbit Foot came closer and spoke to the frog. "He has really got you, my friend."
The frog looked up at Rabbit Foot.
"Wa he! That is so, the frog said.

Rabbit Foot nodded, then said to the frog,
"Do you see the snake's tail there, just in front of your mouth?
Why not do to him what he's doing to you?"

Then the huge frog reached out and grabbed the snake's tail.
He began to stuff it into his mouth as rabbit foot watched both of them.

The snake swallowed more of the frog; the frog swallowed more of the snake,
And the circle got smaller and smaller until both of them swallowed one last time
And just like that, they both were gone.

They had eaten each other
The Peacemaker said
And in much the same way
Unless you give up war
And learn to live together in peace
That also will happen to you."

Black Hawk's chief, Nah-pope, had deceived Black Hawk into believing that the Prophet had invited him to come to the Prophet, Wakieshiek's, village to plant corn and that Black Hawk's people would be protected.
Wakieshiek was imprisoned with Black Hawk, which was justified.
Some American authorities praised Black Hawk for his sense of humanity.

George Catlin told us that the Prophet and Nah-pope were the true instigators of the war.

The first act of the Illinois volunteers was to utterly destroy Wakieshiek's village on May 10th of this year.

Catlin said: "This man Black Hawk, whose name has carried a sort of terror through the country where it has been sounded, has been distinguished as a speaker or counselor rather than as a warrior; and I believe it has been generally admitted that Nah-pope and the Prophet were in fact, the instigators of the war and either of them with much higher claims for the name of warrior than Black Hawk ever had."

"When I painted this chief, he was dressed in a plain suit of buckskin with strings of wampum in his ears and on his neck. He held in his hand his medicine-bag, which was the skin of a black hawk, from which he had taken his name, and the tail of which made him a fan, which he was almost constantly using."
(Catlin, I HAVE SPOKEN)

David returned to Lincoln's band a day later and was home in a week to tell the story. Pearce's friends, in another regiment, slaughtered the children and the women in Black Hawk's band from an armed boat on the Bad Axe River. I believe that these boys will have nightmares about this atrocity.

July 15, 1832

The following is Black Hawk's
account, published in the newspaper:

"On our way down, I surveyed the country that had cost us so much trouble, anxiety and blood, and that now caused me to be a prisoner of war. I reflected upon the in-gratitude of the whites, when I saw their fine houses, rich harvests and everything desirable around them and recollected that all this land had been ours, for which me and my people never received a dollar, and that the whites were not satisfied until they took our village and our grave-yards from us and removed us across the Mississippi.

We are now confined in the barracks, and forced to wear the BALL AND CHAIN!
This is extremely mortifying, and altogether useless. Was the White Beaver (General Henry Atkinson) afraid that I would break out of his barracks and run away? Or was he ordered to inflict this punishment upon me? If I had taken him prisoner on the field of battle, I would not have wounded his feelings so much, by such treatment knowing that a brave war chief would prefer DEATH to DISHONOR.

But I do not blame the White Beaver for the course he pursued – it is the custom of white soldiers and, I suppose, was a part of his duty."
(Black Hawk as a Prisoner of War, 1832)

Black Hawk was obviously an educated chief and he was able to put himself in the other chief's moccasins, as the old Indian saying goes:

"Never criticize anyone until you have walked a mile in his moccasins,"
(THE INDIANS OF ILLINOIS, Op cit.)

August 1832

"Every kind of oppression of man by man rests on the possibility, which a man has of taking another's life and, by keeping a threatening attitude, compelling his obedience."

"Slavery means the freeing themselves, by some, of the necessity of labor or the satisfaction of their needs and the throwing of this labor upon others by means of physical force; and where there is a man who does not labor because another is compelled to work for it, there slavery is."

"In order to obtain and hold power, a man must love it. Thus, the effort to get it is not likely to be coupled with goodness, but with the opposite qualities of pride, craft and cruelty. "
Leo Tolstoy (1828-1910)

Russian author

While in Michigan I heard about John Phipps, wheeling and dealing in the Lead Mines up there. After and during the Black Hawk War, Phipps was also in the Lead Mine area north of Galena, and William was leery of him. With him getting around to a lot of places and meeting with many influential people, he evidently turned his thoughts to the fact that the land in northern Illinois would be up for sale now that Black Hawk was no longer there.

It seems that the Phipps brothers were always in touch, and worked together on various projects. Brother Ben was up in the Lead Mines with John, and George and was always nearby. Old John and I talked about how they were all over the place, throwing their weight around.

It is safe to come home at last. I did leave little Mercy up in Michigan with Old John and her grandma, Mercy. She loves Pearce's new little boy, Clark, so we left them together while Sarah Jane is a baby and I regain my strength. Old John rode down on the ferry with us until we could settle in here at home now that the war is over.

I was glad to see William coming up the trail, looking much older from the war. I ran into his arms. His beard is streaked with gray, but he is whole, not wounded. It's a good birthday present for me, just a month late.

October 1832

"O Liberty! Can man resign thee,
Once having felt thy generous flame?
Can dungeons' holds and bars confine thee,
Or whips thy noble spirit tame?
Claude Joseph Rouget de Lisle
(1760-1836
French army officer

Perhaps the Winnebagos felt that by helping the white men to defeat Black Hawk they would stand a better chance to receive a good deal on a reservation in Nebraska, where most were sent in September, according to the treaty at Ft. Armstrong, Rock Island.

Techumsahantas has come to live in her sweat lodge on our property. Sometimes I wonder if William plans to divorce me and marry her, but he says he has no such plan.

She has begun to teach him and the children about the sacred rituals of the Lakotas.

She stands in the center of the sweat lodge and opens a bundle, saying:
"This is the sacred pipe. With it you and all of the people not yet born will send messages to the Great Spirit."
She held the pipe out as he turned to the center of the sweat lodge and said:
"With this pipe all the people and creatures on the Earth will be joined with the four directions and with the Great Spirit."
Next she taught them how to use the pipe in seven sacred rites. Then she gave the pipe to William.
"Remember," she told him. "Always give the pipe respect and honor. Wherever the pipe is, let there be only peace and harmony."
Next she gave them directions, literally, saying,
"Turn to the east where the daybreak star of knowledge appears. Red is the rising sun that brings us a new day.
Turn to the south. Yellow is the south, Earth, our mother, gives the bounty of summer with the warm wind.
Turn to the west. Black is the color of the west where the sun sets. Black is darkness and protects the spirits. In the dark the spirits come to us.
Turn to the north. North is white. Strength, purity, truth and endurance are of the north. North covers Mother Earth with the white blanket of cleansing snow.
Look to the sky. Father Sky gives life from the sun. Father Sky gives the fire that warms our tepees and the life that moves our bodies.

Look to the earth. Green is the color for Mother Earth. She gives us our food. We all start as tiny seeds. We have grown through what she has given.

Turn to the center. Great Spirit, Creator of us all, Creator of the four directions, Creator of Mother Earth and Father Sky and all related things. We offer this pipe."

That was a healing ritual for William and his brothers who were scarred by fighting in the Black Hawk War, after they had been raised to hate war and to love peace and compassion.

A treaty has recently been signed with the Potowattomi Indians allowing them to stay in this area as long as they do not molest any of the white people here. Their treaty seems to be the only good that has come out of this war for the Indians.

November 1832

"There is a Law that man should love his neighbor as himself. In a few hundred years it should be as natural to mankind as breathing or the upright gait, but if he does not learn it he must perish."
Social Interest
Alfred Adler (1870-1937)
Father of individual psychology

Even though I felt that Techumsahantas was a pure spirit at that time, I didn't trust my husband, since he is a man of charm and passion. I also wanted to study about interracial marriages, since some of the Native Americans were knowledgeable and enthralling enough to attract their European conquerors.

I heard an interesting story. This story of the Framboise family proves that the union of a white man and distinguished Indian woman was more common than we had thought. Francois La Framboise Sr. was born around 1780. By the early 1800s he settled in Ft. Dearborn with his Ottawa wife, Shawenoqua, the daughter of a chief. He taught his wife how to read and write English and she, in turn, taught her own children and became the first schoolteacher there. They had five children: Osette, the first, who married Jean Baptise Beaubien had the first mixed blood child who was recognized by the tribes close to Ft. Dearborn. Leather and beads were brought as presents for the mother and child. The Potawatomis danced all night in celebration the night of January 18, 1822.

Jean Baptists Point Du Sable was born probably of a Frenchman and a Negro mother. At times he said he was from Santo Domingo and at others he claimed to be a Potawatomi chief. After trapping a number of years, he finally built a cabin near the Ft. Dearborn portage in 1779. There he operated a post for the British governor. His first residence was at Peoria in 1778 and sometime in the 1780's he was captured by the British and taken to Ft. Detroit to be tried as a spy. After his release he moved to his Ft. Dearborn post and built a fine house of logs and bark. The furnishings, bought in Detroit were elegant and included paintings. His wife was Catherine, a Potawatomi, and after ten years they had an extensive farm including two barns, a horse mill, a bake house, a dairy, a poultry house and a smoke house. He moved back to Peoria after selling the trading post and died in 1818.

Baptist Peoria was born around 1793 to a French Canadian Baptist and a member of the Peoria along the Des Plaines River. He knew the French and English languages as well as several dialects of the Potawatomi, Shawnee, Delaware, Miami, Illinois and Kickapoos. This ability with languages allowed him to be an interpreter on many occasions. He is working with the United Sates in the moving of the tribes from Indiana and Illinois to the west of the Missouri. We see him often going from tribe to tribe. Early in his life, he represented the Peorias in the Treaty of Edwardsville in 1818.

Alexander Robinson or Chechepinqua is another interpreter and mediator for councils and treaties. Last year on September 28, he married Catherine Chevalier, daughter of Francois and Mary Ann Chevalier of St. Joseph, Michigan.

Both Peoria and Robinson have come here to help settle the differences leading to the Winnebago uprising. Tecumsehantus went to the village of her ancestors and talked with the women who experienced the outrage. She said that she had seen the men kidnap the girls north of Galena. They were boatmen.

The young Indian women, who were rescued by their male tribesmen, also testified to the accuracy of this statement. My husband and several other men, who were indicted had to go to the trial in the Indian village and were much relieved to be found innocent of this allegation. They came home and drank themselves into oblivion after much foolishness at Robinson's tavern at Ft. Dearborn.
(THE INDIANS OF ILLINOIS.).

The reason that the young Winnebago women may have been abducted by boatmen three years ago was that along that stream is a favorite hunting-ground for the Indians and this winter they have quite a large camp in Ash Grove Township of from ninety to one hundred lodges on the west side of West Four Mile Branch on what is known as the William K. Wilson place. The Kickapoos, Pottawatomies and Delawares keep this camp under a chief by the name of Turkey. These Indians are very friendly and considered honest. The camp is a lively place especially on Sunday, when many white people come from settlements for miles around to spend the day, horse racing, shooting, foot-racing, jumping and what we call Indian wrestling. William and the boys still go there, but I have stopped going because of the kidnapping incident. I wish they would not go, but they never listen to me. It's up north, and they are more and more attracted to the area.

December 1832

"Inquiry is human; blind obedience brutal. Truth never loses by the one but often suffers by the other. "
"Rex and Tyrannus are very different characters. One rules his people by laws to which they consent; the other by his absolute Will and Power. That is call'd Freedom. This is Tyranny."
William Penn
Quaker Leader

"The humble, meek, merciful, just, pious and devout souls everywhere are of one religion and when death has taken off the mask, they will know one another, though the divers liveries they wear here make them strangers. "

"Some fruits of Solitude." William Penn (1644-1718)

We are having another bleak Christmas here, although William and the boys did cut down a tree and brought it in beside the fireplace.

I am becoming more and more homesick for my native Pennsylvania. In three months, the beautiful cherry and apple blossoms will be blooming there. Sometimes I wonder why my father had to come out here for his post in the first place and why I had to fall under the spell of the wilderness man that I married.

Now, suddenly my cook and main live-in maid, Matilda, have disappeared. The boys used to go into the kitchen and get treats such as special flans and tarts, while she sang spirituals and they played their fiddles and squeezeboxes. They really liked her, and so did William. I can't see getting that close to the help, especially colored help. They might take advantage. But William always says that the man named Hutcheson in Ulster in Ireland had the philosophy that in his naked, native state man has that spark of divinity within him.

Also being in the Society of Friends has formed William's philosophy. We met in Pennsylvania, when he was there with John, his father, for a meeting of the Friends. George Fox had founded the society in the 1600's, but Elizabeth Harris had brought it to Maryland before he arrived. She said that, while the Puritans had brought about some changes in the Anglican Church, had their own churches and controlled England at that time, she and her Friends felt that there was more to be done. They felt that the urge to good in men's hearts is the result of divine light, the gift of God to each person, that this light, called conscience by some, is the spiritual umbilicus between the soul of man and his Creator, that there is no room for third parties in this relationship, that the relation of man to his Creator is direct, exclusive and continuous. From this followed the notion that ministers, forms and churches are not needed but are in fact diverting. Women should have equal place in meeting with men. Elders should conduct the business of meetings, which should be held regularly and be attended by all. Silence should prevail at meetings until a brother or sister should feel moved to relate an experience. Speech and dress should be simple. Honesty is essential, from which followed that an oath required of a witness creates a double standard of honesty. Oaths were therefore declined. Ultimately affirmations are accepted. War and military service are sinful and are declined. The strength of the faith, William said, is that each person is responsible for himself. All may testify to their experience; all will help comfort the unfortunate and therefore be comforted in adversity.

Jeb MacMurray, a school master friend of ours, says that that is abolitionist talk.

He said the refusal by a Quaker to serve in the colonial militia brought about the first recorded case of an American persecuted for conscientious objection In 1658 Richard Keene, a Maryland Quaker, refused to be trained as a soldier. Fining him heavily, the angry sheriff drew his cutlass and struck young Keene on the shoulder, saying, "You dog! I could find in my heart to split your brains!"

An early trial of Quaker peace beliefs in Massachusetts came during the war with the Indians. The colony had passed a law that imprisoned anyone who refused to bear arms or was unwilling to pay a fine in place of service. The Quaker, John Smith, aged twenty-two, was called to join the militia in 1703. He refused and was tried and fined. When he would not pay the fine, he was sentenced to hard labor in the fort at Boston for as long as would pay the fine. The judge said that only a perverse nature could lead anyone to refuse to fight the enemy. Smith replied that it was not obstinacy, but duty to God according to conscience and religious persuasion, which prevailed with him.

Jeb says that conscientious objectors often love their country as much as anyone else. By saying "no" to war, they speak out of the deep conviction that killing is wrong no matter what the circumstances. He added that many Quakers believe that slavery is also wrong no matter what circumstances exist economic or otherwise. I know that William feels this way and I now believe that he is an abolitionist.

The Revival meetings under the tents tell us of the Great Awakening. The evangelical ministers led by Jonathan Edwards, travel throughout the country explaining to large, boisterous outdoor rallies that God is within everyone and that people can discover and communicate with God without the help of the established church. Part of this creed is that all men and women are humanitarians. They have to help each other and when any people are persecuted, all are persecuted. The ministers said that to hold a man in a state of slavery who has a right to liberty is "man stealing" and in the sight of God is worse than concubinage or fornication.

So many of our hired hands have disappeared that I believe it more and more. William says old Hutcheson, the Scottish philosopher, said that people can be trusted to be free because of that divine spark. They won't cause trouble for society because they are governed by natural law of caring for their fellow men.

My father wrote that in my native state of Pennsylvania, forty peculiar and solemn men and women met in a house in Philadelphia and organized the American Antislavery Society, calling on the free states to remove slavery "by moral and political action, as prescribed in the Constitution of the United States," and announcing, "With entire confidence in the overruling justice of God, we plant ourselves upon the Declaration of Independence and the truths of divine revelation as upon the everlasting rock. We shall organize antislavery societies, if possible, in every city, town and village in the land. We shall send forth agents to lift up the voice of remonstrance, of warning, of entreaty and of rebuke. We shall circulate unsparingly and extensively antislavery tracts and periodicals."

Still I ask, " What about self- preservation?" It means much more work for me now that Matilda is gone. Is woman just meant to be a chattel for her man and the family? Jeb says that Hutcheson believed in the independence of women also and in their schooling, but I never took the chance for education past secondary school, because I fell in love with William. And here I am in the vast mid-waste of the nation.

119

Meanwhile, Abe Lincoln is in Springfield, making his way in politics, but he has not forgotten his colored friend, the itinerate barber, Billy Florville, who has a barber shop not far from the State House, between Sixth and Seventh on Adams Street. Lincoln enjoys swapping stories there, according to William.

Author's note:

On the day before Lincoln's funeral, as visitors flocked to Springfield, Billy Florville had received an invitation to walk up forward in the grand procession with some of Lincoln's closest friends. Finally, the barber decided to refuse and to walk, instead, with the other colored people of Springfield, even though they were given the last position at the tag end of everybody. "He wanted to be among the people 'who felt Lincoln's loss most truly,'" Billy said.

February 1833

"Liberty exists in proportion to wholesome restraint; the more restraint on others to keep off from us, the more liberty we have."
Daniel Webster
American statesman, orator and lawyer

The Potawatomi Indians just gave up 5 million acres that they had occupied a century before Marquette and Joliet reached the northern Illinois area. The Potawatomis have been banished west of the Mississippi, and some say half-breeds and even French, like myself, are also to be banished.

William says he will never let them take me away. He plans to move up near Fort Dearborn and build me a big house some day, he says. This is consoling especially due to my fears of divorce.

Newspaper articles keep lauding the wonders of the fertile Rock River Valley.
On a happier note, the Nez Perce Indians who were such great friends to Lewis and Clark, have decided to search for the accomplishments of

literacy and the white man's "medicine," Christianity. They probably decided on St. Louis because of their memory of Lewis and Clark. A delegation has set out on the two thousand mile journey.

April 4, 1833

"If I cannot be free
To do such work as pleases me,
Near woodland pools and under trees,
You'll get no work at all; for I
Would rather live this life and die
A beggar or a thief, then be
A working slave with no days free"
William H. Davies
Welsh Poet and Novelist

We heard tell of a man named Nathan Cromwell who went with his good-looking wife to the home of a man who had said something to or about Mrs. Cromwell, and Nathan pointed a pistol at the man's heart and made him get down on his knees and beg Mrs. Cromwell's pardon. I wish I had a man who cared that much for me.

Some settlers from New York arrived in these parts to stake a claim. The schoolteacher, Jeb MacMurray, who is a widower with two children has sold his land in New York and wants to settle on part of our land in a leasing arrangement. They are Scottish and had lived in New York twenty years before coming here, but had gotten tired of the rent wars there. Tenants often detest landlords and burn their property. Jeb has a contract on their land to sell it, but it is on a contingency basis and he wants to rent from us until the contract is confirmed. He is one of the Scottish group of Baptists and Presbyterians who have started the Polo Grove area.

Jeb just returned from Springfield, the state capital, where he is seeing about his claim.
He says it was the lawyer and politician, Abraham Lincoln, who log rolled through the legislature the bill that located the capitol in Springfield. He said that there was a near-by town named Sangamon

where Lincoln had built the Offut flatboat to carry travelers down the river and that town had nearly won the selection for the county seat. Commissioners had also nearly selected a town laid out by William S. Hamilton, a young lawyer who was the son of the famous Alexander Hamilton. William vanished after his plans were rejected. That must have been Oregon.

The first time Abe Lincoln had seen slaves being sold was when he was captaining the flatboat down the Mississippi and went to New Orleans. He believed in the steamboats even though it meant trafficking in slaves was smoother. He voted for the steamboat but not for slavery. In New Salem people liked Abe and had voted for him, but he had lost that first election. Still, he was not discouraged. Lincoln was a Paul Bunyan type character. When he laughed, his entire body laughed. Yet, when he thought of slavery he became sad and stern.

On his second trip to New Orleans, he viewed a young colored woman being inspected liked a horse for sale, her breasts being pulled and her lips pulled out from her teeth. He wanted to leave immediately and his law partner, Billy Herndon, claimed that he vowed to avenge this horror in the future.

April 10, 1833

"We, even we here, hold the power and bear the responsibility. In giving freedom to the slave, we assure freedom to the free, honorable alike in what we give and what we preserve. We shall nobly save or meanly lose the last, best hope of earth.
Annual message to Congress, December 1, 1862
Abraham Lincoln

Slaves were brought to Springfield along with settlers. The Kirkpatricks brought their colored boy, Titus, and Colonel Thomas Cox brought his two girls, Nance and Dice. He had come twenty-three years before as register of the Land Office, put up a mill and distillery and hewn-log house with a hall and brick chimney. Then debt and drink broke him, the law turned him out of house and home and he and his wife and two children took shelter in a deserted log cabin a mile and a half from town.

First they had sold Nance and Dice, and this year county records stated that John Taylor "bought at public auction the person, Nance, for $151 and the person, Dice, for $150." The court commission was $15.40.

Lincoln noted parallels between the American abolitionist movement and the long struggle in Britain to end the slave trade.

"There," he wrote, "it required a century of effort before it was a final success in 1807.

I have not allowed myself to forget that the abolition of the slave trade by Great Britain... had its fire-breathing opponents; its Negro equality opponents; and its religion and good order opponents. All these opponents got offices and their adversaries got none. But I have also remembered that though they blazed like tallow candles for a century, at last they flickered in the socket died out, stank in the dark for a brief season, and were remembered no more even by the smell."

April 30, 1833

"I have no race prejudices, and I think I have no color prejudices nor creed prejudices. Indeed, I know it. I can stand any society. All I care to know is that a man is a human being-that is enough for me; he can't be any worse."
Concerning the Jews.
Lincoln

"Loyalty to petrified opinion never broke a chain or saved a human soul."

"Hain't we got all the fools in town on our side? And hain't that a big enough majority in any town?"
HUCKLEBERRY FINN, Mark Twain

"It is curious that physical courage should be so common in the world, and moral courage so rare."

"We are discreet sheep, we wait to see how the drove is going and then go with the drove. We have two opinions; one private, which we are afraid to express and another one-the one we use-which we force

ourselves to wear to please…until habit makes us comfortable in it, and the custom of defending it presently makes us love it, adore it, and forget how pitifully we came by it. Look at it in politics."
From ERUPTION

"In England an illegitimate Christian rose against slavery. It is curious that when a Christian rises against a rooted wrong at all, he is usually an illegitimate Christian, member of some despised and bastard sect.".
"From Europe and Elsewhere"
Mark Twain,
(Samuel Langhorne Clemens) (1835-1910)

Lincoln is a well-revered name in England, where the capital of Lincolnshire in East Anglia is the home of a great cathedral. But Abraham Lincoln expressed little interest in his genealogy. He said that he was the son of "second sons."

His namesake and grandfather, Abraham, had sold a lovely home in Virginia to go West and settle in Kentucky where he held claim to 2,000 acres. In 1786, however, this first Abraham was killed by Indians, while his son, Thomas, watched. Under the rules of Primogeniture, the family's oldest son, Mordecai inherited Abraham's entire estate, and the other two sons were left destitute. Abe's father, Thomas, tried several trades among them carpentry and managed to pay $200 for a 348 acre farm in Kentucky called Sinking Spring where Abe was born.
He said that his mother was the illegitimate daughter of Lucy Hanks and a well-bred Virginia farmer. He also argued that from that source came his logic, analytical ability, ambition and mental activity, which distinguished him from other Hanks descendants.

Lincoln grew up in a series of log cabins, and his rise as a self-made man fit the mold in the years after Andrew Jackson, when many candidates tried to show that they came from such natural and "pure" origins. As a Whig candidate, Lincoln had an early life that indicates the independent, individuality of the platform. We can see that his family never owned slaves.

Slavery has been banned outright in Canada now, so more and more slaves are being sent there. Windsor, a five-hour drive from Fort Dearborn in southwestern Ontario, has been a preferred crossing point for fugitive slaves, as the Detroit River narrows there.

Author's note:

Mark Twain's tales about Huckleberry Finn and his fugitive slave friend, Jim, were a good antidote for racial hatred in the minds of children of America. The author was way beyond his time in portraying this kind of brotherly love.

Still, while the invisible railroad is renowned, the fates of those who reached Canada and their descendants have been largely ignored. An attempt to correct this oversight is a tour, which now sheds light on the fates of slaves such as Josiah Henson, the overly patient former slave said to be the model for the character in Harriet Beecher Stowe's monumental American novel, UNCLE TOM'S CABIN. The Road that Led to Freedom: An African-American Heritage Tour began almost as an after-thought. Group Travel Designers, Inc. was running trips to Windsor for shoppers which included many African-Americans, and the tour operator asked the Ontario Ministry of Tourism to recommend points of interest to that segment of the population.

A full three-day tour includes four points of interest around Windsor: the John Freeman Walls and Uncle Tom's Cabin Historic Sites; the Raleigh Township Centennial Museum in what was the Elgin Settlement, a community built by former slaves before the Civil War; and the North American Black Historical Museum and Cultural Center in Amherstburg, which was a frequent destination for runaways.

May 1833

"I know of no rights of race superior to the rights of humanity."

"The lesson now flashed upon the attention of the American people, the lesson which they must learn, or neglect to do so at their own peril, is that 'Equal Manhood means Equal Rights.'"

Frederick Douglas (1817?-1895)
Letter to W.J. Wilson

"Slaves are generally expected to sing as well as to work.
I did not, when a slave, understand the deep meanings of those rude and apparently incoherent songs. I was myself within the circle, so that I neither saw nor heard as those without might see and hear. They told a tale which was then altogether beyond my feeble comprehension: they were tones, loud, long and deep, breathing the prayer and complaint of souls boiling over with the bitterest anguish. Every tone was a testimony against slavery and a prayer to God for deliverance from chains."
Autobiography
Frederick Douglass

Morgan found a fugitive in the shed, much to his father's discomfort, but our son swore not to tell anyone. He said that her name was Caroline and her skirt was covered with mud. Deeper in the hole behind the tools was a small child of about three. Caroline said that when William had found her as he came home from loading hay she was looking up, her eyes fixed only on the North Star. She was scooping her boy out of the mud.
When William told her he is a "station master" on the underground railroad she didn't believe him at first, but she was so tired, she decided to ride with him in the back of the hay wagon to our house, the next "station."

When Morgan found her outside the shed she said, "I's looking for the drinking gourd," meaning the North Star. We brought her into the house and fed her and her child some fried chicken and mush. William was going to take her to Indiana the next day in the hay wagon. There, her husband was waiting, she said. They had been parted in Kentucky, and dogs had chased her across to the creek near our house. But when she had crossed the water, the dogs had lost her scent.

Spirituals contained codes, urging slaves to "wade in the water" or "cross over the Jordan" for this very purpose of evasion.

In 1819, a small group of devout abolitionists moved from Brown County, Ohio to Bond County here in southern Illinois. They later relocated in Putnam County and then Bureau County where we are.

The Underground Railroad circuit was fully established here in about 1831. There are five main line that run through Illinois, in most cases following old stagecoach routes.
Most runaways cross the Mississippi River from Missouri at Quincy, Rock Island and Alton and angle for Fort Dearborn.

Once in the Fort Dearborn area they can hide out in the free black population or else continue on towards Detroit and from there, into Canada and freedom.

Instead of going to the Fort, some runaways go straight north towards Wisconsin and even Minnesota. I believe that we are going to go up north soon to settle into a new home. There are no recorded cases of slave hunters successfully returning a runaway slave from either Wisconsin or Minnesota. I have relatives in Wisconsin.
I doubt that they want to keep a safe house, but they might.

June 30, 1833

"I beg you to remember that wherever our life touches yours we help or hinder; wherever your life touches ours, you make us stronger or weaker. There is no escape-man drags man down, or man lifts man up."
The American Standard "1896
Booker T. Washington

"I have learned that success is to be measured not so much by the position that one has reached in life as by the obstacles which he has overcome while trying to succeed."

UP FROM SLAVERY
Booker T. Washington
(1856-1915)
American Negro Leader

William has been thrown off a wild horse. He was trying to ride bare back, as the Indians do when they break horses. His shoulder has been dislocated and he may have a concussion. The doctor set his shoulder to the tune of much screaming, and now he has it in a sling but is experiencing excruciating head aches. Last night he walked away at sunset and hasn't been back for two days. I'm worried, but with my clairvoyance, I see him with his Indian princess.

I am going to Michigan for an extended stay to see Mercy and Old John where Pearce and Mary are still keeping little Mercy for me. I miss my little girl so much! They have Clark, born just three years after Mercy, and as cousins, they are inseparable. He is only a year and a half, and she carries him around like a doll baby. She does miss Elizabeth, who is just a year older than she is, Sarah Jane, born around Clark's birthday, and of course, Morgan, who is four years older. I'll take them all to see her. Maybe if I distance myself, William will miss me. He is taking the children and me with our trunk to Lake Michigan to board a boat for Mercy's home in about a week. I am tired of having my children placed in jeopardy over this slavery issue.

Author's note:

The Second Great Awakening of the 1830s was even more powerful than the Great Awakening of the mid-18th century. This new movement whose fiery ministers preached against slavery moved many Christians to see slavery as a political and not just a religious issue. This came at the same time as a growing humanitarian movement whose proponents felt that capitalism and the rapid development of the country required that people take moral responsibility for themselves and their fellow man, which included the ending of slavery.

August 1833

"Love has been in perpetual strife with monogamy."
Ellen Key (1849-1926) Feminist
Liberty and Great Libertarians

Well, William returned this morning, feeling much better. Then, when he thought I had gone to bed, I crept down the back stairs and heard him talking with my son, Morgan and his friend about having been in the purification lodge (the shed) with Tecumsehatas who had gone into a trance state after seeming to electrify some rocks. The rocks were glowing, he said, and she was chanting her appreciation to the rocks that they were going to help her heal William. She also talked with someone named Wakan-Tanka. which is akin to our concept of God, according to William. She said that the healing process goes better if the sick person has faith. Still, people without faith, like William, are cured by medicine people every day, because the body has powers to heal itself and they have faith not in God but in the medicine person. She said that Wakan-Tanka is not really making a choice where the life or death of a person is concerned. He is more concerned with the survival of the nation than with the survival of just one person. She also said that after death every person goes into one of three spirits:

They are Wakan-Tanka, Tankashila or the earth mother. Spiritual people go to a happy place, and the rest to a path where they will suffer all the time. She said that people make their own punishments here on earth, but she didn't blame Wakan Tanka if he shut the door on them, because they turn their backs on Him. Shutting the door means that the dead person's spirit will drift around forever with no place to land. Now and then, it will pass by the happy people who are with Wakan-Tanka, and will see what it has missed.

"When we understand deeply in our hearts, we will fear and love and know the Great Spirit," she stressed. She said that saying was from the Oglala Sioux and again imparted that the Great Spirit is not perfect; it has a good side and a bad side. Sometimes the bad side gives us more knowledge than the good side.

My husband experienced this sweat-lodge healing experience all because of a horse.
He would seldom go to church, but he had a sermon on the divine due to a horse.
It's a country of horsy men. A thirty or forty mile drive is counted an easy day. They speak of one-horse towns, one-horse lawyers or doctors-

even one-horse horse doctors. They tie their horses to hitching posts half-chewed away by horse teeth. We brush off horsehair from our clothes after a drive. We carry feedbags of oats and splice broken tugs with rope to last till we reach a harness shop. A man definitely needs a horse out here where vast distances need covering and work is done by horse-power. In fact, some men feel that their horses are more important than their women.

Author's note:

Not enough horses had come out west to fill the need. By the 1690's some of the plains tribes of Texas had horses, and the animals had reached the agricultural Caddoan villages of the Red River. From there, through raiding and trading, they spread gradually northward. By the 1730's horses had reached the Missouri River. By the 1770s they were well into Canada at the northern limits of their range.

On the Great Plains, the arrival of the horse in this sea of grass dominated by herds of buffalo added the final element in a combination that made mounted nomadism possible.
The Sioux and other tribes, using travois, dragged by **dogs** on the plains now climbed up onto horses. Indians defined wealth in terms of horses. Horses became a bride price; they became the preferred gift at religious ceremonies. The Blackfoot and others call horses "sky dogs," thinking that they had either come from the heavens or from under the earth With the horse came bigger tepees and larger stores of dried meat.

The Conestoga wagons were usually pulled by oxen, not by the riding horses needed for fleet travel. The wild horses, which the Indians had tamed or gotten from the Spaniards, were often stolen from them by white men. Naturally, they felt free to take them back, and Indian sympathizers felt entitled to take horses from the white men they disliked. Sometimes the white men retaliated against the Indians by burning villages and letting the nearly wild horses run free. Horses are deathly afraid of fire, and it takes a long time to break these horses of Indian training, as Indians generally ride them bareback.

The Native American prophesy that the dead person who "shuts the door" on the spiritual life will cause his spirit to drift around with "no place to land" is close to the belief that those who have died by creating violence will become ghosts.

While I have never seen a ghost, I have written about many in my books about famous homes and inns. Nearly all persons who supposedly become ghosts have had violent deaths. Can you imagine how violent deaths through war or the death penalty for crimes impact the life of the spirit, the hope for transmigration into the higher worlds of the spirit?

September 1833

"We ought to strive for the freedom of love; [which] must mean freedom for a feeling which is worthy the name of love. This feeling it may be hoped, will gradually win for itself the same freedom in life as it already possesses in poetry."
Ellen Key (1849-1926)
(Liberty and the Great Libertarians)

"Marriage sets up an indissoluble state of tension, and its very existence depends upon the preservation of this state. Man and woman, both as individuals and as types, are fundamentally different, incompatible and essentially solitary. In marriage they form an indissoluble unit of life, based upon fixed distance."
"Man and woman should never endeavor to be completely merged in one another. On the contrary, the more intimate they are, the more strictly should they cherish their own individuality."
Hermann Alexander Von Keyserling (1880-1946)
German Scientist and Philosopher

"Prejudices, it is well known, are most difficult to eradicate from the heart whose soil has never been loosened or fertilized by education; they grow there, firm as weeds among stones."
JANE EYRE
Charlotte Bronte
(1816-1855)

William has found my diary and has attacked my wish for knowledge.

To know, that is your all," he said. "that is your life; you have one tree, one fruit, the eternal apple. Even your animalism you want all in your head. You don't want to be an animal, you want to observe your animal functions, to get a mental thrill out of them.

Passion you want, but through your intellect in your consciousness. You want a lie, this mirror, your own fixed will. But now when you have come to all your conclusions, you want to go back and be a savage without knowledge with passion. But it isn't passion at all; it is your will. You want to clutch things and have them in your power. And why is that? It's because you haven't any real body, any dark sensual body of life. You have no sensuality, it is your conceit of lust for power to know."

He looked at me in contempt but also in pain because I suffered, and he is compassionate. He knew that he tortured me, but a bitter red anger burned a fury in him.

"But do you really want sensuality from your wife, the mother of your children," I asked.

"Yes", he said, "that and nothing else. It is a fulfillment- the great dark knowledge you can't have in your head- the dark involuntary spirit. You have knowledge in the blood alone."

I cannot abide this dichotomy of my husband's affections any longer. I'm bound for Michigan to stay with Old John and Mercy for a while. William protests that he is only a student of the Indian princess, and he has been able to heal several friends of late, but I have seen Tecumsahantas at a distance, and she looks as though she is expecting a child. William has driven the children and me on a buckboard bound for Lake Michigan where he has put us aboard a steamboat. Old John met us at the dock, and I'm writing now from Mercy's pretty home.

I am so happy to see little Mercy, my precious baby girl!

September 1833

"The first systematical and bloody attempt at Lexington to enslave America, thoroughly electrified my mind and fully determined me to take part with my country."
Ethan Allen (1737-1784

The question of Indian removal is personal for me. I wonder if the Indian Princess would leave if most of her tribe, for which she cares as Shaman, had to be removed across the Mississippi.

It would be good for me if she left, but I don't feel that it's fair for the natives.
Back in 1828, my husband was talking with the boys about Andrew Jackson's nomination for President in this way:
"How can a man fight so hard for his own and his nation's
independence and still not think of the independence of all peoples?
He has quite a record of infuriating the Indians. He became a national hero when in 1814 he fought the Battle of Horseshoe Bend against a thousand Creeks and killed eight hundred with few casualties on his side. His white troops had failed in a frontal attack on the Creeks, but the Cherokees with him, promised governmental friendship if they joined the war, swam the river, came up behind the Creeks and won the battle for Jackson.
When the war ended, Jackson and friends of his began buying up the seized Creek lands. He got himself appointed treaty commissioner and dictated a treaty, which took away half the land of the Creek nation. It took land from Creeks who had fought with Jackson as well as those who had fought against him. When Big Warrior, a chief of the friendly Creeks, protested, Jackson said:

'Listen...The United States would have been justified by the Great Spirit, had they taken all the land of the nation... Listen-the truth is, the great body of the Creek chiefs and warriors did not respect the power of the United States-they thought we were an insignificant nation-that we would be overpowered by the British... They were fat with eating beef-they wanted flogging… we bleed our enemies in such cases to give them their senses.'"

Author's note:
In 1830, Jackson pushed through the Indian Removal Act, thus putting teeth into the policy that his predecessors had long advocated: the "voluntary" exchange of lands by eastern Indians for territory that the federal government would acquire for them west of the Mississippi. Jackson gave the policy immediacy and an assertion that existing Indian treaties did not constitute federal recognition of Indian sovereign rights to the soil of their homelands. The act enabled the president to implement such assertions, putting congressional support and appropriations behind the tragedies to follow.
Lincoln, on the other hand, looked at a nation divided on whether to treat Indians humanely or to kill them off, sided with the humanists, even while clearly advocating western settlement.

December 1833

"I pity the poor in bondage that have none to help them; that is why I am here; not to gratify any personal animosity, revenge, or vindictive spirit. It is my sympathy with the oppressed and the wronged, that are as good as you, and as precious in the sight of God."
John Brown (1800-1859) American abolitionist
Quoted by Thoreau," Slavery in Massachusetts" 1859.

Well we are here with Mercy and Old John. We had a fine reunion with little Mercy, Pearce and Mary Brody. All the children are playing together now.
It's a strange Christmas in a different house from my own, but we have strung popcorn, and old John brought in a tree from the woods nearby. He has a collection of colored men working for him. In the summer they work right along side of him in the fields. This is their last stop before being sent in the hay wagon up to Canada. Some call them slaves, but John pays them "under the table" so to speak.
Matty works as a cook for Mercy in the kitchen near the house. She comes in through a causeway with the food for us and often sings to Old

John's guitar playing after dinner. She sings "Swing Low Sweet Chariot" and other spirituals like "Going Home". I try to help her learn to read during the day in the kitchen, where no authorities will catch us.

I feel so sorry for her children, who have become separated from her on the way to Canada. They all think of that country as almost a promised land, but there are dangers.

She gave birth to her first baby in front of everyone on the boat, coming from Africa. The space she had was no larger that a coffin, she said with tears running down her face. Vomit and excrement were all around her, and her birth cries mingled with the groans of the dying. A corpse was two feet away from her.

She remembered the loving society she had come from in Africa with its community strength and ancient traditions. Her family had what they called slaves, but they were actually serfs, more like tenants and were treated well with rights of their own. She had no idea of the extreme labor that slaves had to undergo in the fields of the South.

I have a letter from my father from Philadelphia, saying that the British Empire has outlawed slavery. This success has inspired American abolitionists to found the American Anti-Slavery Society. Since this organization was restricted to males, Lucretia Mott after the convention, formed the Female Anti-Slavery Society. It helped to gather hundreds of thousands of signatures on petitions, calling upon Congress to abolish slavery immediately and unconditionally in the District of Columbia, where it had direct jurisdiction. Women are learning in this society the basic procedures of political action. In speaking out against slavery they are learning to speak out for their own rights. Popular author Lydia Maria Francis Child has also published "An Appeal in Favor of that Class of Americans Called Africans."

Her husband had persuaded her to attend an abolitionist meeting where William Lloyd Garrison was the main speaker. "Garrison," she said, "got hold of the strings of my conscience."

After that, Child, who had written popular articles for her children's magazine and household books, devoted most of her energies to the abolition cause.

It was Child's book that drew people like Willima Ellery Channing, Wendall Phillips and Charles Sumner to the abolitionist movement. Because of it, Child was ostracized and ridiculed in Boston, however. She received grudging approval from my husband, which was amazing, since she is a female intellectual. She was appointed to the executive committee of the American Anti-Slavery Society when it opened itself to women, because of her friendship with Garrison, and she edited "The National Anti-Slavery Standard."

A year ago after William Lloyd Garrison formed the New England Anti-Slavery Society, a group of African-American women formed the Female Anti-Slavery Society. Later Maria Weston Chapman formed the more aristocratic Boston Female Anti-Slavery Society.

The problem is that public sentiment in the North is still ambivalent about slavery. Over several generations politicians have made little effort to stop it. Abolitionists have no political power and can do little to either free slaves or punish their owners.

Author's note:
The leading cause of the Civil War revolved around the question of the expansion of slavery into the western states rather than the abolition of it. Segments of the North were enraged about the outcome of the Missouri Compromise and regarded Jackson as a potential dictator. They thought, as did William, that his penchant for flouting Congress, the law and the Constitution endangered the Republic. This general feeling led in 1834 to the formation of the Whig Party. They selected the name to identify themselves with the Revolutionary patriots.

I have discovered that I am three months pregnant. I guess I'll stay here with Mercy to have the baby. I am worried about Techumsahantas and my husband. I wonder how long she will remain in Illinois.

In August of 1828, the Treaty of Green Bay had given the United States over 750,000 acres in Illinois of Winnebago land. Now they have only the northeast corner of Illinois for a payment of $20,000 in trade goods.

No wonder they're raiding villages. Soon they'll be stripped of all their land just like the Creeks. Between 1814 and 1824 in a series of treaties with southern Indians, whites took over three-fourths of Alabama and Florida, one-third of Tennessee, one fifth of Georgia and Mississippi and parts of Kentucky and North Carolina. Jackson played a key role in these treaties.

Some of them forbid certain tribesmen to wear the Eagle Feather bustle. It is known to be a powerful talisman. Even the white men fear it enough to forbid it.

June 1834

"The will of man or (woman) is not shattered but softened, bent and guided; men are seldom forced by it (majority opinion) to act, but they are constantly restrained from acting. Such a power does not destroy, but it prevents existence; it does not tyrannize, but it compresses, enervates, extinguishes and stupefies a people."
Alexis de Tocqueville French writer, statesman (1805-1859)

I feel bad about leaving my husband, but life is so much easier here with Mercy to help me with the children, and I am expecting a baby again.

It is a hard life being a pioneer wife. At home, I often cook for my husband, the boys and five hired hands at noon, especially during threshing season or harvest. Washday is really difficult without help. I have little time to read the books I wish to read so much. When I do have a Negro girl to help me, she often disappears as soon as she comes. I attribute this to my husband. The black hired hands don't seem to stay long either. And newspapers rarely appear at the general store. My diary entries become less frequent but I do know something about the politics from talking with my husband's friend Jeb, who doesn't seem to be as friendly with him of late. I wonder if my husband is jealous of my friendship with Jeb MacMurray.

Jeb often stopped by to help me because our mare was birthing and having trouble with a breech birth. When he stopped to pay his rent, he brought me some Shakespeare books and read me one play he likes. He also reads Robert Burns' poetry to me when my husband is driving the cattle to market in Fort Dearborn.
We read until dusk, because we must conserve candles and we do not want to raise suspicions.

Our parents had been Compromisers in the East, but we would not settle for compromise. We are independent to an extreme. My husband is a case in point, a real independent cuss, but our life on the frontier has made us see the interrelationship of all beings. Actually, women are treated more as equals here in the Midwest than in the East where a woman is called Madam and given courtesy but little else. It's lonely, and you often need help and need to share tools and such. The men build barns together, so a man who comes to settle has a barn raised in two days, followed by a barn dance celebration. Jeb plays the fiddle in a sprite-like way, and his barn raising was a great event. He's also a good dancer and I was invigorated to "dosey do" with him during a Virginia reel. But the whole situation became too much of a temptation to me, as I am a God fearing woman, French or not. I had to get away!

July 1834

"In the right to eat the bread…which his own hand earns, he (the Negro) is my equal and the equal of Judge Douglas, and the equal of any living man."
Abraham Lincoln.
Lincoln-Douglas Debate. August 2, 1858

The children really miss their father, especially Morgan. He needs his Pa to go fishing and hunting. Old John takes him fishing but doesn't hunt much any more. The girls love Mercy, with her smiling blue eyes and the crinkles at the corners of her round Dutch face.

They will miss her teas, when they dress up in her big hats with the plumes and long dresses with lace...The children will miss both grandparents when we finally go home.

I have plenty of time to think about events in this country, since Mercy won't let me lift a finger. I have given birth to another boy. We're going to call him Joseph. Perchance, with God's help, he will grow to be able to help his father and Morgan. Then, maybe William will appreciate me more for giving him a son. It gets harder every time.

I can now understand the feeling of the black families that are arbitrarily separated by their masters' whims. I remember the tobacco barn in Ohio that old John showed us where slaves were shackled in an interior shed as they had been shackled in the ships arriving in our nation. The stench and cries were heart rending to any one with a heart.
Levi Coffin, one of the veterans of the Underground Railroad there has written that the owner of the barn has gotten his just deserts. Anderson died in 1834 at the age of 42., having tripped over a grapevine. He fell onto the sharp stump of a cornstalk, which penetrated his eye and entered his brain. He was chasing a runaway slave.

Author's note:
In their "log cabin" adulthood, the share of American population living west of the Appalachians has grown from 3 percent in 1790 to 28 percent now. They were a force to be recognized in politics, and women were also finding a voice in this area.

Fanny Wright, an orphaned Scottish heiress, was the first woman in America to speak out on public affairs. Her speaking tours have attracted thousands of men and women who wanted to hear her views ranging from equal education for girls to birth control. She had studied Greek as a girl and published solid scholarship as a teenager. In 1818 she had traveled to America, accompanied only by her younger sister, Camilla, to see a play produced that she had written. Out of their travels came her first book entitled VIEWS OF SOCIETY AND MANNERS IN

AMERICA, published in 1821. It was widely read in Europe, and Lafayette invited her to join him on his 1824 tour of this country where she met Thomas Jefferson and James Madison.

The tour also introduced her to slavery, which caused her to begin her book, A PLAN FOR THE GRADUAL ABOLITION OF SLAVERY WITHOUT DANGER OR LOSS TO THE CITIZENS OF THE SOUTH. Recently she has purchased 640 acres near Memphis, Tennessee, which she has called Nashoba, a self-help colony for slaves where they can learn skills and attitudes they will need in order to be free. After clearing the site, Fanny fell ill and had to return to Europe in 1827. While she had been away, a terrible scandal has blown up involving the Scottish foreman of the property and the women under his charge.

Legislatures of four southern states were asking that states of the North to "effectually suppress all associations purporting to abolition societies," and governors of New York and Massachusetts had asked their legislatures to take such action. A mass meeting of 1,800 of the wealthiest influential citizens of Boston had declared the abolitionists to be dangerous meddlers, probably because merchants of the North were making a great deal of money importing the slaves for southern plantation owners.

A young Presbyterian minister, Elijah P. Lovejoy, a halfway abolitionist, editing a paper in St. Louis, had written: "Today a public meeting declares you shall not discuss slavery. Tomorrow another meeting decides it is against the peace of society that popery be discussed. The next day a decree is issued speaking against distilleries, dram shops or drunkenness. The truth is, if you give ground a single inch, there is no stopping place. I deem it, therefore, my duty to take my stand upon the Constitution and declare my fixed determination to maintain this ground."

The editorial was answered by a mob that smashed his press and threw his type out of the window. Lovejoy got the press repaired, decided to move up the river to Alton, Illinois, loaded the press on a boat and was met at Alton by a mob that threw the press into the river.

Events slowly changed Lovejoy to an immediate emancipationist. He wrote:

"As well might a lady think to bail out the Atlantic Ocean with her thimble, as the Colonization Society to remove slavery by colonizing the slaves in Africa."

Because of all this legislation and other obstacles, many people in the East began to think about moving west where they could act out their beliefs and help more slaves to freedom.

Author's note:

Elijah Lovejoy's Monument and Grave is at Fifth and Monument Streets in Alton, Illinois. In 1833, Elijah arrived in the Midwest and began to publish "The Observer" in St. Louis. Forced out of the slave state, he began to publish "The Alton Observer," just across the river, in 1836. Mobs wrecked his presses twice and then killed him in 1837. Remains of one of the ruined presses are on display in the lobby of the Telegraph Building, 111 East Broadway in Alton. His home, a safe house in those days, is private.

The Lovejoy Homestead at State Route 61, Princeton, Illinois was owned by Owen Lovejoy, He was Elijah's brother and a fierce abolitionist minister, congressman and political confidant of Lincoln.
He kept up his underground activities through the 1840s despite an indictment in 1843 after which he was acquitted at trial by a sympathetic jury. By the time the Kansas-Nebraska Act was passed in 1854, he was one of Illinois' major abolitionists.

The Abraham Lincoln Home at Jackson and Eighth Streets in Springfield has no connection to the Underground Railroad, but a trip to this museum would "round out" ones' knowledge of the background that led to the Civil War and Lincoln's Emancipation Proclamation

Dr. Richard Eells House is open to the public at 322 Main Street in Quincy, Illinois. Runaways were hidden, clothed and fed there and sent northeast toward Chicago on a network of safe houses. In 1842, Eells was convicted of harboring a runaway and fined $400. He took his battle to the U.S. Supreme Court, which ruled against him.

Zion Baptist Missionary Church at 1601 East Laurel Street in Springfield was founded by a former slave, Thomas Houston, who fled to Springfield from Missouri. He used his home in Springfield as a station in the underground and organized secret raids back to Missouri to free his brother and his brother's family. A descendant, Charles Houston, was a law professor at Howard University. One student of his was Thurgood Marshall, who helped overturn segregation in the public schools as lead counsel in the Brown vs. Board of Education case in 1854.

The Polo Historical Society has an interesting Underground Railroad display at Aplington House, 123 N. Franklin Ave., Polo, Illinois.

The Byron Historical Museum opened an exhibit on the Underground Railroad to be housed in the Lucius Reed home located at 106 Union Street, Byron, Illinois.
Reed a highly respected farmer, justice of the peace and notary republic came from Windsor Vermont in1810. His brother-in-law Kimball built a home in the Greek Revival style for Reed and his wife. Reed took slaves from Buffalo Grove and housed them in the basement of this house and provided food for them in an inn he ran across the street.
They were sent on to Lynnville Station, (where David Driskell "happened" to live) or to Janesville, Wisconsin, where they made there way to Chicago or Canada.

These brave men and their homes were hotbeds of activity when the Driskells lived right nearby close to Springfield and in later times close to Chicago in South Grove, which was the hub of Illinois Underground activities.

September 1834

"Our country is the world-our countrymen are all mankind."
Motto of The Liberator
William Lloyd Garrison

"I determined at all hazard, to lift up the standard of emancipation in the eyes of the nation, within sight of Bunker Hill, and in the birth-place of liberty. That standard is now unfurled; and long may it float, unhurt by the spoliations of time or the missiles of a desperate foe; yea, till every chain be broken, and every bondman set free! Let Southern oppressors tremble; let their secret abettors tremble; let their Northern apologists tremble; let all the enemies of the persecuted blacks tremble."
" The Liberator," first issue, January 1, 1831

"Nothing can take precedence of the question of liberty. No interest is so momentous as that which involves "the life of the soul"; no object so glorious as the restoration of a man to himself."
"The Liberator"William Lloyd Garrison

Abraham Lincoln has spent the past winter months in Vandalia. He knew the legislature was mostly of southern blood and point of view. In the first legislature in which he served there were 58 members from Kentucky and Tennessee or south of the Ohio River, 19 from the mid -Atlantic states and only four from New England. He knew that there was this crimson kinship of like blood between populations in southern Illinois, Indiana, Ohio and in states south of the Ohio River; and that beyond blood kinship there were the closely interlocking interests of the southern planters, buying immense quantities of pork, corn and produce from the southern frontier states and the New England power-loom mills, buying increasing millions of bales of cotton each year.

Amid this welter, Lincoln could understand his fellow members of the legislature when they passed resolutions declaring: "We highly disapprove of the formation of Abolition Societies; the right of property in slaves is sacred to the slaveholding States by the Federal Constitution, and they cannot be deprived of the right without their consent..."

Still, Lincoln voted against these resolutions and was joined by only one other member, Dan Stone, and he recorded a protest spread in the Journal of Proceedings.
On the contrary, he was interested to hear that another travel writer, Anne Royall, often called the "Grandmother of Muckrakers" was convicted in

a Maryland court for "publicly abusing" a group of Presbyterians who objected to her characterization of them. Since most of the Scots are of that religion, it amused him that when a fundamentalist with political ambitions, Ezra Stiles Ely, took her to court as a "common scold," crime only a woman could commit, the proscribed punishment, a public dunking, was changed to a ten dollar fine, because of her advanced age.

The fine was paid for her by John Eaton, the Secretary of War. He was a friend and had testified on her behalf. Her refusal to succumb to pressure as she continued publishing in Washington, established her as one of the first defenders of first amendment rights.

We are also hearing a lot about Susan Brownell Anthony who is an educator and abolitionist and spent much time with Henry Booster Stanton and his wife, Elizabeth Cady Stanton. Her father was a Quaker who believed in the inner light of God, being in each person's soul. Susan also knows Lucretia Mott who established the first female anti-slavery society. Lucretia and Elizabeth formed the society last year in Philadelphia, Susan works full time as a temperance and abolitionist reformer in western New York, her home, and in many other states. She has not married and is free to come and go, unlike Elizabeth Stanton. They make a good team with Elizabeth working from home. They are closely allied with Wendell Stewart and William Lloyd Garrison. We knew of some of these people in Pennsylvania and Ohio..

In 1831, William Lloyd Garrison founded the New England Anti Slavery Society and began publishing "The Liberator." Female abolitionists like Lucretia Mott, Lydia Maria Child and the Grimke sisters play a crucial role. The Grimkes publicize the slave system as no other speakers could, because they are the daughters of a plantation owner and are willing to risk the opprobrium of public indignation.

Liberalized marriage and custody rights have also seen the first American generation to divorce in significant numbers. Around 1820, many joined the rage of canal-building and cloth manufacture in the north or migrated to the southwestern frontier, where they could make fortunes growing cotton. We are up here raising cattle and while the men try to assume the exterior of composure, whatever riot and confusion lurk within, they know that their destiny lies in dutiful expertise, not heroism, as was that of their fathers. Despite rousing victories at New Orleans in the War of 1812 and stirring words of "The Star-Spangled Banner," these young men know that this second War of Independence hardly compares with the first.

Whereas our elders had founded an Empire of Liberty and "stood" for office as citizen-statesmen, we talk of an American System and "run" for office as political professionals. Furthermore, we women cannot replay the young heroine role of our mothers. Instead we embrace the new romantic "cult of true womanhood", emphasizing innocence, femininity and domestic virtue. Still, I feel that both men and women sense in themselves a growing tension between duty and feeling, between the proper division of social labor and this subversive desire for personal fulfillment.

I surmise that this feeling is being acted out in my husband's behavior with this Indian princess, but what about my own longing for a sense of identity and love?

When William picked us up from the boat, the children rushed into his arms, but I was slower to come to him this time. There seemed to be a distance in his eyes, although I had written to him diligently. He seemed preoccupied and concerned unduly about something.

January 1835

"Wherever there is a conflict between human rights and property rights, human rights must prevail."
Abraham Lincoln
The Congressional Record, May 12 1944)

Abraham Lincoln is becoming rather a legend in these parts. He took the office of postmaster, which most Democrats would shun, just to read the newspapers. He is so much in debt because his partnership in the store, Berry and Lincoln, did not work out. Since Berry took too much to the drink they finally got a license to sell.

One of Lincoln's clients, a physician, had forgotten to register a title to his farm in another county A stranger, buying large land tracts for a Philadelphia capitalist came to his home and had dinner one night
.

A few hours later, word came to the doctor that the stranger was riding to Springfield to register for himself the doctor's 100 acres of land. The doctor got on a horse and with the help of neighbors raised the cash to file his land claims. Then he headed for Springfield, but his horse played out a few miles from the capital. Abe on a fresh fast horse came along, listened to a few anxious words, jumped off his horse, shortened the stirrups and swapped horses with the doctor. He said he wanted to get the doctor and the specie into the land office ahead of the shark. That's how the title to the land was saved.

Jack and Hannah Armstrong, out at Clary's Grove, took Abe in two and three weeks at a time when he needed a place to eat and sleep. Abe would drink milk, eat mush, cornbread and butter, bring the children candy and rock the cradle. He would tell stories and joke with people.

February 1835
"As in Adam all men die, even so in Christ shall all be made alive."
(THE BIBLE quoted by Abraham Lincoln to defend the idea of Universal salvation).

Lincoln often stayed at the Rutledge family tavern, where travelers and strangers ate and talked jovially and often loudly. The Rutledges, themselves, are earnest, sober and a little somber. Abe has taken a fancy, they say, to the beautiful and fragile Anne Rutledge.
They often sing hymns together.

The lines of our songs say that the human family has a heavy load of guilt to carry. Man is a pilgrim wandering across barren sands, longing for a cooling stream, a wandering sheep in a howling wilderness, seeking rivers of salvation and paradise.

April 1835

"There must be no compromise with slavery… Nothing is gained; everything is lost, by subordination principle to expediency. "

"The Party or Sect that will suffer by the triumph of justice cannot exist with safety to mankind. The State that cannot tolerate universal freedom must be despotic; and no valid reason can be given why despotism should not at once be hurled to the dust."
The Liberator
William Lloyd Garrison

A St. Louis Presbyterian minister, Elijah Parish Lovejoy, has begun publishing a religious newspaper called "The St. Louis Observer." In it he often calls in fiery words for an end to slavery. His appeals, shrill in the estimation of many Missourians whose state embraces slavery, have become even more strident since he witnessed a horrifying event-a free African-American riverboat worker named Francis McIntosh was pulled from jail by a mob and taken to the outskirts of St. Louis. There, he was chained to a tree with kindling at his feet and burned alive.

McIntosh was accused of slaying a deputy sheriff and injuring another when the lawmen tried to arrest unruly sailors on his ship. McIntosh reportedly interfered, allowing the sailors to escape. After the struggle in which one officer died and another was knifed, McIntosh was hauled to jail. He wasn't there long before the howling mob descended and took him away to his fiery death.

Lovejoy did not defend McIntosh's alleged actions, but he did decry the mob justice. This prompted two raids on his printing office in which presses were seriously damaged, as I noted before.

But last year, Lincoln met with the Illinois legislature in Vandalia. At twenty-five he held his first elective political office, drawing three dollars a day. He was now away from New Salem and Ann Rutledge who had been engaged to marry John McNeil. But then John left for a trip East, saying he would come back to claim his bride after visiting his relatives. Lincoln, who had helped him with deeds, knew that his real name was McNamar.

McNamar was away for months, making excuses about why he could not return in infrequent letters.

Lincoln introduced several bills but always had thoughts of Ann.

Now back to New Salem he has come to Ann. She had written McNamar that she expected release from her pledge to him. No answer had come; letters had stopped coming and her way was clear. In the fall she was to go to a young ladies' academy in Jacksonville. Abraham Lincoln, deep in debts, was to become free of them, and they were to marry.

Lincoln would register in the Illinois College at Jacksonville, where Ann's only brother was studying, and Ann was to go to the Seminary for Women there.

Writer's note:
I was interested in this aspect of their planned education because I had attended MacMurray College there, which was originally the Women's Seminary.

April 1835

"The liberty enjoyed by the people of these States of worshipping Almighty God, agreeably to their consciences, is not only among the choicest of their blessings, but also of their rights."

George Washington
Message to Quakers, 1789

We are having a spring of rain, which is feeding the rich grasses for the cattle and giving the crops a good start. The children are frolicking in the fields. The season seems too perfect. I hope nothing dire is about to happen. I just returned from bringing in the laundry. The billowing sheets smell fresh from the sweet rain.

I'm making biscuits to have for supper tonight and for breakfast with scrapple and sausage gravy. I am praying my appreciation for this peaceful time.

Joseph is slow in developing, but he is a dear child. He doesn't have to talk to make me understand him, but his father seems worried about him and distant.

May 1835

"To correct the evils great and small the spring from the want of sympathy and from positive enmity among strangers, as nations or as individuals, is one of the highest functions of civilization."
Speech to the Wisconsin State Agricultural Society, Milwaukee, Wisconsin.
Abraham Lincoln

This has been one of the worst nights of my entire life. My husband came in at two in the morning, not drunk this time but carrying Tecumsehantas in his arms. She was as white as the sheets that he dropped her down upon as I followed him into one of the boys' rooms and he placed her on a bed of an absent hired hand. He asked me to get water boiling and said that her time had come before he could get her to her people. She curled up on the bed in her fringed deerskin dress, rocking with each pain but not uttering a sound. I was loath to touch her because of my jealousy and fear of her own animosity. She said something to him in her own native language and he took a bullet out of his gun, then sterilized it in the boiling water and some whiskey. She asked him to leave, placed it between her teeth and bit into it with each contraction. I sat silently beside her in an arm chair. Hours went by and I began to doze off into much needed sleep when suddenly she rose up, took off her outer dear skin and crouched down on the floor beside the bed. She began pushing furiously. Blood and fluid gushed around her and when she fell on her side a red baby fell head first onto the floor, screaming lustily with vigorous life. I grasped the sterilized knife next to me and cut the cord for her and she smiled gratefully. Then I helped her up onto the bed and began to wash the baby in a basin nearby. I placed a blanket around him and gave him to her. She held him to her breast as I placed a heavy blanket over both of them, gave her some water and blew out the candle.

William was waiting in the next room, looking drained. When I told him that he had a son, he protested and declared that a white man had raped Techumsahantas.

"I'll find the son of a bitch if it's the last thing I do!" he swore.

I remembered the births of our own sons and how he had paced when Morgan, our first, was born but with further births had gotten drunk. Now, he looked relieved, and while I could smell the whiskey, I knew that the situation was too singular for him to be inebriated. Instead, he looked wary. Had he thought that I might slit the throat of the woman he loves with the very knife with which I cut the cord? Did he think me that cruel or ungrateful for the fact that she had saved our village? I didn't ask him these questions.

He said that she had uttered to him:

"The ones that matter most are the children; they are the true human beings."

She also said, "A man or a woman with many children has many homes."

With all things and in all things we are relatives."

He thanked me with apology in his eyes and told me to save the umbilical cord. It would be carried by the man-child in a pouch for the rest of his life. I just looked at him in my exhaustion and went in to bed. Whether or not he went to talk with her I don't know, because I fell immediately asleep into bad dreams. I was trying to strangle him with the umbilical cord.

May 1835

"A State which is incompetent to satisfy different races condemns itself; a State which does not include them is destitute of the chief basis of self-government. The theory of nationality, therefore, is a retrograde step in history."

Lord Acton (1834-1902)
John E.E. Dalberg, English historian
THE HISTORY OF FREEDOM IN ANTIQUITY, 1877

Finally after a tormented sleep that gave no true rest, I awakened. Tecumsehantas had completely picked up and disappeared. Somehow she was able to tie the umbilical cord and all. I've heard of Indian women going immediately back to work, just as Negro slaves do in the fields after childbirth. Perhaps my husband carried her on his horse back to her tribe. I looked into the shed, and she was not anywhere to be found.

Now, I feel responsible in a way for pushing my husband into this woman's reluctant arms because I was absent. She will lose her Shamanhood. I could see the sadness on her face even in her delight over the child. Whether or not he is William's child I do not know. I do know that I am pregnant again myself.

I picked up my corncob pipe and smoked in resignation. Then, after a while, I looked at myself in the mirror while putting fresh linens on the hired hand's bed.

I am thirty-two this year, and I see more silver streaks in my auburn hair. Four children have changed my figure. I am more rounded in the hips and my breasts are more inclined to droop, but my eyes are still large and shining, my lips nearly as full and my cheeks almost as apple-like as ever. William just doesn't see my good qualities any longer, because I disparage his rustic ways and he loves the Indian princess who, I believe, encourages his deviant tendencies.

Meanwhile, Jeb MacMurray loves my mind, which won't droop with age, but could even improve with his encouragement. What a strange situation. I try to be virtuous, but I wonder what can happen to this seemingly irreconcilable life. Jeb is young and handsome With that forelock of black hair and his well- trimmed moustache, he reminds me of my French father in his younger days. He makes quite a contrast to my rag-tailed husband in his buckskin and coon cap, unkempt beard and wild eyes.

June 1835

"At all times sincere friends of freedom have been rare, and its triumphs have been due to minorities, that have prevailed by associating themselves with auxiliaries whose objects often differed from their own; and this association, which is always dangerous, has been sometimes disastrous, by giving to opponents just grounds of opposition, and by kindling dispute over the spoils in the hour of success."
Lord Acton

The Sioux Indians cut my husband's wrist in a special ceremony admitting him to the tribe as a blood brother. His new name is Free Stallion. When he came home with his wrist bandaged, I asked him what had occurred. He said that the women of the tribe, through whom everyone inherits, had performed a special ceremony for the baby's birth celebration. They had made special moccasins for him and named him Namet, meaning Star Dancer.

My husband now has a distinctly split allegiance. He is endangered, especially since in 1813 a law was passed by the territorial legislature which offered a reward of fifty dollars for each Indian taken or killed in any white settlement and of one hundred dollars for any warrior, squaw or child, taken prisoner or killed in their own territory.

July 4, 1835

"Two tremendous forces have come into moral clash in our time-the newly awakened spirit of liberty and the mighty and ancient spirit of tyranny. The latter undeniably has its seat and stronghold in the Roman system, with its kingcraft and priest-craft and its established control over the motions of men's souls. To it I can no longer adhere...."

"You may not see yet what you will see as you live deeper into this time of ours, that the cause of the Huguenots in France is the cause...of Protestants everywhere. There will be a long struggle, fought out now on one field and now on the other, but the cause is one. A wider question is at stake and a deeper one than many see-not merely a question between

the Mass and the Bible, but a question of the freedom of the human spirit for all time to come…"
William the Silent
Prince of Orange
Father of William of Orange
(1533-1584)

"My earlier views of the unsoundness of the Christian scheme of salvation and the human origin of the scriptures, have become clearer and stronger with advancing years and I see no reason for thinking I shall ever change them."
Lincoln to Judge J.S. Wakefield, after the death of his son, Willie Lincoln.

William's father, John, and brothers, Pearce, David and Taylor have just arrived from Michigan and Ohio. They are full of news about the family. These Irishmen are independent Catholics. With a deeply held view of the moral imperative that helping one's fellowman is comparable to tithes to the Catholic Church, and they always help widows in distress and children.

They are from County Cork, and I think some of the Scotch Irish here may be Orangemen, who are usually from Northern Ireland and protested for the Protestant rule in England. Orange is actually a part of South East France now, but William of Orange was from the Dutch Republic and married the ruler of England, Queen Mary. He also ruled over New Amsterdam, now called New York.

Mercy's title to one of the thirteen patents in New York may have been taken by the Duke of York when he took over Manhattan Island, as I mentioned.
Mercy's parents, the Achens, say that Sarah Pearce, her grandmother, owned most of northern New York State. When they first came to America, they lived in New Jersey, where East and West Orange are cities. The town near David's grove is now called Orange possibly due to their influence or that of the Scottish people here who are protestant.

Mercy and John may move down to the area from Michigan and Mercy would like to see us move there also.

Mercy is glad that it is called Orange because her deed was from William of Orange.
His father, King William The Silent of Holland, had progressive ideas, which his son, William of Orange had adopted. She is happy that David has moved up north Mercy feels that this new area is her birthright now and wants to see us living there.

William's father, John, is talking about hiring an attorney in order to claim their land in New York. He is incensed about the theft of the deed. When determined, he is a formidable force. He has been known to turn the tide in many a dispute in years gone by.
He is a very tall man (over six feet) with a scar on his nose. Some say it was twisted in a fight. He probably weighs about 200 pounds of muscle. He is very intelligent although illiterate. I don't see how he is going to go up against the Eastern lawyers and political forces even if his father's family did have five castles long ago in County Cork.

Most of the Orangemen were from the area of Ulster in Northern Ireland. In 1606, according to Jeb MacMurray, two Scottish noblemen, Hugh Montgomery and James Hamilton, arranged an amnesty for the Irish rebel Con O'Neill in exchange for a third of vast property holdings in counties Down and Antrim. They then encouraged tenants from other parts of Scotland to settle there and establish farms. King James I realized this could be a useful way to pacify the Catholic Irish in the neighboring territory.
In 1610 he set aside nearly half a million acres across six counties, promising land to any settler willing to take the Oath of Supremacy (meaning they recognized James as the head of the English Church, which automatically excluded any non- Catholic Irish. The settlers came in two great waves: first Highlanders from the western islands then Lowlanders and some English.

Even so, the protestant Scots predominated and left their stamp on the six counties of Protestant Ulster.

Some crossed the cold waters every Sunday to attend the Presbyterian churches.

When the tide went out, one could walk over to Scotland. Today Americans call their descendants "Scotch-Irish" but we consider them Scots in every significant respect. In truth, they may be the first representatives of the great Scottish dispersion that changed the rest of the world.

Author's note:
From these forces came the religious revolutionist of the Scottish Enlightenment, Francis Hutcheson.
The Ulster Scots were genuine legatees of John Knox, with their fundamentalist religious zeal and their hope to have an educated ministry. Two of those ministers were Francis Hutchenson's grandfather and father, who was pastor of Armagh when Francis was born in 1694.
Remember that Mercy's ancestor, Countess Philippa Plantegenet who married Hotspur was from Ulster. At that time, of course, everyone in the royal family was Catholic.
This was before the time of the protestant Church of England, promoted by King Henry VIII.

By 1694, the Ulster Scots community had endured massacre by dispossessed Irish Catholics, including the wholesale murder of men, women and children at Portadown in 1641, and had paid them back in kind.

Many had signed the National Covenant, and backed the Parliamentary forces against Charles I., a Catholic. They had submitted to Cromwell's rule and defied James II and the French, my ancestors, at the gates of Londonderry in 1687.

Similar to life in our Frontier West, life in Ulster had hardened and toughened its inhabitants into a tight-knit community. They felt surrounded by hostile forces, not only the native Irish but also, the Anglican officials of a "foreign" government in London. They couldn't even attend Dublin's Trinity College, much less Cambridge or Oxford. Having to be on their own, Ulster Scots clung fiercely to their independent status and Scottish ways.

Still, their faith was already changing. What was called "the new light" was spreading within the ranks of the Scottish clergy from England and Holland, and found support in Ulster. Some ministers had begun to question the fatalistic dogmas of old-style Calvinism, the idea that man was innately sinful and destined from birth to either heaven or hell. They began to cherish the belief that human beings were made in the image of God and the ideal of changing one's life by accepting Jesus as savior.

Francis Hutcheson had begun to rethink his faith early and differed with his father in this regard, especially when he went to study in Glasgow. That city was already sending ships to Europe and America.

In 1648, posters circulated in Glasgow calling for volunteers to "Province of New-East-Jersey in America." Eventually, the English took over Perth Amboy in New Jersey and closed it to all but English merchants. Yet, Glasgow merchants continued to do business along the New Jersey coast as smugglers.

When William III came to the throne, the bloody persecutions of the Killing Time came to an end, and, raised a Calvinist himself, William gave the Kirk (church) its desired independence, throwing out the bishops and recognizing the authority of the General Assembly He also insisted that the Covenant theology was banned.

Francis Hutcheson was starting at Glasgow toward a master's degree in theology, and one of his professors, John Simson, offered to students a more reasonable view of man and divinity. He said that the world is not the realm of the Devil; it reflects the purposes of its Creator, in its orderliness, regularity and amazing beauty. Like the teaching of Jesus in the Gospels, Simson explained about a benevolent God who watches over the fate of His creatures and provides for their needs and desires. He suggested that the belief in Jesus as Savior was not necessary for salvation and cast doubt on the Trinity and on Jesus Christ as the Son of God.

These beliefs of several Scots in the area certainly did not coexist well with Catholic theology. Mercy and John definitely believe in the trinity, and most of the Scots in the area knew of their beliefs.

August 1835

"Upon the subject of education, not presuming to dictate any plan or system respecting it, I can only say that I view it as the most important subject which we, as a people, can be engaged in…"
First public speech; to the people of Sangamon Co., March 9, 1832
Lincoln

While Old John wants to go back to the Island of Manhattan and reclaim Mercy's land, Mercy feels that they are too old to go. She wants to go with us to northern Illinois.

John's real estate transactions in Ohio and Michigan were all signed with an x.
William cannot write and I help him from time to time with certain documents.
He is becoming more appreciative of this help and declares that he will save money for our children to be educated.

Both John and William are talking about moving up north near Fort Dearborn now that the area is being settled. I am shunned, anyway, in most polite society because of my husband's alleged affair with his Indian princess and the abolitionist sympathies of Old John. Some say he killed five men in Ohio.

Writer's note:
(My Aunt Dorothy disproved this allegation. She went to the Ohio Penitentiary and looked up the records. There was no record of homicide by John Driskell or any kin.)

Walking in the field to bring food to the men as they harvest, I found a depression in the ground near the woods and almost fell into it. Covered with crosshatched sticks, it was about six feet deep. I asked William what it was for, and he said it might have been to trap animals, dug by

French trappers in the old days. But I've never heard of such a deep trap, told about by my French relatives. I know they hide slaves in such holes. You might get a horse into it, but you could not get him out. The sides are steep.

September 1835

The corn and grass are stunted with the drought, while the chills and fever of malaria have come to our first born, Morgan, our precious son. I stayed up bathing his face the first night and the second. Then we sent for doctor Armstrong, but to no avail. He has nothing for this mosquito-caused disease. Morgan cried out and I brought a candle to his bedside.

I sat bathing his face and trying to get him to eat some soup when he awoke fitfully from time to time. I prayed to God constantly to save him. Finally, with the dawn his fever broke, and I embraced him and thanked divine Providence that he was spared.

I hear that the fever has taken Ann Rutledge also and that Lincoln is taking it so hard! They buried her in Concord, and Lincoln sat for hours with no words for those who asked him to speak to them. A week after the burial he continued to ramble in the woods and would not speak to anyone.

In the home of Bowling and Nancy Green, he did any job to keep his mind occupied but always ended by returning to her grave. He could not stand to think of the rain beating on her grave.

Those were my same sentiments concerning my Morgan. But he is saved. He can help his father with the farm and the stock and our other living children. There is so much to do and to be thankful for!

I am seven months into my pregnancy now and am feeling a bit better, but I am so heavy.

October 1835
"Liberty, next to religion, has been the motive of good deeds and the common pretext of crime, from the sowing of the seed at Athens, two thousand four hundred and sixty years ago, until the ripened harvest was gathered by men of our race."
Lord Acton
(THE HISTORY OF FREEDOM IN ANTIQUITY)

They say that sorrows come in threes.
A third fateful tragedy has struck! William, white as a ghost, returned in the dead of night, carrying Tecumsahattas. Though bleeding severely, she is not with child this time. It is too soon after the birth of her boy. No, this time she is dead!

At one time, I would have been glad to be rid of the temptress, but now with all the uprisings, I think this is a terrible deed. Surely, her tribe will take revenge on all whites, since she is not alive to intervene.

William found her on the trail to our house, with her papoose on her back. Her son still lives, amazingly enough.. The bullet struck her in the side. She was among the women in Squaw Grove, who were waiting for the men to return from the hunt. They were defenseless, and someone took advantage of the situation to fire on them, killing several women in cold blood.

We have taken care of the baby until now, but decided to return him to the tribe.
They will not take him, because they say the mother swore to be chaste, and his blood is half white, which makes her a traitor to her vow.

Several questions present themselves to us:
What will happen if the Indians plot revenge? Will they attack the village with the son of the princess here?

December 1835

"The souls of emperors and cobblers are cast in the same mold. The same reason that makes us wrangle with a neighbor causes a war betwixt princes."
Michel de Montaigne
(1533-1592)
French philosopher, essayist

"When a white man governs himself, that is self government. But when he governs himself and also governs some other men, that is worse than self government-that is despotism. What I do mean to say is that no man is good enough to govern another man without that other's consent."
Abraham Lincoln

I finally became brave enough to visit the sweat lodge now that my rival has left it. I felt that I might find something that would help me in raising her child, Star Dancer. What I found there was not any thing that I had expected.

I found a parchment book, almost like a diary that told about Techumsahantas' rape! It described her abuser as a tall, thin man with black hair and a mustache. The description of her assailant certainly matches the description of a certain friend of the Phipps I have seen in the newspapers.

I was taking the journal to show to William, but then, I found something even more revealing. In a section of the sweat lodge hidden under the coals in a depression was a Negro child, trembling and hungry. She said that she had been waiting for deliverance, for Techumsahatas to come with a horse, which would carry her to Canada.

"I's make up my mind I's gonna run away first chance I git." she said. "I's travels all day and night. The bloodhounds done tree'd me."

I had had no idea that the Indian princess had been involved in this abolitionist practice.

Now I began to suspect the motive for her killing and who had done the killing.

There are some people here who were rebels in Canada and were ousted from that country. They don't want the Negroes interfering with the jobs that they want as hired hands or renters. They have a constitution and bylaws in their organization, which is a lynching club extending from Ohio to Texas.
THE HISTORY OF OGLE COUNTY, Kett, 1882

William is worried that they will come after him and wants to protect us. He is concerned about the MacCades in particular. John MacCade is from the clan that often picked fights in Scotland and were rebels and land grabbers in Canada. The rebels against the English in Canada hated the Irish. Many educated Irish refused to rebel against the English.

We are considering moving up north near Ft. Dearborn. Jeptha Noe writes us that he has settled in Indian country near the Kishwaukee River, but that the Indians are fairly peaceful. I want to wait until my new baby is older and can stand the adjustment.

Author's note:

Many Sauk and Fox Indians lived in Illinois in 1804, but a treaty in that year called the The Treaty of St. Louis gave the U.S. over 11 million acres in our territory. Payment was only $1,000 first cost and immediate delivery of $2200 in goods and land for relocation of the natives west of the Mississippi. This occurred in spite of the fact that they had been converted to Christianity by Father Claude Allouez, who found them in 1670 in harem situations, often with as many as eight wives. They resented the French attempts to convert them, but when the priest told them the story of the cross and Emperor Constantine, many had emblazoned their bull-hide shield with the cross.

By 1838, most tribes were gone except for the tribe of Chief Black Hawk who was born into the settlement on the Rock River they had formed in the 1690's when they had come from southern Wisconsin. By the time he was born in 1767, the settlement had farms, homes, a cemetery and even some domesticated animals.

In 1680 – 81 Iroquois had invaded the Illinois tribes again, instigated by the British to interrupt the French trade. Many Illinois were slaughtered and others fled west. Commandant Henri de Tonti of Ft. St. Louis at Starved Rock convinced the Illinois to come back again since the French decided to build a fort there. They built it large enough so the Illinois and others could go inside for safety. So, there had been a fort there even before the Sauks had arrived.

January 1836

"If there be human enactments against our entertaining the stricken stranger-against our opening our door to our poor, guiltless and colored brother, pursued by bloodthirsty kidnappers, we must, nevertheless, say with the apostle:'
'We must obey God rather than man'"
Gerrit Smith
New York philanthropist
 and financier of the Underground Railroad.

The annals of Henri de Tonti's son, Deliette, who joined a group of Illinois on a buffalo hunt for five weeks, speak of a sociable people among which the women are treated well. The courtship ritual was a "patient wait" on the part of the young male. The intended young woman herself and her brother, if she has any, had the last say on the marriage match. In some cases, the young woman would wait four to seven days before she made her decision. For the already married, disloyalty on either side was not tolerated.

I wish that we had such a society here in the lawless west among whites. Religion is considered basically for women with Bible readings after sewing bees and itinerant ministers. A man's wife is essentially his chattel still. The double standard insures that he may have his romances, but she must remain his alone. If he finds her with a lover, he may shoot them both and get away with it in many cases.

I have just given birth to a beautiful little girl. We are going to call her Caroline, since William remembered the slave Caroline fondly. She was one of the first he had freed. Our sweet daughter, Caroline, has beautiful red curls and is definitely lovely and our pride and joy. Our little Indian boy likes her too and is not a bit jealous of my attentions to her.

Meanwhile, on the abolitionist front, I have read in the newspaper from Pennsylvania that New York philanthropist Gerrit Smith, one of the most important financiers of the Underground Railroad, is becoming more and more active. The movement is progressing and slaves are beginning to be liberated more often through wills; it is called manumission.

"Free Frank" McWorter has christened his new town New Philadelphia. In this settlement, McWorter is believed to be the first African-American to establish a town in the United States. Nearby Payson, a short distance away from us in Adams County is a definite stop on the Underground Railroad, and McWorter's four sons guide escaped slaves all the way to Canada.

In Springfield and Lexington Kentucky, there is a strain of high society where women may wear eight or twelve starched petticoats with an overskirt of changeable silk. There might be several illusion skirts worn over white satin and a rose or ostrich plume to wear in the hair but not here in the back woods of the prairie state. In these cities, houses also might be two stories high and large enough to hold within their walls a dozen prairie-farmer cabins like ours. Their walls and chimneys are of brick and porches run the length of two sides, according to my husband's account. He saw a large one-story kitchen stretch to the rear of the house and its windows were higher than a tall man's arms could reach. It would be heaven to me to have a kitchen that is that spacious and sunny.

February 1836

"No man will ever be safe who stands up boldly against you, or any other democracy, and forbids the many sins and crimes that are committed in the State; the man who is to fight for justice-if he is to keep his life at all-must work in private, not in public."
Socrates (470-399 B.C.)

My dream may come true! In about two years we will be moving up north to a community about sixty miles from Fort Dearborn, called Groady's Grove. The county was organized last year and included a store, a post office, a tavern, a justice, a physician and an attorney's office. The land has not yet been surveyed, but we are moving anyway. The boys have mapped out a house, including my spacious kitchen and a wide front porch. This will be much more than the log cabin we have here near Springfield. The chimney will be made of brick, for we will need warmth up north. The land has not been surveyed yet, but they have gone up there and staked the claim and with their axes have blazed the line of timber and hitched a team or yoke to the plow to mark out the furrow on the prairie or eighty acres of timber to four of prairie. They can cut down the timber gradually to create the farmland we'll need. This timberland will supply the fuel we'll need for warmth and cooking. William and I are eager to go.

June 1836

"If we ever get free from all the oppressions and wrongs heaped upon us, we must pay for their removal. We must do this by labor, by suffering, by sacrifice, and, if needs be, by our lives, and the lives of others."
Frederick Douglass

I love William now. The death of Tecumsahantas has unified us, but I feel threatened myself here as I try to rear her child along with all of my own. He is certainly brave, true to the Indian appellation for a male, and his skin is light because of his mother's possible distant Illinois ancestry,

I believe. He is a good child, however, and I try to overlook the abusive nature of his conception. William feels that taking care of him is too much for me, however.

We have decided to give him to Old John and Mercy. Perchance, it will distract Old John from his futile quest of looking for the deed to Manhattan Island. They are lonely and will probably adopt the boy.

I am definitely worried about William's abolitionist activities. I don't want to lose him. It was told of various communities that a mob went to the house of a man and took him away and hanged him on a tree. It was a dark night and when morning came they saw they had hanged the wrong man. And they went and told the widow, "The laugh is on us."

Stories such as these make me apprehensive, and soon William will be away from me up north clearing the land and getting our house ready. William has said that I should live with Pearce and Mary who have moved nearby. I'll feel comfortable with them, and the girls especially like them.

We'll have to put the farmhouse up for sale and caution the neighbors to tell nobody where we are living. We also must sell all the stock.

The Black Hawk War has put $4,000,000. into circulation. Land speculators and real-estate dealers are busy. On open prairies many towns and cities are laid out in lots. Men joke that soon no land will be left for farming. A boom is on, overloaded and sure to collapse. It's the pioneer stock, taking its chances, believing in the future, and believing that future will come sooner with a boom.

September 1836

"You may burn my body to ashes and scatter them to the winds of heaven, you may drag my soul down to the regions of darkness and despair to be tormented forever, but you will never get me to support a measure which I believe to be wrong although by doing so I may accomplish that which I believe to be right."

Abraham Lincoln

Lincoln is in the legislature in Vidalia with a vision of himself as a constructive statesman, pushing through plans in transportation, schools and education. He told his friend, Joshua Speed, at Springfield that he aimed at being called "the De Witt Clinton of Illinois," achieving for his state what a constructive Irishman had done for New York in getting the Erie Canal built and in school improvements. Still Lincoln is always high-principled. He wants the capital moved to Springfield, but when he was told of a block of votes he could have if he would give his vote for a measure that he considered against his principles. After an all night session, the members went home at dawn without having brought him their way.

In a second meeting, they tried it again and Lincoln made the declaration above.

Lincoln is such a good man. It is terrible that his ladylove, Anna Rutledge, died last year. They say he went into a deep depression and is still extremely melancholy from time to time.

October 1836
"And what do I deserve to suffer or to pay, because in my life I did not keep quiet but neglected what most men care for-money-making and property and military offices and public speaking and the various offices and plots and parties that come up in the state..."
Socrates
Greek philosopher

All kinds of tales circulate here.
Among politicians there was a tradition of a legislature, which passed a law forbidding small bulls to roam at large. Owners of such small stray bulls would get heavy fines under the law. The small farmers rose in anger, claiming that the law was all in favor of the rich farmers who had only big bulls, and the law let the big bulls roam as they pleased. At the next election, the small farmers revolted and threw out of office every politician who had voted against small bulls.

Some say William McHarry, while herding cattle in Champaign county, rode horseback, snapping off rattlesnake heads with a long cattle whip, sometimes killing twenty-five a day.

Friends of a hunter with a big reputation bragged that he could put a panther under one arm, a hedgehog under the other, and climb a thorn-tree without a scratch.

November 1836

"Why was government instituted at all? Because the passions of men will not conform to the dictates of reason and justice without restraint."

"It is of great importance in a republic not only to guard the society against the oppression of its rulers, but to guard one part of the society against the injustice of the other part."
Alexander Hamilton (1757-1804) American statesman
The Federalist, No. 15

"All communities divide themselves into the few and the many. The first are rich and wellborn, the other the mass of people. The voice of the people has been said to be the voice of God; and however generally this maxim has been quoted and believed, it is not true in fact. The people are turbulent and changing; they seldom judge or determine right.
Give therefore, to the former class, a distinct, permanent share in the government; they will check the unsteadiness of the second, and, as they cannot receive any advantage by a change, they therefore will ever maintain good government."
To Robert Morris, 1780.

People bragged about knowing John Phipps, who knew Francis Scott Key and other Politicians, but William just looked awry at all of this bravado.
He had heard that Phipps was doing a little reconnaissance work heading in a south-easterly direction along the Rock River, and came upon Billy Hamilton, son of Alexander.
Phipps said:

"Billy was doing some surveying of land work for either Illinois or the federal government."

Anyway, Billy was to establish the Standard Line for townships. John probably felt quite comfortable with Billy's work, seeing as how he was the son of Alexander, a Revolutionary War hero and statesman. Billy had also been in the Lead Mines, so John, no doubt, already knew him. The trouble was that Billy never did get around to surveying the land around Sand Hill.

Scouting around in the Rock River Valley, John Phipps was evidently impressed with the beauty there. It was said that at a later hearing of the General Land Office, somebody testified that he had said that Sand Hill would be an "admirable" site for a county courthouse.

Evidently Phipps talked to his brothers about his big plan: form a county, take up some land by the river, have river frontage lots to sell and the county would have a nice site for a courthouse, in the Back Quarter. The Phipps Company would have the Front Quarter and the county the Back Quarter (160 acres), It would take some string pulling but John surely thought it would all work out just right. Later on, we heard that there were some big money men from Chicago and around the state of Illinois who went in on forming John Phipps and Company.

"We knew that John "knew" a lot of people, people in high places. We heard that he got Illinois to have him lay out a road from Chicago to Galena via Oregon City, which is the town they named to be the capital of Ogle County. Phipps claimed he created it. But even I know that with so much work on a project, finding out a few years later that everything had gone wrong might make somebody liable to take a little revenge. I really have no way of knowing all the facts in the matter of the State Locators and all that occurred, but I can put two and two together.

The State of Illinois was to appoint three men from out of town who were authorized to plant a stake on the quarter section of land that was to be used as the county seat, which would be a convenient location for the people who would come to the county. And there were the locators on a June day and where do you think they put the stake?

You're right! The locators put the stake on Sand Hill. But they placed it on the front quarter, not on the back where the Phipps wanted it! Later Francis Scott Key, when he was asked to defend the Phipps claim in Washington, D.C., called the stake "this Magical Post." The quarter section the stake was planted in what would be the seat of justice of Ogle County, thought John. Phipps and Co. would be down along the river, selling lots and would be able to see the courthouse built in just the right place for sales. You can just picture John wiping his brow in relief, believing that was the start of the project for sure. Maybe the Phipps raised a few glasses that night, thinking it was clear sailing from then on out.
Leonard J. Jacobs, THIS MAGICAL POST

Author's note:

You probably have noted that John thought Sand Hill would be an "admirable" site for a courthouse. Well, the man who heard John say that, many years before, was James Giles. It was later said that good citizen James Giles kept a diary or notebook for many years. He was, not so incidentally, the foreman at the second trial regarding the Driskell murders by the Regulators.

There were two volumes of the notebook. After James died, it was decided by the family that "someone" in the family could get hurt by revelations in the second volume. So the family destroyed the second volume.
Can you imagine which family would be hurt if they were painted in a true hue?"
(Leonard J. Jacobs, ARSON ON SECOND THOUGHT)

December 1836
"Democracy arose from men's thinking that if they are equal in any respect, they are equal absolutely."

"Inferiors revolt in order that they may be equal and equals that they may be superior. Such is the state of mind, which creates revolutions."

"Revolutions break out when opposite parties, the rich and the poor, are equally balanced, and there is little or nothing between them; for, if either party were manifestly superior, the other would not risk an attack."

"The real difference between democracy and oligarchy is poverty and wealth. Wherever men rule by reason of their wealth, whether they be few or many, that is an oligarchy, and where the poor rule, that is a democracy."

Aristotle (384-322 B.C.)
Greek philosopher
Nicomachean Ethics

We haven't taken in many slaves lately. Not many try to escape in this weather.

It's just too cold to stay out long. Matches are precious. You don't want the fire to go out.

Without a muffler, your lungs would freeze mornings just as you tried to do the chores. The children can walk to school on the caked snow over the fence posts. They say that Bill Prowder, riding to Springfield, froze to his saddle and had to be carried into a house, saddle and all, to be thawed out.

Sleds don't make a dent in the ice over the snow. Since it is this cold here in the South, I wonder what it will be like when we homestead near Fort Dearborn. I am pregnant again and hope for a boy, a new beginning in a new county. I wonder if the families are close up there. Are there quilting bees and square dances, barn raisings and rodeos?

I am getting ready for Christmas and stringing popcorn on the tree that William and the boys brought in. Not many slaves try to escape. It is just too cold to stay out long.

January 1837
"The man who has half a million dollars in property has a much higher interest in the government, than the man who has little or no property."
"Power is always right, weakness always wrong. Power is always insolent and despotic."
Noah Webster (1758-1843
American lexicographer

Well, here's more on the founding of Ogle County from the newspaper: The elected officials of the county have been installed. Judge Thomas Forbes came in as the Circuit Judge, and Ben Phipps became the Clerk of the Circuit Court. Forbes also had the job of seeing the legal work is done on selling the lots in the Back Quarter. He is called the Commissioner of Lots, and the money he takes in goes to the Public Building Fund. I personally think Forbes is a good man, but it may turn out to be a bad job. He is personally selling those lots and he is a judge. Perhaps, it would be better if he were to stay out of it.

Law and order are practically non-existent in Ogle County. The first sheriff, William W. Mood is a member of a well-organized group of outlaws. At the first session held, the grand jury returned an indictment against him for noticeable omission of duty. A few of the justices of the peace are known to be members of the banditti. These individuals hold court and pass judgment on the guilt or innocence of the other banditti. A few constables are also banditti members and their conduct gives the local people no real help. Hence, all honest people live in constant fear. Because the law enforcing officers could not enforce the laws of the land, the settlers make their own laws and regulations and organize their own local claim societies. Last year the Oregon Claim Society, called Regulators, adopted their own constitution.
(Kett, THE HISTORY OF OGLE COUNTY, 1878)

March 1837
"The whole history of the progress of human liberty shows that all concessions yet made to her august claims have been born of earnest struggle...if there is no struggle, there is no progress."

"Power concedes nothing without a demand. It never did, and it never will. Find out just what people will submit to, and you have found out the exact amount of injustice and wrong which will be imposed upon them; these will continue until they have resisted with either words or blows, or with both. The limits of tyrants are prescribed by the endurance of those whom they suppress.
In the light of these ideas, Negroes will be hunted at the North and held and flogged at the South, so long as they submit to those devilish outrages and make no resistance, either moral or physical. If we ever get free from all the oppressions and wrongs heaped upon us, we must pay for their removal. We must do this by labor, by suffering, by sacrifice, and, if needs be, by our own lives and the lives of others."

Letter to Gerrit Smith, March 30 1849.
Frederick Douglass (1817?-1895)
African American orator and reformer

Well, Van Buren has been elected as Jackson's successor, and William says we shall have more of the same kind of government. The opposition to "King Andrew" seems to have held the Whigs in unity, but they failed to prevent this election of Van Buren.

At the end of the legislative session in Vidalia, the papers say that the "Long Nine," Lincoln's group with their long legs and 200 pounds weight apiece, started home on their horses, with the exception of Lincoln, whose horse had been stolen, leaving him without cash to buy another.

Later, as he rode with his long legs straddling a borrowed horse, he had seven dollars in cash in his pockets and was more than a thousand dollars in debt. Arriving at Springfield, the "Long Nine" sat down for a fine supper while spokesmen for Springfield expressed gratitude to those who had arranged to move the capital to their own city.

Lincoln would now be practicing law in the firm of Stuart & Lincoln. Like all lawyers, he had been certified to the Supreme Court as having good moral character. He was leaving the town on the hilltop at the curve of the Sangamon River with its memories of being the pilot on the

Talisman, of the Offut store that had gone bankrupt, of being captain in the Black Hawk War, the store of Berry & Lincoln that had failed and left him struggling under debts it would take years to pay off. He was leaving the town where he had won the girl with the wavy corn-silk hair, the terrible taking her away that he would never forget.

In the legislature that winter over the nation the question had come up whether the slavery of the Negro race under the white race was right or wrong and whether any man or woman, believing it wrong, should be free to state the belief. In the southern states it was no longer lawful to speak against slavery; any person found guilty of an agitation that might cause an insurrection of slaves would be hanged, in accordance with the statutes. The State of Georgia offered $5,000 for the person of one Boston agitator to be brought to Georgia for trial. The three million Negro workers in the southern states are considered property, livestock valued by tax assessors at more than one thousand million dollars. In the Senate at Washington, Henry Clay has named the total slave property value as twelve hundred million dollars, and the cotton belt is spreading westward, adding thousands of acres every month.

My father has sent me an article from the "Richmond Whig" of Virginia. It stated that: the North must go to hanging fanatics if they would not lose the benefit of Southern trade, and that they will do it. Another paper he sent was "The New York Courier and Enquirer," which declared, that (the Abolitionists) have no right to demand protection of the people they insult.

And we are definitely in peril for our lives at this point, even out here on the prairie.
I wonder what my father, an officer in the army, would think if he knew that William and his family are abolitionists. My mother came from a Quaker family, called Friends in Pennsylvania. Quaker is a derogatory term, which my father sometimes used. He did not believe that a man should "quake" before his duty to fight.

Riots in Philadelphia lasted three nights, ending with forty-four houses smashed, a colored Presbyterian church battered, one Negro beaten to death, and another drowned in the Schuylkill River.

The meek, soft-spoken little Quaker, Benjamin Lundy, editing a paper with the mild title, "The Genius of Universal Emancipation;" was beaten by a Baltimore mob.

On March 4th, by the ballots of North and South, the New York Tammany Democrat, Martin Van Buren, took office as President of the nation, telling the country that he is "an inflexible opponent of every attempt of Congress to abolish slavery in the District of Columbia against the wishes of the slaveholding states," saying he is determined to resist the slightest interference with it in the states where it exists."

April 1837

"I would respectfully suggest the propriety of passing such a law as will prohibit under severe penalties, the circulation in the Southern States through the mail, of incendiary publications intended to instigate the slaves to insurrection."
Andrew Jackson
To Congress

We are in the midst of a terrible Panic nationwide, which may evolve into a depression.
Land grabbing and exploitation seem to be the order of the day.

After the first settlers staked their claims and Indian land was "purchased", the federal government claimed all the land under "eminent domain." Settlers like the Driskells said that they had staked their claims and they were theirs. The government surveyed the land and that meant that the Driskells could sell it for $1.25 per acre.

William says Jackson is true to his prejudiced form. He treated the blacks as he treated the Indians. He says that John Phipps served under

Jackson with the Tennessee Volunteers and fought in the Battle of New Orleans. He is bragging about it, while building his courthouse.

He participated in all of the firefights around New Orleans. It is a known fact that Jackson's army lacked an adequate supply of blankets, food and small arms, and it is possible that Phipps made note of those problems and thought to himself that if an entrepreneur had the foresight of bringing those supplies to Jackson, a neat profit could have been realized. He could have turned a good profit, a "race horse" that could have been invested in by a group of citizens. It could have been that "Old Hickory" who did hold short conversations with his men, might have entertained the idea of such a deal with Phipps.

(Leonard J. Jacobs, Ogle Through a Glass Dimly, pg. 9, Oregon, Illinois 2001)

Just last January, there was a parade, commemorating that Battle of January 8, 1815.
John Phipps marched in it as much a hero as the veterans of Lexington or Valley Forge.
William definitely has a bias against John Phipps, and I don't think it's just because John fought with Andrew Jackson. He and William have had some kind of words with one another. As I've mentioned, John had interests in mines in Michigan that I heard about while there with Mercy.

William said that he was down in the town of Dixon where Phipps stopped to talk with John Dixon, the founder of the town and its innkeeper. William heard Dixon's wife say to Phipps, "It is a good thing for you, Mr. Phipps, that Mr. Dixon is not at home today, for it is you who would get hurt. There would be a fuss."

William said that John replied:
"It is a good thing for Mr. Dixon, madam, that he is not here for if he was, he would surely be hurt. I was born in a fuss, and nothing pleases me better than to be engaged in a fuss."

John was born in Virginia in 1796 where his parents were engaged in farming. In 1810, the family moved to middle Tennessee where they again took up rural pursuits, that area being the frontier of development at the time. John was not interested in farming.

He had an indomitable spirit of adventure, an untiring will to move forward geographically and financially. His unbending streak of stubbornness caused him to keep fighting for what he thought was his right, even though signs read "It can't be done."

(Leonard Jacobs, ARSON ON SECOND THOUGHT)

Pearce remembers him in the Black Hawk War. When Black Hawk's Band threatened to re-cross the Mississippi and move up Rock River Valley, John happened to be in Schuyler County at the time, so he joined the local militia company with a lieutenant's commission which was given to him by the then Governor Reynolds, a personal acquaintance of Phipps. Pearce remembers how he hated Indians.

When Black Hawk decided against the crossing, the scare went away, and everybody went home. Then when Black Hawk's Band did actually re-cross into Illinois in 1832, setting off the little war, it forced the settlers and miners to "find a hole" and stay there until the chastened Band went back across the Mississippi in August.

Pearce recalled some of the antics of John Phipps and told us this history of him:

After the little war, John again went out on a search scout, starting in southern area east of Michigan and moving in a southeasterly direction. He soon came onto Billy Hamilton, son of Alexander, who was camped in the area just north of Oregon City. Billy was carrying out a contract he had with the federal government. He was evidently instructed to lay out the Standard Line, which was required every so many townships. Up to that time of 1833 the land locally had not been surveyed to lay the land into townships and sections. In order for this public land to be put up for sale by the U.S. government, it had to be surveyed.

Somehow, John Phipps encouraged Billy Hamilton at some later date to survey the land around his proposed courthouse.

In 1833, John and his brother Ben were now both in JoDaviess County, which later became Oregon County. JoDaviess had Ben act as an election clerk in the White Oak Springs Precinct when that precinct was then in Wisconsin.

Court documents show that Ben was paid for his services as an election clerk in 1830. (JoDaviess Commissioners Court records, pg. 155.) (Ogle, Through a Glass Dimly)

While they were moving about the lead mining region, the brothers Phipps had the opportunity to meet James M. Strode and J.D. Kirpatrick. Kirkpatrick wore several hats in the affairs of J.D. County as a business man and as a deputy sheriff.

James Strode was an attorney in Galena and served as the colonel of the 27th Regiment of militia in the Black Hawk War. He created a problem with the military when he declared martial law in Galena. He had the new J.D. County jail converted into a fort as a defense against possible attacks by the British Band of Indians.

Recently, he and Kirkpatrick have become involved with Phipps in several investments.

Because the brothers Phipps were in J.D. County, they were able to see how a new county got "on its feet" after being created by the Illinois legislature. John would be able to see the various pitfalls that awaited the unsuspecting entrepreneur. The brothers made their way east to the area where John had talked to Billy Hamilton, John liked the beauty of the region and especially liked Sand Hill. He thought it would be an admirable site for a county courthouse.

John, Ben and George found a site for a saw mill. Here they whip sawed lumber to be used to build a ferry that would be made to cross Rock River. The ferry went into use in 1834 after John went back to Galena to get a license to operate it legally in Jo Daviess County. The Commissioner's Court records say that John Phipps was to charge the same ferry-crossing rates that John Dixon charged for his crossings downstream. (That may have been the "fuss" that Phipps was referring to with Mrs. Dixon.) The more important note is that John Phipps and Company were "in business" and that the ferry was to be operated in

"Oregon City" where John and Company had subdivided a claim and where lots were being sold adjacent to the admirable Sand Hill proposed courthouse.

Author's note:
Ogle County was created 16 January 1836, but the Jo Daviess commissioners Court handled Ogle County's business until January of this year, 1837. At that time Judge Thomas Forbes arrived and became the circuit judge of the 6th Judicial Circuit.
And we find that Ben Phipps on the same day became the county's Circuit Court Clerk.
The papers say that the so-called "Prairie Bandits" are a threat to the citizenry at the time, especially in the eastern part of Ogle County, and Judge Forbes says that he will condone the citizens' right to take the law into their own hands.
The spotlight was being directed to the Driskell family as alleged members of the Prairie Bandits because the Phipps and Forbes thought they were in the same league with the Groadys, who were bandits before the Driskells arrived at the grove.

David Driskell, our brother sued Fred Groady, who owned Groady's Grove, for poaching on the land Groady had sold to David. The Commissioners Court records testify to this. Why would one family of a gang of thieves publicly sue another family of that same gang? It makes no sense, but we are now condemned by association.
(Ogle, Through a Glass Dimly-
Ogle County Court Records, pages 50 and 244.)

John Phipps definitely has southern sympathies along with others in Ogle County. They, no doubt, include an interest in the continuation of slavery and possibly the extension of it.

June1837

"We do firmly believe that, if the Southern States do not quickly unite, and declare to the North, if the question of slavery be longer discussed in any shape, they will instantly secede from the Union. That the question

must be settled, and very soon, by the sword, as the only possible means of self preservation."
"The Augusta Chronicle of Georgia"

In Boston an agitator who came to a meeting of the Female Antislavery Society had his clothes torn off, was dragged at a rope's end through the streets, and, after being rescued by the police, borrowed coat, hat and pantaloons to go to jail for further safety from those hunting him, who were respectable citizens of Boston.

When Miss Prudence Campbell opened a school for Negro children at Canterbury, Connecticut, she was sent to jail for violation of the state law forbidding the teaching of colored children from other states. At Concord, New Hampshire, an academy was wrecked where colored children were being taught reading and writing.

July 1837

" A man protesting against error is on the way toward uniting himself with all men that believe in truth."

"Histories are a kind of distilled newspapers."
"Every new opinion, at its starting, is precisely in a minority of one"
Thomas Carlyle (1795-1881 Scottish historian, critic, sociological writer

I see in the papers that the Sioux, Mandan, and other tribes have been ravaged by Small Pox. These natives never had any of the white man's diseases before we came.
America was a pure land, free of such epidemics. Then the "pox" swept the plains from Mexico in the late 18th century and the Mandan, Ojibwa, Pawnee and Arikara populations diminished by two-thirds. But by this decade, the tribes of the upper Missouri have outlived their acquired immunity. It seems that a fur company, headed by Francis A Chardon, steamed upriver from St. Louis to pick up furs and drop off annual supplies. The nearby Mandan and Hidatsa tribes had gathered hundreds of packs of bison robes.

The St. Peters docked at Fort Clark on June 19 and unloaded trade goods and Indian provisions. Also aboard was Chardon's 2 year-old son, Andrew Jackson Chardon, whom he had fathered with a handsome Lakota Sioux woman named Tchonsumonska. That night, the crew members of the St. Peters joined in a boisterous frolic, singing and dancing with the men and women at the Mandan's village of Mittuttahandkush.

Since the steamboat had been carrying several passengers and crewmen infected with a lethal virus, Variola major, feared for thousands of years by it better-known name: smallpox, the boat's arrival triggered one of the most catastrophic epidemics ever recorded, according to this St. Louis paper.

The disease had announced itself when a St. Peters crewmember had showed symptoms on May 2, two weeks after the boat left St. Louis. Ignoring suggestions that the man be put ashore, the 33 year-old captain, Bernard Pratte Jr. said he needed every available hand to bring back to St. Louis the packs of profitable furs his company was expecting.

Less than a month after the boat left Fort Clark, the Indians began dying at an accelerating rate-at first two or three a day, then entire families of eight or ten at once.

"I keep no a/c of the dead, as they die so fast it is impossible," Chardon wrote. Soon his young son Andrew would join them. The deaths were horrifying with fever, chills and excruciating pain. With blood pouring from their mouths and ears, they often died even before the appearance of smallpox's pustules. Husbands and wives committed mutual suicide, stabbing themselves with arrows or knives or leaping from cliffs.

Bodies pile up in villages too rapidly to be buried and are dumped into the river.

William Fulkerson, who oversaw local Indian affairs from his base at Fort Clark, wrote to the explorer William Clark, superintendent in St. Louis "the small pox has broke out in this country and is sweeping all before it- unless it be checked in its mad career I would not be surprised if it wiped the Mandans and Ridkaree tribes clean from the face of the earth."

Clark forwarded Fulkerson's letter to his superiors at the War Department in D.C. But most of the federal government appeared to shrug off the impending disaster except for one U.S. official, Joshua Pilcher, a 47 year old Virginian who had been appointed to take care of the Sioux agency at Fort Kiowa in South Dakota. Traveling to his new post on Board the St. Peters during its fateful trip, Pilcher had observed the disease spreading before traveling to his new post. He quickly sent out messengers from Fort Kiowa to warn the nomadic Lakota and Nakota Sioux still hunting on the plains to stay away from the river in order to avoid contagion.

Later after the disease had reduced the Mandan from 1,600 to thirty one persons and had reached the Blackfoot of the Rocky Mountains, Pilcher proposed a brave experiment. He went up the river with a doctor and $2,000 in presents, located the Sioux and vaccinated them with cowpox, a vaccine developed by the Englishman Edward Jenner in the 1790's. It had proved so effective that Jefferson had urged Lewis and Clark to carry it with them on their historic expedition.

The doctor was Joseph De Prefontaine, who was an erstwhile physician/theatrical manager who had been ordered out of his employer's theater for rolling on the floor and Singing during a performance of Hamlet.

Amazingly, the Sioux accepted the vaccinations and were saved along with some other tribes. Thus, Techumsahantas's relatives were saved to roam the plains.
Pilcher was able to tell his superiors that the epidemic had finally subsided and eventually went to serve as Clark's replacement as Superintendent of Indian Affairs.
(THE INDIANS OF ILLINOIS)

Author's note:
My friend Leonette, descended from the tribe of Pocohantas, told me that sometimes the white men gave the Indians blankets with the small pox germs infested within to cause the natives to sicken and die.

July 1837

"Those who profess to favor freedom and yet depreciate agitation are men who want rain without thunder and lightning. They want the ocean without the roar of its many waters.
Letter to Gerrit Smith, March 30 1940
Frederick Douglass (1817-1895.

Regarding the abolitionist agenda which is so much in our thoughts, the conflict has hit us out here now. James Gillespie Birney, a brilliant Kentucky-born lawyer who had been an Alabama planter and had given all his slaves freedom, can't get a paper printed nor hire a hall for a speech in Owensville, Kentucky. "The Philanthropist," which he published in Cincinnati, was refused delivery by postmasters in the Southern states. He had traveled southwest and heard dreams of southern empire while listening to planters talking about the big land stretches west of the Mississippi and how to make them slave territory.

He writes: "There will be no cessation of conflict until slavery shall be exterminated or liberty destroyed. Liberty and slavery cannot live in juxtaposition."

While Birney and his group tried to bring gradual emancipation by lawful and constitutional methods, the Garrison group demanded immediate emancipation by moral persuasion and Christian wisdom, or somehow otherwise, maintaining that the United States constitution in its silent assent to slavery was "a compact with Hell".

The first Abolitionist convention in Ohio met at Mt. Pleasant with secretary Gamaliel Bailey, who later founded "The Cincinnati Herald." Others at the convention were John Keep, William Donaldson, Christian Donaldson, John Rankin, A.A. Guthrie, Major Nye, President Finney of Oberlin, Asa Mann and others. The Quaker, Lundy's newspaper enterprise was also tied up with Mt. Pleasant after he returned from St. Louis.

A favorite point of crossing the Ohio was at the northern end of Wheeling to Martin's Ferry and the first "stations" were the residences of Joel Wood in that town, Jacob Van Pelt on the hill and Joshua Cope at the head of Glen's Run in Belmont County.

Wheeling was avoided at all costs because it had a public slave market where human beings were publicly sold at auction and from all accounts the scenes are fully as repulsive as any related to New Orleans or St. Augustine. To visitors from the Ohio side this was a festering sore. The lower end of the county as well as the upper end of Belmont county adjoining had been largely settled by members of the Society of Friends who accepted the words of the Declaration of Independence as meaning just what they said and had migrated from North Carolina and other slave states for the express purpose of getting out of the slaveholders' domain. These people definitely influenced my husband when we were young and just married in Ohio's Jefferson County.

Jefferson County also became the first freed slave colony. In 1825, Nathaniel Banford of Virginia liberated seven of his slaves and sent them to Benjamin Ladd at Smithfield, who had been a neighbor of Mr. Benford. Mr. Benford, who was a Quaker, was said to have been influenced in his actions by David Minge, another neighbor who had freed eighty- seven slaves and sent them to Cuba. The problem for Mr. Benford, as with all who desired to free slaves, was whether their condition would really be improved thereby. He concluded to try the experiment of a colony and in 1829 gave manumission papers to nine families of slaves on his plantation and sent them to Smithfield. He furnished Mr. Ladd with guns, and the latter, under his instructions purchased two hundred and sixty acres of land in Smithfield, erecting cabins and furnishing the immigrants with farming implements.

The settlement was on McIntire Creek from which it took its name, sometimes called Haiti from the West Indian black republic. All the property was divided into parcels of from three to fifteen acres and distributed according to number of children in each family. The heads of the original families were: Nathaniel Benford, who took his name from his master, Ben Messenburg, Collier Christian, Lee Carter,

Paige Benford, David Cooper, William Toney, Fielding Christian and Fitzhugh Washington. All are known from miles around and many were expert gardeners, hired out for their knowledge.

As time goes by, we may see how long these people live in freedom, compared to the length of life of the typical slave.

The abolitionist papers published articles and items about mobs North and South and about auctioneers of slaves calling for bids in Washington near the Capitol and about the tactics of John Quincy Adams in Congress against the so-called "Gag Rule," a resolution passed by Congress providing that all petitions relating to slavery should be laid on the table without being referred to a committee or printed. Events are splitting the churches into northern and southern divisions.

Author's note:

Beginning in 1802 with the end of slavery in Haiti, the Caribbean and South America, the slave empire had begun to crumble. Slavery was banned in Venezuela in 1810, in Chile in 1823. The United States soon found itself as the last great nation on earth with slavery, but with the invention of the cotton gin, King Cotton reigned and the problem intensified.

According to Polo historian, Betty Obendorf, there were three main lines that ran through Ogle County in the early 30's. Starting with Garden Plain in Whiteside County, one line ran to the Asa Abbott Farm on Route 30 between Morrison and Fulton. From there the line continued to the Jacob Baker family property on Blind Corner near Fulton.

From Milledgeville, the line ran through Eagle Point Township to Buffalo Grove, Byron, Kilbuck and on to Mayfield in DeKalb County.

A third route ran along the east side of the Rock River. From Bureau County, the line ran through Lee County into Ogle. It included stops in Princeton where Reverend Lovejoy was and where our David and Taylor lived later, La Moille, Amboy, Franklin Grove, Nashua Township, Paynes Point, Lynnville, where David lived in the later '30's and then to Deacon David West's home in DeKalb County, ironically, only two blocks south of the DeKalb County courthouse. Most of the underground railroad activity in DeKalb County took place in the Sycamore area, where Margaret's family resides in our story.

As was mentioned before, Ogle County came to be avoided because of the Ku Klux Klan that was so active there. The Driskell murders set an example for avoiding Ogle County.

One of the stops between Sycamore and Chicago was in Bolingbrook. Just recently in 2003, an old farmhouse was being uprooted and moved to another location. It once had belonged to the abolitionist, George Dyer. Under it, workers found a five-foot cavern that was four-feet across where local historians figure Dyer hid runaways on their way to the Windy City.

Back in Ogle County, the runaways passing through Nashua Township were taken to the Ruel Peabody Farm. As his fellow underground agents, Peabody was born in the east and moved to Ogle County as a middle-aged man in 1836. He transported runaways to Capt. Thomas Stinson's farm near present day Paines Point. The good captain then moved them on to Lynnville Station, where David lived at the time of this story. Stinson was born in New Hampshire in 1799. In 1839, he and his wife, Naomi, bought 300 acres of farmland next to Aaron Paine at the intersection of what is now near the Chana Blacktop.

At the time of the second Fugitive Slave Act, David Driskell was pointed out as an abolitionist.

(Three Underground Railroads, second story in a series about the Underground Railroad in Ogle County. By Doug Oleson.)

Remember that the offending plaque, declaring my ancestors to be horse thieves and murderers, is in Chana.

August 1837

"Hangman's gallows ought to be the fate of all such ambitious men who would involve the country in Civil War and all the evils in its train so that they might ride on its whirlwind and direct the storm.

The free people of the United States have spoken and consigned these demagogues to their proper doom. The tariff was a mere pretext and disunion and southern confederacy the real object. The next pretext will be the Negro or slavery question."
Andrew Jackson

In Texas, men of southern kinship are fighting, the Alamo garrison of 187 men trying to the last man to try to hold out against a Mexican army of 5,000. This is part of the march of the South or the southern planters, to wider regions and more cotton-planted land. Sam Houston's men took victory from a Mexican army at San Jacinto and won independence for Texas. Planters had come; slave ships had arrived at the coastline of Texas direct from Africa. Abraham Lincoln is against this war and the expansion of slavery.

Now the South is openly declaring its defense of slavery as an inevitable institution and a necessary practice, but there seems to be no clear vision of the southern empire. There was an attempt of South Carolina to break out of the Union of states in 1832, medals were struck reading "John Calhoun, First President of the Southern Confederacy," the flag was ready a palmetto tree coiled with a rattlesnake, "Don't tread on me."

Past-President Andrew Jackson had publicly warned that if any State may at pleasure secede from the Union, the United States is not a nation.

Now, with Martin Van Buren in office, from the Government at Washington and the national church organizations on down to business partnerships and families, the slavery question is beginning to split the country. At the one end are Abolitionist agitators who want to take away a billion dollars' worth of property from Southerners (I guess that means our family also) and at the other end is the Southerner who cries, " The people of the north must go to hanging these fanatics."

At the two opposite ends of this issue are passionate, reckless, stubborn men whose grandfathers had fought side by side in open combat to overthrow by violent revolution the government of the British Empire over the American colonies.

August 1837

"There is no safety where there is no strength; no strength without Union; no Union without justice; no justice where faith and truth are wanting. The right to be free is a truth planted in the hearts of men."
William Lloyd Garrison

We had a knock on our door on a sultry evening yesterday. It was a man from southern Kentucky hunting down his runaway slave. My heart beat at a furious clip. He looked in our shed. Fortunately, no one was there just then. He didn't find the hole behind the shelves anyway. But he could have knocked down the shelves. He was in such a lather.
"H'its my property that's being stolen away from me," he proclaimed.

It's hard to tell the difference between a real slave owner and the bogus slave hunters who kidnap free Negroes (like the ones who sometimes help us as hired hands) and take them to St. Louis or across the Ohio River into Kentucky and sell them.

Wagons from Tennessee and Kentucky drive across Southern Illinois with movers who call out from the wagon seat that they are driving to Missouri where a man "had a right to own a 'nigger' if he wanted to." Hostile feelings are developing between Illinois and Missouri people; the Missourians call Illinois the suck hole and its people as "Suckers," while the Illinoisans let it pass by alluding to Missouri residents as "Pukes."

I've decided to go up to Michigan to be with Mercy for the delivery of my child.
I'm boarding the ferry tomorrow with the children.

Sept. 1837

"Distribute the earth as you will, the principal question remains inexorable-Who is to dig it? Which of us is to do the hard and dirty work for the rest, and for what pay?
Who is to do the pleasant and clean work and for what pay? Who is to do no work and for what pay?"
John Ruskin

Lincoln knows that the legislature is mostly of southern blood and viewpoint. In the first legislature in which he served there were 58 members from Kentucky, Tennessee and south of the Ohio River, 19 from the Mid Atlantic states and 4 from New England.
He knows that the blood ties between populations in Southern Illinois, Indiana, Ohio and in those states south of the Ohio River are firm and are closely interlocked with interests of southern planters buying huge quantities of pork, corn and produce from northern frontier states and the New England power-loom mills buying increasing millions of bales of cotton every year.

Surely, he can understand his fellow members of the legislature when they passed resolutions declaring: "We highly disapprove of the formation of Abolition Societies; the right of property in slaves is sacred to the slaveholding States by the Federal Constitution, and… they cannot be deprived of that right without their consent…."
Lincoln voted against these resolutions and only one other member joined him. Dan Stone. The two recorded a formal protest spread on the Journal of Proceedings as follows:

"Resolutions upon the subject of domestic slavery having passed both branches of the General Assembly at its present session, the undersigned hereby protest against the passage of the same.
They believe that the institution of slavery is founded on both injustice and bad policy, but that the promulgation of abolition doctrines tends rather to increase than abate its evils.

They believe that the Congress of the United States has no power under the constitution to interfere with the institution of slavery in the different States.

They believe that the Congress of the United Sates has the power under the constitution to abolish slavery in the District of Columbia, but that the power ought not to be exercised unless at the request of the people of the District.

The difference between these opinions and those contained in the resolutions is the reason for entering this protest."

November 1837
"A day, an hour, of virtuous liberty
Is worth a whole eternity in Bondage."
CATO
"Liberty or death." Confederate flag
Joseph Addison (1672-1719)
English essay writer and poet.

William has written to me to tell me that that his brother, David, sent a letter saying that Lincoln has just given a speech before the Young Men's Lyceum at Springfield where David is going to school. Lincoln asked the question: "Shall we expect some transatlantic military giant to step the ocean and crush us at a blow? Never! All the armies of Europe, Asia and Africa combined… with a Bonaparte for a commander could not by force take a drink from the Ohio.

At what point then is the approach of danger to be expected? I answer, if it ever reaches us it must spring up amongst us; it cannot come from abroad. If destruction be our lot we must ourselves be its author and finisher. As a nation of freemen, we must live through all time or die by suicide."

He went on to declare: Accounts of outrages committed by mobs form the everyday news of the times from New England to Louisiana. In Mississippi they first commenced by hanging the regular gamblers-a set of men not following a very useful or honest occupation but one which so far from being forbidden by the laws, was actually licensed by an act of the legislature passed but a single year before. Next, Negroes suspected of conspiring to raise an insurrection were caught up and hanged in all parts of the state; then, white men supposed to be leagued with the Negroes; finally strangers from neighboring states, going thither on business, were in many instances subjected to the same fate. Thus, the process of hanging from gamblers to Negroes, from Negroes to white citizens and from these to strangers, till dead men were seen literally dangling from the boughs of trees upon every roadside and in numbers that were almost sufficient to rival the native Spanish moss of the country as a drapery of the forest.

December 1837

"The Party or Sect that will suffer by the triumph of Justice cannot exist with safety to mankind. The State that cannot tolerate universal freedom must be despotic; and no valid reason can be given why despotism should not at once be hurled to the dust."
William Lloyd Garrison

It's another spare Christmas with just oranges in the children's stockings and dolls made of straw, but we are saving for the house that is being built by William and the bigger brothers. Now they are home, because the snow up north precludes the finishing of the house and outbuildings until spring. But we do have that to anticipate.
Stores advertise velvets, silk, satin, and Marseilles vestings, fine calf boots, silk and morocco pumps for gentlemen and for ladies silks, bareges, crepe lisse, lace veils, thread lace, shawls, lace handkerchiefs and fine prunella shoes, but we have none of these. We are spending money releasing the slaves.

We are lucky that now we can go to town wearing shoes, where we used to go barefoot and the men have changed from moccasins to rawhide boots and shoes. We no longer spend time killing deer, tanning the hide and making leather breeches to tie at the ankles. Instead we raise corn and buy pantaloons, which come from Massachusetts over the

Ohio River or the Great Lakes. I can fit into them now that my belly is not so large.

Springfield with its 1,500 inhabitant is the bog town of Sangamon County, selling to the people of the county a large part of their supplies, tools, groceries, grain, pork, beef and produce. We went into town the other day, passing churches, schools, banks, newspaper offices, courts, lawyers, offices of government, taverns, saloons and other places of entertainment. It is a town where people are ready to say there is no more wilderness here; the land has been surveyed and allotted. Streets are made of plain black Illinois soil underfoot, except for gravel here and there for footing in rain or snow, and stone and sticks for street crossings.

There are in Sangamon county 79 Negroes, 20 registered indentured servants and 6 slaves. We still will be better off in the north where nobody suspects us of harboring slaves, sympathizing with Indians or stealing horses.

March 1838

"An idea that is not dangerous is unworthy of being called an idea at all.
It is not book learning that men need, nor instruction about this and that, but a stiffening of the vertebrae which will cause them to be loyal to a trust, to act promptly, concentrate their energies, do a thing- carry a message to Garcia."
Elbert Hubbard American writer, publisher, lecturer
THE PHILISTINE
(AN AMERICAN BIBLE)

Well, we're on our way. I'm writing this diary on the wagon drawn by four yoke of oxen. It contains family, bedding, clothing and provisions. Another wagon contains our chickens in coops, pigs in pens, and cows, calves, colts and horses follow on foot.
Sometimes, I have to get out and lift the wagon wheel out of the mud, since we do not yet have a son old enough to do that.

I can't write well because of the rumbling motion, so I'll close.

April 5 1838

"Laws that do not embody public opinion cannot be enforced."
Elbert Hubbard
EPIGRAMS

We just got the log cabin raised, and I have had my baby son. We have named him Theodore Decatur- Theodore, which means adorer of God, and Decatur after Stephen, my uncle who fought as an admiral in the War of 1812.
I feel in my bones that he will be an admirable man and a strong devoted son. We have a new start in a new land.

We staked our claim of 150 acres of land this month. It is the first claim made in the township by permanent settlers. There are no neighbors, except for the Grodies who seem to be rascals. The nearest mill is at Ottawa, 50 miles away. We have to make our way there with an oxen team.

We are glad to have the liberty of choosing this land and taking it.

June 1838

"The only foes that threaten America are the enemies at home, and these are ignorance, superstition and incompetence."
Elbert Hubbard
.

It's been a hard and busy time, but we're almost settled in. I have just begun to feel that I could start fresh in my new house away from Techumsahantas' land and her control over my husband, who loves his new son so dearly.

This area has about 400 acres of woods mainly. The first settler, Joseph Seaman, came to Squaw grove where the Squaws often waited for their men to return from the hunt and sometimes still do. He is rather far away and supplies are obtainable only from remote points. The nearest mill is way down in Ottawa, 56 miles away.

The courthouse is being built to contain a doctor's office, a lawyer's office and the post Office. We have called our grove Driskell's Grove. Before we came, it was Groady's Grove

The Groady's who were disreputable, have left that grove. They were known to kill salesmen and hide their wares in deep depressions in the earth that we have found in the woods. The nearby neighbors are glad that they are gone. I wonder if those depressions down south in our field were of a similar nature.

July 1838

"No society can surely be flourishing and happy, of which the far greater part of the members are poor and miserable."

"In order to make every man feel himself perfectly secure in the possession of every right that belongs to him, it is not only necessary that the judicial should be separated from the executive power, but that it should be rendered as much as possible independent of that power."
Adam Smith (1723-1790)
Economist and philosopher

Two tremendous forces have come into moral clash in our time-the newly awakened spirit of liberty and the mighty and ancient spirit of tyranny. The latter undeniably has its seat and stronghold in the Roman system, with its kingcraft and priestcraft and its established control over the motions of men's souls. To it I can no longer adhere.
William the Silent (1533-1584)
Father of King William of Orange

The Scottish people who have settled nearby in Polo are not highlanders. Highlanders are rather barbaric people who lived in tribes, much like our Indians with chieftains. They tend to be Catholic, as they fought for Bonnie Prince Charlie's ascendancy to the throne but were soon put down when the English realized what they were about after their sudden shocking uprising.

No, these Scottish people are from Dumfriesshire by and large. Some are from the village of Eskdalemuir, near the town of Dumfries, where Robert Burns was born and raised. This village is where Jane and James Byers are from. It is where Robert the Bruce fought valiantly against the English. Also the great engineering genius, Thomas Telford, who built bridges and much-needed roads all over Scotland was born and raised in that village. His greatest project was the Caledonian Canal, a sea-to-sea navigable waterway, connecting the Atlantic Ocean to the North Sea. It took almost fifteen years to build, using tens of thousands of workers at the astronomical cost of nearly a billion pounds. It opened up the central Highlands to commercial traffic for the first time, marking a new era in the history of that remote region.

Another Scot from that village was Charles Pasley who created the idea of the British Empire. Like Telford, he had prodigious intellectual gifts. He translated the NEW TESTAMENT from Greek at eight. His gifts, however, found their main outlet in solving technical problems as he served in the Royal Engineers in the Napoleonic Wars and became Europe's leading demolitions expert and siege warfare specialist. In 1810, he published "An Essay on the Military Policy and Institutions of The British Empire," which completely changed the way Britons thought about their empire in relation to the rest of the world. In fact, Pasley had created modern geopolitics. He warned his fellow Britons that they could no longer rely on their isolation or the British navy to keep them secure in the future. He said that true national security rests on policy and power-especially military power. That includes large overseas colonies, which could supply sailors for its navies and soldiers for its armies.

Actually, England is acquiring quite an empire. I'm glad we're not a part of it, thanks largely to my ancestors, the French. But at each turn of the acquisitions, Scots take the lead. They operate sheep farms in New South Wales, grow rye and barley in Lower Ontario, work in lumber camps in British Columbia, or trap beaver and otter along the Mackenzie River. Part of their success is due to the fact that most Scottish emigrants have more skills and education than their other European peers. This is due to the fact that the Presbyterian religion required its adherents to be able to read the Bible and write about it. They were the most literate nation in Europe in the 18th century.

Their bravery and loyalty were legendary. The first Highland "Watch," or armed patrol, was raised in 1667 under Charles II. However, the Jacobite wars led the English Royalty to lose faith in the loyalty of its Scottish contingents, and they were disbanded. After that time, clans loyal to the Stuarts raised a levy of troops to suppress the remaining Catholic rebels. General Wade issued a dark-blue-and green tartan for these companies of Highlanders, which gave them their name, the "Black Watch." Regiments such as Campbell's Highlanders, served with distinction in George 11's wars in North America and Europe, then they fought loyally against the American colonists and Napoleon. By 1800, they were the backbone of the British army.

It was the "clearances" that sent so many of the Scottish people here to these shores. Faced by an increasingly competitive agricultural market and the need to pay off enormous debts, chieftains looked for ways to make the land pay. This meant rewarding farmers who could afford higher rents or specialists in cost-effective agriculture, such as sheep and cattle farming and getting rid of the rest. This was the clearing of the land for grazing. The Scottish economist Adam Smith's " Division of Labor" had arrived in the Highlands and swept everything else aside. It spelled the end of the traditional Highland village community, the Baile, with its rights, powers and obligations of military service. The chief began to think in terms of progress and improvement rather than in terms of rewarding loyalty and service.

This was how the Scots who arrived here, even from the lowlands were able to sympathize with the Native Americans. The native culture was being destroyed to clear the land for cattle ranches.

Even Sir Walter Scott, for all his genuine sympathy with ordinary people, did nothing to stop the highland clearances directly. He hated revolution for the same reason that he loved his country. The outbreaks of popular unrest in the 1790s terrified him. He saw the blue-collar instigators as traitors and grimly supported the government's harsh repression as the Black Watch patrolled Ayrshire.

What drew educated Scotsmen such as Scott to the conservative Tory Camp rather than to the liberal Whigs? Under William Pitt, the Tories had supported the cause dear to the hearts of many Scottish Presbyterians, antislavery. This they share with people like Old John.

Also, of course, Tories were the party of patriots. The Whigs in Parliament had opposed war against France, and had gone on strike to undermine it, but Tories had been "hawks" from the start after the French Revolution, promising no peace with a regime built on terror, regicide and conquest.

Ironic to me, with my French upbringing, is the fact that these Tories thought of Great Britain as the last bulwark of Europe's freedom.

The wars against the French Revolution and then Napoleon struck a strong nerve in Scotland. The middle-class Scottish commitment to the British Union had found a new outlet, and even Sir Walter Scott found the attacks on the principle of property to be abhorrent. However he did write this disparagement: "In too many instances the Highlands have been drained, not of their superfluity of population, but the whole mass of the inhabitants, dispossessed by an unrelenting avarice..."

Yet, he also felt that there was nothing that he, even as Scotland's spokesman, could do to prevent the day coming when no one would be there to list to the bagpipe's call to arms.

The people who were being expelled from their burning homes in 1814 could have warned of this. But no one was listening to them. Scott, became their voice, however indirectly. Through the Highland shepherds, crofters and fishermen he placed in his novels, the voice of rural Scotland reached a wide audience. For his precedent in the historical novel. Dickens, Tolstoy, Hugo and especially his Scottish successor, Robert Louis Stevenson, all owed him appreciation.

August 1838

"Education is the leading of human souls to what is best and making what is best out of them; and these two objects are always attainable together, and by the same means. The training which makes men happiest about themselves also makes them most serviceable to others."
Stones of Venice 1853
John Ruskin.

Jeb and I have been reading the Waverley novels of Scott to the boys and to his smaller children at night. Jeb is fond of some of these Scottish families from Polo. Most of them lived in Toronto before coming here. They were rebels against the English in Canada. They don't want the slaves freed to go to Canada, where the English will be able to use them as cheap labor.

Some families, such as the Byers, are from New York and do not live in Polo. While in New York they had the misfortune of seeing their homes burned by rebel tenants during the Calico rent wars.

Another Scott, Zenas Aplington, a close friend of Lincoln, has come to Buffalo Grove and founded the small village of Polo. When the Illinois Central Railroad was projected through the region, he became a contractor on the line and succeeded in securing the establishment of a depot on his farm where he plated the town. His free-hearted and generous ways have won him hosts of friends. He is liberal in the aid of all public enterprises and contributes generously to the building of churches. He is a Baptist

He was born in the town of Deposit, in Broome Co., N.Y. in 1815, the son of James and Mary Aplington. He was reared on a farm and now at 22 years of age is a Free Mason. His ladylove, Caroline Nichols, also came this year from Delaware County, N.Y. She is the daughter of William and Jane (Look) Nichols. Her brother, John Nichols, was born in the same area as James Byers and Janet Scott in 1826.

197

Caroline has told us about the Byers family. Jane, also called Janet, was named after her aunt, Jane Scott who lived to the venerable age of ninety. She died in 1800, before Jane married James Byers. They made the perilous voyage in 1818 to the new country of America shortly there after. During one winter before they left Scotland, a blizzard lasted from November until April. In 1823, the winter and epidemic took the life of Jane's mother at 52 and the lives of Jane's brother and sister the year afterward. Her sister, Elspeth, was only 20 and her brother, Thomas, only 24. Jane feels fortunate to be alive and here on this earth. Her parents forbade the marriage, because James was rather poor, but he did well in New York. In fact, Jane was able to return home in 1829 with her little daughter Christie Anne, named after James' mother Christian Anderson, who is still living at age 80. The story is that they arrived in all their finery and were welcomed happily even by Jane's father, William Scott II, who saw that James and Jane had "made good" in the world and forgave their elopement. The next year he died. So, it was good that they made the trip.

Jane, James, Christie Anne and sons William, John and James II live in New York in the town of Andes in Delaware County and have owned property there for the past 23 years but barely escaped with life and limb when the Calico Rent Wars erupted and their tenants rose up against them. The tenants refused to pay the rent for houses on their estate and ultimately burned their manor house.

James was a teacher, but had felt for some time that he would like to explore the wilderness in the Midwest.

William Byers, eldest son of James and Jane, who walked here from New York nearly all the way except for hitching a few rides, encourages his parents in letters to come away from their tenants who are pillaging their belongings even while they try to live in an inn near their ruined house. It will take his parents at least three weeks to get here even in good weather. The oxen will have to go through a great amount of mud.

Author's note:

Immigration began to increase in the Ogle county area about 1836 when word was sent back to the relatives and friends of the settlers about the wonderful Rock River Valley. There were several books printed, such as ILLINOIS IN 1837 by S. Augustus Mitchell, and PECK'S NEW GUIDE TO EMIGRANTS, published in 1836 which describe the country, the best routes to take, how to build their cabins, etc.

They came by wagon, some using horses, but oxen were the most popular since they were cheaper to buy and easier to feed. They could choose an all-land route or a combination of land and water. Albany, N.Y. was the principal starting point from the eastern states. They traveled across New York State on the Geness turnpike, which paralleled the Erie Canal, or on boats on the canal to Buffalo, N.Y. where they had the choice of loading teams and wagons on steam boats for Detroit or following an Indian trail along Lake Erie.

Another factor, which hastened immigration, was the "Panic of 1837 which caused many people to start over in a new place.

There were four main entrances of the Underground Railroad into Canada. The western most route was across the Detroit river at Detroit and into Ontario Province at Windsor. Fugitives, crossing the river usually by ferry, settled in the communities of Fort Malden, Windsor, Sandwich, Dawn, Buxton, Chatham, Elgin, Dresden and Amherstburg.

In the latter town is the North American Black Historical Museum, 227 King Street, Ontario. Its archives contain numerous letters and diaries of early black leaders.

The John Freeman Walls Historic Site is at County Road 25 in Puce, Ontario. It contains several restored buildings, including the home of Walls, a slave who lived in Canada in 1846. A trail winding through a nearby wooded area is where visitors can hear the sounds of the Underground Railroad, such as shouts and barking of bloodhounds.

On County Road 40 in Dresden, Ontario is the Uncle Tom's Cabin Historic Site. It was the home of Josiah Henson, born in 1789, who fled Kentucky with his family to Dresden in 1830. He entered Canada at Fort Erie, after walking all the way from Kentucky, carrying his two small children in a knapsack. It was his story that inspired Harriet Beecher Stowe to create the character of "Uncle Tom" in UNCLE TOM'S CABIN.

August 1838

"Liberty is not to be found in any form of government; she is in the heart of the free man; he bears her with him everywhere. The vile man bears his slavery by himself; the one would be a slave in Geneva, the other free in Paris."
Jean Jacques Rousseau (1712-1778)
French writer, philosopher.

"Supreme happiness consists in self-content; that we may gain this self-content we are placed upon this earth and endowed with freedom, we are tempted by our passions and restrained by conscience. What more could divine power itself have done in our behalf?"
Rousseau

"The first (religion of man), which has neither temples nor altars, nor rites and is confined to the purely internal cult of the supreme God and the eternal obligations of morality, is the religion of the Gospel pure and simple, the true theism, which may be called natural divine right or law."
Rousseau

We were the first settlers in the South Grove area. But there were some Groadys, who are not our relatives. They are disruptive, and we have had to sue them. Finally, we agreed out of court, but John's brother, David, sued Hugh and John Groady later.

John S. Sebree made the first permanent settlement in this county in the fall of last year at Squaw Grove. He had the only frame house.

Some say that Peter Lamois located nearby. Early this year, settlements were made at Paw Paw by David Towne, Reverend Benoni, Benjamin Harris, Edward Butterfield and others. In Somonauk, Reuben Root, William Poplin, Joseph and William Sly, Thomas and William Brook, Captain William Davis and others settled. In Orange, Peter Lamois, Cpt Wharrey, the Watermans, Marshall Stark and Lysander Darling settled. Other settlements were made in Kingston, Clinton and Mayfield Townships.

As in other parts of the nation, we settled in the groves or in the timbers along the streams. Each man made claim to a tract of timber, covering as he supposed, about 80 acres and generally about 160 acres of prairie land. There is no land association here and many degenerate characters try to jump claims.

The Oregon Claim Protecting Society was organized in 1836 and drew up by-laws to adjust differences in over-lapping claims. The Society would protect anyone's claim up to 320 acres and required $50 worth of improvements on every 320 acres. There are land speculators who claim large tracts of land, and then sell land to settlers. This is a hardship for many settlers as some of the claims sell for $1,000 and more, and The settlers still have to buy the land from the government. The reason the land offices are not open is that the land has not been surveyed. William S. Hamilton started surveying the township corners in 1833, but the sections have not been completed.

A peace society has begun near Quincy, Illinois called the Mission Institute. Women participate equally in the antislavery societies. Baptists are neutral, believing that the Puritanical Law of God remains binding upon rulers and people. Only with divine law can there be perfect liberty.

In northern Illinois here the Presbyterian and Congregationalist churches give testimony of the sin of slave holding.

David Driskel is located a short distance east of the old village of Lynnville, which is a hub of abolitionist activities. He is reserved and fearless.

Samuel Ackin and his son Charles are in Washington Grove, while Thomas and Richard Aiken are in Lafayette Grove, just a short distance away from Samuel. William Ackin was Mercy's father who married Sarah Pearce. They are respectable, law-abiding citizens but have suffered loss through speculation.

William Bridges is also at Washington Grove. He is a man of more than ordinary ability and has the bearing of a gentleman. Being a man of fine conversational powers, hospitable in the extreme, he receives the visits of the best people in Ogle, Lee and DeKalb Counties. Few men would ever suspect him of being connected with law-breakers of any description.
(Portrait and Biographical Album of Ogle County, Chicago; Chapman Brothers, 1886.)

The Indians are often very unceremonious about the use of our cabins and out buildings. They will often open a door and throw in a blanket. If they are suffered to remain, they walk in, lie down upon it and take a nap; if it is immediately thrown out, the native picks it up and moves on. No Indian is ever known to knock at a door. The women are often frightened by one of the tribe who has noiselessly entered, looking for something to eat. When his wants are supplied, he will usually go away.

September 1838
"Liberty is obedience to the law that one has laid down for himself."
Jean Jacques Rousseau

The last payment was made last year to the Indians at Shabbona Grove, and those who are here, with the exception of Shabbona and his family, must remove across the Mississippi River to their new reservations. Shabbona's Indian name is Shaubenee. He was born near the Maumee River in Ohio in 1775. His father was an Ottawa and his mother a

Seneca. Around 1800, Shaubenee hunted in the Potawatomi country along the Illinois River. There he met chief Spotka and his wife. They decided to give him their daughter, Wiomex Okono, in marriage. Spotka died around 1815 and consequently Shaubenee was made chief of the village. This year his village numbers about 130 and his own family consists of about 25 individuals.

Sometime during 1807, Shaubenee was down on the Wabash and met Tecumseh. He was quite impressed by the leader. Shaubenee and Billy Caldwell accompanied Tecumseh all over Illinois, visiting tribes along the Illinois, Fox and Rock Rivers. Shaubenee fought with Tecumseh's forces in the War of 1812 and was in the field with Tecumseh when the chief was killed in the Battle of Thames on October 5, 1813.

Shortly afterward Shaubenee reluctantly pledged his allegiance to the United States. He returned to his village in the grove.

Gordan S. Hubbard who worked for the American Fur Company in Chicago remarked that he first met Shaubenee in 1818 and was acquainted with him until he died. Hubbard stated that he was impressed "with the nobility of Shaubenee's character. Physically he was as a fine a specimen of a man as I ever saw-tall, well proportioned, strong and active with a face expressing great strength of mind and goodness of heart. Shaubenee was not much of an orator, but whenever he talked, others listened.

Bill Caldwell gave Shaubenee a citation in 1816, commending him for his war efforts.

He said: "I have been witness to his intrepidity and courageous warrior conduct on many occasions and he showed a great deal of humanity to those unfortunate sons of Mars who fell into his hands."

(Amhurstburg, August 1, 1816 B Caldwell, Captain I.D.)

It was Shaubenee and Caldwell a few years later in 1827 who calmed Big Foot and persuaded him not to wage war with the Winnebagos, Techumsantas' tribe. I mentioned before that William was there.

In 1829, Shaubenee and his people were granted land near Orange and he lived there together with his people in peace until settlers wanted his land. Last year Shaubenee and his village were ordered to move to a new reservation in western Missouri. About 130 moved to new homes there, but it was not long before some other tribes in Missouri began terrorizing Shaubenee and his people. As a result Shaubenee lost his eldest son and a nephew.

People can be so greedy. There's no scarcity of land here. If it costs anything, it's about a dollar and fifty cents an acre.

I feel a great deal of sympathy for the old chief. Especially since we are raising this Native American boy, I can see traits of nobility in the race.

The leaves are falling, and some people call this season "Indian Summer". They say its just like the old Indian braves falling in their war paint and "biting the dust."

October 1838

"The power of the press, in the hands of highly-educated men, in independent position, and of honest purpose, may indeed become all that it has been hitherto vainly vaunted to be."

The Veins of Wealth

John Ruskin

I do not want to be pregnant again. I wish that I could resist the advances of William, but he is so irresistible. When he plays his guitar, I watch his tanned hands that I find so sensual. I then want him to play me, and I am lost to having a huge body once again. Sometimes, I think its better to have the pregnancy than the mess and pain of menstruation with washing of the rags and all. Elizabeth is of some help to me now with the younger children. Even Sarah Jane is learning to do some chores. Joseph is a slow child mentally and a disappointment to William, who needs help with running the farm competently when he is away. He loves Joseph but almost like a pet, which is incapable of speaking and can only express thoughts by noises. Fortunately, Old John and Mercy have offered to take Techumsahantas's little boy, Star Dancer.

Life is hard. We have only this log cabin, no neighbors. The nearest mill is in Ottawa, 50 miles from here, but this land is so much better than where we were before. I thank God.

In a town seventy miles from Springfield, a wild drama has been acted out. A young man in the town of Alton told men he must speak what he believed ought to be spoken about abolition. And the men answered that if he did speak what he believed, they would kill him. He had brought a printing press from St. Louis, intending through his paper to speak what he believed; they threw his printing press into the Mississippi River. He brought another press to Alton; they wrecked it. And a third time he brought a press to Alton, they circled by night with torches and guns around the warehouse where his press was, set the warehouse on fire and shot him dead.

Over the Illinois prairies and from the frontier to the eastern coast there was discussion about whether this young man Elijah P. Lovejoy, was right or wrong to say what he believed; discussion flared up, sank down, flared up again about gag rule and gag government.

November 1838

"In a community regulated by laws of demand and supply, but protected from open violence, the persons who become rich are, generally speaking, industrious, resolute, proud, covetous, prompt, methodical, sensible, unimaginative, insensitive and ignorant."
Ad Valorem
John Ruskin

William is acquainted with William H. Herndon, whose father took him out of Illinois College at Jacksonville when the killing of Lovejoy started abolition bonfires among professors and students. Young Herndon is thinking of studying law. He has seen Lincoln on some stumping trips and at the time he piloted the Talisman over that broken dam at New Salem. He began clerking in the Speed Store and sleeping upstairs in the big room with Speed and Lincoln.

William is a counselor to people here and often helps them to settle disputes among neighbors. He is friendly with Billy Herndon. If he could read and write, he could study law. We would be much better off. I would like to teach him.

205

Lincoln is stumping for his law partner, John T. Stuart, who was elected to Congress. When Stuart was running against Steve Douglas the two struck, grappled and "fought like wildcats" back and forth over the floor of Herndon's grocery till each was too tired to hit another blow. Then when Stuart came to, he ordered a barrel of whisky for the crowd.

Douglas later said that he was "in favor of confining citizenship to the white men of European descent, instead of conferring it upon Negroes, Indians, and other inferior races."

Interest in politics and the destiny of the human race is running so keen at this time that the young Democrats and Whigs had a debating tournament, lasting eight straight days. The future holds the thoughts of young men. With railroads coming West the border will move, the Great Plains fill up with settlers, the frontier will shift from the Mississippi River to the Rockies and after that to the Pacific Coast.

Peoria runs stages daily to Springfield, three times a week to Galena, Ottawa and Rushville. Seven steamers make trips between Peoria, St. Louis and Pittsburgh; another runs between St Louis and the Rock River. History and destiny are in the very air; the name of Stone's Landing is changed to Napoleon; the name of Goose Run to Columbus River.

The land is now all surveyed; fences are coming; if timber for rail-fencing is not handy, there is the Osage orange hedge which with some growth years can keep cows in pasture and out of a cornfield. Land speculators now hold the larger part of Illinois land.

December 1838

"You may either win your peace or buy it; win it by resistance to evil, buy it by compromise with evil."
"The Two Paths"
John Ruskin.

We now have seven children, but Mercy is with Pearce and Mary, and Namet, Techumsahantas' son, is with Mercy and Old John. Both children have come home for New Years and Christmas.

We are stringing popcorn and berries for the tree. William has constructed a crèche to place on the mantel of the fireplace. We are enjoying this holiday season in our new home, but it is still lonely without neighbors.

We have heard that bids are being made on the job of building the courthouse and the jail on Sand Hill. A man by the name of Jacob Crist has done a lot of the construction. This had been instigated by the Phipps with a large company from Chicago.

January 1839

When a bill came up in the legislature to throw off to the territory of Wisconsin the fourteen northern counties of the state of Illinois, Lincoln fought to defeat it. He wanted Illinois to have Chicago as port on one of the Great Lakes within its border connecting the West with the East. If the measure had won, we would have been part of Wisconsin, and the bill would have left Illinois depending on the Ohio and Mississippi rivers for water transportation, with its main economic outlets toward the South, with its future tied more closely to the South. The bill was beaten by 70 votes to 11.

February 1839

"The effects of unlimited power on limited minds is worth noting in Presidents because it must represent the same process in society, and the power of self-control must have limit somewhere in face of the control of the infinite."
Henry Brooks Adams
(1838-1918)
American historian

A school for young ladies in Springfield has announced that besides ordinary branches of education in 'intellectual and moral science it will conduct a class in Mezzotint painting. Sarah is so talented that I think

I'll suggest to William that she attend. A store nearby has offered on sale cloth, comb, tooth hair and nail brushes. Civilization and culture are stirring in Illinois.

The Alton Literary Society has met in the courthouse and debated the question "Was Brutus justified in killing Caesar?"

I also read in the Sangamon Journal sent to me from Springfield that the Northern Cross Railroad will pay cash for timber to make the grade from Springfield to Meredosia. Shipments of rifles are arriving in Illinois, "all lengths and sizes, mounted brass, silver and gold, single and double barrel, with shotguns to fit the same stock, some very fine in mahogany and leather cases."

Another newspaper column has the heading "Estrays" and tells of lost horses, sorrels, bays, dapple bays, some blaze-faced, some with saddle-marks or spots and scars or "bit in the ear" or long tailed or switch tailed.

Lincoln, having lost a horse ran, an advertisement stating:
"Strayed or Stolen: From a Stable in Springfield on Wednesday, a large bay horse, star in his forehead, plainly marked with harness, supposed to be eight years old... Any person who will take up said horse and leave information at the Journal office shall be liberally paid for their trouble." A. Lincoln.

Advertisements also are put out for abolitionists, calling them horse thieves, rather than slave thieves, which the slave owners consider us to be.

Along the confines of advancing civilization toward the west, there has always hovered a swarm of bold, enterprising adventurous criminals. The broad, untrod prairies, trackless forests, rivers unbroken by keels of commerce furnish refuge for those whose crimes have driven them from the companionship of the honest and law-abiding.
People say that Old John has killed five men in Ohio, for example. They are trying to frame him for horse thievery.

Courts and civil process can furnish only a thin veil of protection for life or property. The temptation to prey upon the unprotected sons of toil, rather than to gain a livelihood by slow process of peaceful industry is too strong for these pirates to resist.

A strong and well-constructed network of organized crime stretches over this whole section and few are fortunate enough to preserve their property.

No possessor of a fleet and famous horse dares to leave him for a single night, unless secured in a strong, double-locked stable, guarded by faithful dogs and sometimes by the owner himself. Many owners a obliged to keep an armed watchman every night in order to secure the safety of valuable horses. They are more cautious because of the fact that a fleet horse once gone was usually gone forever. So skillful are the plans of the prairie pirates who put so much ingenuity into rapidly forcing the stolen steeds quickly to a safe distance and so many rascals are connected that the pursuit and capture is difficult, dangerous and almost always unsuccessful.

(History of Ogle County)

Not only are people who suspect Old John of being an abolitionist trying to indict him.

There is talk that William has stolen horses, but I have never seen a horse around the farm here that I couldn't identify.

March 1839

Power concedes nothing without a demand. It never did, and it never will. Find out just what people will submit to, and you have found out the exact amount of injustice and wrong, which will be imposed upon them; and these will continue until they have resisted with either words or blows or with both. The limits of tyrants are prescribed by the endurance of those whom they suppress.

Frederick Douglass.

Letter to Gerrit Smith, March 30. 1849

William does not want Sarah to attend the school for young ladies. I don't know why. He doesn't want her down south, he says. He usually is interested in having the children educated. He must feel that there is a threat in the South.

My father has written to me concerning a one-time slave named Frederick August Washington Bailey who escaped last year from Baltimore, Maryland.

While Frederick was in Talbot County, his slave master had rented sixteen–year-old Frederick to a poor tenant farmer known as a "nigger breaker".
This farmer, Edward Covey, worked him sixteen hours a day, six days a week no matter what the weather. Frederick's back was scarred from Covey's whippings. Soon he began to dream of suicide rather than freedom.

One day Frederick pitched a last forkful of hay down from the loft to feed the horses. As he climbed down the ladder he felt a rope tighten around his right leg. Even without turning, he knew that it was Covey who had come to torment him. He jerked away and fell off the ladder into the dirt. Covey leaned over him clucking his tongue in victory. Frederick looked into Covey's sneering face and decided what to do. He was not going to let Covey beat him ever again even if he was hung for it.
He sprung forward and seized Covey by the throat. He pressed so hard that he pierced the skin and blood rushed out. Then, he kicked Covey in the ribs..

Then, Covey grabbed Frederick's arms to drag him. Frederick wrenched himself free and flung Covey to the ground. For nearly two hours they rolled in the dirt. With each punch, Frederick felt more like a free man.

At seventeen, Frederick took a large canoe from St. Michaels, floated eighty miles up the Bay, with forged papers in his master's name stating, "I the undersigned have given the bearer, my servant, full liberty to go to Baltimore." When he stepped into the kitchen of a house, he was grabbed by constables and thrown into the Easton jail. After being detained for a short time, he was sent to Baltimore to live with his master's relative.

Four years later, Frederick escaped to New York, taking the name Frederick Douglass. He now speaks regularly before abolitionist societies.

My father writes that the Mother Bethel AME Church in Philadelphia is the center for the Underground Railroad in his city.

April 1839

"This declared indifference, but as I must think, covert real zeal for the spread of slavery, I cannot but hate. I hate it because of the monstrous injustice of slavery itself. I hate it because it deprives our republican example of its just influence in the world-enables the enemies of free institutions to taunt us as hypocrites-causes the real friends of freedom to doubt our sincerity..."
Lincoln
Peoria Speech

There is so much sickness here and so little medical attention. A friend went shaking with ague to the doctor, walking seven miles on foot for a dose of quinine, but the doctor told him solemnly, "No, young man, I can't let you have it; you are young and can wear out the disease. I must save my little supply for cases in which it is needed to save life, for I don't know when I shall be able to obtain more."

Deaths are many and the few carpenters who are able to work are at times busy night and day making coffins. It is said that the disease results from our being close to groves and streams. The bad surface water from the sloughs, which we use from the want of wells of proper depth has caused the outbreak.

One settlement in Franklin is quite free from the diseases, since the three or four houses are two miles from the timbered land in the middle of the prairie

Still the citizens near the county seat have found time to build a new Court House. The survey lines, ordered by the County Commissioners, had been brought down from the neighborhood of Rockford, where some Government surveying had already been done, and the village of Sycamore has been staked out. Broad streets have been laid out in the hope that they will be needed to accommodate future business. From this time on, the name of Orange, originally given the settlement, has been dropped and Sycamore adopted by common consent.

Writer's note:
I think this was because the people didn't want to be associated with Orangemen who were for William of Orange, the Dutch leader of the army and symbolic head of the Dutch State. He had married Mary, the daughter of King James, but he was a Dutch Protestant and had supplanted the Catholic rule of King James. Perhaps because the Duke of York had taken over New York City, then New Amsterdam, the English pioneers decided upon a different name.

The Island of Manhattan changed ownership five times in three decades in the 1600's, but it forced the inhabitants to solidify their identity and their ties to traders, shippers and family in other parts of the world. What mattered was that cache of rights, which they noisily insisted be honored by whoever had just won control of the place, and which enabled the separate minority communities to flourish.

Under English law, for example, the governor tried crimes with no independent prosecutor, but the Dutch instituted the Schout or Scout who traveled the countryside settling disputes and later became the first District Attorney.

These facts are of interest to me, since my daughter, Michelle, is an assistant states attorney and head of the States Attorney's Office here in Annapolis. Also, my cousin, Scott Larson, descended from the Driskells, was an assistant states attorney for several years in Oregon, Illinois and is now in private practice.

During the previous winter, Captain Barnes had gotten together materials for building a spacious tavern at the new county seat, Sycamore, and it was erected, the first building in the village. It was directly east of the

Public Square and occupied as a hotel. As an inducement for building it, it was agreed that the block on which it stands should be given to the captain free of cost. Commissioners directed by Mr. Jewel proceeded to sell lots at public auction, and with the proceeds they contracted for building a courthouse and jail. The auction was held and the bidding was spirited. Some fifteen or twenty lots were sold at prices ranging from twenty to fifty dollars. Among purchasers were Frederick Love, J.C. Kellogg, James Waterman, Harvey Maxfield, Daniel Bannister, Almon Robinson, Erastus Barnes and Timothy Wells.

June 1839

"Poverty is a great enemy of human happiness, it certainly destroys liberty and it makes some virtues impracticable and others extremely difficult."
Samuel Johnson (1709-1784
English lexicographer, essayist, and poet

We read in the papers that several Mendi Africans, captured in their homeland, have mutinied aboard the Spanish schooner Amistad. They were on their way to a South American slave market in Guanaja, Honduras. These Africans overpowered their guards, killed the captain and cook and seized the ship in a bloody battle. The 36 remaining slaves ordered the three Spaniards who did not flee the ship into rowboats. The three remaining crewmen agreed to sail the Amistad to Africa, but the Spaniards tricked them and sailed instead to Long Island Sound off the Connecticut coast. There the ship was seized by a U.S. Navy cutter and taken to New London, Connecticut, where the Africans were arrested and charged with piracy and murder. As soon as the seizure of the ship was made public, the Cubans who purchased the slaves sued to have them brought to Cuba.

The Africans have been taken to a jail in New Haven to await trial. Three days after their arrest, leaders of the abolitionist movement in New England started efforts to free them. A special Amistad committee has been formed consisting of Lewis Tappan, a wealthy New York businessman, Reverend Simeon Jocelyn of New Haven, and Reverend Joshua Levitt, an abolitionist editor. They engaged lawyer Roger Baldwin to represent the Africans and with the help of Yale professor Josiah Givvs, located James Covey, a seaman who speaks Mendi, to be the interpreter.

Mr. Solomon Wells has purchased from us the south end of our grove a hundred acres or more for sixty dollars. He is entitled to all the adjacent prairie land he chooses to claim.
We need this money to feed our growing family.

Near our grove settled the Orput family, naming their grove Orput Grove, of course. The Beeman and Hatch families arrived about the same time.
The majority of the inhabitants of these groves are from the State of New York; a few came from New England and the foreigners are Scottish, English and Irish.
Only a few are of German descent.

Usually in this country 85% of the English persecute the Irish in some way. They don't allow them to work for their families. They also keep the Irish out of their public inns and schools.

We have changed our grove's name to Driskell's Grove.
It is over three hundred acres, fortunately. It abounds in a variety of wild fruits: the native plum, sometimes very sweet and rich, I use to make divine plum jam.
The wild crab and thorn apples are good for pies, too. We also like the mandrake and gooseberries and nuts of various kinds.

The slaves in the Underground Railroad love groves. Deep in the woods, they create secret places of worship. While berry picking, I once stayed out until twilight and found them in what they call a 'hush harbor." Here, led by an old woman of about seventy, they retell stories from the Old Testament, stories of how God delivered the Hebrews out of years of slavery. They create their own songs to comfort and empower themselves.

Uniting Groadie's Grove and ours was an Indian trail over which Big Thunder sometimes led his braves and often made the area a place of encampment. They dined on mushrats cooked over a spit and made beautiful jewelry. They would show the white men how they made it, letting them watch, but would not let the white women see. They knew that the women would be able to copy the jewelry designs with their nimble fingers.

July 1839

"Among a people generally corrupt liberty cannot long exist."
"People, crushed by law have no hopes but power."
As wealth is power, so all power must infallibly draw wealth to itself by some means or other."
"The only thing necessary for the triumph of evil is for good men to do nothing"
Edmund Burke(17829-1707)
English political writer, orator

The Groadies,who lived north of our grove before we came, were reputed to be horse thieves. John Groadie came from Ohio. He has a low forehead. His three sons are destitute of character and are feared and despised. It was also said that they robbed traveling salesmen of their wares, which they hid in depressions in the ground.

In some areas there are also caves where outlaws hid their plunder. Some of these caves we have used to hide horses, saddled and bridled and ready for the fugitives to use.

One day one of the Worden men was walking over the prairie in search of his cattle and found the ground sinking beneath his feet. He was precipitated into a large, square cavity, which had been excavated, covered with planks and soil and turfed over with growing grass. It didn't help that our son had married a Brody, sweet Mary, who was

now suspected of being a cousin of that clan whose grove was only six miles from ours.

She is not a cousin. We married into the Brodys a way back in Ohio, and it's a completely different family.

These Groadies run a gang. Benjamin Worden had two horses he guarded some times even at night. Old man Groadie heard about it and had taken a liking to Ben. He told him that he didn't need to worry about the horses and gave him a warrant to that effect.

He said that he would see to it.

September 1839
"A body of men holding themselves accountable to nobody ought not to be trusted by anybody."
Thomas Paine
American Revolutionary

Ben Phipps and his brother John have been involved in a fiasco regarding the building of that courthouse over in Ogle County.

After working in Michigan on the lead mines, John Phipps had set out on a little reconnaissance work along the Rock River. Just north of where Oregon is now, he came upon Billy Hamilton, son of Alexander. Billy was doing some surveying of land for either Illinois or the federal government. He was to establish the Standard Line for townships. John had probably known Billy from when he was working in the lead mines, and he of course felt comfortable with his work because of Bill's famous father, Alexander.

Evidently Phipps talked to his brothers about his big plan: form a county, take up some land by the river, form a company and have river frontage lots to sell near a courthouse. The company would have the Front Quarter and the county the Back Quarter (160 acres), and Billy Hamilton would survey it, while a group of men, a "race horse" from Chicago would finance this venture.

A lot of work had been done on the courthouse, laying foundations and so on when on October 1st, the government suddenly threw a "wagon spoke" into the proceedings. Actually, it was kind of like a bomb. The new federal survey showed that the magical stake was placed in the Front Quarter, not the Back Quarter.

Author's note:
The state surveyor said, in effect, that the line dividing the front Quarter and the back quarter is not at about where 5th Street is now, no, the line is a little bit west of 7th Street. The Commissioners Court called a special Term and announced that the county seat stake had been planted in the Front Quarter, not the Back Quarter, and that all work be stopped on the public buildings, and no one was to trespass on the Front Quarter, because the Front Quarter was now the county seat of Ogle County.

Another strange thing happened. The Illinois legislature ordered the locating commissioners to plant the county stake on a spot that would be "convenient" for the citizens who would arrive in future years.

When we examine the records, however, we see that one of the locators, James MacCade, failed to carry out his assigned task. It turns out that he was among the men from Chicago, who were known as pillars of the community and were actually the financiers of this "race horse" project..
Ogle County Commissioners Court Records, page 51

Should we care that this leader of the community was not there to squelch the deal? He had promised to finance Phipps Company's land grab? Why would he want to locate the courthouse in the right place? No records say that he was related to John MacCade, so we can't claim that was the case.

The court took this action: three written notices to be posted in the Front Quarter forbidding any person trespassing on or in any way taking possession of any portion of the Front Quarter,
(Ogle County Commissioners Court, page 112.)

I can just imagine what John and Company may have said to the Commissioner's Court: "Well, come on now; the difference is only about 40 feet, surely, you don't have to be all that accurate about this thing, considering all the work we have put into it. And you make a big fuss about 40-some feet!"

The court my have replied something like this:
"It's not our fault that you relied on a preliminary survey done by Hamilton, and furthermore, those two men, Reed and Kirkpatrick were appointed by the state of Illinois who ordered them to put the county stake on a spot convenient to the citizens. We can't just say, 'Well, that's all right, what's 40 feet?'"

Even I know that when so much work has been done on a project and you find out a few years later that everything has gone wrong and there will be no courthouse up on Sand Hill, you've got to be fit to be tied and might even feel like taking a little revenge. You can imagine John's reaction to that bit of news. But knowing how John looked at this project, I think he must have said something like this:
"No, no, there's been a mistake somewhere!"

On account of the error in the original survey, the court went on to say that nobody was to build any thing on the Front Quarter until somebody who knew the law could advise the Commissioners Court what they should do now that the shoe was on the other foot. The Court didn't take long to say that those people who had bought the seat of justice had the Front Quarter and the town was to be known as Florence, not Oregon City. So the Commissioners Court began plans to find a new location for the courthouse in the Front Quarter on the County Square. That meant the plan to build the courthouse up on Sand Hill had gone up in smoke, especially for John Phipps & Co. Evidently Phipps thought he could work things out against the odds. He tried to collect money from those who he thought still owed him money for the lost land around the courthouse, which did not exist.

Ogle County Commissioners Court hired a Congressman from Ohio to represent Ogle County's interest in the land dispute. That was in answer to Phipps and Co. hiring Francis Scott Key to represent the company at the General Land Office in Washington. The arguments featured Key calling the locator's stake "this magical post" and the Congressman getting in his licks by calling John Phipps and Co. "squatters." Chalk one up for the Congressman and for the citizens of Ogle County! (Leonard J. Jacobs, OGLE THROUGH A GLASS DIMLY) (Jo Davies Commissioners Court Records.) (KETTs, BICENTENNIAL HISTORY OF OGLE COUNTY, pages 379, 351,339, 233. Ogle County Circuit Court records 10 January 1837. Also see longhand minutes of the hearing at the General Land Office from Leonard J. Jacobs, THIS MAGICAL POST.

November 1839

"As the patriots of '76 did to the support of the Constitution and laws, let every American pledge his life, his property and his sacred honor; let every man remember that to violate the law is to trample on the blood of his father and to tear the character of his own and his children's liberty."
Abraham Lincoln " The Perpetuation of Our Political Institutions" address before the Young Men's Lyceum, January 27, 1838.

Lincoln spoke in the courthouse in Springfield as a candidate for presidential elector and Stephen A. Douglas, in "The State Register," a Democratic sheet, commented:

"Mr. Lincoln's argument was ingenious. He has, however, a sort of assumed clownishness in his manner which does not become him, and which does not truly belong to him. Mr. Lincoln will sometimes make his language correspond with this clownish manner and can thus frequently raise a loud laugh among his Whig hearers, but this entire game of buffoonery convinces the mind of no man and is utterly lost on the majority of his audience."

In another column "The Register" acknowledged that Douglas was the loser in one debate:

The second editorial had the heading, "Mr. Lincoln and the "Register." It opened stating: "On last Wednesday night, Mr. Lincoln in the course of his reply to Mr. Douglas, traveled out of his way to attack the veracity of the editors of this paper. Under the rule agreed upon by a committee, governing the discussion, the editors of this paper could not reply to Mr. Lincoln."

"Lincoln had asserted that he did not advise the running of John Bennett for the Legislature, but was in favor of Bowling Green; and that the editors of "The Register" had lied in making such a statement. Mr. Lincoln said further that we had no authority for making the statement and that having no authority, even had we published the truth, we were still liars. To the indecorous language of Mr. Lincoln we make no reply."

In the same issue of "The Register," Lincoln could turn a page and read an advertisement of a sort common in newspapers then. Usually such advertisements were scattered among the lost-horses and strayed-cattle notices. One read:

"$50 reward. Ran away from the subscriber, living in Lewis County, four miles from Tully, a slave named Charles, about 20 years of age, five feet six or seven, well made, free spoken among whites and pleasant in conversation, had a white speck in the ball of eye, a scar at the extremity of the left eyebrow, also a scar on the right wrist and one between the neck and collar-bone, had also scars on his back."

Then followed particulars about the payment of the reward for the delivery of the property.

Now there are a thousand slaves in the North. As late as 1810, thirty thousand blacks, one fourth of the black population of the North, remained slaves. In the upper South, there are more free Negroes than before, leading to more control legislation. In the lower South, slavery has expanded with the growth of rice and cotton plantations.

Author's note:

The situation of black slaves as a result of the American Revolution had been to create space and opportunity for blacks to begin making demands of white society. Some were from black elites in major cities. Pointing to the DECLARATION OF INDEPENDENCE, blacks petitioned Congress and the state legislatures to abolish slavery Thousands of blacks had fought with the British forces. Five thousand were with the Revolutionaries, most from the North but some free blacks came from Virginia and Maryland. Amid the chaos, many had taken their freedom –leaving on British ships to settle in England, Nova Scotia or the West Indies and Africa.

Underground leaders were mostly white men and women such as Levi Coffin in Indiana, John Rankin in Ohio, The Brown family in Rhode Island, Laura Haviland of Michigan and Thomas Garett in Wilmington, Delaware, but there were many freed blacks and former slaves, such as Lucretia Mott and William Still in Philadelphia, John Parker of Ohio, David Ruggles in New York, and Josiah Henson of Canada who were instrumental in running the railroad. It was never a white line; it was always black and white.

By the 1840's, slaves were valued at between $300 (children) and $800 each and some as much as $1,500 each (about $40,000 in today's monetary value.) White laborers hired themselves out as slave catchers. The gangs of pursuers became like a fox hunt with blood hounds prized for sniffing out the runaways. A number of slaves drowned trying to cross the Delaware Bay and Ohio River in small boats. Some slaves escaped by riding on the roofs of trains. One black man, Henry "Box" Brown, had himself nailed inside a box in Richmond and shipped to Philadelphia. There, underground workers retrieved the box and opened it to a chorus of applause from other workers.

Some stowed away on the ships of captains, sympathetic to the cause or willing to take bribes ($50 was the regular bribery rate in the 1830s and 40s.)

Those who stayed on plantations asked for their rights in many cases. In Norfolk, they asked to be allowed to testify in court. In Boston, blacks asked for city money, which whites were getting to educate their children. In 1780, seven blacks in Dartmouth, Massachusetts, petitioned the legislature for the right to vote, linking taxation with representation.

A black man, Benjamin Banneker, who taught himself mathematics and astronomy and had predicted a solar eclipse accurately, was appointed to plan the new city of Washington. He wrote to Thomas Jefferson:

"I suppose it is a truth too well attested to you to need a proof here that we are a race of beings, who have long labored under the abuse and censure of the world; that we have long been looked upon with an eye of contempt; and that we have long been considered rather as brutish than human and scarcely capable of mental endowments… I apprehend you will embrace every opportunity to eradicate that train of absurd and false ideas and opinions, which so generally prevails with respect to us; and that your sentiments are concurrent with mine, which are, that one universal Father hath given being to us all; and that He hath not only made us all of one flesh, but that He hath also, without partiality, afforded us all the same sensations and endowed us all with the same facilities…

Banneker asked Jefferson "to wean yourselves from those narrow prejudices which you have imbibed."
Jefferson tried his best, as an enlightened, thoughtful individual. But the structure of American society, the power of the cotton plantation, the slave trade, the politic of unity between northern and southern elites as well as his own weaknesses kept Jefferson a slave owner throughout his life.

December 1839

"I insist that if there is anything which it is the duty of the whole people never to entrust to any hands but their own, that thing is the preservation and perpetuity of their own liberties and institutions."
Abraham Lincoln

I have written to Jane Scott, the wife of James Byers, who, we hope might be our tenant, about her home in Eskdale Muir, near Dumfries, the hometown of Robert Burns, the famous poet. She does miss the village but not the severe winters.

Of her childhood there, she reminisced that it was a community of about 300 men and 400 females. Her mother, Mary Armstrong, used to tell about the terrible winter storm of 1774 that tore through the area from 26 November until the end of March in the next year! Obviously, life was not easy. The soil was deep, but not very fertile. Hills were green in summer with good pasture. More people farmed before 1775, but then they stopped because of the uncertain climate. At one time, they raised black cattle among the sheep whose wool was of good quality.

By 1755, her mother had told her that plantations were proposed. One was to be from the church, where the road from Dumfries ended.

When the area became part of the Abacy of Melrose, a Presbyterian priest with the name of Book I Bosom came from time to time to confirm marriages. Before this time, they had an annual fair. People of both sexes who were unmarried chose a companion with whom they were to spend a full year. They continued to live together for life if they were pleased with each other after that year; if not, they separated. The fruit of their connection was always attached to the disaffected person, who had not wished to end the connection.

All persons belonged to the Church of Scotland, if they were religious Christians. None owned land. The land is owned by a Duke.

Eskdale Muir is at the head of the Esk River and is famous for battles fought on its banks between the Scots and the English. Robert the Bruce was a famous warrior. The river's breadth was 8 miles and its length 11 ½ miles. Once a part of Westerkirk, it erected its own parish in 1703 with its present name.

On the farm of Coatt, there are two circles in the form of Druidicat temples. One is 90 feet and the other 340 feet. Part of the temple circles was washed away by the river. Jane does not remember people speaking much about the ancient Druid religion.

She was glad to get to New York safely. She and her husband were married in Eskdale Muir but rather against the wishes of her family, which had the means to afford a comfortable life for the times. Her husband's family was quite poor. So, in a manner of speaking, they eloped and soon boarded the clipper ship for the new country of America. She was sick almost the whole journey.

When they finally got to New York, they found that huge blocks of land had been granted to individuals or groups, just as they had seen advertised. The possessors of these grants sometimes sold their lands and sometimes leased them to the settlers. The Hardenberg Patent was the largest of these grants. It included all of Delaware County as well as several other counties. Some of the leases were almost feudal, lasting forever and requiring annual service by the person leasing the land. James worked for some years this way and eventually was able to buy a few acres of land, but wars and inflation had taken their tolls. People who were still holding leases began to object to the interminable amount of time and toil involved. There began a movement, which culminated in the Rent Wars or "Calico Wars," during which time Delaware County was declared to be in a state of insurrection and the National Guard was sent to restore and maintain order.

But Jane and James may leave before it gets so bad, before the financial bust is coming. Banks are starting to close. This has to do with the falling prices of Southern Tier New York forest land when the Erie Canal opened, making northern lands much more valuable.

William, who walked our here and persuaded his folks to come, is now twenty and thinking of marrying sweet Mary Anne Adee. The Adees moved here just a short time ago and are a very nice family.

Now a canal is being dug between Illinois and Michigan, sparing immigrants the bumpy travel overland. The work on the canal is being done by Irish and Negro laborers. Plagued by mosquitoes and leeches, they work on in the deep mud. At Ft. Dearborn, planks are being set across the mud. Horses have to be dug out of it frequently. Signs say: "No bottom here; shortest way to China."

Chinese workers are undergoing the same horrible travail to build the railroads.

January 1840

"A thousand starve, a few are fed.
Legions of robbers rack the poor,
The rich man steals the widow's bread,
And Lazarus dies at Dives' door;
The Lawyer and the Priest adjust
The claims of Luxury and Lust
To seize the earth and hold the soil.
Under the heels the white slaves toil,
While children wail and women weep!"
The New Rome
Robert Buchanan (1841-1901)
Scottish poet, novelist, playwright

The Amistad trial has begun. The African leader, Cinque, gave an emotional plea, charging that he and his fellow Africans had been illegally seized and sold into slavery.
"We are men, too," he declared.

U.S. District Court Judge Andrew Judson ruled that the Africans were free men, not slaves, and therefore could not be returned to their alleged owners in Cuba. The defendants were overjoyed and through Hartford, church bells rang.

The jubilation was soon marred, however. The government of Spain insists that the Africans were "cargo", not people, and must be returned. The case has gone to the Supreme Court.

All of this news makes it harder for us to be undetected. With abolitionists in the news, every one who is not of our leaning wants to find an abolitionist to persecute. To make matters worse, land-grabbers are flooding the country and obtaining contracts of sale at outrageous prices.

When Indians try to hold land by individual title, misrepresentation occurs such as: the Indian not knowing what he is signing, the use of intoxicants; the misuse of notary seals on blank instruments which were filled in at the swindler's convenience, and outright forgery or the bribing of some subservient Indian to impersonate the owner and sign in his place as well as rigged probate procedure in the state courts.

The Driskells have been called land-grabbers, but they have established themselves in Pennsylvania, Ohio, Michigan and here legally and have never jilted the Indians. Because the Irish have had so much prejudice against them, they have compassion for the underdog, be he Indian or black.

There is an element that continues to land-grab, however. We have seen a log hut being erected on our back forty and believe it is lived in off and on by relatives of the Canadian expatriate named John MacCade. If found, they may claim "Squatter's rights."

The Phipps have also been foiled in their plans to erect a courthouse in Oregon City. Now the Commissioners Court has finally announced that they are "satisfied that the true location of the county seat of Ogle County is located [in the Front Quarter] The order for the erection of the court house and Gaol or jail [in the Back Quarter] is hereby rescinded, and it is ordered that the Court House and Gaol be erected on the eastern end of Lots 2 and Block 21 in Florence in said county of Ogle."
(Ogle County Commissioners Court,
Page 121.)

In the extra term, the Commissioners Court also tried to bring itself up to date by dealing with the past sales of lots in the Back Quarter. They said that "money and notes taken in payment on that account will be returned to the purchasers, provided said purchasers return to the County or its agents the certificates and bonds for deeds made them by the county and its agents."
(Commissioners Court Records, pg. 120)

The Court at this same time, ordered that the foundations of the courthouse and jail be taken off of Sand Hill and removed to the new County Square to the dismay of the Phipps.

Contractor Jacob Crist was given the job of building the new courthouse at the above site. But he seemed to have some difficulty in proceeding with the project caused by John Phipps. The matter was not publicized until sometime later, but John attempted to stop Crist. (Commissioners Court Record, page 229.)

Author's note:

From HISTORY OF OGLE COUNTY, 1843
"The idea that John Driskell was an abolitionist is very interesting. I know that he and John Phipps were two of the oldest men in the 1840 census. John Phipps was very much an anti-abolitionist. He owned slaves.

At the 1883 Old Settlers meeting, Judge Petrie said that Driskell was an early abolitionist among a few others: Martin Reynolds, John Wallace, Phillip Sprecher, James McCoy, and Dr. Price. Deacon Perkins led four fugitive slaves through Mount Morris to freedom on the Underground Railroad.

There were so few abolitionists that men laughed when they put together an antislavery ticket for elections in John Driskell's time.

At Driskell's Grove near Vernon, David Driskell was the first landowner."
(Horace Kaufman, HISTORY OF OGLE COUNTY)

February 1840

"I am in earnest. I will not equivocate-I will not excuse-I will not retreat an inch-AND I WILL BE HEARD! The apathy of the people is enough to make every statue leap from its pedestal and to hasten the resurrection of the dead."

William Lloyd Garrison
"The Liberator," first issue, January 1, 1831

Old Shabonee, the Indian chief, was forced to return to Illinois to save his own life after his son, Pypeogee, and a nephew, Pypes, were killed In Missouri. Only his immediate family returned with him to his old grove, but they found strangers living there, who ordered him to leave. A few of his old friends, William among them, realized his plight and bought him a tract of land of 20 acres of timber on Mazon Creek south of Morris. There, he built himself a double log cabin.

We have taken a Christmas present basket to Shabbona's Grove. Old Shabonee is grateful, and the 25 children and women in his family are jubilant to have warmer clothing and even some fruit plus straw dolls, bows and arrows.

It is terribly cold and blustery. William can hardly make it to the barn some mornings at 4 a.m. when he goes to milk the cows. Jane Byers writes that in the old country, the barns were attached to the houses, and the animals kept the houses warmer that way. Sometimes, they grazed on the thatched roofs. But now we keep the animals separate. Some of them are sick from a disease. I wonder if the humans are getting the disease from the animals.

Caroline coughs much and wants to stay in bed. This is so unusual for her. It's not at all like her to stay in bed; she is usually so vivacious. I'm afraid she may be coming down with the "milk sick" which some of the children are getting. It makes them tired, cranky and feverish. They say that Lincoln's love, Ann Rutledge died from it. We don't know whether or not people are catching this fever from the animals, but it is a possibility. Morgan is his father's only help. I hope he does not get this sickness. Since he is 15, he is old enough to be of real assistance with the chores.

William is out tilling the land for a widow who lost her husband only two weeks ago. He is always doing acts of kindness for people, participating in barn raisings and other compassionate activities here in the community. John also helps in these undertakings.

A world anti-slavery convention met in London. After fierce discussion, they voted to ban women. The women sat in the back row in protest, and William Lloyd Garrison sat with them.

March 1840

"In the nature of things, those who have no property and see their neighbors possess much more than they think them to need cannot be favorable to laws made for the protection of property. When this class becomes numerous, it grows clamorous. It looks on property as its prey and plunder and is naturally ready at any time, for violence and revolution."
Daniel Webster (1782-1852)
American statesman

"Lying rides upon debt's back."
He that builds before he counts the cost acts foolishly and he that counts before he builds, finds that he did not count wisely."
Ben Franklin
Poor Richard's Almanac

We sent for the doctor, but there was nothing he could do. Our beautiful Caroline has departed this world! It seems so terrible to place her vibrant red curls in the grave!
She was such a joy to us all…I don't know when I can get over this. Everything seems so gray and depressing, and people seem to be getting meaner.

We read still more about John Phipps. He was brought to trial for beating a man whom he thought owed him funding for land in the lost deal on the courthouse.

The Court record states:

"Before me, one of the Justices of the Peace for said County, personally came Benjamin T. Phipps who being duly sworn according to Law deposeth and saith that on the 4th day of March 1840 in the County aforesaid that John Phipps did strike, wound, & beat Isaac Wooley, and this deponent says that John Phipps is guilty of the fact charges, and further this deponent saith not."
Sworn to & subscribed before me this 4th day of March 1840.
Joseph Knox J.P.
B.T. Phipps
Circuit Court Record March 4, 1840

Ogle County officials went on ahead with their plan of putting the courthouse in the front Quarter, and John Phipps went ahead with his plans to hire a lawyer, who turned out to be none other than Francis Scott Key. He presented his case at the Dixon Land Office and tried to stop the construction of the courthouse. He forcibly entered and tried to detain the builders and J.B Crist brought suit against him.
(Longhand minutes of the hearing at the General Land Office.)
The Land Office at Dixon said, in so many words, that where the locators planted the stake was the quarter section where the county seat would be located.
(THIS MAGICAL POST by Leonard J. Jacobs.)
(Ogle County Court Records, page 199. Also OGLE, THROUGH A GLASS DIMLY.)

April 4th 1840
"But from the moment one man began to stand in need of the help of another, from the moment it appeared advantageous to any one man to have enough provisions for two, equality disappeared, property was introduced, work became indispensable, and vast forests became smiling fields, which man had to water with the sweat of his brow, and where slavery and misery were soon seen to germinate and grow up with the crops."
Jean Jacques Rousseau
French writer, philosopher

Using the slogan "Tippecanoe and Tyler, too," Van Buren and Tyler have run on the same national ticket this year. Because sectional wings of the two parties supported a common candidate only once every four years, in presidential elections, Northerners and Southerners can usually take different positions from each other on slavery. This year, John Tyler, a slaveholding Virginian, has been elected Vice President on the Whig ticket and now that William Henry Harrison has died, he is President. Tyler promptly vetoed some of the Whig party's most crucial economic legislation. He is now trying to resurrect his reputation with the Whigs, but since he is a proponent of slavery, he is using the annexation of Texas as an issue on which to win the Presidency in 1844.

Zenas Aplington visited us and told us that Abe Lincoln has met his match in a young woman from Lexington, Kentucky named Mary Todd. She comes from an educated and highly cultural background and is the granddaughter of the Todds who had fought with Washington in the American Revolution and with Daniel Boone in Kentucky at the time that Boone had said he was "an instrument ordained by God to settle the wilderness." Mary's father, Robert Smith Todd, had been a captain in the War of 1812 under my uncle, Admiral Stephen Decatur, who died in 1820, Her father had also served in both houses of the legislature in Kentucky and was president of the Bank of Kentucky in Lexington. He is a slaveholder, but it was said that Mary does not approve of this.

Zenus said that she is twenty-two, plump and quick with remarks. She has a smooth soft skin, soft brown hair and bright blue eyes along with a sparkling vitality that wins friends. She is the first brilliant woman who has impressed Lincoln with the resources of her accomplishments. She is fluent in the French language and has read the classics of French literature.
She is at times a wildcat and at other times a sweet angel, and she is certainly ambitious. She resists when the restraints of life for women are too many.

The Todds trace back to Scottish Covenanters who fought the king and the established Church of England. Among Covenanters transported

231

to the American colonies were two Todds, whose blood runs in Mary Todd's veins. Her faith is of Presbyterian lines crossed with Episcopalian. She had told a Kentucky friend before leaving for Illinois after a dispute with her stepmother that she was going to be the wife of some future President of the United States.

During this, her first year in Springfield, both Abraham Lincoln and his old nemesis, Stephen A. Douglas, took turns at entertaining Mary Todd in the parlor of her sister's house, the Edwards house. She has been asked which of the two she intended to have as her husband and answered that it would be the one who has the best chance of being President.

May 1840

"A firm bargain and a right reckoning make long friends."
Thomas Paine

American Revolutionary and Statesman.

Zenas Applington founded the town of Polo for the habitation of fellow Scottish friends. James Byers does not wish to live there just now. He is renting from us with plans to quickly own his own land here in the area we now call South Grove in DeKalb County. Polo is in Buffalo Grove and many Scots live there. Many are revolutionaries from Canada, Buffalo Grove is in Ogle County.

In October of last year, the U.S. land office in Dixon opened a part of Ogle County for sale. People who had moved into these areas before the land was for sale had nothing but claim titles for their land, and such titles had no legal status.

Law and order are practically non-existent. Claim jumper and land speculators act freely. The first sheriff of Ogle County, William W. Mull is presumed to be a member of a well-organized group of outlaws. At the first court session held in Ogle County, the grand jury returned an indictment against him for noticeable omission of duty. Some of the justices of the peace are known to be members of the banditti, or prairie pirates. A few constables are also banditti members, and their conduct gives the local people no real help.

About 1835, three families, apparently farmers, settled in the southern part of Ogle county, at Inlet Grove. Later events show them to be counterfeiters. However, the heads of these three families were successful in being elected to law-enforcing offices, which gave them an excellent cover-up. After their real business was discovered and they were convicted, investigators found five sets of dies to make counterfeit money sewn into a feather mattress. Barns with trap doors allowed stolen horses to be kept in the basement under the barn during the day and moved on to another place at night. Some caves where the plunder was kept have long since caved in, but the approximate location of the caves is still known.

One of Lincoln's main themes in speeches is that of social disorder. Too many changes have happened too quickly, Canals and railroads brought about the transportation revolution, which he acclaimed. But the needed immigration was a threat to American jobs and sectionalism was becoming more divisive as the controversy over slavery mounted.

The political battles of the Jackson Era had destroyed the national political consensus. A mulatto man was burnt to death in St. Louis after being accused of the murder of a prominent citizen.

May 1840

"It would be a very strange thing, if six Nations of ignorant savages should be capable of forming a scheme for such a union, and be able to execute it in such a manner, as that it has subsisted ages, and appears indissoluble, and yet that a like union should be impracticable for ten or a dozen English colonies, to whom it is more necessary and must be more advantageous; and who cannot be supposed to want an equal understanding of their interests."
Ben Franklin in the 1750's
Regarding the Iroquois Confederacy

Fort Dearborn was named Chicago some time ago. The city's namesake is Chief Chicagou who was head of the Metchigama tribe, a division of the Illinois nation, which has long ago disappeared from the state. LaSalle reported in 1680 that he had seen three children of Chicagou's brother baptized. They were Pierre, Joseph and Marie. In 1682, when La Salle again visited Illinois country, Nicanape, Chicagou's brother, treated him and his men to a feast.

In 1725, Chicagou was one of the delegates selected by the French authorities of the India Company to visit the country of France to see King Louis XV. It was reported that the chief was very well built physically and strong, but that he had been sick all the time he was in France. Native Americans have no ancestral immunity to our diseases.

Six other tribal representatives made the trip. They arrived in France on September 20 and met with French officials the following week. The visit caused a sensation as reported in the popular journal "Mercure de France."

The article showed that the members of the court regarded the Indian delegation as a novelty and not representative of a legitimate culture. This lack of respect was similar to that evidenced in England. In return for pledges to support the French, the Indians were presented with extravagant gifts that were utterly useless in the wilderness.

Chicagou was quite taken by all the extravagance of the French Court, but he did not dress in the clothes given by the French to the delegation He usually stood before the French in his pentagonal cloth blanket with a silver border just above the edges. His loin cloth was made of a quarter-yard of scarlet embellished with a silver band. His moccasins were cloth –half red and half blue and held high by thongs tied to his belt. He attracted more attention than the others.

Of the experiences in France, Chicagou was most impressed when he had an audience with the Duchess of Orleans whose husband was next in line to the French throne if there were no male heirs born to Louis XV. Chicagou said this to her:

"I see with great joy that you are the beloved of the Great Spirit since, after making you the daughter of so many great chiefs, he gave you for a husband, him who is himself a great Chief and the son of a great warrior. Your virtue gave the Great Spirit reasons for watching after you and loving you just as your good heart makes all Frenchmen esteem and admire you."

"Always be as happy as you are now; Even more, be fruitful in producing warriors and great chiefs who will resemble the grandfathers of your husband and yourself. Finally, live a long enough time so that the children of my children can one day come to see you, as I have the good fortune of seeing you today." ("An Indian Delegation in France," 1725.)

As a gesture of her generosity, she allowed him to visit her apartments. Chicagou received a magnificent snuffbox of black tortoise shell with a gold-embossed lid, having in its center a gold flower, adorned with several precious gems. Chicagou still treasured this gift five years later and refused to part with it.
In 1918 A. Milo Bennet referred to Chicagou as the most famous of the Illinois and surmised that Chicago, the city, was named after the chief. (THE INDIANS OF ILLINOIS)

June 1840

"Prejudices, it is well known, are most difficult to eradicate from the heart whose soil has never been loosened or fertilized by education; they grow there, firm as weeds among stones."
Charlotte Bronte (1816-1855
English Novelist
JANE EYRE

Chicago is nothing better than a great overgrown village, set down in what appears to be the lowest, muddiest spot in all creation. Farmers like William unload wheat or other grain into a hopper and the elevators are no better than will be seen in country towns. It usually takes about six days to get a load of wheat to market. Since there are few good hotels

235

along the route, the farmers generally sleep in their wagons and prepare their own meals along the road. I send William with a frying pan and coffee pot. Before he starts out, I provide him with enough coffee and bacon for the round trip and sufficient bread to last to Chicago, where he buys fresh loaves.

Lately some hotels have been appearing along the road as Rock River Valley becomes better settled. Close to us there was that old house at Groady's Grove, but I've already described what may have happened to wayfarers there, before the Groadys were driven away and the grove renamed Driskel's Grove. Then, there is Huntley's Hotel at DeKalb.

One way that grain could be quickly turned over into money is the making of "moonshine." It is said that James Byers has made his fair share of home brew and consumed quite a bit of it. It is reported that he would return home inebriated from sharing his stored grain and while under the influence, he would be berated by Jane. But by the following morn, when he was able to understand, she had usually let off steam and forgotten about it.

Part of their house is the school with a puncheon floor, shake roof and mud chimney. Twenty-five pupils learn there, but Mr. Byers is paid by the barter system in potatoes and such. A dollar would buy twenty pound of coffee, but he rarely gets a dollar. Everyone is so happy that he is there with his kind, genial voice softening its rugged Scottish accent and cheering students over the frightful Alps of a, b c and two times one are two. His eyes are always blind to any fun, and his laugh is as long and loud as the merriest urchin's.
And the Irish are allowed to attend his school.

June 1840

"No man is good enough to govern another man without that man's consent."
Abe Lincoln
An American Bible

DeKalb is named after Baron Johann DeKalb (1721-80), the German major general under Washington in the American Revolution. He visited this area after the war.

In the southern part of the town of DeKalb is the highest point of land between Chicago and the Mississippi river. A pleasant stream of water called Owen's Creek passes nearly through its whole length, rising in that southeast portion and flowing towards the northwest, where in the adjoining town of Franklin it empties into the Kishwaukee River. Our South Grove has a population of 774, and DeKalb County has 1697, according to the recent census.

I mentioned that we have just seen the first marriage in our grove. George Crill married Lucy Wells, the daughter of the couple to whom we sold part of our parcel of land. It was a simple wedding outside in an apple grove. The bride wore a white muslin dress and had a band of apple blossoms in her golden hair. We named the road to their farm after the Crills in their honor as a gift to start out their married life.

Another family, the Tindalls, have come to stay from New York. Jesse Tindall and his wife, Mary Barber, were born in New England and New York respectively. Their son, Thomas J., had been born in Michigan early this year. Chauncey Barber, brother of Mary Barber Tindall was buried last week after a long illness. A carpenter here made the casket of fine walnut.

Baptists hold meetings twice a month, but Methodist meetings are starting to be held in Mayfield at Mr. Ira Douglas' house. The Methodists have espoused the abolition cause for many years.

We were discussing Emerson yesterday. Concerning the Cherokee relocation, which has been called the "trail of tears," he declared: "This thought has served to blacken many days and nights."

The Cherokees had pretended to take black people into their culture as slaves in order to help free them. Soon the Negroes had married into the tribes, but when the Cherokees were relocated, they again said that the Negro members were their slaves to protect them.

July 1840

"No other occupation opens so wide a field for the profitable and agreeable combination of labor with cultivated thought as agriculture. The mind, already trained to thought in the country school, or higher school, cannot fail to find there an exhaustless source of enjoyment. Every blade of grass is a study; and to produce two where there was but one is both a profit and a pleasure."
Abraham Lincoln

James and Jane Byers have arrived and have rented some of our land. I had tea with Jane and told her how I had enjoyed her letters. She is a petite woman with hair the color of Burgundy wine, bright blue eyes and rosy cheeks. She lost one boy, John, a short time ago in New York, and her son, William, came out here to see the lay of the land before they decided to come. We put him up for a while.

Over tea, Jane told me that her parents, who were prominent in the village of Eskdale Muir, had not approved of her wish to marry James, who was from a less advantaged family. They married in 1818 and came to New York, where James did well and bought some land to farm, as she had mentioned in letters.

Jane was able to take her daughter, Christie Anne, back to Scotland. When they arrived in their finery, her father greeted them happily, seeing that James had made good. The Scottish people base their regard on hard work rather than elitism, as I mentioned before.

John Byers, Jane's father had died the year after they had married, and Jane's brother and sister had died in an epidemic in 1824. But Jane's mother, Christian Anderson, is still alive and was especially happy to see her namesake, Christie Anne, who is a beautiful, vivacious girl with her mother's gorgeous red hair. James' grandmother was named Christina Nichol. So Christie Anne is actually named after both of her forebears.

Strangely enough, we have neighbors with the last name of Nichols who are related to Zenas Aplington, the founder of the town of Polo nearby which has many Scottish residents. Christie Anne and John Nichols are close friends already in James Byers' one room school house. They are sixteen.

James and Jane Byers have a son, James, who seems to be upstanding although very curious, always asking questions. He is probably kind of an intellectual, like his father. His son James is thirteen years of age. His son William has the legend attached to him that he walked all the way out here from New York. His father-in-law-to-be, Mr. Johnathan Adee lives nearby and Mr. Matthew Thompson has just moved here. The Beemans have also moved in.

Morgan, Elizabeth and Sarah Jane are also doing well at James Byers' school. They help me with "Cate" as we call Theodore Decatur, who trails William even to the barn when he does his chores early in the morning.

It takes 61 hours of labor to grow an acre of wheat and Chicago is becoming the wheat capital of the world.

July 1840
"Believe nothing, O monks, merely because you have been told it... or because it is traditional, or because you yourselves have imagined it. Do not believe what your teacher tells you merely out of respect for the teacher. But whatsoever, after due examination and analysis, you find to be conducive to the good, the benefit, the welfare of all beings-that doctrine believe and cling to, and take it as your guide.
Gautama Buddha (563?-483? B.C.)
Indian Philosopher

My father writes me that in New York an announcement was put in the "Seneca County Courier" calling for a meeting to discuss the "rights of woman" the 19th and 20th of this month. Three hundred women and some men came. 61 women and 32 men signed a "Declaration of Principles." Then came the grievances: no right to vote, no right to her wages or property, no rights in divorce cases, no equal opportunity in employment, no entrance to colleges. They ended by declaring:

"He has endeavored in every way that he could, to destroy her confidence in her own powers, to lessen her self-respect and to make her willing to lead a dependent and abject life..."

The great State Road from Ottawa to Beloit has been laid out. It is eighty feet in width, entering the County of Somonauk, passing Sebra's, Esterbrooks and Lost Grove to the southeast corner of the Public Square, then to H. Durham's to Deer Creek and north to the County line.

We now have Hick's Mill Post Office with Henry Hicks as postmaster. Mail comes by way of a stage coach on the State Road, running between DeKalb and Sycamore and Hick's Mill is the only cross road between Kirkland and Fairdale. At this time one half mile north of State Route No. 72, Hick's Brothers Co. has also established a sawmill.
James and Jane Byers used to walk almost all day to the mill to haul for their neighbors, because when they arrived here they had only 16 cents to their name.

The land office is located in Dixon, where Mr. Dixon had his ferry.
The first resident lawyer in the County has been admitted to the practice, the County Commissioners Court certifying that he is a man of good moral character. His name is Andrew J. Brown. He settled in Sycamore. But most of the practice at the bar at this time is monopolized by W.D. Barry, A.N. Dodge, B.F. Fridley and Crothers Champlain.

As Lincoln was, many lawyers are itinerant, roaming the state to practice.
For many years, it has been the custom of the sheriff to keep his prisoners manacled but to board them at the same table with guests at the hotel. They come shuffling in at the first table, usually taking the head seat. It sometimes astonishes strangers, but is considered all right by the regular boarders.

August 1840

"Life is short, but truth works far and lives long; speak the truth."

"As the world is in one aspect, entirely idea, so in another it is entirely will.
THE WORLD AS WILL AND IDEA, preface, 2nd edition
Arthur Schopenhauer (1788-1860)
German philosopher

In one of his first murder cases tried in Hancock County, Lincoln failed to save William Fraim, who was convicted on April 25, 1839, and, by court order, hanged by the neck till dead.

Murderers, horse thieves, scandalmongers and slanderers come often and tell their stories at the Stuart & Lincoln law office.

Zenas said that on one hot summer day a farmer came to the law office wanting to prove ownership of his farm at Macomb. He had to have the testimony from a witness near Springfield. Court had closed for six months, Lincoln explained, but they would go out to Judge Thomas' farm a mile east and see what they could do. Lincoln took off his coat and with papers in one hand and a handkerchief for wiping sweat off with the other, he and the witness walked out to the Thomas farm.
The judge's wife said the judge had gone to the north part of the farm to help a tenant put up a corncrib. She showed them how to cut across the cornfield.
When they came to where the judge and his men were raising logs for the corncrib and hog pen, Lincoln put the case to the judge, who looked over the papers, swore in the witness and with pen and ink from the tenant, signed the documents. Lincoln remarked that it was kind of a shirtsleeve court that they were holding.

January 1841

"What is a man born for but to be a Reformer, a remaker of what man has made; a renouncer of lies; a restorer of truth and good, imitating that great Nature which embosoms us all, and which sleeps no moment on an old past, but every hour repairs herself, yielding us every morning a new day, and with every pulsation a new life?

Every great and commanding moment in the annals of the world is the triumph of some enthusiasm."
The Reformer, lecture, Boston, January 25, 1841
Ralph Waldo Emerson.

"If you put a chain around the neck of a slave, the other end fastens itself around your own."
REPRESENTATIVE MEN

"The philosopher and the lover of man have much harm to say of trade; but the historian will see that trade was the principle of liberty; that trade planted America and destroyed feudalism; that it makes peace and keeps peace, and it will abolish slavery. We complain of its oppression of the poor and of its building up a new aristocracy on the ruins of the aristocracy it destroys. But the aristocracy of trade has no permanence is not entailed, was the result of toil and talent, the result of merit of some kind and is continually falling, like the waves of the sea, before new claims of the same sort.
THE YOUNG AMERICANS. 1844
Ralph Waldo Emerson (1803-1882)

Something strange has happened with respect to Lincoln. He has been busy all year since he and Mary Todd had plighted their troth. He couldn't escort her to parties, dances and concerts because of so much work; she flared with jealousy and went with other men. Still, the wedding was set for New Year's Day. The bride was ready. The groom didn't come. It was a phantom wedding, mentioned in hushes.

On the day set, Lincoln took his seat and answered roll call in the legislature, and during two months was absent from his seat only a week. He worked with the Whigs on an "Appeal to the People of the State of Illinois" on circulars and protests trying to rouse public opinion against the Democrats.

And yet, he was a haunted man. He had torn himself away from a woman; she had stood ready and waiting; his word had been pledged. He had failed to meet her. He had sent word that he didn't love her, and there could only be pain and misery in a marriage where the man knew he didn't love his wife.

But was he sure he didn't love her? .

Once he had written it all out in a letter, how he had made a mistake in telling her he loved her, and his friend, Speed, had read the letter and thrown it into a fire, saying words may be forgotten but letters are permanent. Speed advised him to tell her himself.

And he had gone from the Speed store, saying he would be careful not to say much and would leave Mary as soon as he told her. And he was gone an hour, two hours…

It was past eleven o'clock that night when he came back and said to Speed that when he told her he did not love her, she had burst into tears. The he had suddenly caught her in his arms and kissed her.

Meanwhile his friend, Speed, had fallen in love and wrote glowingly of his sweetheart. He married her in a few months and told Lincoln that he was blissfully happy.
Then, at his invitation, Lincoln went to visit the Speeds.

The trip also fostered Lincoln's political sense. The Speeds were slave owners as well as moderate abolitionists, who had tried, unsuccessfully, to persuade their black farmhands to return to Africa.

Lincoln observed the family's moral anguish, which helped him to realize that slavery was a curse on both its victims and its perpetrators. On their return to Illinois, he and Speed traveled the Ohio River in a boat that also carried a dozen manacled slaves.
"That sight was a continual torment to me," he recalled later.

Author's note:
Asked by Speed a decade later why he had never fulfilled the worst fears of his friends that he might end his own life, Lincoln replied that

he could not bear to leave the world without having done anything to make other human beings remember that he had lived.

February 1841

"The loss of enemies does not compensate us for the loss of friends." Abraham Lincoln

"We better know there is fire, whence we see much smoke rising, than we could know it by one or two witnesses swearing to it. The witnesses may commit perjury, but the smoke cannot." Abraham Lincoln

Finally Mrs. Simeon Francis, wife of the editor of the 'Sangamon Journal' has come to Lincoln's rescue. She believed with her husband that Abraham Lincoln had a famous career ahead of him and that her friend Mary Todd was a rare, accomplished brilliant woman. In her eyes the pair were a perfect match. She invited them to her parlor, brought the two together and asked them to be friends again.

I wonder what will happen in Lincoln's troubled mind and heart.

William has read to me that the U.S. Supreme Court ruled in Prigg v. Pennsylvania that all captive slaves who were aboard the Armistad, are legally free because they were illegally transported. This is a landmark case for abolitionists and all blacks.
It was ruled on March 9th.

I've had little time to ponder about Lincoln's melancholy plight.

I have mentioned the corruption in the governing body of Ogle County where Old John and his other sons live. The Ogle County courthouse was designed in 1838 and it is now ready for occupancy. It is in the position that the government wanted it rather than where John Phipps desired it to be.

This night of the 21st we were just beginning to sleep when we heard an outcry from our neighbors. James Byers was at the door with a lantern. He said that Old John, David, Pearce and Taylor along with John Groadie who now lived in Dement and his three sons, had all been apprehended for horse thievery. They are now in jail near the courthouse.

They are to stand trial tomorrow, "but the courthouse is now on fire!" shouted James.

We could see the flames from our window.

William went to try to put out the fire, thinking that it might kill his father and brothers. Some of the constables who were members of the Banditti chased him and restrained him.

Mr. John MacCade of White Rock Grove was head of the Regulators. He was considered an exemplary man, a good Christian, a member of the Baptist Church, a father and grandfather, just as Old John is. But MacCade had been Old John's nemesis for many years, suspecting him of running slaves into Canada, from which MacCade had been expatriated. MacCade wanted to hold "slaves" as low cost farm help, leaving them only the hope of freedom after years of being enslaved or indentured.

Old John was seven years old when the Constitution was written and nineteen when George Washington died. His brother, Phoenix, had married into a family that was close to William Penn and he had picked up the philosophy of the Society of Friends, which was largely abolitionist. He also had developed a friendship with a Native American man named Jerome and had taught William and his other sons to be open minded toward other races, although he couldn't read or write. He knew that persecution or any "cruel and unusual punishment" of captives was against the law. He knew that the U.S. always viewed itself as the one true haven of the world's oppressed, but he also knew only too well, that once here, the oppressed were often again oppressed, especially if Irish or Negro.

March 22, 1841

"Avarice and happiness never saw each other; how then, should they become acquainted?"

"Don't throw stones at your neighbors if your own windows are glass."

"Sell not virtue to purchase wealth nor liberty to purchase power."
Ben Franklin.

The alleged evidence against our men was not destroyed by the fire. Ben Phipps, clerk of the court, had taken it home with him because he had known that his brother was going to burn down the courthouse where evidence existed against the Phipps family and Judge Forbes for selling property by the water under false pretenses. Ben Phipps said he had an "intuition" that something would happen to the courthouse. What does that tell you about his family's involvement in this arson?
When the jury started its deliberation, one jury member was thought to be a member of the banditti and would not consent to a guilty verdict. The other 11 men on the jury seized this member and threatened to lynch him in the jury room unless he changed his mind. Our men on trial were found guilty and sentenced to a year in prison. They were denied counsel. They were tried as horse thieves.

Writer's note: The following is the testimony of Leonard J. Jacobs after much research into this fire:

"One of the charges against the Driskell "Bandits" is that they committed arson on the just completed Ogle County courthouse in 1841. But if we research the Ogle County Circuit Court records, it seems that no one was ever charged with arson and brought to trial. If we really look closely at the court records and that of the County Commissioners Court, we might ask ourselves:

'Hey, maybe the Driskell/ Bandits didn't burn the courthouse, maybe one of the 'good guys' did it! Anyway, as far as he was concerned, he had good reason to burn the house down-revenge! One wonders what the Driskells would have to say, then and now, to bolster their defense? Did they ever have a chance to defend themselves in a court of law or to ask the court to put that "good guy" on trial for arson?

One might say: "Us Driskells have pretty much taken the blame for burning the courthouse, but I hope you will take a long look at John Phipps as being the "good guy" that did the job. In our family, we talked about him as being the guy who did it. John Phipps had a whole sack-full of self-confidence. He was the guy that was always right, and if you don't believe me, just check the court records. It seems like he was always suing somebody or the other way around."

The Groadies didn't get the blame as much as we did but they got painted with the "criminal" brush too, in the "history books," but if you look at the records of the Circuit Court, we Driskells and Groadies weren't skeered to take each other to court. Now, why would we do that if we were both Bandittis?"

(Ogle County Court records, page 51)
"OGLE, THROUGH A GLASS DIMLY," Leonard J. Jacobs.

April 3, 1841

"A mob's a monster: heads enough, but no brains."
Ben Franklin

"But what is liberty without wisdom, and without virtue? It is the greatest of all possible evils, for it is folly, vice and madness without tuition or restraint."
Edmond Burke

"Whenever a separation is made between liberty and justice, neither in my opinion is safe."
Edmond Burke
English political writer, orator

Through the help of William Bridges and Norton Royce, our old father and brothers have escaped along with John Groadie, who was also being detained for horse theft.

Now 15 men who say they are victims of gang members of the banditti have met and entered into a compact, calling themselves the Regulators. They are also members of the lynching club. They agree that their method will be to notify suspects to leave the country "under pain of whipping if the order is not obeyed." The activities of the club members are such that many people have become indignant, feeling that the Regulators are carrying on activities little better than the conduct of the banditti. Some have used the organization to obtain personal vengeance on their enemies as had MacCade, their chief. Some of the most active and prominent Regulators, such as the principals in the Oregon government, have turned out to be horse thieves and are lynching other horse thieves and innocent individuals. No one is safe. The Regulators appointed a man who they thought could act as their captain, but that man, John Chang, was "persuaded" by Bandit members to resign his position. Then, MacCade of White Rock was asked to be their captain.

April 15, 1841

"I believe each individual is naturally entitled to do as he pleases with himself and the fruit of his labor so far as it in no wise interferes with any other man's rights."
Abraham Lincoln

"Stand with anybody that stands right. Stand with him while he is right, and part with him when he goes wrong."
Abraham Lincoln

"Agonies are one of my changes of garments, I do not ask the wounded person how he feels. I myself become the wounded person."
Walt Whitman

The Regulators have had several leaders since their inception. A few months ago, the Regulators met and elected John Chang as Captain of all companies. John has just completed the construction of a sawmill on Stillman Creek. He along with other club members found Jim Ducket, a hired man of our family who was residing near the town of Franklin and who had been lame as long as I've known him. They thought him to be a member of the banditti and he was given a severe beating by them and then freed amid threats at Paine's Point. They warned him to leave the country. He came dragging his leg to our house and fainted on the front porch. I picked him up, put him to bed and cleaned his wounds. Shortly after this, another man named Ross was made to cling to a tree while he was horribly beaten.

John and Aaron Long had already been hanged for horse thievery and therefore, we decided that the situation needed legal intervention.

The Bridges and others obtained from Esquire Wood, an attorney sympathetic to us, a warrant against those who whipped people.

Soon after this event happened, Mr. Chang's sawmill was burned. The victim of a beating was thought to be the arsonist, but no one could point exactly to him. About the same time, Lyman Powell was seized upon the road between Driskells' and Kilbuck. He is a really harmless, inoffensive man, lame and destitute of any settled occupation. But being an associate of ours, working at threshing and other odd jobs for us, he was questioned closely. They tried to draw from him some evidence of our criminality or his. Not succeeding to their liking, they flogged him horribly with hickory withes and took from him his horse and turned it adrift. He afterwards went to the place where he had bought his horse and, furnishing satisfactory proof that it was honestly obtained, had it returned to him.

About this time Mr. Chang said that a threatening letter was sent to him. He resigned as Captain and Mr. Reilly was the second Captain of the organization. He soon received a letter featuring a skull and crossbones, warning him to leave his position as captain. He resigned and John MacCade of Rock Grove in Ogle County had become the third Captain. William was blamed for sending the letter, but neither William nor Old John can write.

Jim McCade had led an insurrection in Canada and was thrown out of the country for his part in it. One revolt was master minded by a Dr. Charles Ducombe of Burford he gathered 500 men near Brantford. It is supposed that he worked in concert with William Lyon Mackenzie, leader of the revolt near Toronto. He had heard an erroneous report that Mackenzie had taken Toronto.

The rebels revolted and were crushed by the loyalists in 1837. Most of these rebels were from either America or from southern Canada. This was a narrowly localized movement, seeking political reform. Twelve of the insurgents were hanged, but MacCade escaped.

Last night, John MacCade visited our home and warned the Driskels, one and all, to leave the country within twenty days. MacCade said: "If after that time you are found east of the Mississippi river, we will brand your cheeks with R. S., meaning runaway slave, and crop your ears, so that none shall fail to know your character as a rogue and a scoundrel wherever you may be seen."

One of the first to receive a visit from the Regulators was John Harl, charged with being instrumental in having his neighbor's horse stolen. He was taken out of his house and ordered to strip. After tying his hands behind his back, the Regulators proceeded to give him 39 lashes with a raw hide, well laid on, the blood flowing at every stroke.
An ex-Baptist minister, named Dagett, was also visited. He was charged with being an accessory to the stealing of several horses. After an informal

"trial", he was sentenced to receive 500 lashes on his bare back. He was stripped for that purpose, and as they were about to proceed with the execution of the sentence, his young daughter rushed in among the men and frantically begged for mercy. Upon his promise to leave the county at once, Daggett was finally permitted to go free. About two o'clock that night, however, some of the Regulators returned to his house, took him outside and gave him 96 lashes.

May 20, 1841

"The proposition that the people are the best keepers of their own liberties is not true. They are the worst conceivable, they are no keepers at all; they can neither judge, act, think or will, as a political body."
John Adams, second President of the United States
"Defense of the Constitution."

Old John was captured last night on the road to his home. Thugs brought a flaming torch in front of his horse, which reared and threw him off. Fortunately no bones were broken, but the masked men pulled down his britches and branded him with the inscription R.S.
He lay there on the ground in agony for hours until his wife, Mercy, went looking for him. She placed him over her gentle horse and led him home. He is sixty years old.

Now, there is a gathering at our house of some of our neighbor families, the Brodies, the Driskels, the Bridges, and the Barrets. Stern and fearless, the men are exasperated nearly to madness by the threats served upon them, indignant as most honest men would be at the rigid summons to abandon their homes and firesides to their enemies and fly like hounds before them.

The men are making preparation all over our house. I have sent the children up to friends who live nearby. The house is like a magazine, filled with various kinds of weapons. I have tried to talk sense into both William and Old John who seems to have a plan, but is not talking about it.

June 22, 1841
Dawn

"When men take it into their heads to hang gamblers or burn murderers, they should recollect that, in the confusion usually attending such transactions, they will be as likely to hang or burn someone who is neither a gambler nor a murderer as one who is; and that, acting upon the example they set, the mob of tomorrow may, and probably will, hand or burn some of them by the very same mistake."
The Perpetuation of Our Political Institutions"
Address before the Young Men's Lyceum of Springfield, Illinois, January 27, 1838

One hundred and ninety six men, mounted on horseback, are appearing over the horizon.
The sun is at their back. They are led by Captain Jim McCade and with a bugler and American flag they head east toward DeKalb. It is like a war of the two counties.
The horsemen march two abreast and finally they arrive at our home. We have seventeen men barricaded in the house, armed with five different kinds of guns.

But now, the seventeen men, who are well outnumbered and know it, have broken out and run away just as the messenger of Captain MacCade neared the house.

The messenger returned to Captain MacCade, followed by a Mr. Bowman. The messenger said that John Driskell would talk with MacCade and to send word back with Mr. Bowman if they would like to talk with John. My William sent word that he had 300 men they could call upon for support in Sycamore.

John Driskell arrived on the scene accompanied by the Sheriff of DeKalb County and other men. The Sheriff wanted to know the purpose of 196 men from Ogle County coming to DeKalb County. Captain MacCade told the Sheriff the purpose of the expedition. The Sheriff, Morris Walrod, Frederick Love, the Probate Judge, District Attorney Farewell of Ottawa and William A. Miller, a well-known citizen, had been sent by Judge Forbes to find out the purpose of this invading army.

After a long and friendly conversation, Captain MacCade displayed the constitution of the lynching club for inspection. It required its members to scour the country, investigate the character of suspected persons, warn them if probably guilty to leave the country and lynch them if they refused. MacCade explained that they did not desire to interfere with the courts, but to aid and assist them in the enforcement of justice in cases, which they were unable to reach.

Old John sat on his horse and said nothing while Captain MacCade was making his speech. Later, I learned that MacCade could hear old John's teeth grating as MacCade was telling his side
The commission had a friendly visit and returning, made a very favorable report to the Judge Forbes, who seemed indisposed to make any opposition to their proceedings, but rather to favor them more than otherwise.

As it came out, the Driskells promised to leave the state within 20 days. (History of DeKalb County, Henry Boies, O.P. Basset Printing, Chicago, Ill.)

June 26, 1841
"Justice, sir, is the great interest of man on earth. It is the ligament which holds civilized beings and civilized nations together."
Daniel Webster
(1782-1852)
American statesman, lawyer, orator
Funeral Oration for Justice Story.

I knew the men were not going to be cowed. They were going to meet at the home of William Bridges in Washington Grove. I am not sure what took place there. They talked about the problem confronting them. A similar problem with Regulators was handled in Iowa by shooting the leader. The first leader quit when his house was burned. The second when threatened in a letter. If they discussed killing MacCade no one will know. No record of the meeting was made.

June 27, 1841

"History is not a web woven with innocent hands. Among all the causes, which degrade and demoralize men, power is the most constant and the most active.
Lord Acton
Essays on Freedom and Power

John Driskell was supposedly seen riding his horse near the home of John MacCade at White Rock this Sunday. He walked around the grounds, passed up to a clump of bushes, closely observed the location and soon went away. He might have easily gone home, but he did not. He stayed at a neighbor's without any apparent reason and slept there. Was it because he knew that a crime was about to be committed and wanted an alibi?

Late in the afternoon when John MacCade started to walk from the house returning from attending the Baptist church at Rockford, he was passing from his dwelling to his stable, when he was accosted by two men who inquired about the road to Oregon. He stopped and asked what they wanted. His answer was met with a volley of shot.
Mrs.MacCade was alleged to cry "Driskell" as she appeared at the door. As she rushed to her husband, he fell into her arms. The three men walked away. John MacCade was said to have lived but a few minutes.

The son of MacCade, a lad of thirteen years, reportedly seized his father's gun and rushed toward the retreating murderers. He snapped the gun at them three times, but the gun did not go off. It was thought that Hugh Groadie was at the site, and of course, it could have been that the other two Groa]]die boys were involved.

I don't believe that our David and Taylor could have done such a terrible deed. But, of course, since I am their mother, I would be considered biased.

William was the first to tell the story of the murder to me and to other settlers at the grove. He had been in Sycamore on that day, and while there Mr. Hamlin, the post master, had called him into his office and read to him the startling news which the postmaster at Oregon City had written on his package of letters bound for Chicago in order that passing through all of the offices on the route, the news would spread far and wide.

William seemed surprised and saddened by the intelligence. He said that it boded no good for him. Because he had already been forewarned at the post office, perhaps he had expected to be taken and tried, for he went quietly with his captors. It was a dark night full of foreboding for us all.

July 4th, 1841

"The history of persecution is a history of endeavors to cheat nature, to make water run up hill to twist a rope of sand."

"The human spirit is equal to all emergencies, alone, and man is more often injured than helped by the means he uses."

"Grief, like all the rest, plays about the surface, and never introduces me into the reality, for contact with which we would even pay the costly price of sons and lovers."
Ralph Waldo Emerson

I am writing this from a neighbor's home. All we have is destroyed. Both William and John have been murdered. I am trying to understand how this could have occurred in a so-called free country. Here it is the birthday of our independence from arbitrary rule of unchallenged authority. Yet, in this frontier state we have no real justice.

For my part, the worst has happened. The regulators burst into our house. They dragged William away and set fire to the house. I have followed him in the buggy with some of the younger children in tow. Conscious of his own innocence, William had said the he felt sure of acquittal. They told him that they merely wanted him to go before Mrs.

MacCade at White Rock, -so that she might see if he was the man who had killed her husband.

Toward evening we arrived at the house where the corpse of the murdered chief of the lynchers was still lying, and the wailing widow still mourned in her sudden bereavement. Pearce and William were brought to her view and she said that neither of them was present at the murder. The son, who had followed and tried to shoot the assassins, seemed equally confident that neither of the prisoners was part of the guilty pair. Yet, this party of excited men who had gathered at the scene of the assassination was eager to avenge the death of their leader and cried aloud for victims.

So saying, they placed them for the night in the upper chamber of the MacCade house and a guard was set round to prevent their escape. I was in the buggy for the night, and since it was the dark of the moon, and the guard seemed asleep, I crept to the house and threw pebbles against the window. William soon appeared and indicated that I should return to the buggy. He said that Pearce wanted to escape, but he felt that they could prove their innocence, and the proof would be so strong that they would not fail to discharge them.

With the dawn on the next morning, a large gathering of the lynch mob had collected. Many of the most respectable citizens, such as the Chanceys, who hitherto had looked with some disfavor upon the summary proceedings of the lynchers, now gave up their opposition and began to drink from the community keg of whiskey. Those from remoter settlements soon joined them. There was a company from Payne's Point led by Spark Walls. From the Pennsylvania settlement came Dr. Dillard and his group, from Oregon City, a group came led by a Methodist clergyman named James Crisk, and from Daysville came a mob led by one Captain August Bellet.

White Rock Grove had been selected as the place of rendezvous for the lynching clubs, and to that area went the band with Old John, Pearce and my dear husband in the wagon. Ropes were tied around their necks.

When we arrived at White Rock, we knew that the trial was a terrible miscarriage of justice and we had no hope of reprieve, but soon a couple of wagons drove up containing a few defenders. Among these I was glad to see Timothy Wells, J.R. Hamlin, Frank Spencer of Sycamore as well as Benjamin Worden and Solomon Wells of Driskell's Grove.

Near the place of the mock trial was a distillery, and during the delay, while they waited for the lynching club of Rockford, the barrel of whisky was rolled out from it.
Its head was removed and the thirsty crowd regaled themselves with its fiery contents. Maddened by a sense of indignation at the outrages of the banditti whom they were organized to oppose, infuriated by the brutal murder of their own honored chief and driven to frenzy by the fiery fluid, they were in no mood to be merciful.

The little band of those who knew William and believed him to be innocent endeavored to encourage him to hope for an acquittal. Yet, he declared, "No, they will kill me, but they will kill an innocent man." (History of Dekalb County, Boies)

Pearce was brought out for questioning, but no evidence could be shown that he participated in any of the activities, and he was released. I breathed a sigh of relief. He is so young.

Mr. Hamlin, the postmaster at Sycamore, asked permission to say a word or two. This request was met with a storm of hisses and shouts of "No, not a word."

I know Mr. Hamlin would have said that William was astounded when he heard word from him of MacCade's murder and said that it did not bode well for him or our family.
The club from Rockford finally arrived, led by Jason Morsh, Mr. Robinson, the postmaster and by Charles Letiter, a young lawyer. Upon their arrival a circle was formed, and a lawyer named Lemand was chosen as the presiding officer.
Seating himself on the ground at the foot of a tree, he had Old John brought into the ring and arraigned before him.

One hundred and twenty men were selected from the group of 500 that formed a circle around the large black oak tree.. Mr. Lemand asked if there were any objectionable men in the group of 120 and if so, to point them out and remove them. Nine men were removed.

John and William were led into the center of the 111 members of the "Jury." They were told that David and Taylor had been identified as the murderers of Captain MacCade and also that there was evidence to prove that they, John and William, were accessories, as they were present in the Bridges house the previous Saturday night when the plan to kill MacCade was made.

The postmaster tried to interject remarks on the innocence of my husband, but the crowd again hissed. Then, Mr. Leman asked for an expression of opinion upon the guilt of the prisoners by raising the right hand. The vote was almost unanimous.

An opinion was expressed that the action was a little hasty, but this was met with shouts that "if these men are released, we will not be safe in any part of the country." Other shouts exclaimed that the Driskells shot Captain MacCade and these men were Driskells.
One of the vigilantes was from Winnebago County, where William was hated because of his influence over and possible impregnation of Tecumsehattantas. These events had stirred up the members of her tribe, since she had been a pure shaman with incredible powers prior to knowing William.

This Winnebago County vigilante declared:
"Nothing but blood will palliate the crimes that have been committed, and as long as the outlaws are permitted to remain upon the earth, the community will not be free from their depredations and crimes."

He also said that the Driskells, if not the center and instigators of untold robberies and murders that had been committed in the country, were at least accomplices and shared in the plunder.

"What are the charges against this man?" he asked.

It was a pertinent question, but it rather confused the lynch mob. They hesitated, but at last one and another charged him with certain minor offences. The main charge was a general cry that he was one of the horse-thieving fraternity, and that they were afraid for their lives if he should be released.

Old John stoutly denied most of the charges, but he admitted that he had stolen a yoke of cattle in Ohio and a few horses. The horses were to enable slaves to escape, but he did not bring up this point because of the threat to the abolitionist movement after his demise.

A very few minutes were spent in the mockery of a trial, when Leman put the question,
"What shall be done with this man?"
Some one started up from the back and moved that he be hanged.

Old John said, "Don't hang us like dogs. Shoot me." He asked Chancey to remove the rope from his neck, and this was done.

Of the 111 men selected to be on the jury and firing squad, very few, if any, knew my husband. Yet, if a trip to the barrel did not convince them of their duty or strengthen their shaking legs, there were others present out of the 500 in the mob who could and would replace them.

The old man was taken out of the ring, and William was taken in. He looked so noble. If the party hadn't been frenzied with liquor, he would have commanded respect as he normally did. Few could charge any crime whatever; but then a circumstance that excited suspicion and had been much discussed was mentioned. It was that he must have been in on the secret of the murder of MacCade, because he first reported it at Driskell's Grove and in that section of the country. He had gotten the information about it from Mr. Hamlin, the postmaster at Hamlin, who had come especially to explain this suspicious circumstance and now tried to get a hearing. Hamlin asked again to be permitted to say a word or two, but he was met with a storm of hisses and shouts. The mob yelled, "No, not one word."

William was asked if he had instructed David to go to Captain MacCade's at twilight on the previous Sunday evening and say that he was lost and wanted to know the way to the saw mill after which he shot Captain MacCade.

William answered, "I did not."

Spencer and Wells, who had made some defense of the accused and had gotten excited, raising their fists, were seized and placed under guard. A move was made to take Hamlin also, but Leland cried out that he had a right to be heard.

The Catholic practice of confessing sins before death now was evident in the behavior of my husband and even Old John who said that he had stolen a few horses in Ohio but had decided to change his ways when he arrived in the Midwest.

William also spoke, saying that he had lived honestly and done no injustice to anyone, unless it was that in a certain trade on one occasion, he had afterward thought he did not do quite right. Both he and Old John had been perfectly straightforward but it was to no avail. Their honesty was just fuel for the fire. The crowd cried, "Shoot him, shoot him," and he was led out of the ring.

There was no evidence, fortunately, against our boy Pearce, and he was discharged.

There was a motion, then, to give them an hour to prepare for death and to give them the benefit of clergy, which as they construed it, was furnished by the clergyman Crisk, the captain of the band from Oregon City. That preacher went to the barrel of whisky, drank a dipper full and then knelt down and prayed long and noisily. William joined him, without the liquor, and I could hear him praying:

"Oh, Lord, forgive any offenses that I have committed and take this cup from me or let me be with Thee today."

Hamlin, meanwhile, moved around, talking to the lynch mob, endeavoring to secure a postponement of the execution or if possible a commutation of the sentence to banishment beyond the Mississippi, within twenty-four hours.

Lemand, the presiding officer, favored the project, and while unwilling to do much himself, urged Hamlin to keep up the excitement in favor of mercy. Ben Phipps, clerk of the Ogle County Court, favored it. McFarland was also active in support of this movement, and they finally got the party called together again and moved for an extension of time.

But the majority, led by the Chanceys, Morsh and others, were bitterly opposed to it and hooted it down.
(HISTORY OF DEKALB COUNTY)

I could see William talking to Pearce who was at his side, but I could not hear what Pearce was saying. I heard William say, "Oh my God, I can't do it now."
He was being dragged away and blindfolded.

The time had now expired, and our gray-haired old grandfather, John, was brought out blindfolded and told to kneel upon the grass. The lynch mob drew up in a long line, with guns in their hands. A number, unwilling to take part in the execution, stood round in the field with their guns leaning against the trees. Morsh shouted that all must join in, and he moved that all the guns left standing there be whipped up from against the trees. Upon the order the guns were all taken, and the men fell into line, there were one hundred and one of them. A Justice from White Rock gave the order to fire. The fatal one, two three was called and at the word all the guns were discharged and the lifeless body of the old man fell over like a bag of wheat.

Then, they led William out by the side of the bloody body of his father, which was all but demolished. He knelt bravely and in a volley of gunfire, less than that fired at Old John, William was crushed to the ground. He fell before the volley was over.

So many bullets had pierced Old John that, but for the bandages that covered his eyes, his head would have fallen into fragments. The bodies were thrown into a brush-heap, and the crowd dispersed to their homes. Some of the neighbors in pity covered the corpses with a foot or two of earth, and left.

I came out of hiding and made my way to the bodies. I heard an indistinct moan. It was William! I rushed forward and grasped his bullet-riddled body to my breast. He murmured, "Peggy, my darlin'" in a deep strained gasp.

I was able to drag him to my wagon, using all the strength I still had after that nerve- racking ordeal. I hoisted him up on the wagon and whipped the horses. I could see our home that we had dreamed of, burning in the distance, but the corncrib was left still intact. The children were all standing in it, and the pillagers had not been able to hurt them, I discovered after looking inside. I thanked God for that blessing.

Morgan helped me lift William who was moaning pitifully, and take him to the corncrib. He got water from the horse trough and I tore my dress to make bandages for William. He could no longer speak but could only moan and suffer with wounds in his chest, arms and legs, like Christ on the cross, until he breathed his last strangled breath as the dawn shown in gold and rose on the land he had loved and for which he had died.

We buried him secretly with the few remains of his father's fragmented body. Then, I returned to our property only to find that my new home was burnt to the ground. The older children had taken refuge in the corncrib. I took the younger ones, who had mercifully slept through the devastation, into the corncrib where we remained for two weeks until our neighbors were brave enough to rescue us.

Because of my pregnancy, this has been almost unendurable. I would get out of the corncrib just at dawn to vomit before the children awakened. I am just a month and a half along at this time.

263

July 7, 1841

"Let every American, every lover of liberty, every well wisher to his posterity swear by the blood of the Revolution, never to violate in the least particular, the laws of the country and never to tolerate their violation by others. Let reverence for the laws be breathed by every American mother to the lisping babe that prattles on her lap. Let it be taught in schools, in seminaries and in colleges, let it be written in primers, spelling books and almanacs; let it be preached from pulpits, proclaimed by legislatures and enforced by courts of justice. In short, let it become the political religion of the nations."
Abraham Lincoln

"When out of favor, nobody knows thee, when in, thou dost not know thyself."
Ben Franklin

Now, I have a taste of what the slaves must have endured below decks with their own excrement so close to where they lay. I am finally out of the corncrib with my children, yet, I will never be the same. I will never forget the indignity of that experience or the loss of my dear husband just when we were beginning to become close in spirit.

I am now at the home of our tenants, James and Jane Byers, where I have taken refuge. My own relatively new and beloved home was set afire and is leveled. I can see that John's home has been burnt also. I wonder where Mercy might be.

I am grateful that Pearce and I were able to reclaim the bodies and bury them in secret. He didn't do that when told to do it by the vigilantes, because he felt that William was still alive. Only we know where they lie, and I can't go there to take flowers and mourn for fear of their discovery.

Mr. R.P. Watson, a good friend, dared public opinion so far as to make coffins for them.

To those neighbors who were too frightened to take me in and who now pity me, I say:
"Well, I had a run of bad luck this month." That is all I shall say. I won't give into their pity. We still have our pride, at least.

And I was better off than Mercy, the heir to part of New York State, who nearly died on the open prairie during the week after the regulators burned her home. Imagine a woman of over sixty, surviving by keeping fires alive on the open prairie!
Old John had told her to do her best and nothing more, because he didn't want the mother of his children to die for the abolitionist cause. That would leave no one to take care of the grandchildren if anything happened to me.

The sheriff of Ogle County had arrested Old John at David's home. But David has made good his escape. His house is burning and his family was left on the open prairie until some friends took them in.

The sheriff came to our home, but when he arrived it was too late. William had told me to run as fast as I could to get the children and a few prized possessions together. Here I will stay with Jane and James Byers. They have offered to buy a portion of my land for $300, which will give me a chance to rebuild the house.

I now know what William was trying to say to Pearce before he was killed. He was trying to tell him where the money was hidden for the children's education. But Pearce couldn't hear him, and then William exclaimed the words I had heard:
"Oh, God, I can't do it now."

The money is buried somewhere near here. I wonder where it can be. He said that he had buried it so that they could have a liberal education. Now, I know that William had changed in his thinking about education. He came to understand that it was vital for all fields of endeavor, even for farming.

I also feel now that O.B. Lynleys, son-in-law of the Regulator Leader, MacCade, orchestrated the entire mock trial. It is strange to think that the Byers family, which has been so good to us, is from the Lynley clan also. The difference is that the Byers family knows and cares for us and is not prejudiced.

July 8, 1841

Now that I am out of isolation I can read the papers.

"The inherent right in the people to reform their government I do not deny; and they have another right, and that is to resist unconstitutional laws without overturning the government."
Lincoln

"We are all agents of the same supreme power, the people."

"I shall oppose all slavery extension and all increase of slave representation in all places at all times, under all circumstances, even against all inducements, against all supposed limitation of great interests, against all combinations, against all compromises."
Abraham Lincoln
Senate address, Oregon debate

"Given a free press, we may defy open or insidious enemies of liberty. It instructs the public mind and animates the spirit of patriotism. Its loud voice suppresses everything which would raise itself against the public liberty, and its blasting rebuke causes incipient despotism to perish in the bud."

Daniel Webster (1782-1852)
Second reply to Hayne, January 26, 1830.

The Rockford Star expressed the editor Mr. P. Knappen's opinion about the execution to my great relief and appreciation. He declared:
"A short time since we received through the post office a copy of the proceedings of the Ogle county lynch mob up to the latest date,

embracing the following resolution. 'Resolved that the proceedings of the Volunteer Company be published in the Rockford newspapers once a month."

Now let it be known to all the world that we have solemnly resolved that the proceedings of Ogle County or any county volunteer lynch company cannot be justified or encouraged in our columns. The view we take of the subject does not permit us to approve the measures and conduct of the said company. If two or three hundred citizens are to assume the lynch law in the face and eyes of the laws of the land, we shall soon have a fearful state of things, and where, we ask, will it end if mob law is to supersede the civil law? If it is tolerated, no man's life or property is safe. His neighbor, who may be more popular than himself, will possess an easy and ready way to be avenged by misrepresentation and false accusation. We live in a land of laws and to them it becomes us to resort and submit for the punishment and redress as faithful keepers of the law and thus extend to each other the protection and advantages of the law. Would not this course be much more satisfactory and agreeable in a Christianized country than to resort to mob law?

We repulse every attempt to deprive a fellow citizen of the precious privilege granted in every civilized country-namely, the right to be tried by an impartial jury of twelve good men of his country. But perhaps, it will be argued by some, that we have in this new country no means or proper places for securing offenders and breakers of the law.

To it we answer, 'Then, build them.'

The time already spent by three or four days at a time this season would have built jails so strong that no man or dozen men on earth deprived of implements with which to work and confined in them, can ever escape and guard them sufficiently strong by armed men outside to prevent assistance from rescuing them from the arm of the law.

We wash our hands clear from the blood of lynch law."

In the same issue of "The Rockford Star," a letter appeared expressing one person's opinion of the affair of June 29. The writer signed his letter," Vox Populi," the voice of the people. This writer said:

"Banditti like, these fiends in human shape commenced to traverse the country for plunder, not perhaps of valuable goods, but the liberty and lives of fellow citizens. Every one who happened to fall under suspicion of one or more of this gang was at once brought before their self-constituted tribunal where there was no difficulty in procuring testimony for convicting him of any crime named, when he was sentenced and men appointed to inflict the adjudged punishment which is the embryo existence of the clan,' from twenty to three hundred lashes were laid on."

The letter then continues in a different vein, he states:
"No man pretends that John and William Driskell had committed murder. How can they say they merited the punishment they received? Even had they been found guilty by an impartial jury of their countrymen of the crime alleged by the mob, even had unimpeachable testimony been brought to prove them guilty of that for which circumstantial evidence has horribly distorted to convict them, the punishment would have been but three to five years in the penitentiary. Has it come to this, that in a land of civilization and Christianity, blessed with as wholesome a code of laws as man's ingenuity ever invented, that a few desperadoes shall rise up and inflict all manner of punishment, even death, upon whomsoever they please? Shall our civic law be sacrificed and trampled in the dust at the shrine of mobocracy? Shall the life and property of no one receive protection from the civil law, but both be subject to the nod of an inconsiderate and uncontrollable mob?"

Vox Populi

July 9, 1841
"Nothing is dead: men feign themselves dead and endure mock funerals and mournful obituaries and there they stand looking out of the window, sound and well, in some new and strange disguise."

"It is said [that] all martyrdoms looked mean when they were suffered. Every ship is a romantic object except that we sail in. Embark, and the romance quits our vessel, and hangs on every other sail in the horizon. Our life looks trivial and we shun to record it."
Ralph Waldo Emerson

Another newspaper has printed the following first hand account of a sixteen–year-old boy,
Michael Seyster, who witnessed the murders of my husband and father-in-law.

Here is the printed account:
"Michael Seyster was 16 years old when the [Bandits] were shot to death by the Regulators. He was plowing a field near Oregon City when the Regulators stopped with John in the big lumber wagon.

The regulators took one of Seyster's horses from the plow, and harnessed it with the other horse, already hitched to the wagon, the one horse belonging to the Regulators having given out [tired]. (This may mean that the Regulators themselves were horse thieves.
They may have projected their sin upon the Driskells.)

"They started east toward the river when young Seyster jumped into the wagon to keep track of his horse.

Soon the sheriff came on the run, hatless and coatless, and seizing John [Bandit] as his prisoner, intending to take him to jail. Then John Phipps sprang from the wagon and said: 'If we are going to be men, let us act as men, and not like a pack of boys!'
This aroused the Regulators, and they by force took John [Bandit] away from the sheriff, and pitched him into the wagon and drove to where the Regulators had decided to try [kangaroo court] and then execute these criminals.

Mr. Seyster said he did not want to see John [Bandit] killed, so he made for a ravine nearby. After the volley had been fired, and John [Bandit] was dead, he returned just in time to see William [Bandit]

fall face forward, pierced with a number of bullets from the guns of the Regulators. He says some of the Regulators were opposed to the execution and wept like children at the dreadful scene."
(Indictment for Murder, the Grove Creek Incident, Jacob J. Jenkins)

The place where the two were executed is about 200 yards east of Prairie Road, just south of Grove Creek in Pine Rock Township.

When we consider the number of men, 111, who fired at the two Bandits, it comes as a shock to learn the details in the files of the Ogle County Circuit Court about the death of William [Bandit].

The files list the names of the 111 or 110 who were charged with the murder of the two Bandits. The names that appear in these pages include Jonathan Jinkins, George Phipps, Benjamin Phipps, John Phipps and James Crisk.

It goes on to say that William was badly wounded but did not die until the next day, June 30, 1841.

We can search the records of local histories and accounts of the execution but we will not see any if then in the court files. Therefore, it would seem that many of the Regulators were "poor shots" or that they discharged their pieces, firing high. It was said that half of the 111 fired at John and the other half fired later at William. "

This account mentioned that the files listed the names of the 111, listing the ubiquitous Jonathan Jinkens' name first, possibly suggesting that he was the "leader of the Regulators."

I wonder if Jonathan Jinkins sympathized with John and William and for fear that he would swear them away, was indicted with the 110 other men. No one can testify in his own behalf and in this way Jinkins' mouth was stopped. There is no evidence that this is the case, but I feel that Jinkens was rather against citizens taking the law into their own hands. Other people feel the same.

July 10,1841

"Be not intimidated, therefore, by any terrors, from publishing with the utmost freedom whatever can be warranted by the laws of your country, nor suffer yourselves to be wheedled out of your liberty by any pretenses of politeness, delicacy or decency. These, as they are often used, are but three different names for hypocrisy, chicanery and cowardice."
John Adams (1735-1826)
2nd President of the United States

Now I learn that the Rockford Star's press has been destroyed. Their entire office has been burnt. I don't see how the truth will out. Type was dumped on the floor and machines wrecked. Mr. Knappen's business and hopes were wrecked. He sold "The Rockford Star" and the paper is out of business.

This year Emerson has written about persecution stating:

"The martyr cannot be dishonored. Every lash inflicted is a tongue of fame; every prison a more illustrious abode. Every burned book or house enlightens the world; every expunged word reverberates through the earth from side to side. Hours of sanity and consideration are always arriving to communities, as to individuals, when the truth is seen and the martyrs are justified."
Ralph Waldo Emerson

July 14, 1841

"If persons and property are held by no better tenure than the caprice of a mob, if the laws be continually despised and disregarded," Lincoln warned, "citizens' affection for their government must inevitably be alienated."

"Nature has a higher end, in the production of new individuals, than security, namely ascension, or the passage of the soul into higher forms."

Emerson

Still, at least there is now an open appeal for a trial of the Regulators. Some form of law and order has arrived in the county. The first resident lawyer has been admitted to practice, the County Commissioners Court certifying that he is a man of good moral character. His name is Andrew J. Brown. He settled in Sycamore, but most of the practice at the bar is monopolized by W.D. Barry, A.N. Dodge, B.F. Fridley and Crothers Champlain.

I don't know who will defend the Regulators, but we will prosecute. Seth B. Farwell will be the prosecutor, and the trial will be held in September.

I have petitioned to Zenas Applington that he might talk to Abe Lincoln concerning the trial.

August 4, 1841

"Let us not be unmindful that liberty is power, that the nation blessed with the largest portion of liberty must in proportion to its numbers be the most powerful nation upon earth."
John Quincy Adams

Pearce has moved to Sycamore. As he was freed, he can now go about building a home for the children and me. Our one hope of making a living seems to be in real estate. The land office is located in Dixon, not far away. Now that the Mexican War is over, land warrants have been issued, giving each soldier 160 acres of land, located wherever they choose. These can be bought on the market for $112, making land value 70 cents an acre. Some of these soldiers seem to want to move even further west, and I am buying up their land. Meanwhile, we are living with Pearce, and I am preparing for the birth of my last child. I shall probably never marry again as I am mourning William now more than before.

I am so glad that James and Jane Byers are here to empathize. Their beautiful daughter, Christie Anne, is 15, just a year younger than Morgan. James Jr. is only 13 and their youngest, a tiny girl named after Jane is just four, the same as Theodore Decatur who we have started to call Cate.

James Byers is teaching school, and we are living in the school portion of his house at night. My children, including Cate, are staying in school and learning a great deal from James, who is as impish as the children in some ways and often joins in their fun on the playground and in the schoolroom.

He is the first teacher in the community. The school is one half of his double log house, which has a puncheon floor, shake roof and mud chimney. He has twenty-five pupils with my seven added to it. He boards himself for $10 from each of the children, which is usually paid in kind in potatoes and such. A dollar can buy twenty pounds of coffee in Chicago.

In addition to the school duty, James and Jane often travel 8 miles a day to husk corn for 30 cents a day.

Author's note:

The second schoolhouse was built on the present site, donated by James Byers Senior in 1854 near the cemetery.
That year of 1841, a post office was established and Timothy Wells was postmaster. Later James Byers was postmaster. His compensation for that year was $2.64. The year of 1847, the compensation was $7.16. In 1853 it was $12.64

Before the construction of railroads, when all travel was by team, the tavern and wayside inn were numbered among the great institutions of the day. News was disseminated here, and businessmen met and passed on messages to one another through salesmen.
When Mr. Beeman and Mr. Adee each ran a tavern for some years, a York Shilling, 12 ½ cents, was the customary price for a meal or a nights lodging. The State Road ran through Sycamore and St. Charles and

entered Chicago on Lake Street. Just about two miles from the Grove is the highest point between Chicago and the Mississippi River.

August 21, 1841

"I admit that slavery is at the route of the rebellion or at least its 'sine qua non'."
Abraham Lincoln

At least some important rulings for abolition have happened this year, although too late for William and Old John to learn of them.

The first issue of the "Christian Recorder" has appeared in Philadelphia, my father writes.
This is the first Negro newspaper, published by the African American Methodist Episcopal Church.

.

Authors note. This newspaper is the oldest continuously published African American periodical in the United States

.

Another important item is that Great Britain, France, Russia, Prussia and Australia have agreed to the search of vessels on the high seas for illegal slave transportation.
The slaves who rose up against their captors on the Amistad have won. Their trials have lasted from 1839 through this year. Lewis Tappan was the chief fund raiser for their legal defense and John Quincy Adams came forth to defend them.
They cannot be returned to slavery and are free men.

The year 1840 found the County of DeKalb increasing in population, if not wealth. The total receipts and expenditures of the county amounted to the sum of $452,15, a very moderate amount considering that a courthouse had been constructed, although built from another fund it increased the counties expenses.

DeKalb County had a population of 1697. All travel was by horse team. The state road ran through Sycamore and St. Charles and entered

Chicago on Lake Street. The inhabitants of Sycamore can thank Captain Eli Barnes and James S. Waterman for its wide streets, which are one hundred feet wide, because they thought that this capital would become a city.

Many of the settlers were from the Southern States, a pleasant, hospitable, generous people but not sympathetic to the abolitionist cause and lacking the energy and shrewdness of the New Englanders and other citizens of northern origin. Mr. James H. Furman, later editor of the Sandwich Gazette, had just moved from New York City and taught school in Squaw Grove to a settlement of Virginia and North Carolina people.

There was one framed house in the settlement owned by Jack Sebrees. All others lived in log cabins. One large double log house was a favorite resort for all in the neighborhood. Huge roaring fires of logs upon the broad open fireplaces at each end, could hardly keep the winter chill out of these dwellings. At night, they slept between two feather beds, as was the custom of the Southern country.

Just about two miles from South Grove is the highest point between Chicago and the Mississippi River, making it prime selling land added to the fact that the rich humus soil is the best in that entire area. It was wise of Margaret to buy up land in order to sell it for $1.50 to $3.50 an acre. This is how the family survived.

September 12, 1841

Pearce does not have our house ready quite yet, but it will be finished next month. It is a small cottage compared to the one we had before it was burned. I am almost completely dependent on my husband's brother.

Tomorrow is the day of the trial, and I'm sure it will not be fair, since it is to be held in the new courthouse in Ogle County. Rumor has it that some of the jurors were actually indicted for complicity in the executions. The newspaper said that Johnathan Jinkins and one hundred and eleven others would be tried.

September 20th 1841

"Pardoning the bad is injuring the good."
"The wise and brave does own that he was wrong."
Ben Franklin

Judge Thomas Forbes, Associate Justice of the Ninth Judicial Circuit Court presided at the case. Seth B. Farwell, Circuit Attorney, was the prosecutor. Messrs Peters, Dodge, Champlin and Caton appeared for the defendants.

Benjamin Phipps was the clerk and also one of the defendants. William T. Wall, Sheriff of Ogle County was also present on the jury. Can you believe that? He had to be biased. Remember that Old John had brought him out to reprimand the Regulators, but he had been taken in by MacCade and had taken back a favorable story about the Regulators to Judge Forbes.

The Grand Jury came into court and presented the following bills of indictment as true bills, to wit: The People of the State of Illinois against Jonathan W. Jinkins, JOHN F. GILES, GEORGE W. PHIPPS, PHILIP SPRIHER, ANTHONY FETZER, JACOB M. MIERS, JAMES H. ROLDS. MOSES T. KROWELL among many others.

Anthony Fetzer, Philip Spriher, Moses T. Krowell., Jacob M. Miers, John Fridlley, John Price, Samuel Funk, C. Burr Artz, Leonard Andrus, Salmon C. Cotton, Rodolphus Brown, Robert Wilson, John Waterbury, William M. Mason, John Carpenter, David Pembrook, Samuel Patrick, George Taylor and Oskin Webster were grand jurors. John F. Giles was foreman, and Ben Phipps was Clerk of the Court.
(Illinois State Genealogical Society Quarterly, Vol. 28, No. 4.)
The Ogle County, Illinois, Circuit Court Records.)

By comparison of the names of these jurymen with the names of the defendants, one can plainly see that some of their own number in the jury itself were the murderers indicted for complicity in that tragedy at Washington Grove on June 29, 1841. Jury members Anthony Fetzer and

Philip Spriher, Jacob Miers, Joseph M. Roland, Moses Krowell George Phipps, Clerk of the Court, Ben Phipps and foreman John F. Giles were all among the vigilante murderers who appeared at the original mock trial! How could they judge their own innocence or guilt?

The jury met in a small building then belonging to an attorney named John Chancey. Could he have been Phinias Chancey's relative? Other Chancey at the mock trial were Osburn, and Rolf Chancey.

When arraigned for trial the defendants pleaded not guilty. The trial proceeded and a few witnesses were called but no direct evidence was presented. Without leaving their seats in the jury box the jury returned a verdict of not guilty.

The Ogle County Circuit files (as printed by the "Independent" declare … [to} the said William did then and there feloniously, willfully and of their malice aforethought, did strike, penetrate and wound to the said William, then and there, with the leaden bullets aforesaid, so as aforesaid shot, discharged and sent forth out of the guns aforesaid, by them, the said Jonathan Jinkins, Seth Halls, and the others in and upon the head of him, the said William, one mortal wound of the depth of four inches, of which the said William from the said 29th day of June, in the year of aforesaid [1841]until the thirtieth day of the same month of June, in the year aforesaid, at and within the county aforesaid, did languish and languishing did live, on which thirtieth day of June in the aforesaid of the said mortal wound died."

The files listed the names of the 111, listing the ubiquitous Jonathan Jinkins name first, possibly suggesting that he was the leader of the regulators, but that is not what was suggested by one Ogle County history book.

It said: "Jonathan Jinkins, whose name appears first in the bill of indictment, was supposed to be in sympathy with the [bandits], and for fear that he would swear them away, he was indicted with the 110 other men. At that time [in history] no one could testify in his own behalf. In this way, Jinkins' mouth was stopped."

(Horace Kauffmann, HISTORY OF OGLE COUNTY 1909, page 734.)

Abraham Lincoln had appeared in the courtroom silently during the trial. In spite of his melancholia over his broken engagement and other troubles, he had made a point of attending this trial.

He rose from his seat to protest the verdict by saying it was false justice to have those who should have been defendants as grand jurors, and he recalled another speech he had delivered:

"Back in 1834, I warned about accounts of outrages committed by mobs which even then formed the everyday news of the times from New England to Louisiana. In Mississippi, they first commenced by hanging regular gamblers, a set of men certainly not following a livelihood that is a very useful or honest occupation but one which, so far from being forbidden by the laws, was actually licensed by an act of legislature passed but a single year before. Next, Negroes suspected of conspiring to raise an insurrection, were caught up and hanged in all parts of the state. Then, white men alleged to be in league with the Negroes and finally strangers from neighboring states going about their business were sometimes subjected to the same fate.

Thus went on the process of hanging till dead men were seen dangling from limbs of trees upon every road side, similarly to the native Spanish moss of the country as a drapery of the forests.

When men take it into their heads today to hang gamblers or burn murderers, they should recollect that, in the confusion usually attending such transactions, they will be as likely to hang or burn someone who is neither a gambler nor a murderer as one who is; and acting upon the example set, the mob of tomorrow may and probably will hang or burn some of them by the very same mistake. And not only so, the innocent, those who have never set their mind to any act of violence, alike with the guilty fall victim to the ravages of mob law and thus it goes on step by step, until the walls erected for the defense of persons and property of individuals are trodden down and disregarded. Good men, who love tranquility, who desire to abide by the laws and enjoy their benefits who would gladly spill their blood in the defense of their country become tired and disgusted with a government that offers them no protection."

It was heart warming to hear this admonition from" honest Abe" and I walked up to tell him so as he stood awkwardly near Zenas Aplington, who had summoned him. He only declared: "I certainly wish I could have done more, Mam."

October 30 1841

I haven't been able to write much since the trial,-just haven't had the heart. My feelings of loss are monstrous, and Mercy may never be the same. She had to live on the open prairie for five days until some of the hired hands of neighbors found her emaciated and filthy. It was a wonder that she wasn't eaten by wolves. Her house was also burned to the ground. This is the heiress to Manhattan Island who had been so mistreated.

My only son old enough to take his father's place in tending the crops for harvest is Morgan, and he is working 16 hour days in the fields. He has borrowed equipment. We have a house being built in a barn raising way by neighbors. Pearce is organizing it still. Taylor went back down south, where the abolitionists are more active, but no one here knows where he is except for us. Decatur is a big town for the movement as the slaves come from Indiana through Paris and Independence to go north at that point. Coming from Chicago, the Underground Railroad goes through Elgin, Pleasant Grove and Belvedere just north of our grove and on North to Beloit and Madison, Wisconsin. Our grove is just miles from the meeting place of those slaves coming from the South and those coming from the East, which is Belvedere.

Our remembrance of Decatur, once the capital city, is another reason that we named T.D. Theodore Decatur. He seems to have done fairly well in the corncrib, even though he is only about four years old. He is smart, and I took him outside at night to go potty at dusk along with the girls.

November 20, 1841

"There is always some leveling circumstance that puts down the overbearing...
Though no checks to a new evil appear, the checks exist and will appear...
The dice of God are always loaded."

"Every reform was once a private opinion and when it shall be a private opinion again it will solve the problem of the age.
Every revolution was once a thought in one man's mind, and when the same thought occurs to another man, it is the key to that era."
Ralph Waldo Emerson

It is getting very cold, and we are living in our unfinished house. At least we have the hearth for warmth and a place to cook. Mercy has moved in with me. I nursed her for several weeks because she had lost so much of her resistance and had pneumonia.

Morgan now has bronchitis but is still getting up at four to try to get the crops in. He weakens daily. I am so worried about him. He can't go to school at James Byers' place since we need him to work. The girls and I take lunches to him in the field as we must hurry to bring in the harvest. It's going to be a spare Thanksgiving. We are trying to can food night and day in preparation for a hard winter.

November 24, 1841

"No man [should] be sorry he has done good, because others have done evil! If a man has acted right, he has done well, though alone, if wrong, the sanction of all mankind will not justify him."
Henry Fielding (1707-1754)

English novelist, essayist, dramatist

Morgan shot a wild turkey and we have yams and potatoes, so we are thankful and expressed our appreciation to God, but Morgan's barking cough can be heard at all hours. After dinner I had him lie down and placed hot compresses on his chest after he drank herbal tea.

Janie Byers, the little daughter of James and Jane who is only four is also gravely ill. Jane is up with her most of the night. She shakes and heaves with the milk sick.

November 28, 1841
"The loss of enemies does not compensate us for the loss of friends."
Abraham Lincoln

The strongest bond of human sympathy, outside of the family relation, should be one uniting all working people, of all nations and tongues and kindreds.
Abraham Lincoln

I held Morgan's head helplessly all last night and he passed away at daybreak. My heart is now completely broken. I don't see how we can make it without him. I loved my first born so… How can life be so cruel? I fainted for a moment when he drew his last breath.
But no one knew. I told no one.

The neighbors have gathered around to hold me up. They say that they will help me just as William and John helped widows all along here.

November 30, 1841

Though loath to grieve'
The evil time's sole patriot
I cannot leave
My honied thought
For the priest's cant,
Or statesman's rant
Ode (inscribed to W. H. Channing) 1847

Janie has passed from this existence. It is hard to believe that such a lively child with her bright red hair and rosy cheeks is no more. A neighbor has prepared two coffins, one for our Morgan and one smaller of pine for the Byers' Janie.

We had a blessed slight thaw and we can now bury the bodies of our precious children.

A heavy coating of snow fell on the 8th of this month and seems determined to stick to the Earth. Forage for the stock is becoming unusually scarce and hundreds of cattle have died from starvation. Hay is selling at twenty dollars per ton.

December 4, 1841

"Property is the fruit of labor; property is desirable, is a positive good in the world. That some should be rich shows that others may become rich, and hence is just encouragement to industry and enterprise. Let not him who is houseless pull down the house of another, but let him work diligently and build one for himself, thus by example, assuring that his own shall be safe from violence when built."
Abraham Lincoln

The continuing saga of John Phipps' revenge came in the form of a court action, granting Jacob Crist twenty five dollar in the case of forcible entry and detainer for erecting a courthouse in Florence. In other words, Crist was finally paid for his labors on the foundation of the courthouse that never was. We already know that Phipps was fined for hitting Crist, but no one was published for burning our homes.

The snow has now crusted over, and the deer entrapped in it are slaughtered with axes and clubs. They "yard" together in great numbers in the wood where they live on the bark of trees. When driven out onto the crusted snow, they make no progress and are soon killed. We've had some venison feasts, but we haven't really enjoyed them, as we are still in mourning for the darling children.

Jane Byers and I have become very close over teas in the afternoon, when she has been coming over to visit in the sleigh. I am becoming very large, as I'm due to deliver in February.
I guess she and Mercy will help with the delivery,
Jane's boy, Asahel is only ten, James is 13. Christie Anne is 15, and William, 20.

I have Theodore Decatur, who is three, Joseph, who is 4, Mercy, who is 12 and living with Pearce, Sarah Jane, 11, and Elizabeth, 13. Sarah and Elizabeth are at least of some help around the house and beautify everything.

It will be a bleak Christmas, but we shall pop corn to string around the tree.

My baby will be born next month. This will be my last, since I'll probably never marry again. I'll probably have to send this baby to Pearce just as I sent little Mercy in 1829.

I have met Solomon Shaver, the blacksmith who founded Buffalo Grove with John Waterbury in 1835 just west of Polo. They also journeyed from New York. Buffalo Grove got its name from the great many buffalo bones found there after the severe winter of 1777-78. Shaver and Waterbury liked the area and returned here with 70 of their friends and family. They are avid abolitionists.

Most of the men who migrated west with Solomon and Waterbury were professionals or held prominent positions. Why would they leave New York? John Clark owned a saw mill. Captain Stephen Hull was a ship carpenter. Samuel Reed was a sheriff. Waterbury himself ran a woolen mill. The Shaver clan even allowed itself to be broken up as our family did for the cause. One brother was sent to Mercer County along the Mississippi to forward runaways to Brother Solomon in Buffalo Grove. Another brother was stationed in Canada to receive the slaves and help them get settled. The operator of the Byron ferry Jared Sanford is also a part of the Railroad.

Author's note:

Doris Vogel is an Ogle County historian, a genealogist and the great-great granddaughter of Adam Shaver, Solomon's Uncle. She claims that it wasn't mere chance that brought Shaver and Waterbury to Buffalo Grove; rather, they were sent there by none other than John Brown.

Brown, the most famous abolitionist in the country, was hung for treason in 1858. for trying to lead a group of slaves to insurrection. Like many other abolitionists, Brown had been so outraged by the Second Fugitive Act of 1850, that he formed his own anti-slavery society. But before that time he was already running a secret school in the East, instructing other abolitionists in how to operate the Underground Railroad. He then sent them to specific parts of the country.

Historian Vogel also said that Shaver visited Brown at least twice in Kansas and that Brown stopped at "Shaver Hollow,"the Shavers' home, on his way to Hagerstown, Maryland where he was arrested.

This view was supported by one of Shaver's fellow abolitionists, Henry Elsey. In the February 28th 1907 issue of the Tri-County Press, Elsey recalled a rally he attended in Kansas in which Shaver and Brown were the main speakers. In the Polo area, local historians claim the names of many who were involved in the Underground Railroad. From 1842 to 1860, the Polo area agents transported runaways to Byron.

Historian Vogel said that the agents purposely avoided Oregon. Oregon housed the sheriff's office and the county jail. Helping runaway slaves was an illegal activity back then. Plus, there were a number of Southern sympathizers in the Oregon-Mt. Morris area, including members of the Ku Klux Klan.

The Byers family has become active also. Even though James is a Justice of the Peace he has consented on several occasions to pay twenty-five dollars a head for the slaves to be transported, fed and lodged, placing himself and his family in jeopardy.

Author's note:(A case in point, which occurred on one July 4th, was mentioned in one of the chronicles of the times.)

John Nichols married Christie Ann Byers and his sister married Zenus Aplington, Lincoln's friend, and the Nichols are definitely active in the cause. So the tradition continues. Even though I cannot afford to be a very active part of it, I'll always open my new shed and even my humble abode to poor disenfranchised colored people, continuing my husband's legacy of liberty for all.

Epilogue

"A great revolution in just a single individual will help achieve a change in the destiny of a nation and further, will enable a change in the destiny of all humankind. This is the main theme of my story."

Daisaku Ikeda
President of the Soka Gakai International
(THE HUMAN REVOLUTION. Volume II, The Seikyo Press, Tokyo, 1966.) Page viii)

I hope that the depiction of these dreadful acts will show how gun violence should be brought to a halt in this country by the restriction of guns. Meanwhile, gun control laws are easing. Supporters say the easing of restrictions can head off greater violence. Members of the National Rifle Association say that the only thing that can stop a bad person with a gun is a good person with a gun. This is the same rationale that the vigilantes used against my ancestors.

Gun control advocates argue that weakening laws is disastrous. While it wouldn't necessarily lead to more shootings it would certainly increase the number of gun related murders in the U.S. There are currently more than 11,500 each year, and America has the highest firearm homicide rates. Per capita our rate is 39 times that of England, 13 times Australia (like America, a country where England often sent criminals), and 6 times that of Canada. Selling more guns is not working as a deterrent.

According to the Johns Hopkins Center for Gun Policy and Research, we have the equivalent of a Virginia Tech Massacre every day in this nation. It is just not happening in one place and if the angry person had not had the gun, this would not have happened at all!

Seven years after the "trial," Taylor Driskel was brought to trial. He had changed his residence to McHenry county and secured a change in venue which helped his case. It was prejudged that no one in Ogle County could be expected to be unbiased against the Driskels.

David Driskell was shot in an argument over his dog when he was about 35.

According to records of John & Barry of St. Charles and Arnold of Chicago, Taylor Driskell was acquitted of the charge of killing John Campbell. His attornies, Issac & Newton, secured the change of venue to McHenry County. The trial was held April 12, 1847.

Moreover, at the trial, held in Woodstock, Mrs.MacCade, who was so sure that she could identify her husband's murderer said that Taylor was the killer but then said that she had seen Pearce in Ogle County just a short time before. Several witnesses said that Pearce was not in the county but was in another state. Finally Mrs.MacCade stated that neither David nor Taylor was present at the time of the shooting, thus changing her original testimony. Therefore, it was decided that her account was inadmissible and Taylor was set at liberty.

David and his wife, Hannah Brody, went to Michigan. They had a daughter, Mary in 1842, probably named after Mercy. Then they had Jacob and Angeline later. David was shot years later in a dispute with a man who was trying to shoot his dog.

Theodore Decatur," Kate", the first white child born in the county who had been so loyal to his mother, married a schoolteacher in 1876 named Harriet Tindall. She was my grandmother, Harriet Byers' mother. Harriet Tindall. Her father, Jesse, was from New England and her brother, Thomas, was born in Michigan. She and Thomas went to college at Wheaton and Thomas fought in the Civil War. Their mother was Mary Barber Tindall.

During the Civil War there were 103 men in the service from South Grove township. There are seven buried in the South Grove cemetery: William Ward, George Newell, Warren Decker, Thomas Tindall, Julius Thompson, John T. Becker and one unknown soldier. The cemetery was donated to the school district by James Byers, Sr. who was also the Justice of the Peace for a time. He also donated the East West Road which went through Mayfield.

The Tindalls arrived in South Grove in 1842 and helped James and Jane Byers to get settled as well as Margaret Driskell. Hariet Tindall was born in South Grove in 1843, just two years after the murders of her husband-to be, Kate Driskell's father and grandfather. In spite of these problems Kate had 600 acres of farmland by 1870 and later built three spacious homes.

James Byers' son, James II, married Jane Gibson, born June 8, 1849 in Glasgow, Scotland. Her father, James, came from Scotland and purchased the Orput place in 1848 from Margaret. James and Jane had a daughter named Olive, who married Charles Black in California and became the grandmother-in-law of Shirley Temple, the darling movie actress and our delegate to the United Nations.

In 1844, John S. Brown purchased the Beeman place on the northwest side of South Grove and became a great help to Margaret. He and James Byers, Sr. purchased the first reaper in 1847 for $130. His wife was buried in the late '50s.

Levi Lee was the first Methodist preacher to hold meetings at the Grove School house adjoining the cemetery, which had been given to the community by James Byers, Sr.

Early in 1842, Ogle County Commissioners Court hired a Congressman from Ohio to represent Ogle County's interest in the land dispute that was in answer to Phipps and Company hiring Francis Scott Key to represent the company at the general Land Office in Washington. The arguments featured Key calling the locator's stake "this Magical Post" and the Congressman getting in his licks by calling John Phipps and Company "squatters.".

At last, Phipps was beaten.

You may recall that John thought Sand Hill would be an "admirable" site for a courthouse. Well, you will remember also that the man who heard John say that, many years before was James Giles, foreman of the jury during the second travesty of justice.

It was earlier said that good citizen James Giles kept a diary or notebook for many years. There were two volumes. After James died, it was decided by the family that "someone" in the family could be hurt by revelations in the second volume. So the family destroyed the second volume.

Can you imagine which family would be hurt if they were painted in their true colors?

Years after the murders, members of the Driskell family, Margaret's grown children, saw strangers digging on their land. The strangers fled with a parcel when they saw that they were being observed. When T.D. and Joseph arrived at the dig site, they found their father's money bag discarded there. This was the site that William had tried to tell Pearce about. This is where he had hidden the money for his children's education. The "luck of the Irish" had not prevailed, and Pearce had not been able to hear his father's "will" before William was dragged to his death.

Theodore Driskell was still living with his mother according to the census until he was over thirty.. Margaret Lozier Driskell lived to be 85, and "Cate" dedicated a beautiful obelisk tombstone in her memory. It is still the tallest in the cemetery that James Byers had given to the community before he passed away in Polo.

Still, future generations of Driskells prevailed by ignoring or refuting insults and lies. Through hard work and determination, they gained numerous doctorates and professional honors, in spite of the tragedy that had occurred when their forebears had aspired to help the disadvantaged and abused.

Bibliography

Boies, Henry L., HISTORY OF DEKALB COUNTY, O.P.Basset Printing, Chicago, 1868.
Debo, Angie, HISTORY OF THE INDIANS IN THE UNITD STATES,
University of Oklahoma Press, 1970
Ford, Thomas, A HISTORY OF ILLINOIS, 1854
Gross, Lewis M., PAST AND PRESENT OF DEKALB COUNTY, the Pioneer Publishing Co., Chicago 1907
Hubbard, Alice, AN AMERICAN BIBLE, The Rosecrofters, New York, 1911.
Ikeda, Daisaku, THE HUMAN REVOLUTION, Vol II, The Seikyo Press, Tokyo, 1966.
Jacobs, Leonard J., OGLE: THROUGH A GLASS: DIMLY, Arson on Second Thought,
"The Grove Creek Incident," Illinois State Genealogical Society Quarterly, Vol. 28.
Jacobs, Leonard, THIS MAGICAL POST.
JoDaviess Commissioners Court records.
Kaufmann, Horace, HISTORY OF OGLE COUNTY, 1909.
Kett's HISTORY OF OGLE COUNTY, 1878
Kett's BICENTENNIAL HISTORY OF OGLE COUNTY
Portrait and Bigraphical Album of Ogle Co., Chicago, Chapman Brothers
Tregillis, Helen Cox, THE INDIANS OF ILLINOIS, Heritage Books, Inc. Bowie, MD. 1991.
Zinn, Howard, A PEOPLE'S HISTORY OF THE UNITED STATES, 1492 to Present,
Harper Collins Publishers, 1980.

OHIO RECORDS used by Dorothy Driskell:

Dourhir, Ruth Long, References for Genealogical Searching Published by Detroit Society for Genealogical Research.

Ohio Resources for Genealogists (1961)-same publisher.

Ohio Genealogical Records, compiled by the Genealogical Advisory Commission

of the Western Reserve Historical Society, Cleveland, Ohio (1968)

The Ohio Genealogical Society, Route I, Box 3326, Ashland, Ohio 46885 Ohio Records and Pioneer families.

1820-1830 Federal Population Census of Ohio, Index (1964), Ohio Library Foundation, Columbus, Ohio.

Index to 1840 Federal Population Census of Ohio, Compiled by Cleo Goff Walkens (1970).

PENNSYLVANIA RECORDS

Federal Courts Inventory of County Archives (1942-1946).

Printed Census Records 1790 Heads of Families and 1810 Index to 1810 Census of Pa.

PEARCE GENEALOGY

Henry de Percy, Baron of Alnwick III, b.1321, d.1368, m. Marry Plantagenet b. 1821.

in Tutbury Castle, England.

I

Henry Percy, Earl of Northumberland I, b. 10 Nov. 1341, m. Margaret Neville, b. 1346,

daughter of Ralph Neville and Alice Audley in Brancepeth, England on 12 July,1358.

I

Sir Henry Percy, (Hotspur) b. 1364, d. 1403, m. Elizabeth Mortimer, b. 1370, d.1417 daughter of Earl Edmund Mortimer of March III, (b. 3 March 1350-1381) and Countess Philippa Plantagenet of Ulster (16 Aug. 1355-1 Jan. 1381) in England.

I

Henry Percy, Earl of Northumberland II. b..3 Feb. 1391, d. 22 May 1455, m. Eleanor Neville.

I

Ralph Percy, b. 11 Aug. 1425 in Leconfield, York, England, d. 15, April 1464, Hedgeley. Moor, England m. Eleanor Acton, daughter of Lawrence Acton, b. 1429.

I

Peter Percy, b.about 1457 in York, England, d. After 1485.

I

Richard Percy PEARCE, b, about 1478. d. in Pearce Hall, York, England

I

Richard Pearce, Jr. b. about 1563 in Pearce Hall, York, England.

I

Richard Pearce. b. in 1590 in Bristol, Somerset, England. d. in Newport, Road Island
October 7, 1666 m. Martha about 1613 in England b. about 1597.

I

William Pearce b. about 1619 in England m. Hannah, b. about 1621

I

John Pearce. b. 18 JULY 1643 in Boston, MA. d. 8 April 1720 m. Eliza Carter d. Feb. 1742, daughter of Edmund Carter (1615-before 1715) and Ann Brewster (about. 1615-before1715)

I

John Pearce. b. 20 April 1682 in Flatbush, N.Y. d. 3 June 1744. m. Maria Delamater, daughter of John Delamater (9 March or Nov. 1653-Oct. 1702) and Ruth Waldron (10 May 1657-1707) in Mamaronech, Westchester, N.Y. Maria was b. 8 Aug. 1696 in Kingston, Ulster, N.Y.and Christened on 26 Aug. 1696 in Harlem, New Amsterdam, N.Y. d. 20 Oct. 1734. in New Jersey or New Harlem, New York. Buried on 24 Oct. 1734 in New Jersey.

I

James Pearce. b. 8 Aug. 1717 in Mamronech, Westchester, New York. d. in Elizabeth, Allegeny, PA 15 March 1778. m. Sarah Van Horne. b. 30 March 1721 in New York, N.Y. d. in Colombia, Ohio on 20 Nov. 1806 at 85.

GENEALOGY OF Phillipa Plantagenet who married Hotspur

King of England Edward III Plantagenet, b. 13 Nov. 1312 in Windsor Castle, Berkshire, England, d. in Sheen Place, Richmond, Surrey England on 21 June 1377, buried in Westminster Abbey, London. m. Philippa of Hainault, daughter of Count William III & Jeanne de Valois in York Minster, Yorkshire, England. Philippa b. June 1311, d. 1369.

I

Lionel Phantagenet, Duke of Clarence. b. 29 Nov. 1338 in Antwerp, Brabant. Oct. 17 1368 in Alba, Piedmont, Italy. m. Countess Elizabeth of Ulster, b.6 July, 1332 in Tower of London in August 1352.

I

Countess Philippa Plantagenet of Ulster, b. 16 August 1355 in Eltham Place, Kent, England. D. in Wigmore, Hertford, England 1 Jan. 1381. m. Earl Edmund Mortimer of March III, son of Roger Mortimer, in Queen's Chapel, Reading Abbey, Berkshire, England. Earl Edmund d. in 1350.

I

Elizabeth Mortimer, b. 12 Feb. 1370 in Usk, Monmouthshire, England, d. in Trotton, Sussex, England 20 April, 1417. m. Sir Henry Percy (Hotspur), b. 20 May 1364, d. 1403.

I

Henry Percy, Earl of Northumberland II, b. 3 Feb. 1391, d. in St. Albans 22 May 1455.
m. Eleanor Neville.

Pearce/Delamater Genealogy

John Pearce, b. 20 April, 1682 in Flatbush, N.Y., d. in New Harlem in 1744, m. Maria Delamater, daughter of John Delamater in 1696. John Delamater,b. 1657, m. Ruth Waldron, daughter of Baron Resolve Waldron, b. 1608, Hall Holland, d. 1690, New Amsterdam, N.Y.m. Taneeke Nagle. (John Delamater owned a patent to Manhattan..)

I

James Pearce, Sr. b. 8 August 1717 in Mamaronech, Westchester, N.Y. d. Jan 1807 in Elizabeth, Allegeny, Pennsylvania at 89, first M. Sarah

Van Horne, daughter of John Van Horne and Rachel Webber, b March 1721, d. Columbia, Ohio, 20 Nov. 1806 (Old Bullskins Cemetery) at 85

I

Sarah Pearce, b. Sept. 23 1751, m. William Achin (1757)

I

Mercy Ackin, b. 4 Nov. 1788 Columbiana C., Ohio, d. in Ogle Co., Illinois 11 April1848
Buried in Lane Station Cemetery, Ogle Co. M. John Driskell, b. 15 Nov. 1780, d. June 29. 1841.

DRISKELL GENEALOGY

Daniel Driskell, d. 1820 in Ohio, Granted citizenship to West Bethlehem Township, Washington Co., Pennsylvania, in 1790. M. Eleanor Brooks in Swedes Church, Philadelphia, PA. March 1, 1779.

I

John (1780-1841)
William d. 1842 in Medina Co., Ohio, m. Mary Brody, Feb. 1804 in Ohio.
Dennis, d. 1843 in Medina Co., Ohio two years after Old John and William.
　　m. Hannah Taylor in Columbiana Co., Ohio July 21, 1809.
Sarah "Sally" was on the census for Brown County. Ohio in 1820.
Unnamed. Born before 1790
Unnamed, Born between 1781 and 1790
Phoenix. b. in 1790 in Pennsylavania, d. in Cass Co., Missouri on March 1864 at 72. He was on the census for Wayne County, Ohio in 1820.
John Driskell, b. 15 Nov. 1780, d. in Ogle co., Illinois on 28, June 1841 at 60.
m. Mercy Ackin on Jan. 1803.

I

William, b. 1804, d. 1841.
Pierce, b. March 1806 in Ohio. K. 19 April 1866 at 60. Buried in Forest Hills Cemetery, Glen Ellyn, DuPage Co., Illinois.
Sarah. b. 12 April 1808 in Columbiana Co., Ohio, d. 28 Dec. 1853 at 45, buried in Poe Cemetery, Cass Co., Newberry township, Minnesota.

David, b 25 Jan 1811 in Ohio, d. in Dadeville, Dade Co., Missouri on 4 Dec. 1848 at 37.

Reason. B. 12 May 1815.

Elizabeth Cedelia, b. 13 March 1816 in Ashland Co., Ohio.

Emeline, b. 5 Jan 1818 in Ohio

Delilah, b. 11 March 1810 in Ohio.

Taylor. B. 27 August 1822 in Ohio.

Phoenix, b. 11 Nov. 1824 in Ohio.

John. b. 26 Jan. 1828 in Morgan City, Ohio. d. in Juno City, Wisconsin in 1880.

William Driskell b. 16 March 1804 in Ohio, d. in Ogle Co., 29 June 1841 at 37 m.   Margaret Lozier, b. 8 September 1806 in PA. m. 28 April 1825. Margaret died in South Grove Township, Illinois on October 1887 at 81. She was christened on 7 May 1815 in Columbiana Co. Ohio.

I

Morgan, b. 11 Nov. 1825, d. as a child on 9 October 1841 at 15.

Elizabeth, b. 18 Nov. 1828, d. in Jefferson City, Ohio, 21 Nov. 1913 at 85.

Sarah Jane. B. in 1832

Mercy Jane. B. 2 May 1833, d.. 1851 at 17.

Joseph, b. in 1834 in Illinois.

Caroline b. in 1835, died as a child in 1840.

Theodore Decatur, b. 1838, d. 1917.m. Harriet Augusta Tindall, (b. Jan 21, 1843, d. Feb. 1907), daughter of Jesse Tindall (20 Jan. 1812-July 1880) and Mary Barber. Cate and Harriet were married. Jan. 6 1876. She was a teacher.

    Children   I

            Arthur

            Elizabeth

            Jessie

            Harriet m. Asabel Byers

Hannah, b. 1842 in DeKalb County, Illinois

BYERS GENEALOGY

John Byers, b. August 14, 1753, d. July 17 1819 at 66 in Eskdale Muir, Dumfries Co., Scotland. m. Christian Anderson, b. May 28, 1756, d. in 1843 at 87.

I

James Byers, b. 1797 in Eskdale Muir, d. 9 Dec. 1874 in South Grove, Illinois, M.

Jane Scott (b. August 5, 1798) on 10 May 1818 before emigrating to New York. Her grandfather was William Scott and her grandmother, Margaret Bold,

(b. 1680, d. 1720, age 40). Their son, William II (d. 1830 at Bankhead, age 71), m. Mary Armstrong (d. at Holm Dec. 28, 1823, age 52), the mother of Jane Scott.

I.

William M. Byers, b 20 March 1821 in Delaware Co., N.Y. d. 4 Oct 1908 Dekalb. Co. Ill. At 87 He was a road commissioner, supervisor, township treasurer.

M. Jane Adee, born in New York. Children John T., Jennie and Anna.

James Byers, Jr., b.1828 in Delaware Co. N.Y., d. 15 Jan1909 at 81.

M. Olive Mason in DeKalb Co., Il. (b 1825 in N.Y. d. 1879 at 54.) Sept.29, 1850.

Christie Anne, b. April 14, 1826, d. 17 April, 1847, DeKalb Co. Illinois

M. John Nicols, b. 19 Jan. 1844 whose sister Caroline married Zenas Aplington.

     Robert Bruce (1853-1937)

     John

.   William

     Olive was the grandmother-in-law of Shirley Temple. Shirley Temple marred Charles Black.

Robert Bruce (1853-1937) son of James Byers and Olive Mason
m. Jane Gibson of Glasgow, Scotland

I

Olive B. Waldo of Aurora, Illinois

Asahel Bruce Byers, b. March 1, 1889, d. 9 March, 1950 in Clare, Illinois, April 1, 1901 m. Harriet Driskel, b. Sept. 1881 in South Grove,

d. Dec. 28, 1961 in Sycamore. She was a kind, humorous, patient and religious woman.

I

Louise Marie Byers, b. 22 Dec. 1902
Robert Bruce Byers, b. 16 Dec. 1903.
Theodore Driskell Byers, b. 20 March 1905
Harriet Jane Byers, b. 28 April 1907.
Olive Lucille Byers, b. 11 November 1910.
Opal Beulha Byers b. 6 February 1912.
Margaret Amelia Byers b. 14 December 1815.
Charlotte Katherine Byers, b. 21 January 1922.

The authors cousins Byers/Driskell

Printed in the United States
by Baker & Taylor Publisher Services